Ghost in the Tamarind

Ghost in the Tamarind

A Novel

S. SHANKAR

UNIVERSITY OF HAWAI'I PRESS | HONOLULU, HAWAI'I

Printed in the United States of America

Library of Congress Cataloging-in-Publication Data

Names: Shankar, Subramanian, author.
Title: Ghost in the tamarind : a novel / S. Shankar.
Description: Honolulu, Hawai'i : University of Hawai'i Press, [2017] | Identifiers: LCCN 2017025978 (print) | LCCN 2017027879 (ebook) | ISBN 9780824867232 (e-book) | ISBN 9780824867218 | ISBN 9780824867218 q(cloth qalk. paper) | ISBN 9780824867225 q(pbk. qalk. paper)
Subjects: LCSH: Caste-based discrimination—India—Fiction. | Brahmans—India—Fiction. | Dalits—India—Fiction. | India—Politics and government—20th century—Fiction. | LCGFT: Novels.
Classification: LCC PS3569.H332614 (ebook) | LCC PS3569.H332614 G48 2017 (print) | DDC 813/.54—dc23
LC record available at https://lccn.loc.gov/2017025978

University of Hawai'i Press books are printed on acid-free paper and meet the guidelines for permanence and durability of the Council on Library Resources.

Designed by Mardee Melton

For Amma, K. S. Champakam,
first and best teller of stories

Contents

Part One

Past Is Prologue

TEN MINUTES. THAT WAS ALL it took him to rush home, stumbling and falling, from the dreadful discovery under the tamarind tree. That was how long it took him to stagger back utterly transformed. His faithful sword—lost. When he had set out for the tree he had held it fast in his hand—King Vikramaditya resolute on his mission. He had left with his shining crown sitting proud on his head. By the time he returned, the crown too was lost, dashed unnoticed into the mud in his mad flight back. With what guilty terror in his heart he came back!

He had set out on his mission—brave innocence—holding his sword in front of him like a bright talisman against the darkness. The darkness: it was exactly as foretold. Inky gloom surged spiteful and restless around him. His mission? To carry back the undead corpse hanging from a branch of the tamarind tree for the sage's ritual. The darkness was his enemy. Was determined to stop him from doing this. To put fear in his heart, it sent mysterious spirits, flitting shapes wailing and cackling, against him. From deep within itself, it spawned terrifying shadows with glowing red eyes and white translucent hands that reached for him, clung to his legs and his arms, weighed him down as he walked the distance to the tamarind tree. With his sharp sword, he hacked at the shadows and strode purposefully on toward the tree. How he hacked and how they wailed as he did so!

But darkness, enemy, too was purposeful. Out of the ocean of gloom came a great monster. Shoving its head forward. Peering at him with malevolent eyes, swinging its sharp horns from side to side. Massive head mottled with bright spots of red and green and brown. Mouth champing on loathsome food, vicious teeth chewing without pause. Dauntless, he stared back at the monster and watched as a foul fluid collected between thick black lips and drip-drip-dripped into the darkness. The monster lowered its head menacingly, shoved its blood-soaked horns into his face, flung its menace at him. *Watch out! Look out! Go back, fool!* Boldly he lifted his sword and thrust it into the monster's face. The sword shimmered blue in the darkness. A roar of frustration. A frightened heave of the colossal body. The monster slunk away, tail lashing in disappointment at the flowing veil of darkness.

He continued through the murk, passed two giant ghosts screaming incantations over an immense pit in the ground filled with a magical potion, a vile potion of vast power that the ghosts were raising rapidly in a great vessel. Their black hands flashed over the rope that drew the vessel up, up, up. He knew what they meant to do with it. He would have to be swift and sure in passing them. Should they manage to fling even one drop of the noxious fluid onto him, his body would break out in sores and all his strength would drain out of him. Swift and sure—that is what he had to be. And he was. He judged the moment confidently and nimbly darted past. The ghosts saw him, but it was too late!

It was all, all of it, as described—the monsters, the spirits, the magic pit, the implacable darkness. Every last bit of it. Exactly as foretold.

Except the tamarind tree. That was not as predicted. What he saw there froze his heart, shattered his world, in an instant. The darkness blasted apart. Bright sunshine, stabbingly hurtful to the eyes, came pouring in. He came to an abrupt, frightened halt, trembling at what he saw.

The tamarind tree was known to him. It was a large tree, towering high up into the air, even as branches weighed down by brown pods trailed low to the ground. His touch knew the scabrous feel of the tree's bark well; he had clambered up the gnarled trunk many times, for his mission was never-ending. Every time he fetched the undead vetal from the tree, it found a way to return. He would have to go back for it again. And again and again. Until he solved the riddle of the undead corpse. So it was ordained. Was it any surprise that he knew the tree so well?

But now both the familiar tree and its usual terrifying fruit were utterly transformed, utterly unlike anything he had ever known! The corpse was not hanging from a branch high above. It was lying on the ground beneath the tree.

Ramu stopped abruptly at the shocking sight. The body lay before him, throat cut and arms and legs flung wildly in different directions. Involuntarily his hand flew up, afraid for his own throat. His breath caught there, beneath his hand. He struggled to breathe. He rocked back on his heels, in his fright lurching instinctively away from the body before him. It lay close to the trunk of the tree with head flung back and a jagged red line across the neck. Blood from another wound on the forehead seeped out and clotted the thick white thatch of hair. Blood pooled on the ground beneath the head and the neck. The dirty brown waistcloth, miraculously free of blood, was bunched up around the crotch. Ramu was so close to the body—had managed, lost in his dramatic reverie of King Vikramaditya and the vetal, to arrive so near before noticing it—that he could make out stained teeth. Beneath the scraggly mustache, also white like the hair on the head, the mouth was wide open. And beneath this mouth was the other mouth, the terrifying tear in the throat, a gaping, jagged second mouth to rival the natural one between hollow cheeks in the face above.

Ramu knew well the gaunt-faced dead body with two mouths. It was Murugappa, who had worked for his family all his life. Murugappa lived in the hut he had been allowed to build in the coconut grove Ramu's family owned. Now Murugappa's bulging eyes, as watery in death as they had been in life, stared straight at Ramu, as if they were watching him with great deliberation. Ramu had the terrifying feeling that any moment now Murugappa would get up from the ground and speak to him in his familiar high-pitched voice, only now through the second mouth that had appeared in his throat. The thought made him stagger back, away from Murugappa, dead on the ground under the tree. The wooden stick his Uncle Siva had shaped into a sword for him tumbled unnoticed from his hand.

Suddenly the midday sun was hot and dazzling. Ramu wildly cast his eyes around, searching for whoever might have done this to

Murugappa. The tamarind tree marked one end of his family's lands. Behind him, bright in the sunshine, lay their garden of vegetables and turmeric, and beyond that their paddy fields. In the distance was their coconut grove, in which Murugappa's hut, now suddenly a dark smudge of accusation, bulged from the ground under two tall coconut trees. In another direction stood the Brahmin houses of Meenakshisundareswarar Temple Street, which bounded the village of Paavalampatti on one side. The voices of two hidden men chanting a work song came to him faintly. In the paddy fields, women were working, bending and straightening among the green stalks. In the far distance, two bullock carts trundled slowly on the road to Thirunelveli Town. Ramu could find nothing suspicious, identify no terrifying intruder, in these tranquil surroundings—which only made everything more terrifying still. He turned and ran, ran blindly down the path through the garden toward Meenakshisundareswarar Temple Street.

The path took him through patches of onions, turmeric, and spinach to the immense well that provided water to his family's lands. Here the voices singing the work song were loud. Two men, lean black bodies dripping with sweat, worked a rope that lifted water in a great leather sack. When the rope, pulled over a creaking and complaining wheel, had brought the dripping sack to the mouth of the irrigation ditch that ran from the well, one of the men tipped the sack with his hand and the water fell into the ditch. Then the sack went crashing back into the well and the men began their work again, their bodies contorting and relaxing, contorting and relaxing, as they worked the rope to raise the next sack of water. The water in the irrigation ditch—it seemed such a modest trickle—flowed hissing and gurgling past a mango tree into the vegetable garden. As they raised the bucket of water by the naked strength of their bodies, the men sang their work song, passing call and response back and forth between turns of the wheel:

Manne numbi! Maram irukke! Ailasaa!
Maruthe numbi! Kalai irukke! Ailasaa!
Kalaiya numbi! Pazham irukke! Ailasaa!

Pazhatha numbi! Naam irukke! Ailasaa!
Nammba numbi! Mannu irukke! Ailasaa!

So the song went. Ramu had heard the words all his life without ever giving a thought to what they meant. Now the words cut through the turmoil in his mind with a peculiar clarity:

Trusting the soil! Lives the tree! Ailasaa!
Trusting the tree! Lives the branch! Ailasaa!
Trusting the branch! Lives the fruit! Ailasaa!
Trusting the fruit! Live you and I! Ailasaa!
Trusting us! Lives the soil! Ailasaa!

So went the song. "*Nammba numbi!*" called one man, as he pulled on the rope. "*Mannu irukke!*" replied the other, as he did his bit. "*Ailasaa!*" Ramu's mind clung to the words, focusing desperately on every call and every response, eager for anything that would push the sharply etched image of the dead body with the two mouths out of his mind. To no avail. A loud sob burst out of him. Startled, the man reaching for the sack to tip its contents into the ditch lost his grip and the water from the sack went hurtling back into the well.

"Fool!" his companion cursed him, forgetting in one fickle instant the profound camaraderie of the work song.

"It's the master's son," the first man said, excusing himself. "Why is he running like this, as if he's seen a ghost?" To make amends, he gripped the rope once more and gave it the greatest pull he could. The sack lifted out of the well again, heavy with water.

Ramu bounded past the mango tree that stood on the other side of the well. In the shade of the tree, a bullock, tethered to a peg driven into the ground, was munching on fallen mangos pecked loose by birds. The bullock too belonged to his family. It was a fine, well-muscled beast, the best of all the cattle owned by the family, used to work the fields or to draw the cart the family owned. It had a beautifully shaped head with soft, brown eyes and two black spots on one cheek, just below a throbbing vein. Ramu had often stroked the face of the bullock or placed the tip of a forefinger against the vein to feel life pulsing through it. The sharp horns that crowned the head were painted a gay red. As Ramu careened down the path toward the paddy fields that lay between him and home, the bullock stopped and lifted its head. With calm eyes, it observed the barefoot boy in khaki shorts rushing by. Then it gave its horns a quick shake, as if of disapproval, and, nosing aside the toxic mango leaves, returned its attention to the fallen half-ripe fruit.

Ramu plunged into the paddy fields, hurrying through them on the familiar path. Disturbed by his headlong flight, paddy birds flashed into the sunlight on their white wings. Beady-eyed and watchful, they hovered and circled in the air until he was gone, and then settled back into the paddy to wait patiently for tiny fish in the shallow waters of the fields. One of the working women unbent her back to watch his flight. The world was busy around Ramu, but Ramu could not bear to turn his head to left or to right for fear of what he might see. Still, his feet slipped and he tumbled headlong from the path when he was almost through the fields. Muddy water filled his mouth.

Panic. Quickly he picked himself up from the slime and burst out of the paddy fields, racing now across the open ground that lay between the fields and Meenakshisundareswarar Temple Street. He did not notice the blood pouring from a deep gash in his knee, nor that he had lost the precious crown that he had had his grandmother make for him years before out of sticks and old sheets of newspaper. The crown was copied from a picture in one of his English books. It showed King Vikramaditya striding firmly forward with the undead corpse on a shoulder. When it came to crowns, the artist responsible for this picture had had an intricate imagination. Gomati Paati had spent hours laboring patiently with scissors and glue to copy it in a manner worthy of her grandson. After several aborted attempts, the crown was ready. The picture in the book was black and white, but Ramu had had no doubts about the color the crown should be: gold. He had painted his crown of paper and sticks the brightest possible yellow, thickening the paint over the newsprint in layer after layer; and then he had added several red and blue diamond shapes for priceless stones embedded in the gold. A most impressive crown it was, so fine in fact that Gomati Paati was every bit as proud of it as Ramu. And now the crown was lost in the muddy water of the paddy fields.

As Ramu swung past the outhouse (the smell of human refuse wafted from it subtly) and approached the back entrance to his house, Gomati Paati called out, "Ramu! Ramu! Slow down! Why are you running so hard? You'll hurt yourself!" She noticed his bare head and added, "Where is your crown? What a fine crown I made for you. Don't tell me you've lost it!" And then she became aware of his besmirched condition and the wound on his knee.

Gomati Paati was in her customary place, guarding the back door to the house in a wooden chair placed in the shade of a neem tree. The chair was large and sturdy and comfortable. It had to be, for Gomati Paati spent hours in it. It was the throne from which she kept watch over her domain—the house with the attached cattle sheds behind her, and in front the groves and fields and gardens stretching away into the distance. Ramu's father, Vishwanathan, known to the world as Vishu, too was present. He was tall and were it not for the thinness, bordering on emaciated, of his limbs and body, he would have made an imposing presence. He stood framed in the doorway leading into the house, hardly filling it, and gazed with a bemused and uncertain look in his deep-set eyes at his son racing toward it. But Ramu did not notice his father. He came to a halt in front of Gomati Paati, his chest heaving with his desperate panting, and looked down at his grandmother through eyes brimming with tears.

Gomati Paati was a widow. She wore no blouse and was dressed in an austere white cotton sari, its cloth pulled tightly across her chest and over her shaved head. She wore no jewelry or, indeed, adornment of any kind. As befitted a widow, her forehead was entirely bare. She was small in size, but the features in her face were striking. The lips were firm but quick to smile. The eyes were large and, when one had the opportunity to observe them at leisure, evoked a life of varied experiences beyond those of most men or women. There was an elusive wisdom in them. At the age of fifty, Gomati Paati had already been a widow for almost half her life, but her condition had done nothing to reduce her undeniable beauty, which had changed and matured over the years but not disappeared. Even widowhood seemed only to have augmented it.

Gomati Paati reached up, placed a calming hand on Ramu's shoulder, and said to him, "Look at what you have done to yourself. Look at how you've been hurt! Aren't you too old to be playacting like this? I thought you were all done with this game of pretending to be King Vikramaditya gone to fetch the vetal from the tamarind tree. What made you dig out your crown and sword today? I called out to you when you set off a little while ago but you did not hear me. What happened, child? Did you find your vetal there on the tree, then?"

At the question, Ramu's thin body shuddered. He flung himself into his grandmother's lap and nodded in terrified reply.

Ten minutes—all the time that had transpired since Ramu's chilling discovery under the tamarind tree. Ten minutes, a lifetime.

⁓

WORDS. CLAMORING VOICES. THREE OF THEM. *Refusing to be kept out.*

"Who could have done such a thing? I keep asking myself, who was such an enemy to Murugappa that he would do such a thing to him?"

"Murugappa bothered no one. His family and himself—that is all he cared about."

"Such a hard worker. So responsible. How will we find someone to take his place? He was with us for so long. He built his hut in the coconut grove when you two were still boys. I don't know if you remember. Your father saw what kind of a man he was. When the previous overseer died, your father called Murugappa and said, 'I want you to do the work the Padaiyanar was doing. I want you to build yourself a hut in the coconut grove and keep a watch on the fields and on the other workers.' Murugappa said, 'But I am a Paraiyar, ayya. How can I do this job? It is a job for a Padaiyanar.' Your father said, 'I don't care if you are a Paraiyar. Be honest and loyal and I'll take good care of you.' And that is how he has been: honest and loyal."

"I remember. I was ten or eleven. I watched him build the hut."

"You two don't know half the things that go on in this village.

I don't want to say anything about Amma, but Vishu here, he remembers Murugappa building his hut years ago, but does he know about what goes on in the village now, these days? He is always gone on tour, or to his office in Ambasamudram. When he is home, he doesn't go anywhere, doesn't talk to anybody. He stays at home reading his books. Once in a while he should go out and meet a few people in the village."

"What are you trying to say, Siva? You know I have to be away because of my work."

"Why do you need to work? Don't we have enough lands for all our needs? And about this Murugappa. What do you *really* know about him? The number of times I have found Murugappa drunk! Murugappa hasn't been the same for years. Not since his wife died."

"Who doesn't know about that? I may be a woman, but don't forget I have managed everything around here since you both were children . . ."

"I have no wish to find fault with you, Amma. Didn't I already say that? I am talking about Vishu here."

". . . I talked to Murugappa three times a day. You think I didn't know about his drinking? The drinking made him look old. He must have been the same age as me, you know. Once or twice I had to speak to him about it myself. When I brought it up the first time, he threw himself flat on the ground and began banging his head in the dust in shame. 'Why do you want to talk to me about this filthy matter, Amma?' he said. 'I don't do any harm to anybody with my drinking. When I drink a little, I forget everything—my wife who is gone, my children, my troubles, everything. That is all it is. Don't worry yourself about it, Amma. It won't happen again.' But of course, Murugappa couldn't stop. And what did it matter? What he said was true. He did no one any harm with his drinking."

Ceaseless voices. Pouring out of three mouths.

"Siva is right. I didn't know how bad Murugappa's drinking was."

"You should pay more attention to the affairs of the family."

"What can I do? It's not easy being Health Inspector. I am on tour for so many days of the month. You know that."

"Tell me something—am I the only one with responsibility for things at home? Amma is getting on in age. You are the eldest son. Do you even know how much help she needs these days?"

"No, no, Siva, that's not what I'm saying at all. It's lucky I'm posted in Ambsamudram and can live at home. Imagine how much harder it would be if the Sanitation Department posted me somewhere far away."

"Siva, I am sitting here, right in front of you. I can talk for myself. I'm not so old. Fifty. These days, that's hardly any age."

"Much help your living at home is! Amma doesn't like to admit she needs help. How long can a woman manage things the way she has? I don't want to criticize Amma, but . . ."

"Enough, Siva! Any moment of the day you want to start bickering. If Vishu's job takes him away, what can he do? It's not as if he doesn't bring in money to the household."

"Maybe Siva is right, Amma. Maybe I can take more interest in our lands."

"That is what you always say, Vishu. When have you actually done it? Anyhow, let it go now. Let's not talk about it anymore. I can manage everything. I'm not trying to quarrel with you. All I'm saying is that there is more to this Murugappa than meets the eye. It's a serious matter. You shouldn't think it isn't."

"How could I not know how serious it is, Siva? My son is the one who found him, under that tamarind tree, with his throat cut. Now Ramu is lying in bed sick."

"All I'm saying is that in the end everything to do with this murdered Murugappa is going to fall on me. But what is the point in complaining? Isn't that how it's always been? Murugappa worked for us. His murder does not show us in a good light. Sub-Inspector Chandran has been poking around, making inquiries, you know. He will want to talk to Ramu too when he is better. The year is 1939, not 1839. We may be a little village far from Madras but even here things are not like they were before. I hope you two keep that in mind. Somebody has to take care of things so we don't get dragged into this mess. Who will do that? Siva, of course. Fine! I can take care of it!"

"Shh! Lower your voice. Ramu might hear."

A long pause.

"He is all right. He is still sleeping."

Three mouths talking. What kind of mouths? Fine, proper ones? Or bloody and jagged and torn? Like the vetal's frightening second one.

"Hunh, hunh, HUNH, HUUNH . . ."

"See, he is moaning. You have disturbed him. Stop bickering, the two of you!"

Another pause. Longer. Then the voices start up again, softer, gentler.

"Murugappa's brother has arrived. From Madras. Didn't you say you saw him, Siva?"

"Yes. Chellappa came to see me when I was out in the fields yesterday."

"What did you say to him?"

"What is there to say? I told him how sad it was that such a thing had happened to Murugappa. I told him what I think happened. I thought he would want to know. Murugappa got drunk, got into a quarrel with someone who also was drunk, and that person killed him in a rush of anger. That is what I think happened. It makes sense. That tamarind tree is on the way from the Nadar's toddy shop to Murugappa's hut."

"How did he respond?"

"He started to say something, and then stopped himself. He looked straight and hard at me. Impudent fellow! Then he just nodded his head and went away."

"Chellappa was never like Murugappa. He was never afraid to say what he wanted."

"He's been gone a long time. When he visits, it's for really short periods, and it's like no one even knows he's here."

"That's because of what happened years ago, when he came for that long visit. Remember?"

"Who could forget? He'd better be careful how he behaves around here this time. This is not Madras. When he came to see me yesterday, he was dressed in shirt and trousers like some durai."

Ramu was back fully in the world now, drawn unwillingly into wakefulness by the voices. He lay quietly, tasting the bitterness in his mouth. His left knee felt stiff. His eyes felt heavy. He knew opening them would require an immense effort, one that he felt no desire to make. He had been sick, very sick. He knew that much. He felt as if he had been gone somewhere far away. How long he had been gone he did not know. He remembered his sickness, but as if in a haze.

He remembered terrible images, of corpses with two mouths and monstrous trees with menacing branches.

He remembered the heat, the great heat within him. He remembered tossing, turning, turning, tossing, while the heat raged within. So hot: too hot, much too hot. And then cool water on his forehead. Rubbed over his body. The cold touch on his chest. It made him think of a clear pool of water. Cool, inviting. So inviting. Until he saw Murugappa rising slowly out of the pool. With bulging, sad eyes and two mouths, one monstrous and terrifying. He wanted the water gone then! But the hands that were rubbing the wet cloth over him would not go away. He struggled with them. A protest broke out of his dry mouth. And then he was tossing and turning again, lying on a bed of flames, his head on a pillow of fire. He wanted the water back. He wanted the water gone. He did not know what he wanted. He was grateful, so grateful, when a deep darkness came to gather up his broken thoughts and put them away.

He remembered voices. One was a woman's voice. It called him "son." But it was not his mother, could not be his mother. His mother was dead. He had never even seen her. The voice told him to be strong. But he did not want to be strong. He wanted to sleep. He was angry with the voice. He wanted to be left alone with his hard-won darkness. He protested until the voice obliged. He slipped into his very own darkness and then there was the pool of water again and dead Murugappa rising out of the pool. Now he wanted the voice back. He wished it would speak to him.

He remembered being lifted up from the bed and being carried. He was squatting over a smelly trough. The smell thrust itself into his nostrils and punched a little lucidity into his mind. He was in the outhouse at the back of the house. The stench was familiar, a friend. He was almost happy for its companionship. When he was done, he saw it was his father who was there to help him. When he came out of the outhouse, Gomati Paati's hands were there once again—yes, that had been his Gomati Paati before, hadn't it?—to support him and lead him back to his bed. He was happy for Gomati Paati's hands when he was back on his bed of fire and ice. They were comforting.

There were other hands, another face, a young man's face, leaning over him and peering at him. The fire within had abated a little. "Oh, you are awake," the face observed. The hands that belonged to the face reached out and touched him. They felt his wrist. They removed the sheet covering him. They examined the bandage his father had placed on the wound on his left knee. Later, the face disappeared from his view, but he could hear voices conferring in whispers. This is what the doctor said, and this, and this, his father's voice explained. Why had he fallen sick? Not clear. Perhaps the fright, perhaps the wound on his knee, perhaps the muddy water he had swallowed. Various things were fed to him: rice gruel, powders, potions. The darkness, when it came, was no longer so complete. He could sense different objects as he drifted around in it. A wooden almirah, which contained the family's finer clothes. A second cot and a deep armchair. A calendar on a wall, a wooden loft high above him, a door, a window. Slowly, the darkness around him resolved itself into a familiar room. He was in the room his father shared with his uncle. He was in his father's bed. The darkness now began to develop a taste. Every time he moved his tongue in his mouth he tasted it—a bitter taste that grew stronger and stronger over time. And then the bitterness became unbearable. The voices in the darkness became clearer, more insistent. He awakened, moving his tongue this way and that way in his mouth, trying to escape the bitterness. He heard his father in conversation with Gomati Paati and with his Uncle Siva. Whenever Murugappa was mentioned, he felt a flutter in his chest, but he did not move.

His father, Uncle Siva, and Gomati Paati were in the central courtyard of the house, open to the sky above except for a secure grille. The window of the room in which Ramu lay recovering from his sickness opened onto the verandah that fronted this courtyard on all sides. Just outside the window, in one corner of this quadrangular verandah, a swing hung from the ceiling. When she was not in her chair looking out over the fields and gardens at the back of the house, Gomati Paati loved to perch on the broad and smooth wooden plank of this swing. Now Ramu could hear its regular creaking as she swung back and forth, with his father and uncle keeping her company. His father probably stood leaning against a pillar of the verandah, while his uncle sat cross-legged on the floor with a wooden tray arrayed with betel leaves, areca nuts, and chunamb by his side. That was how it usually was when the three of them were gathered in the verandah in the afternoon.

By this time of the day, the mild December sun would have shifted to the other side of the courtyard, where it could throw a bright yellow dazzle into the shallow tank of water with the hand pump perched over it. The corner in which the swing hung would be shaded and cozy. The stone floor, which could grow hot and uncomfortable from the onslaught of the summer sun in April and May, now would be slowly releasing the stored warmth of the day. Between words, Uncle Siva, folded legs warmed by stone, would spread chunamb in a thick white layer on a leaf, wrap areca nut in it, and place the leaf in his mouth with great relish. Sometimes he would pass one such preparation to Gomati Paati. His father would be leaning against the pillar, watching without partaking, his white veshti folded above his knees. From his present position, Ramu could not see out of the window of the room; but were he to lift himself even a little, he knew, he would have been able to witness just this scene out in the courtyard. He did not attempt to do so, though the certainty of his knowledge comforted him. He lay quietly listening to the voices drifting in through the window, over the creaking of the swing as it moved back and forth at the gentle pace Gomati Paati liked. He found the creaking restful.

The sound was about to put Ramu back to sleep when Kumar and Sharada stole into the room and placed themselves next to the bed. They stared at him with wide, curious eyes, as if he were something special, perhaps a hero returned from some great adventure. Ramu looked impatiently back at them.

"You are awake," Kumar whispered, because he had been told not to bother Ramu. Everyone agreed he looked like his father, Uncle Siva. His six-year-old face was pudgy, but he would be as handsome as his father when he was a man.

Ramu made no reply. He shut his eyes, hoping to make Kumar and Sharada go away. Even at the best of times he had little patience for Kumar and four-year old Sharada, who followed her brother everywhere he went. Years before he had been excited at the arrival first of baby Kumar and then of Sharada. But he was twelve now, going on thirteen. He liked to consider himself beyond the likes of Kumar and Sharada.

"Tell us about Murugappa," Kumar whispered.

Ramu kept silent, not even deigning to open his eyes.

"Did he speak to you?" Kumar asked. When Ramu still refused to break his silence, he persisted, "Tell us. Is it true he tried to catch you before you ran away? That's what Subbu says." Subbu was a boy who lived on Meenakshisundareswarar Temple Street. He went to the same school as Ramu and was his best friend.

"Go away," Ramu whispered back, without opening his eyes. "Both of you."

"Why won't you tell us?" Kumar demanded. It was clear Ramu's non-cooperation was annoying him.

"Yes, tell us," Sharada chimed in.

Encouraged by his sister's support, Kumar added, "You were afraid. I would not have been afraid." Of late, he had begun to show a new tendency to challenge Ramu directly. Kumar's mother doted on him and he was becoming puffed up, Ramu had decided, with his own importance.

Reluctantly, Ramu opened his eyes. Sharada was leaning her chin on the mattress of the bed, gazing up at Ramu with big, guileless eyes. Ramu focused his attention on Kumar. He fixed him with a glare and said, "You want to hear about Murugappa? I'll tell you about him. When I found him he was hanging upside down from a branch of the tree, just like a vetal. His hair was long and white. Just like a vetal's." Images flashed through Ramu's mind, so vivid his words almost faltered. "His head was split open all the way down to his neck. Red blood poured out of his head, onto the ground below. When he saw me standing there, he stretched out his long arms toward me and said, 'I beg you. Do something for me.'" Ramu paused, confused by his own image of a split bloody head speaking. He looked at Kumar and Sharada and asked, "You still want to hear what really happened?"

Sharada looked back at him with stricken eyes, but Kumar said boldly, "I'm not afraid!"

"Is that so? I'll tell you, then. But don't say later I didn't warn you," Ramu said. He made his voice hoarse, ominous, and stretched his arms out toward Kumar and Sharada. "Murugappa reached out for me like this. But I was quick. I stepped back so he couldn't catch me and asked, 'What is it you want, Murugappa?' He replied, 'I'm hungry. I want you to bring me a child. Any child will do. But if you can find Kumar, that would be best of all. Will you bring me Kumar?'"

Sharada's face trembled and then dissolved into tears. She turned and ran out of the room, shouting, "Amma! Amma!" Kumar held out for a few moments longer, and then he too whirled around and fled in search of his mother. Ramu watched his cousins' flight without satisfaction. He heard Uncle Siva call after them, asking why they were running so. The images he had conjured up for Kumar and Sharada were vivid, too vivid, in his head—startling enough to frighten he himself who had made them up. He had witnessed the real Murugappa dead with his throat cut under the tamarind tree. Should he have spoken the way he had? He felt a nagging disquiet at what he had done.

In a few moments, Aunt Malati came bustling into the room, trailing Kumar and Sharada behind her. Sharada was crying inconsolably. Kumar's face quivered in a brave attempt to keep the tears away. Ramu felt sorry when he saw Sharada.

"Why did you scare the children?" Aunt Malati asked. "You've been lying here sick. You open your eyes for the first time after days and this is the first thing you can think to do?" She spoke calmly but Ramu could not mistake the iron in her voice. Aunt Malati's straight hair was ever well oiled and braided, without a single strand out of place. She was a small, compact woman, sturdy and solid. She was very fair, almost white, and because of this she was envied, although as a matter of fact she was rather plain featured.

"Kumar insisted that I tell them about Murugappa," Ramu said, defending himself.

"So what if he asked you about Murugappa? Have you no sense? Don't you know what to say to a child? When will you learn to act your age?"

"He said Murugappa wanted to eat me!" Kumar declared, and burst into tears.

"Why would I say that? Why would Murugappa want to eat you?" Ramu asked. He stretched out his hands and made claws of them. "Is he a vetal, or a bhootam? Don't you know there are no such things?" At the sight of the claws reaching out in his direction, Kumar let out a stricken whimper. Sharada clung to her mother's sari, wailing louder than ever.

The commotion brought Ramu's father and Gomati Paati into the room. Ramu dropped his hands back onto his chest. Uncle Siva was at the window, looking in. He stood with his two hands holding the window bars and a superior look in his eyes, while his imposing chin was thrust forward in his usual arrogant manner. Below his well-groomed mustache, his mouth worked busily on betel leaf and areca nut.

"Are you awake, Ramu? How do you feel?" Gomati Paati inquired as she came up to the bed.

"Not so good, Paati," Ramu lied. In actuality, he was beginning to feel quite recovered.

"Leave the sick child alone," Gomati Paati admonished Aunt Malati, and started shooing her and the children out of the room. "Why are you pestering him now?"

"I have a pot of sambhar boiling on the stove," Aunt Malati said. The tart, tamarind smell of sambhar was indeed wafting through the house. "If Ramu hadn't made the children cry, would I be here? Ask him what he said to the children!" She flounced out just as she had come, taking her children with her. Uncle Siva disappeared from the window.

Ramu's father placed the back of his hand against Ramu's forehead. He looked at Gomati Paati and informed her, "No fever."

Gomati Paati came over to the bed, took Ramu's face in her two hands, and said, "Look how thin the child's face has become. Small and dry and brown. Like a sapota left out in the sun too long."

Supported by Gomati Paati, and feigning more weakness than he truly felt, Ramu sat up in bed. He liked the bed, his father's bed, in which he lay. He wondered whether, now that he was recovered, he would have to return to his usual sleeping arrangement—the mat rolled out for the night in a corner of the portico of the central courtyard. It was only because he was getting so much bigger now that he slept out in the portico. Until recently, Ramu had slept in the same room as Gomati Paati—how well he knew the delicate fragrance of her well-washed cotton sari!—for Kanchana, his mother, had died giving birth to him. Kumar had joined them when he was three, insisting on sleeping with his grandmother just as Ramu did. Sharada, however, was content to remain with her mother, in the room opposite the one in which Ramu had been sick all these days. The windows of these two rooms faced each other across the central courtyard of the house, out of which light was now draining rapidly.

The sun had dropped low in the sky, relinquishing the village of Paavalampatti from its bright clutches. The house had darkened considerably. Ramu's father pressed a switch on a wall of the room. An electric bulb ensconced in a glass fixture hanging from the ceiling directly above Ramu sprang into light. This was part of the magic of the room for Ramu—part of what made it special. Electricity had arrived in Paavalampatti only recently. Very few houses yet had electric lights. Theirs was one of the select, and even in their house only this room and the front room in which his father and uncle received guests were provided with these glowing markers of modernity. Petromax lamps, or else oil lamps of brass or clay, illuminated the other rooms.

As the harsh brightness flooded the room, Ramu forgot he was still pretending to be sick and leaped up on the bed, shouting, "Can I do it, Appa? Can *I* switch on the light?"

Ramu's father lifted Ramu up from the bed and carried him over, huffing and puffing and laughing as he did so. Why he was carrying Ramu in this fashion was not clear, for Ramu was certainly tall enough to reach the switch, which was set in a wooden box on the wall. Dangling like a puppet in his father's tight embrace, Ramu flipped the brown Bakelite switch up to the off position, and then down again. He did it again and again, the room leaping into brilliance only to plunge into darkness, until his father pulled him away from the switch, saying, between pants, "Enough. You will damage the light bulb. Do you know how expensive one of these is?" He carried Ramu back to the bed and plunked him down on it, still panting, and observed, "How heavy you have grown. Soon *you* will be able to carry *me*."

"Heavy? He has lost weight in his sickness," Gomati Paati declared from the other side of the bed. "He is still such a baby. Playing at being King Vikramaditya! If I had known something like this would happen, I would never have told him the stories about the vetal. Or made him that crown. Aren't you too old for this kind of game, Ramu? You're almost a man now. You don't know how sick you made yourself with your silly game. You've been out for five days straight."

In response, Ramu bravely leaped down from the bed and said, "Stop it, Paati. How can I be a man when you treat me like a baby?" He stood next to his grandmother and drew himself up to his full height. He had indeed lost weight because of his illness and his ribs showed through starkly above his loose shorts; but it was also true that he was already as tall as his grandmother. "See how tall I am. I don't want you to baby me anymore."

"Nonsense," Gomati Paati said. "I baby you? Never!" But then she immediately added, "Be careful. You are not fully recovered yet. You need rest still." It had been this way ever since Kanchana had died. On that day, also the very day Ramu had been born, Ramu had become Gomati Paati's third son. And she had begun to love him with a love both fiercer and more fearful than any that she had ever felt for her own children.

~

Kanchana's pregnancy had been difficult. She was a small-framed, anemic woman, only eighteen years old when she died, much too young to be dead. A few months into the pregnancy she had fallen ill with a mysterious fever. She had recovered but not without being severely weakened. For the rest of the pregnancy, she was prescribed complete rest. Custom demanded that she return to her mother's home for the delivery of the baby. But Ramagramam, the village in which she was born and had grown up, the village in which she had lived until her marriage to Vishu the previous year, was far away, involving many hours of travel by bullock cart along bad roads. Given her condition, it was not advisable to move her. Kanchana was bitterly disappointed, but there was nothing to be done. The risk, both to the baby and to the expecting mother, was simply too great. It was decided that instead of Kanchana going, a week before the baby was to arrive her mother would come to Paavalampatti.

After the fever, Kanchana lay night and day on a thick jamakaalam in the room now occupied by Malati. Gomati Paati's two daughters, Saroja and Vasantha, were still living at home at that time. They were betrothed but not married yet. They nursed Kanchana, who was the same age as Saroja, the elder of the two. As the day of the baby's arrival approached—Kanchana's mother would be here any day now—new and disturbing complications arose. Kanchana saw a powerful vision in her sleep. She was in the main temple of Ramagramam. It was night and the temple, dedicated to Lord Rama, was dark. She was alone in the stone portico of the temple, with the familiar paintings of scenes from the Ramayana adorning the walls. Suddenly the wooden doors of the sanctum sanctorum flew open with a clatter, and a booming voice, accompanied by a great glowing yellow light, rang out, calling her name. "Kanchana! Kanchana! Come to me, Kanchana," the voice exhorted. "Come back to me. What are you doing so far away from me?" This vision so frightened Kanchana that she woke up sobbing and drenched with sweat. It took great patience on the part of Saroja, keeping her sister-in-law company through the night on a mat spread out next to her, to ferret out what Kanchana had seen.

By morning, the whole household knew of the harrowing vision, and soon after, all of Meenakshisundareswarar Temple Street. Neighbors stopped Gomati Paati, on her way for her morning devotions to the temple from which the street took its name, to express concern at her daughter-in-law's vision. In the temple, between her respects to the idol of Meenakshi on one side and the Shiva lingam on the other, more neighbors stopped to ask their questions. The inquiries—so solicitous, too solicitous—deepened the irritation Gomati Paati already felt at the singular experience her daughter-in-law had had. She cut short her visit to the temple, foregoing the customary circumambulation of the sanctum sanctorum, and hurried home. She marched straight into the room in which Kanchana lay and demanded, "What kind of thoughts are these you have in your head? Is this what you should be thinking of when you are about to bring a baby into the world?" She stood outlined against the window opening onto the central courtyard. Her white widow's sari glowed palely in the dim room, which was lit only by a single oil lamp and the gray morning light from the window.

Kanchana, already distraught from the night's experience, stared back mutely at her mother-in-law. She was lying on her side on her jamakaalam with her enormous belly, stuffed as if to bursting with new life, bulging out from her. Her mouth felt sour from the thin, acidic bile that had forced its way up from her stomach. Her back hurt. Her head hurt. These days some part of her body or the other was always hurting. In her unquiet mind, memories of her life before her marriage moved around boldly like guests who had overstayed their welcome. Her father, her dear mother, the green irrigation canal by which she had played with her brothers, the dear, dear house in which they had all lived, the temple to Lord Rama she would visit every day—she could not keep these and other such visions out of her mind. Even at this dire moment, with her mother-in-law standing demandingly over her, her mind was filled only with thoughts of her own mother, who was to have arrived by now but had not.

It was left to Saroja, seated cross-legged on the mat next to the prostrate Kanchana, to say soothingly to Gomati Paati, "Let it be,

Amma. She has had a difficult night. She keeps asking whether her mother has arrived. See how big her belly is? She must be in much pain."

"When Vishu was born, I was the same age as this girl here," Gomati Paati retorted. "I did not ask a single person to help me. I cooked in the kitchen, because your father was devoted to my cooking, until it was time for Vishu to come. Then I sent for the maruthavachi and came and lay down in this very room. In no time at all Vishu was born. That is the way it was with all four of you. The girls these days . . ." But then she faltered, for she saw how wan Kanchana looked in the flickering light from the oil lamp. She aborted her sermon and abruptly left the room.

Kanchana was a trial to Gomati Paati. She agitated her no end. Perhaps it was because Gomati Paati saw in Kanchana the young bride that she herself had once been—and, she could not stop herself from thinking, also *not* been. Kanchana was frail, moody, listless. She was sensitive. She hardly spoke, hardly took any interest in the new family and home she had entered. Between her and Vishu the relationship remained formal, studied, proper. Gomati Paati saw little intimacy between them—Vishu had always been a retiring type, and Kanchana seemed grateful to be left alone. Occasionally Kanchana was found sitting in a dark room, crying. It was true that the pregnancy, which had begun quite soon after their marriage, had turned out difficult. Even so, Kanchana had been withdrawn and uncommunicative from the very first day of her arrival in the house after the wedding. Gomati Paati made many attempts to reach out to her daughter-in-law, inviting her to come and sit next to her on the swing in the central courtyard while she told her stories about her new family. "You are the eldest daughter-in-law," she would tell Kanchana, while she braided her long, black hair. "Don't you need to know everything about your new family?" She would gently run her fingers through the hair as she braided, moved to tenderness at the misery so clearly visible on Kanchana's face. Kanchana, however, remained silent, unresponsive. Gomati Paati would feel her sympathy souring, and, forcing herself to swallow the sharp words springing to her lips, would continue, "Do you know at what age I was married? Do you know how old I was when I became a widow?" And then she would launch with great deliberation into some story from her past.

Gomati Paati had grown up the third daughter of Neelakanta Sastrigal, an impoverished but respectable priest in the distant village of Korurpatti. The Brahmin section of this village was small. The village temple, of which Gomati Paati's father was priest, was accordingly modest, with no endowed fields attached to it. Her mother had died years before, forcing Neelakanta Sastrigal to devote himself to the difficult task of raising his three suddenly motherless daughters. Despite his spiritual vocation, Neelakanta Sastrigal was a practical man, combining acute consciousness of his own poverty with a deep sense of familial obligation. Made exceedingly aware of the trials and tribulations of life by his poverty as well as the unexpected demise of his wife, he brought up his daughters to be independent minded. "After me," he often declared to them, "who will care about you poor girls? Rely only on yourself."

He raised his three daughters with little financial or other assistance from relatives—it helped that the eldest was already twelve when their mother died—and he found himself forced to marry the first two into families even more impoverished than his own. It was the best he could do, given what he was able to provide as dowry. The marriages were not happy. Money was a constant problem in both the marriages, the lack of it poisoning trust and harmony and hope. One daughter, it soon became clear, had married a proud but tyrannical man embittered by his straitened circumstances. There were beatings. There were stormy quarrels. The other daughter faced no direct abuse in her marriage, but her husband seemed determined to make up for this virtue by his hecklessness and indolence and complete inability to provide for his family. Neelakanta Sastrigal grieved privately for his two eldest daughters and regretted his inability to find better grooms for them.

When it came to Gomati, however—no Paati at this point in her life—he was determined to do better. She was his favorite. Already, at the age of fourteen, she was an acknowledged beauty, with mesmerizing eyes and a finely shaped face. One day, he called her out to the thinnai fronting their modest house, where he was resting for the afternoon. Their house was at one end of the short, mean Brahmin street of the village. At the other end was the Shiva temple at which Gomati's father officiated as priest. When Gomati had settled herself next to him on the red stained floor of the thinnai, he said, "You and I are left alone in this house now." He spoke in a low voice so that the neighbors passing along the street would not overhear their conversation.

"Yes," Gomati agreed.

"It is time to get you married. When that is done, all my obligations will be finished. It has not been easy with three mouths to feed. You are my last worry in life. Already you are a woman. You have been one for more than a year. I should have found you a match before you became one. The neighbors make hurtful remarks every chance that they get about how I keep a grown daughter at home." The neighbors were scandalized: whoever had heard of a girl remaining unmarried till puberty, like some vulgar, low-caste woman? Neelakanta Sastrigal felt their censure keenly, but his hindrances and anxieties were not theirs. What did they know about how he had to struggle to save for a dowry? Or how he worried about making the right kind of match for his third daughter, the kind he had not been able to make for the first two?

"I don't care about the neighbors. I like being here with you," Gomati replied.

"Yes, child, but two offers of marriage have come for you. In both cases, the size of the dowry will not be a concern. I am not a rich man. How can I ignore fortune when it comes knocking on the door like this?" He did not clarify that one offer had come searching for Gomati, while the other he himself had pursued.

Gomati, young though she was, understood her father's predicament.

"One offer is from the village of Vandanad, not far from here. I have seen the boy. Everyone speaks very highly of him. The family is not rich. The boy is a cook. When there is a big wedding or a similar occasion, he goes with his father to do the cooking. That is why I have seen the boy. Father and son have been in charge of the food at weddings I have attended as priest. The boy is very handsome. Let me be frank here: I have been both father and mother to you, and I have always spoken freely about all matters. You have great beauty, more than your sisters. The boy is a match for you. He is eighteen years old. He will be a companion to you in your life. Your horoscopes match very well."

"You said he is a cook?" Gomati asked, for she knew the boy her father was describing.

A few months previously Gomati's father had taken her with him to a wedding at which he was officiating as priest. The wedding was in a neighboring village. Both of Gomati's sisters were already married by this time and it was not possible to leave her alone at home. At the wedding, she had seen and been seen by a young cook with bold, searching eyes that singled her out from the crowd. Tall, straight-backed, he was striking in appearance, though clad in a dirty white vest and veshti stained with sweat and food. He was dark, almost black, with a broad brow and a firm, determined mouth. He stood in an open clearing between two mango trees some distance away from the portico of the wedding hall, where she had found a group of girls her own age. She was wearing her one silk paavaadai, grown so short now that it did not quite reach her ankles. The paavaadai was a deep green that she loved, but it was a hand-me-down from her sisters and had a long tear in it that had been rendered barely visible only because she was so adept with needle and thread. In the clearing, pots and pans sat over wood fires burning between low, blackened brick walls. Over an enormous shallow pan was bent a balding older man dripping with sweat. He was expertly squeezing swirls of dough into the spluttering oil with bare hands. Was this the boy's father? The moment the swirls met the oil they began to turn orange, into jelebis dancing and hissing in the hot oil. In another pot, the finest Elephant's Tusk rice cooked, sending its delicate aroma wafting from the clearing toward Gomati and the other girls gathered in the portico of the wedding hall.

In the midst of it all, staring impudently at her, towered the young cook from whom an offer of marriage had now arrived. His white sacred thread, grimy with sweat and soot from the fires, dangled awkwardly from a long tear in his vest, which was full of holes. His bare feet were callused and knobby and encrusted with mud. Wooden ladle in hand, he stood next to a large black pot of aviyal, his curly hair falling into his eyes. The heat from the pots made the air around him undulate in the bright sunshine. Eyes met, she looked away, but when her gaze inexorably returned, he was standing just as before, still looking at her. He held her eyes again for a long moment, until the older man sniffed, as if smelling something, turned, noticed his idleness, and yelled at him, "Idiot. Quick! The aviyal is beginning to burn." Deliberately—too deliberately—the young man returned to his work, stirring the green and yellow vegetables bubbling in the pot with the ladle grasped firmly in both his hands, while the older man's abuse rained down on him. Now his back was turned to Gomati and the muscles of his arms and shoulders rippled as he turned the boiling broth this way and that. Gomati could not help contemplating his fine appearance as he stood there leaning over his pot. How very handsome he was! She looked away only when one of her companions, giggling, shoved an elbow into her ribs.

"That is what I said. A cook," Gomati's father replied to her question, abruptly ending her reverie. He misunderstood her reason for asking it and continued, "The family is not rich. It appears they do not care that you have already become a woman. What kind of comfort this marriage will bring you I cannot say. You have been the daughter of a poor priest. You know what that is like. You will be the wife of a poor cook." He paused. "But as I said, there is another offer. They too do not care that you have become a woman."

"Yes. The other offer."

"This man is rich. His name is Kumaraswamy Iyer. His village is far from here. The name of the village is Paavalampatti. The man is not young. You should know that."

"How old is he?"

"Thirty-five."

"Thirty-five?"

"Yes, child, he is only a little younger than I am. I have never seen him, but I'm told he does not really look his age. He has only a little bit of white in his hair. Just a little on the sides. Nothing to speak of. He has been married before. His wife died a few years ago, and now he wants to marry again."

"I will be his second wife."

"Yes, but there are no children from the first marriage. There was a son. He too died and now the man wants to marry so that he has heirs."

Gomati was silent, thinking of the two offers of marriage that had been made for her.

"The man from Paavalampatti is rich. He is a big landlord. If you marry him, you will never have to worry about money again. How many days we have gone to bed after eating just one meal in the day, and that being no more than rice gruel with a little bit of lime pickle. You will never have to do that again if you marry the man from Paavalampatti. I have made careful enquiries. I'm told he is a good man. The horoscopes match. I have gone over them myself. Initially, I thought they didn't. But then I looked at them again and now I think they do. As for the man, he does not care about horoscopes."

"You want me to marry the rich man."

"No, child, I don't know what I want. Sometimes I think one thing and sometimes another. It is true that the rich man is much older than you. My heart falters when I think about that. I keep asking myself what your mother would say. The cook is handsome. He is a good match to your beauty and perhaps he will be a better companion to you because of his age. But, then again, what pleasure is there in being poor? Right now I don't know what to tell you, child. Let us think about this some more."

At first, Gomati could only think of how the cook had stood in the clearing and boldly looked at her. She felt once again the thrill—the powerful stir of deep desire—she had felt then. But then her mind turned more and more to her sisters. She thought especially about her eldest sister, who had been a kind of surrogate mother to her after their own mother had died. This sister's husband, too, was handsome. And what good had that done? Gomati remembered the sister as gentle and loving. Her life was a misery now. How bitter and angry she was all the time. The anger her husband took out on her, she took out on her children. When she visited, she hardly spoke, instead taking every opportunity to curl up in a corner and sleep. Dark circles were etched permanently around her eyes—indeed, darkness lurked deep within the eyes too. Gomati thought of those eyes filled with darkness and felt dread.

Soon, without any prompting from her father, Gomati herself broached the subject of her marriage: "Appa, I have decided."

"What have you decided?"

"About my marriage. I will marry the rich man from Paavalampatti."

"What are you saying, child? When you are still young, he will be an old man." Neelakanta Sastrigal could not help recalling at this moment of decision that Kumaraswamy Iyer was old enough to be Gomati's father.

"You say he is a good man. If God wills it, I will spend a long, happy life with him. I have seen what poverty does to men. What guarantee is there that I will be happy with the cook? What do I really know of him as a person?"

But in the end, what she had wished for, God had not willed. At fourteen, she was married to a husband who was thirty-five; fifteen years later she was the widowed mother of four children. Was God punishing her for the uncommon resolve she had shown at such a young age? Neelakanta Sastrigal could not help wondering. None but Gomati herself knew of the way she had agonized until the very day of her wedding, and indeed after the wedding too for a while, about the decision she had made to marry the rich man from Paavalampatti. Once the decision had been made, once ritual promises had been given and accepted, what was the point in burdening other people with useless doubts and fears? This was the way Gomati thought, and so her father knew nothing about all the reflecting and deciding and wavering and redeciding she had done lying awake on her mat night after night. Many were the nights the handsome cook had come visiting in her thoughts—only to be followed at once by her two unfortunate sisters.

Gomati Paati was not yet thirty when she discarded her ornaments (her nose ring, her diamond-studded earrings, her marriage necklace of the purest gold) and her colorful saris (how she loved the green ones especially!) and gave up decorating herself with flowers. In their stead, she put on a plain white widow's sari. She shaved off her thick, long, lustrous hair, the smell of which had been such an intoxication to her husband in intimate, conjugal moments—as much as the gentle flutter of his fingertips on her lips had been for her. Such intoxications, given or received, were forever forbidden to her now. As the barber rasped his blade back and forth over her beautifully shaped skull, her father wept, but she herself shed not a single tear, at least not right there, right then. If she wept at all, her father did not know it. Or perhaps he did not notice it, for he was consumed by the thought that he had made an error over the horoscopes. He remembered how, when he had first compared the horoscopes, it had seemed their conjunction through marriage would give inordinate power to the malignant influence of Saturn on the bridegroom. But he had read the horoscopes again and again until he had been persuaded that that was not the case. And now the bridegroom was dead. What if the *first* reading had been the correct one? The thought was unbearable when he considered all that his young daughter would have to endure as a widow.

Whenever there was an auspicious event, widow Gomati Paati made sure to stay out of sight as custom demanded. The very sight of her was now contaminating. There were a hundred rules about what she could and could not do. She followed them all—no, not all: many she broke, quietly and unobtrusively, if the interests of her children demanded it, or on her own behalf if she felt a great need to. But mostly she observed the rules as best she could. She put up with the remarks of relatives on her husband's side who wondered loudly in her hearing what kind of an ill-starred woman she was to have thrust her husband so speedily onto the funeral pyre—it took time for her to firmly, gradually, remove the interference of these relatives in her affairs. To these remarks she found it easy to turn a deaf ear, for she had in fact had a mutually and profoundly caring relationship with her husband, so much older though he had been than she. And perhaps it was because she realized just how rare her relationship with her husband had been that she did not grieve his death as desperately as she might have. How much worse it would have been if she had never had such a relationship at all!

On both sides, the caring had come slowly, with growing knowledge of the other. Kumaraswamy Iyer was a thoughtful man. He did not summon Gomati to his side as wife until she was seventeen. Mere girl though she was when he married her, he quickly recognized Gomati's qualities. Drawn to her first by his need for heirs, then by her beauty, he grew eventually to love her—yes, *love* her, she knew it was true—for those aspects of her not visible to the naked eye. She too had come to love him. Rich though he was, she saw that he himself had suffered at the hands of his domineering father. He was a learned and progressive-minded man, who did not think it beneath him either to discuss the affairs of the world with her or to share his hopes and fears. He was famous in the village for his free thinking. Defying caste laws and village custom, he gave Murugappa a place of prominence on his lands. Similarly, he defied custom and practice at home in the way he made Gomati his intimate partner in accepted and unaccepted ways. Had he not been a man of sober dignity and great learning in three languages—Sanskrit, Tamil, and English—he would no doubt have been made to pay for his independence. But who in the village had the temerity to challenge a rich man who was more a Brahmin in the depth of his knowledge of rituals and scriptures than the most orthodox Brahmin among them? Moreover, Kumaraswamy Iyer was not rash or recklessly unmindful of the opinion of the village. He could be formal, careful in his observation of custom when he was with Gomati in public. At first, she had been confused by this public formality, and then she had realized that it was a way for him to respect her, so much younger than he, when they were with others. She had loved him both for observing custom and for breaking it, and in loving him had learned to do both herself.

Before his death, Kumaraswamy Iyer had made it clear in legal documents and in informal instructions that she was to be in charge of his lands until the eldest son, Vishu, came of age. He trusted no one else to safeguard the interests of his children. The trust was not misplaced. Gomati Paati grieved the loss of the man who, though old enough to be her father, had given her the respect due to her because of her character and her status as his wife, and who had in the little time he had spent with his children shown himself gentle and sensible. She was determined to honor him by living up to his assessment of her. She invited her father to her side—what need now for the priestly position in the poor little temple?—and proceeded to manage with rare ability the lands left behind by her husband. It was another matter that later Siva, the younger son, took the avid interest in the land that Vishu was meant to. Vishu's mind was always far away. He proceeded to earn a Licensed Medical Practitioner's diploma and joined the Sanitation Department rather than working the land. There was no need for him to make such a living. Gomati Paati could not understand the attraction of such a job, but she did not stand in his way.

Widowhood was, Gomati Paati found, difficult in both expected and unexpected ways. She missed her husband terribly for the man he had been—in the world and at home. She missed his familiar presence by her side at the auspicious village events she was no longer permitted to attend. She missed the comfort as well as the arousing throb of his body in the night. All this was expected. Unexpected was the way she missed him because she found herself now in a strange new situation with other men. Now, she found, she moved all manner of men powerfully. It was as if men could not bear to find such beauty widowed; as if they felt a mighty impulse to right what callous death had wronged. She did nothing to incite such feelings in the men; it seemed to be just the way things were. Men, even the most innocent, yearned to be near her, to do things for her, to warm their cold selves in the glow of her beauty. Gomati Paati became all too aware of her allure. In her marriage, she had felt desire's ability to affirm; now she felt its power to constrict and confound. In the end, she refused to be governed by it; but only she knew how much firm calculation it had taken her over the years to preserve herself, widow that she was—to never let the desiring men too near but sometimes, when it suited her, to let them do one or two things for her. It had not been easy, any of it.

Over the years, Gomati Paati became a doughty presence in Paavalampatti, not only in the Y-shaped Brahmin street commanded by the Meenakshisundareswarar Temple but beyond. Like those of her neighbors who too were rich, Gomati Paati's house was in the stem of the Y, which led up to the tall wooden doors of the temple located at the very center of the street. The houses of the street's two short branches, which extended behind the temple in the direction of the Tamarabarani River, were smaller, less imposing in appearance. Less well-to-do Brahmin neighbors lived in them. In this street and beyond, Gomati Paati was known and respected.

Gomati Paati shared many stories from her life with Kanchana during the first few months after Kanchana's arrival in Paavalampatti. With these stories she hoped perhaps to draw Kanchana out, to make her feel at home. Kanchana, wide-eyed and innocent, remained immured from these advances, the walls of her isolation apparently tall and insurmountable. Gomati Paati queried Vishu about his new wife, but her son, a wisp of a boy himself, was clueless about the new person to whom he had irrevocably hitched his life. In response to his mother's probing questions, he was able only to voice a shy bewilderment. So Gomati Paati had turned to her father, still with her in Paavalampatti and two years away from his death, to help her understand Kanchana. The old man's response, delivered in a quavering voice, was to observe that Kanchana, as befit a bride of the family of Kumaraswamy Iyer, came from a well-to-do background. The rest he left for his daughter to infer. The passage of years had deepened Neelakanta Sastrigal's appreciation of the differences between those two great tribes of human beings—the rich and the poor. Gomati Paati, however, had been born into one tribe and married into the other; she did not know what to make of her father's speculation. A resolute and strong-willed woman herself, she could not easily understand the difficulties of a timid personality such as Kanchana's. What problems could a woman such as Kanchana, pampered in the home into which she had been born and destined to be equally pampered in the home into which she had been married, have? Perhaps in time Gomati Paati would have discovered the answer to this question and opened a new chapter in her relationship with her daughter-in-law. But time there had not been.

Kanchana had promptly become pregnant and entered into the complications that had ensued. And then, warm life was shadowed by cold death: at the moment of celebration, tragedy. Kanchana's labor pains began prematurely the night following the extraordinary vision of the Ramagramam temple. Kanchana's mother had still not arrived from Ramagramam. The maruthavachi was summoned. She was a plump, white-haired woman who was generally confident and optimistic. But one look at Kanchana on the jamakaalam, frail and fatigued, and her face grew grave. She gave instructions for boiling water, clean rags, a candle in addition to the two oil lamps already burning in the room. From a fold in her sari she drew a sharp knife, sterilized it in the flame of the candle, and placed it next to herself on the jamakaalam. Then she pushed aside Kanchana's sari and, with closed eyes and pursed lips, proceeded to press and feel the great mound of flesh that was now Kanchana's belly. From inside the quivering mound she could feel the baby stir, push back, as if eager to reply to her inquiring hand. Reassured about the baby, the maruthavachi opened her eyes, turned to Kanchana's face, and looked deeply into it, prising open the eyelids drooping from exhaustion. Again her face grew melancholy. Gomati Paati, squatting next to the maruthavachi, noticed her expression. Taking Kanchana's hand in her own, she asked anxiously, "What is it? How is the baby?"

The maruthavachi said, "The baby is fine."

"And the mother?"

When the maruthavachi made no reply, Gomati Paati understood. She thought of Vishu restlessly pacing the floor outside. Her poor son. If something should happen to Kanchana, how would he take it? And then she thought of Kanchana's family so far away at this time of her need, and of Kanchana's mother who was to have been with her at this moment. Why had she not arrived yet? Perhaps she was on her way even now, oblivious to how her daughter's life hung perilously in the balance. When she thought of all the people whose lives would be forever stained by sorrow should Kanchana die, she felt shame for the testiness she had displayed during the preceding months. And then dread washed out shame, for her mind remembered the life inside Kanchana hungry to be born. Had she not been a motherless child herself? Did she not know what that meant? Gomati Paati's stomach churned at the awful prospect.

Hours later, the baby was born and Gomati Paati's worst fears about Kanchana had come true. Kanchana had died—pale, silent, and barely conscious—in a flood of unstoppable bleeding. All the clean rags in the house did not suffice for the blood that poured out after the baby—a red torrent, it seemed to Gomati Paati's helpless gaze. She clutched Kanchana's hand—the weight of it almost non-existent—and willed the girl to fight, fight, fight. A doctor was summoned, but before he could arrive it was over. Kanchana was dead. Sometime during the bleeding she had drifted away forever, fading out without opening her eyes or speaking a word. Gomati Paati had felt the going in the hand she was holding, and when she had, it was as if a part of her too was leaving.

At the end of the ordeal, Gomati Paati wearily picked up the little wrinkled baby, washed clean of the bloody agony of its entry into the world, and carried it out to the backyard by the well. Dawn light filled the yard, tingeing everything with its gentle, pearly beauty so that the things of the world appeared soft, beguiling. The smell of cow dung and hay rose from the stalls in the back. On the high back wall, a stray black cat paused, back arched gracefully, head turned to take in the widow in white sari who had suddenly appeared holding a newborn baby in her two extended hands like an abject offering to the world. And then the washerman's donkey brayed from the direction of the river, its daily morning complaint harsh and grating to the ear. In a dark blur, the cat leaped from the wall into the neem tree beyond, driving the birds in the branches to burst into the air, calling shrilly to one another in panic.

Once again—she had done it many times already—Gomati Paati checked the fingers and toes and ears and nose and eyes and penis of the baby, holding it up in her two hands in the strengthening natural light of the rising sun. All as should be. A perfect little baby. A little rheumy encrustation in the corners of the eyes, but otherwise perfect. Satisfied, she drew the baby protectively to herself. The baby stirred, as if to burrow deep into the warmth of her body. She could not help smiling sadly when she looked at the small shape nestling close against her breasts; inside, her heart was stone. She was exhausted from watching over Kanchana for hours as her fate swung first one way and then another, like a heavy overripe mango threatening to snap and fall from its branch. The poets liked to sing about dying in the fullness of time. But Kanchana, young as she was, was no overripe mango at the end of its life. No matter: the mango, sweet and fresh, had snapped, fallen, to be crushed into the dirt below. A girl of eighteen dies. A newborn child is left motherless. Where was the justice in it? The poets knew nothing. The world was not just. The world was not fair. The world was a burden. Gomati Paati decided then and there that she would be a mother to the motherless child in her arms.

Later that morning, the bullock cart carrying Kanchana's mother from Ramagramam arrived belatedly in Meenakshisundareswarar Temple Street with a creak of wood and a gay tinkle of bells. Kanchana's mother had expected to arrive the previous evening but midway the wheel of the cart had come undone and the journey had had to be suspended for the night while repairs were made. When she entered the house, eager to see her daughter, it was Gomati Paati who met her somberly with the newborn baby in her arms. Vishu was too devastated to be able to face his mother-in-law. And the next day, when Kanchana's mother suggested in a lifeless voice (she had spent the previous day weeping by the body of her daughter) that the baby be named Raman, Gomati Paati could not deny her.

According to custom, the baby should have been named Kumaraswamy, after the paternal grandfather, Gomati Paati's deceased husband. But Kanchana's mother had been told of the vision of the temple in Ramagramam that Kanchana had seen the night before her death. "My daughter is dead," she observed to Gomati Paati in a desolate voice. "Who knows what the vision she saw means? If you ask me, don't anger Lord Rama unnecessarily. Name the baby Raman in His honor." Was it love for her lost daughter? Or resentment arising from what she had learned of Gomati Paati's annoyance at the vision her beloved daughter had seen? Whatever the reason, Gomati Paati, who had been looking forward to naming this first male grandchild after her husband, had not been able to refuse the request of a grieving mother. Years later, it was Siva's son who got to be named Kumaraswamy, Kumar for short.

~

DURING RAMU'S DAYS OF CONVALESCENCE, his father did not go on tour or to his office in nearby Ambasamudram. He stayed at home, lounging in an easy chair drawn up next to the bed on which Ramu lay. The day after his fever had subsided, Subbu, who went to the same school in Ambasamudram as Ramu, was asked to find out what Ramu could do to keep up with his schoolwork during his days of absence. Subbu returned with pages and pages of instructions—Ramu must do *this*, *this*, and *this* from his English textbook and *this* and *this* from Tamil; in math he must do *these* exercises and also *these,* and since math was his weak subject he must make sure to brush up on *this* during his absence. To Ramu the instructions were galling—what point was there in being sick if you could not escape schoolwork? It felt like double punishment. He felt let down by Subbu, who took great pleasure in scrupulously detailing all the work that was to be done. Since his father was such a constant companion by his bed, there was no escaping the assigned work.

While Ramu did his schoolwork, his father sat in his chair and read his newspaper, or else quietly watched Ramu. As had ever been his wont, he spoke little. Sometimes he brooded with his arms folded across his chest, a fugitive expression on his face, a mysterious longing lurking in his eyes. And then he seemed even more distant and unreachable than usual. Ramu could not help feeling his father wished to be elsewhere, perhaps on tour. It was not that he doubted his father's love for him. Rather, he sensed an unspoken restlessness in his father that he did not fully understand.

Father and son spoke little (the terrible incident that had occasioned Ramu's sickness was especially avoided), but when the silence between them became so unbearable as to bother even his generally taciturn father, the newspaper came in handy. Ramu's father was one of the few men in Paavalampatti to receive an English newspaper, from which he sometimes read to Ramu. In this way,

Ramu came to know a little about the great events unfolding in India as well as around the world. At awkward moments during Ramu's convalescence, his father would pick up the newspaper from where it lay on the floor by the chair, indicate some story in it, and ask, "Do you know what it says here?"

Ramu would make his typical reply: "No. What?"

"Indian soldiers will be fighting in Europe soon."

All too often the stories were about the war in Europe. The war was very much in the news, and also, it seemed, on his father's mind.

"Against the Germans?"

"Yes."

"Why? What did the Germans do to us?"

"Nothing. But, as you know, the British have thrown us into the war on their side against the Germans."

"Will the Germans come to India, then?"

Intriguing prospect. Ramu imagined German soldiers marching through Paavalampatti, tanks rumbling along in their wake, past the banyan tree where the bullock carts halted. He imagined German planes bobbing and weaving in thrilling battles with British planes high in the sky above the gopuram of the Meenakshisundareswarar Temple.

"I hope not," Ramu's father laughed. He paused, and then continued, "What do you think, Ramu? Do you think we should fight for the British against the Germans?"

"Yes . . . No . . . What do you mean?" Ramu was not sure what answer to give.

"The British will be sending Indian soldiers to fight against the Germans in Europe." Ramu's father tapped the newspaper. "Every day there is some item in here about young men signing up to go to the war. Do you think Indians should fight in this white people's war?"

"No," Ramu decided. "Why should we fight in somebody else's war?"

Ramu's father nodded. He looked contemplative. "Hitler is a bad man. But he is not our enemy. He is the enemy of the British. Gandhi and the Congress want no part of this war. That is why all the Congress governments all over the country resigned a few months ago. You know about that." He looked at Ramu searchingly. He liked to be reassured that his attempts to inform his son about the larger world were not wasted.

Ramu did remember the resignations. His father had told him about them. Two years previously the Congress Party had decided to participate in elections at the provincial level and then had formed governments in those provinces where they had won. But when war broke out between the British and the Germans, the Congress governments had resigned, because they were not ready to support the war effort without some promise of freedom after the war. Gandhi's experience during the previous war between the Germans and the British had been a disappointment. Fresh from South Africa, he had supported that war effort by encouraging military recruitment among Indians, only to have hopes of political concessions from the British dashed after the ending of hostilities.

Thinking about the last time the British and the Germans had fought—long before his birth—made Ramu remember something else. "Didn't the Germans come to India the last time they fought the British?"

"Germans in India? During the Great War? . . . Yes, you're right. I know what you mean. You are thinking about the *Emden*, the German ship that fired on Madras. Something like that could happen again. This war the British and the Germans are fighting will not be over soon."

Now Ramu's mind filled with images of the guns of a great ship out at sea thundering against a blue sky. He had never been to Madras. He imagined a city with high white towers rising up among palm trees. Under the deadly assault from the *Emden* the towers collapsed in great clouds of dust. The vision in his head was rousing. What a shame that Paavalampatti was not on the coast! "Do you remember *Emden* firing on Madras, Appa? How old were you when that happened?"

"Very young. I don't remember the firing itself. But people talked about it for years afterwards. If I did something bold and naughty Gomati Paati would say, 'What an *Emden* you are.'"

"She still says that to me," Ramu observed.

"The *Emden* created a huge panic just by firing at Madras from out at sea. People fled in the thousands. Fires broke out in the city. Afterward the ship sailed down the coast firing here and there. The British didn't know what to do." Ramu's father was silent then, as if he too were imagining a great ship firing at a great city by the sea. Such abrupt and inexplicable silence in the midst of a conversation was his eccentric way.

As the silence grew, Ramu's anxiety grew with it. He enjoyed it when his father initiated these conversations that wandered across the world, stopping now at this event and now again at another; at these times he felt a rare intimacy between himself and his father. He glanced encouragingly at the newspaper lying open in his father's lap and asked, "What is that story there?"

Ramu's father stirred himself. "This?" The story was small, no more than a brief paragraph. The headline read *Men of Different Castes Come Together for Meal.* "There is an organization called the Inter-Caste Dining Association. This is about them."

"What do they do?"

"The Association is against caste discrimination. They don't believe there is anything wrong if people of different castes eat together. How can eating together make you impure? So they organize meals where people of different castes come together to eat."

"Even Untouchables?"

"They are not called Untouchables now. Gandhi calls them Harijans—it's Hindi for God's People."

"Hari . . . jans . . . They too eat with people from other castes at these meals?"

"Yes."

"And Brahmins like us too?"

"Yes. That is what it says here in the newspaper."

"Murugappa was—how did you call them?—a Harijan."

"Yes."

Corpse with two mouths. Terrifying, untouchable corpse.

"He never ate with us."

"No." A faint smile flitted across Ramu's father's face.

"What do you think, Appa? Do you think it is fine if people of different castes eat together?"

Ramu's father considered the question with his usual deliberation. "I think so," he said. "Didn't Tiruvalluvar say it two thousand years ago? 'Flawless conduct is flawless birth; flawed makes birth low.' What does it matter what caste someone is? What matters is what a man does. If a man is good, why not eat with him?"

"That's not what Paati says."

"Gomati Paati was brought up in a different world. India has changed a lot since she was a child."

"It's not just Paati. Uncle Siva too does not think like you."

"True."

"And he is younger than you, Appa."

"True again."

"So then?"

"So then what?"

"So then is Uncle Siva wrong when he says what he says about people who are of other castes?"

"I suppose India hasn't changed very much then."

"Have you ever eaten with someone who is not a Brahmin, Appa?"

"Sometimes. When I am away on tour."

"Never at home. Only Brahmins come inside our home."

"That's not exactly right. The Kanaku Pillai comes to do the accounts for us, for example."

"I know that. But he sits at his desk in the front room. No one ever comes into our kitchen. Or eats with us."

"True."

"And have you eaten with a Harijan ever?"

"No. Never." The look on Ramu's father's face suggested he was amused at Ramu's question.

"How can you be so sure?"

"I just know. It's hard to explain. I can tell who is a Harijan."

"Uncle Siva says a Paraiyar's body is made differently than ours."

"I don't know about that . . ."

Ramu remembered more. "He says they have hot bodies. Much hotter than ours. That is why they can work for such long hours in the hot sun, when we would fall down and die."

"Uncle Siva talks a lot."

Ramu looked at his father slyly. "Are you saying Uncle Siva doesn't know what he is saying?"

"I can see you are feeling much better now."

"I think that's what you mean," Ramu declared. "Uncle Siva does blabber a lot. I think so too."

"I did not say any such thing. You'd better learn to be respectful of your elders." Ramu's father paused for a long moment, thinking. "And pay attention to what they teach you in science in school. The world is changing. Everything is based on science now."

Ramu laughed triumphantly. "Uncle Siva knows nothing about science," he whooped. "Why should he talk about things he does not understand?"

⁓

FOR THE FIRST FEW DAYS of his convalescence Ramu stayed in bed, kept company by his father in this fashion. Gomati Paati and Uncle Siva were busier than usual because of the unexpected demise of Murugappa. Uncle Siva was out in the fields a lot, resentfully overseeing work Murugappa would have done. Gomati Paati still liked to keep a close watch on the affairs of the family. She sat in her wooden chair under the neem tree at the back, coming in every now and then to check up on Ramu. She was present when Sub-Inspector Chandran came and Ramu repeated what he had seen and done on that terrible day. After that interrogation, Ramu's spirit did not lift until Subbu came by, full of gossip about school. Hari had a new top that was fantastic. Nobody dared play against him anymore—not even Subbu. Neelu, whom they both disliked, had been made to stand up on his chair during history for not knowing who Queen Elizabeth the Great was. It was only when he heard stories like this that Ramu missed school. What fun it would have been to see that huge, hulking Neelu perched on his chair like a mouse! Otherwise he did not miss school at all; indeed, now that he was more or less recovered but still not ready to return to school, he enjoyed how he had become the object of envy for Subbu and Rajan and the one or two other friends who came to see him.

It quickly grew difficult to keep Ramu in bed. Sometimes Ramu followed Gomati Paati out back and stretched himself out on a mat spread on the ground. Ramu enjoyed doing this. It felt special to be lying under the neem tree in the middle of the day when he should be in school. The wind blew in gently from across the rice fields, making the green paddy wave in the bright sunshine. Above, the leaves of the neem tree too fluttered, so that the yellow sunshine falling through the branches danced over him. The rains, which had been plentiful this season, were almost over. In the distance, the mountains rose in a hazy greenness. Closer was the mound with the fort built by the Naicker chieftain who had founded the village, ruined now. The ruin was small, with most of the walls crumbled almost to the ground—at this distance, it was but a vague hint on the crest of the mound. Hardly anyone went up there. Until recently, only Ramu and his friends had gone up to it to play; but now they too had stopped, because the abundant rains had made the overgrowth—the weeds and wild bushes that grew all over the fallen stones—worse. The sight of the familiar mound comforted Ramu. He drank in the scent of plants and trees bursting with fruitfulness that pervaded the air. Harvest would be soon. And then it would be Pongal. The December air was soft, seductive, full of pleasurable anticipation. Ramu lay on the mat and looked out across the rice fields toward the tamarind tree and it was almost as if he had imagined everything—that he had not gone playing King Vikramaditya that fateful day, that he had not stumbled on the corpse with two mouths, that Murugappa was not dead.

Almost. Not quite. The feeling did not last.

Sometimes men came to see Gomati Paati while Ramu lay on his mat by her chair. The Chettiar from Thirunelveli Town with a money bag under his arm came to find out how the crops were doing and how many sacks of rice he could expect to buy from her this year; the priest of the Meenakshisundareswarar Temple dropped by to apprise her of the arrangements for Pongal. When each visitor was gone, Gomati Paati would detail for Ramu the work that had brought them to her. Ramu understood that Gomati Paati was trying to teach him with her elaborate explanations, but try as he might he could not make himself pay attention to her words. He enjoyed the visitors when they came, for he who had discovered Murugappa's dead body under the tamarind tree was an object of near universal interest. With Gomati Paati present, no one dared to raise the subject of the murder directly, but Ramu could nevertheless sense the curiosity directed toward him.

"Oho," the Chettiar had said during his visit, his earrings flashing in the sun as he bobbed his head in Ramu's direction, "this is your grandson." The words were innocent; it was the pregnant pause at the end of them, as if seeking permission to say more, that was significant.

Gomati Paati's reply was admonitory: "Yes, this is Ramu. He is not well."

Now that more than a week had passed since the terrifying encounter with the body under the tamarind tree, such interest in him was not without its perverse and guilty pleasure for Ramu. But what pleasure could there be in learning about the different aspects to be taken into account in calculating the correct price of a sack of rice, or about how to harvest turmeric root and dry it in the sun? Such were the topics of Gomati Paati's lessons. "I know you are not listening to me," she would interrupt herself suddenly in the midst of a long explanation. "You are thinking of something else."

At such moments, Ramu responded aggressively, "No, I am not! I have listened to every single word you have said. You don't believe me? You want to test me?" Though nothing could ever be said with certainty of Gomati Paati, he knew this tactic generally worked. He alone could bully Gomati Paati in this manner.

On the same day that the Chettiar visited, a short man came walking across the fields toward the house. He was dressed in black trousers and a white shirt. Though he was small and slight of build, he had an air of cockiness that demanded notice. He came striding boldly, scandalously, as if he meant to come right up to where Gomati

Paati was seated in her chair; but then, while he was yet a little distance away, his steps faltered and he came to an uncertain halt.

Gomati Paati said, “What now, Chellappa? How are you?”

When Ramu heard the name, he sat up on his mat to take a closer look at the stranger. This was Chellappa, Murugappa’s younger brother, returned from Madras because of his brother’s death.

Though they were brothers, Chellappa was much younger than Murugappa. Ramu studied Chellappa, so different from Murugappa in both clothes and manner. Not only did Chellappa differ from Murugappa, but he was nothing like Murugappa’s son Manickam, whom Ramu had often seen working in the fields. Ramu had never noticed Murugappa or Manickam in anything other than the faded pieces of cloth they wrapped around their waists. Indeed, he had seen few men other than his own father in shirt and trousers, which he wore when he went to his Sanitation Department office in Ambasamudram or when he was called away on tour. Even Uncle Siva never wore trousers, though his shirts and veshtis were always the purest white. And here was Chellappa in shirt and trousers! Chellappa’s physical appearance and general demeanor—the eyes so hooded and watchful—were a stark contrast to Murugappa’s. Chellappa was more wiry and compact than Murugappa, and his hair was jet black where Murugappa’s had been white. Ramu could see a faint resemblance to Murugappa only in the broad forehead and the shape of the mouth beneath the mustache.

“Murugappa worked faithfully for you for years,” Chellappa began abruptly, without so much as a greeting.

“It’s true, Chellappa. I don’t deny it. He was a good man,” Gomati Paati replied.

“He was loyal. Loyal as a dog.”

“Why say such a thing, Chellappa? What do you gain by demeaning your own brother? He was a good man. Let it go at that.”

Chellappa had his face turned away. He was running both his hands down the front of his shirt, carefully smoothing it. Ramu noticed that the bottoms of Chellappa’s trousers above the leather sandals were badly frayed.

Chellappa did not look at Gomati Paati, instead focusing his attention on his hands, as if what they were doing to his shirt was more important than the words he was speaking. "How will Manickam and Ponni live now?" The words were spoken as if to no one, as if he was embarrassed to speak them.

Manickam and Ponni were the only two of Murugappa's children still living in Paavalampatti, in the hut under the coconut trees. Manickam was grown up and worked in Gomati Paati's fields.

Gomati Paati said to Chellappa, "Don't worry about them. Manickam will work in the fields as he always has. How old is Ponni? As soon as she is able, she can work in the fields too. Don't worry. We will take care of them."

Chellappa jerked his head up and darted a quick, angry glance at Gomati Paati. He dropped his hands to his sides and drew himself together and said, "No need. I wasn't asking for help. We take care of our own."

"You always were a proud man, Chellappa."

Chellappa dropped his head again and went back to smoothing the white front of his shirt. Gomati Paati waited patiently for him to speak. Ramu too waited in the gap between word and word, keenly feeling the weight of the moment as it filled with unspoken thoughts and memories he could hardly imagine.

Into this gap, drawn by the voices, Uncle Siva rushed, appearing suddenly in the doorway to the house. When he saw Chellappa, he leaped forward, crying, "Chellappa! What are you doing here? How dare you come here like this, bothering Amma? Have you no shame?" He addressed Gomati Paati: "This is what happens when these people go off to the city. They forget everything they have learned." Turning back to Chellappa, he added, "Careful! This is not Madras. We know how to teach you your lessons here."

At Uncle Siva's appearance, Chellappa's manner changed sharply. He dropped his hands to his sides again and looked straight at Uncle Siva. The watchful expression in his eyes was gone. The shadow had lifted from his face. "And what are my lessons, Ayya?" he asked calmly. The emphasis on the last word was subtle; nevertheless, the challenge was unmistakable. Ramu listened with wonder. It was clear that Chellappa meant no respect by the use of the honorific. He had never heard anyone speak to Uncle Siva in this way before.

"Hey, you!" Uncle Siva cried. "Have you forgotten how you left Paavalampatti like . . . ?" but before he could finish Gomati Paati interrupted, "Siva, be quiet. Have you no sense?"

Chellappa laughed mirthlessly. "Ayya, what were you going to say? How was it that I left Paavalampatti? Like a dog?"

"If you act like a dog, you will be whipped like a dog," Uncle Siva cried, his handsome face ugly with anger.

Chellappa looked back at Uncle Siva steadily. "I am not the man you knew years ago, Mr. Sivaraman Iyer," he said. "I have met people and learned things in Madras. You don't frighten me." He spoke quietly, as if he knew what he was doing now, as if he had had occasion to speak in this way many times before.

There was a sharp intake of breath. There was the quiet rustling of the leaves of the neem tree in the wind. A child called loudly from inside the house. It was Kumar calling for his father. Uncle Siva stood motionless, stunned, bereft of words.

Gomati Paati said, "Chellappa, go now. There is no use in your saying anything more. Come back later if you wish to speak to me. I would be happy to hear anything you have to say."

"If you say so, Amma," Chellappa said. "I can come back another time if you like. Murugappa and I did not always agree about things. But he was still my brother. I have questions about how he died." Then he turned deliberately on his heels and, before Uncle Siva could speak, left as he had come, striding toward the paddy fields beyond which stood Murugappa's hut. The confrontation was over almost as soon as it had begun.

At last, Uncle Siva found his voice. "Did you see how he called me Mr. Sivaraman Iyer?" he cried. He spoke loudly so that Chellappa, who had just reached the path leading through the paddy fields, could hear. "He had better not forget that Murugappa's hut stands on our land. I can have him thrown off."

"Siva," Gomati Paati said. "Sometimes you show the sense of a buffalo. I told Manickam that Chellappa could stay in the hut."

"I will kill the rogue if he talks to me that way again!"

"Nonsense," Gomati Paati said. "I don't want to hear such talk. What's happened to you, Siva?"

"Don't think I can't get it done," Uncle Siva said, darkly. Then, he seemed to calm down and said, "This is what we get for having a Paraiyar living on our land. Why did Appa give Murugappa the job of supervising the lands? Appa even let him build his hut in the coconut grove. That's not the way it was before. We never had a Paraiyar doing this kind of work. It is one thing to hire Paraiyars to do fieldwork. But to have a Paraiyar live on your land and be an overseer to other Paraiyar workers? Unheard of! See what you get if you do that? You give these people a fistful of rice and they want the whole sack. Ungrateful wretches!"

When Gomati Paati spoke, her voice was scolding. "Really, you have no sense, Siva. Stop babbling and think for a change."

"What is there to think about? I hear Chellappa is going around saying he is determined to find out what really happened to Murugappa."

"Why would he not, Siva? His brother has been horribly murdered. Think about that. Or, if you can't rouse yourself to think, at least understand how the times are changing and that you have to learn to behave in a different way."

"Think? I will tell you something that will make you think, Amma. I hear the assistant superintendent of police himself will be coming from Thirunelveli Town to look into Murugappa's death. A white man. Robinson is his name. What do you think about *that*, Amma? Nothing but trouble, these Paraiyars."

"The assistant superintendent of police? A white man? To look into Murugappa's murder?"

"That's right."

"What about Chandran? Wasn't he investigating the murder? He came to see me a few days ago when I was sitting out here, when Ramu was still sick. He seemed a nice man. His wife is from our village. Did you know that? Markandayan Pillai's daughter."

"You didn't tell me the sub-inspector came to see you."

"I'm telling you now."

"What did you say to him?"

"What is there to say? I told him what a good man Murugappa was and hoped that the police would do all that they could to catch the killer."

"You have to be careful, Amma. This Chandran is a smart one. He comes from a poor Pillai family. They have no land, but this Chandran is young and ambitious. See how he's managed to make his way into Markandayan Pillai's family? I know the daughter. She looks like a horse, but you know how much land and money Markandayan Pillai has."

"I don't know about all that. Chandran seemed a nice young man. That is all I know. But, tell me, why is this white man taking so much interest suddenly?"

"Why? Because of this Chellappa. There are all kinds of rumors about him. About all the unsavory types he's involved with in Madras. Troublemakers. That's all they are. Now the British are at war with the Germans, they will tolerate no nonsense from anyone. The smallest peep and it's straight to the jail with you. I'm sure that's the reason this Robinson is on his way to Paavalampatti. I just hope he doesn't come bothering us. He'll probably want to talk to us."

"Vishu will talk to him. He has probably heard about Vishu."

"Vishu is only a health inspector—not so important that the assistant superintendent of police would know about him, Amma."

"Even so. Vishu will be able to talk to him in English. He will know how to talk to a man like this Robinson."

"I should be there too. I know more about Murugappa and his affairs than Vishu."

"You are a hothead, Siva. Go with Vishu to talk to Robinson if you like. But watch your tongue. Don't be running your mouth like you always do."

After Gomati Paati and Uncle Siva had gone back into the house, Ramu continued lying on the mat under the neem tree and considered all that he had overheard about this fascinating man Chellappa. One thing intrigued him particularly: Chellappa's abrupt departure from the village years before. What had happened to make him leave in that way? Ramu wanted to know. Many people probably knew what had happened, but who could he ask?

His father surely, but that very morning his father had gone back on tour. The district health officer was visiting distant villages to vaccinate against smallpox, and every available health inspector and assistant health officer was needed for the camp. Since Ramu was fully recovered and would return to school the next day, his father did not need to remain at home any more. That left Gomati Paati and Uncle Siva to ask about Chellappa. Ramu certainly could have asked Gomati Paati, but she had gone into the house for her prayers, and would remain busily engaged in them for quite a while. Uncle Siva? Ramu remembered how ugly his face had become during his quarrel with Chellappa. No, he could never bring himself to ask Uncle Siva anything about Chellappa. A bold thought suggested itself to him. Why not ask Chellappa himself? Ramu hesitated for a moment as an image of Murugappa with his throat slashed came into his mind. Then he thrust the image away, sprang up from his mat, and set off in the direction of Murugappa's hut.

⁓

THE HUT UNDER THE COCONUT trees was larger than Ramu had expected—he had never before been this close to it. Its thatched roof sloped low over sturdy mud walls, on the brown surface of which a child had drawn pictures of a cow, a bird, a cart, and the sun shining over them all. The black charcoal lines were faded now. The pictures had been drawn a long time ago. A little distance from the hut, a clay pot with a blackened bottom was perched aslant on equally blackened stones. Underneath, dead gray ash showed. No fire, it seemed, had been lit under the pot for days. At Ramu's appearance, a dog began barking, straining at the rope that tethered it to one of the coconut trees. Ramu halted. The dog was not large, but it looked ragged and mean. It flung itself again and again in Ramu's direction, yapping madly. In response, a girl emerged from the dark doorway of the hut.

The girl looked at Ramu and said, "What do you want?" She was dressed in a faded cotton paavaadai and blouse. As she spoke, she unwound a wet cloth from her head. Thick hair, still dripping with water, tumbled out. Ramu was relieved to see the dog grow quiet at the sound of the girl's voice.

Ramu knew who the girl was. She was Murgappa's daughter, Manickam's sister. Sometimes she had come up to the house with Murugappa. He had seen her around, though if he remembered correctly she had also been gone from the village for some time. He seemed to remember Murugappa talking to Gomati Paati one time about how he missed her. The girl's name was Ponni.

"Chellappa . . ." he began, and then stopped abruptly. Murugappa's daughter! He had not expected to encounter Murugappa's daughter. What would he say to her? How should he speak to her? He thought of the corpse under the tamarind tree. The corpse with two mouths. Suddenly, he felt terrified. What was he doing here under the coconut trees by Murugappa's hut? Why had he come?

Murugappa's daughter looked at Ramu and said, "You are the one who found Appa." Her voice was steady. Firm. As if unaffected by who he was. As if what he had found was not quite, exactly, her murdered father.

Ramu nodded. The dog had settled back on its haunches but its head was up and pointed alertly in Ramu's direction. Ramu looked at the dog, so he would not have to look at Murugappa's daughter. The dog let out a low growl and rose menacingly from the ground.

Murugappa's daughter ignored the dog. "What do you want?" she repeated. She was about as tall as Ramu, but not as thin.

"I came to see Chellappa."

"He is not here."

"I'll come back later."

But Ramu did not leave. Where could Chellappa have gone? Had he not seen him walking toward Murugappa's hut moments before? Where had he disappeared to? Manickam was in the fields. Ramu had seen him from a distance on his way to the hut. Where was Chellappa?

Murugappa's daughter turned and shook the water from the white cloth she had unwrapped from her hair, snapping it high in the air so that iridescent drops of water went flying in the sun. She did this a few times, expertly causing a loud crack to sound every time. And then she twisted the cloth so that more water was squeezed out from it. Ramu had seen Aunt Malati do exactly these same things with her towel after her bath. The wet hair, black and heavy, fell across Murugappa's daughter's face as she twisted and squeezed the water from the cloth. When she finished, Ramu was still standing there, watching.

"Your name is Ramu," Murugappa's daughter said. "I'll tell him you came." The way she spoke made Ramu think of a woman, not a girl. A woman, like Gomati Paati, or Aunt Malati. Except that Murugappa's daughter was no Paati and seemed nothing at all like Aunt Malati.

"When will he be back?"

"I don't know." And then she turned suddenly and pointed and said, "I went to see for myself."

Ramu saw that she was pointing in the direction of the tamarind tree, clearly visible even from such a distance. Again, the voice was calm, as if unaffected by the terrible subject that had just been broached. But her body: Ramu noticed it had gone strangely still. He thought of the blood that had seeped into the ground from Murugappa's wounds. He thought of Murugappa's daughter standing under the demon tree—the tree he had come to think of as the demon tree—looking at that patch of blood. "Why did you do that?" he blurted out.

Murugappa's daughter did not reply, only looked back at him with steady, unwavering eyes.

Before Ramu could query her again, Chellappa appeared from behind the hut, calling, "Ponni!" The dog, seeing Chellappa, began barking madly once again. It twisted and turned at the end of its tether as if possessed. Ponni turned now to throw an irritated look at the dog. She said sharply, "Stop that, Insect! Stop it!" The dog grew quiet. To her uncle, Ponni said, "He's come to see you."

Chellappa's surprise showed. "Does your father know you are here?" he asked Ramu.

"My father is away on tour," Ramu replied.

"Your uncle? Your grandmother? Do they know you have come here?"

Ramu shook his head. From the corner of his eye, he could see Ponni spreading the wet cloth she had taken from her head on the thatch roof of the hut.

"You should go back," Chellappa said. "They would be angry to hear you were here."

Ramu felt irritated. "I can go where I want to go. I don't need anyone's permission," he said.

Chellappa laughed, and Ramu saw a look of amusement dart across Ponni's face too as she ducked back into the hut through the low, dark doorway.

"I don't know about that," Chellappa said cryptically. "You can't go where you want any more than I can." Then he added in a softer, kinder, tone, "What do you want?"

Ramu felt a sudden lightness, a freeing within, now that Ponni had disappeared into the hut. He said, "I found her father under the tamarind tree." Unnecessarily, he added in a self-important way, "Murdered."

Chellappa looked at the hut. "Ponni . . ." The look was quick, fleeting, but it was enough to turn the dark doorway of the hut into a quivering, listening ear and to make Ramu ashamed for the thoughtlessness of his words.

Chellappa stepped away from the hut. Drawing Ramu along with him, he entered one of the paths through the rice fields. He stopped some distance from the hut and repeated, "What do you want?"

"You are Murugappa's brother." Custom made Ramu use the familiar pronoun, even though Chellappa had been using the more polite form in addressing him. It was the way Ramu had always heard his father and uncle and grandmother address people like Chellappa. At the same time, he could not stop thinking of the thoughtless way he had spoken of Murugappa moments before. He felt a desire to make amends. Gomati Paati's words came back to him. He added, "Murugappa was a good man."

Anger flashed across Chellappa's face. He said, "Go back home before somebody comes looking for you." He too was using the familiar pronoun now, but Ramu did not notice.

Chellappa's anger made Ramu remember why he had come looking for Chellappa. "Why did you leave the village?" he said to Chellappa. "What Uncle Siva said . . . What made you go away all those years ago?"

"Ask your Uncle Siva. He'll tell you."

Ramu knew better than to tell Chellappa why he could not ask Uncle Siva. Instead, he said, making up a reason, "There's this white man who's coming here because of Murugappa. Uncle Siva is busy with that."

"White man?"

"Yes. A police officer. Rob . . . Robin . . . I don't know how to say his name."

"Robinson. Douglas Robinson?"

"Yes. I think that's what his name is."

Chellappa said, as if to confirm the fact to himself, "Douglas Robinson is coming here."

"Uncle Siva said it was because of you."

"Do you know why I was made to leave all those years ago?" Chellappa asked curtly. "Because I drew water from the well in the village."

Ramu was confused. "But why would you do that?" he asked. "The village well is for other people. You have your own." He tried to remember where the well for people like Chellappa was but could not.

Chellappa spoke bitterly. "Other people? You talk like a child. You're not a child any more. Why should there be one well for you and another for me? What would happen to the water in your well if I drank from it? You asked me why I left the village. That's why. Because I drew water from a well." He paused and said, "Now, go. Go back home to your grandmother. You have your answer."

⁓

It was not much of an answer. There was much that Chellappa did not tell Ramu. From his answer, Chellappa had left out everything that mattered.

The path that had brought Chellappa to that moment at the well in Paavalampatti was long and circuitous. When Chellappa was eleven, his brother Murugappa, at twenty-eight much older than Chellappa, had been given the job of overseeing the workers by Kumaraswamy Iyer. Their father too had worked for Kumaraswamy Iyer before his death, but only as an ordinary laborer. It was unusual that Kumaraswamy Iyer had plucked Murugappa up from the abject conditions of an ordinary Paraiyar laborer—hardly anyone in Paavalampatti used "Adi Dravidar," the alternative term Chellappa himself preferred—and conferred such an important status on him. But dependable agricultural labor was becoming hard to find. Adi Dravidar laborers were fleeing, migrating to cities like Madras and Madurai, and even far-off lands like Malaya and Ceylon. Perhaps Kumaraswamy Iyer thought Murugappa, who was Adi Dravidar himself, would have greater success in recruiting and keeping workers. Murugappa's elevation was, everybody seemed to think, a great privilege. Whoever had heard of an Adi Dravidar given such a position by a Brahmin landlord? Because of it, many benefits flowed to Murugappa: he and his dependents had more to eat, certainly, than most of the other Adi Dravidars around Paavalampatti. But there was also more money to spend. And more respect from the other Adi Dravidars, and even from people of higher caste.

Kumaraswamy Iyer was, by conventional standards, an exceptional man. When reports reached him, soon after Murugappa's elevation, of Murugappa walking about in a shirt in Thirunelveli Town—Murugappa would of course never dare do such a thing in front of Kumaraswamy Iyer himself—he was amused rather than angered. And when he came to know that Chellappa had learned to read and write a modicum of Tamil from a Nadar Christian in an adjoining village, he approved. No Adi Dravidar, it was widely felt, could ask more than to have a master of such graciousness, such munificence. What was more, upon Kumaraswamy Iyer's death two years after Murugappa's elevation, Gomati Ammal had called Murugappa to her and let it be known that she had every intention of continuing the unusual arrangement initiated by her husband.

Nevertheless, despite these privileges that had been given to his family, or perhaps indeed because of them, Chellappa grew restless as he grew older. He was not like everyone else. He could not bow his head in appreciation for the so-called beneficence of Kumaraswamy Iyer and his family as his brother Murugappa did. He began to ruminate critically—those who thought him ungrateful would say too critically—on his situation. When he was only seventeen he took his first important step on the long path to that moment when he had drawn water from a well not meant for him. Already he had been working for many years alongside his brother on Kumaraswamy Iyer's land—out in the fiery sun tending the vegetable garden with his bare hands; down in the enormous dank well, keeping the water flowing during the dry season with his iron bar; or up on the dizzyingly tall palm trees, pruning with his sickle the sharp-edged leaves that cut nastily into his arms and chest. Already his hands were covered with thick calluses. He knew all too well the smell of cow dung and the peculiar itching of your bare feet that came from standing for hours in the muddy ankle-deep water of the paddy fields. When he looked ahead down the unfolding years, he saw exactly how his life would turn out if he stayed in Paavalampatti. And something within him could not accept it, would not accept it.

One night, soon after turning seventeen, he fled Paavalampatti in the company of Kovalu, a young Adi Dravidar man many years older who had befriended him. They stole away in the middle of the night, so that Murugappa would not notice his brother's disappearance until it was too late. Chellappa had never been away from Paavalampatti before. He took with him only a handful of roasted peanuts, wrapped in an extra waistcloth, freshly washed. There was nothing else in the world for him to call his own. He walked past the rice fields, Kumaraswamy Iyer's well, the great tamarind tree. He came to the small shrine to Muniappan, the deity of the western boundary of the village, fierce with his prominent black mustaches and sword. There he met Kovalu, and then with a single long stride he followed Kovalu out of the village. He had taken his first steadfast step away from the narrow place that had been ordained his, that had held and confined him ever since his birth.

With Kovalu, Chellappa made for the mountains to the west separating the British territory of Thirunelveli from the Princely State of Travancore. Kovalu was from Paavalampatti, but he had gone over the mountains before. He knew the way well. They walked through the night, and by the time dawn broke they had left the lowland villages and the rice fields behind. Chellappa saw by the brightening light that they had already climbed a good distance into the mountains. They kept climbing, and by late morning Thirunelveli District lay spread out below, a distant flat plate shimmering in a yellow haze. Where exactly was Paavalampatti on that enormous brown and green expanse undulating in the waves of heat? Kovalu could not tell. The village was not far from the mountains, but in which direction? They did not know. Kovalu did know that far to the east, way beyond the horizon, the plains of Thirunelveli District met the salty waves of the Bay of Bengal. Kovalu had soaked his feet in those waves one time. Chellappa hoped to do the same in the not-too-distant future.

Kovalu and Chellappa walked for hours. Chellappa grew tired, but Kovalu would not halt. Up ahead lay the vast plantations of the British—neat rows of tea plants spread out on the slopes of the mountains. Among the workers on these plantations, many of whom were Adi Dravidars, Kovalu had friends. His plan was to press on until they had reached one such plantation, where they would be able to find shelter with men he knew. They would rest with these men for the night and continue on their way into Travancore the next day. So they thrust fatigue out of their minds and walked through the rows of tea until they came to rough shacks that clung to the mountain slopes. The shacks had tin roofs weighted down by sandbags. In one such shack they sheltered with a family Kovalu knew. The next morning Chellappa crossed over the mountains into a new life.

In Travancore, where few spoke Tamil, Chellappa drifted for months from town to town in the company of Kovalu. Kovalu knew enough Malayalam, learned during previous visits, for them to manage. To make money, they worked at the markets carrying loads, or else hired themselves out as apprentices to carpenters or bricklayers. Kovalu introduced Chellappa to the pleasures of drink and women. Whenever they had a little bit of money, Kovalu would locate a toddy shop, and from there their inebriated steps would naturally find the way to dark places where alluring women of the night dwelt. In the arms of a woman, Chellappa found, you could forget everything. He learned how the hot press of flesh on flesh could empty the mind of all its demons, at least for a while. When they were not drunk or losing themselves between the legs of a woman, they got into fights, for Kovalu had a mean temper and was quick to violence. When offended, he thought nothing of smashing his fist into a face. And then Chellappa too would find himself laying his fierce hand on someone's throat.

Chellappa followed Kovalu in everything. Like Kovalu, Chellappa too came to live for the toddy and the women. But, alas, when they had no money, which was often enough, there was neither toddy nor women. There was no food even. Indeed, there were days when they could not scrape together rice gruel and lime pickle. Certainly, Chellappa was exploring the world, to the extent that Travancore could be called the world, but he was also suffering hunger of a kind he had never felt before. When in the grip of such hunger, Chellappa forgot the condition of bondage that had driven him from Paavalampatti and thought longingly of his older brother Murugappa, who saw himself as a father to him. It was, however, too late for regret.

Late one typical day of hunger and longing, Kovalu and Chellappa found themselves on a dark and deserted road, walking behind a foolish Muslim trader going home alone with his load of printed Manchester cloth over one shoulder. A faint sliver of a moon cast a weak silvery light onto the road. Kovalu took a sturdy stick from the roadside and silently gestured to Chellappa to grab a stone. The hunger within Chellappa was a ravenous monster. Together, he and Kovalu crept up on the trader, and to this day Chellappa could not tell whose blow, his or Kovalu's, had made the blood spurt from under the trader's skull cap and into his thick beard. The trader had gone down with a muffled groan. They had left him bleeding there in the faint moonlight—dead or alive, who knew?—and fled into the night with his money purse.

That was how Chellappa found himself a few days later in Vaikom, money in his hand but guilt in his heart, even as a great uproar was convulsing the town. It was not long before he found out, from some young Tamil men as it happened, that the commotion concerned the famous Shiva temple. He was in the main street of Vaikom late one morning, surrounded by the barely comprehensible sounds of Malayalam, when a group passed speaking Tamil. Tamil was not unknown in Travancore; but such a large group, all speaking Tamil? Chellappa, still groggy from a night of lust and liquor, unthinkingly stumbled after them. The young men stopped when they noticed his pursuit. He explained where he was from and learned that this group of men had come from Erode in British India with their leader, one E. V. Ramaswami Naicker, known to the world as EVR, to participate in a political agitation. The agitation had begun when a so-called low-caste man had been forced to dismount from his bullock cart. His bullock had been allowed to pass down the road by the temple with the cart, but not he—a man! The roads around the great Shiva temple had been traditionally barred to people called low-caste, and the caste of the man had been deemed lower than that of the bullock! The incident, small as it was, had sparked a protest that grew stronger day by day and drew in people from all over India. Even the Mahatma, Gandhi himself, had voiced his support for the protestors. The group from Erode had arrived only a few days earlier to join in the campaign to open the roads to all people.

"I am of a low caste," Chellappa exclaimed when he heard the Tamil men's account. "The lowest."

One of the young men shook his head. "We are all men here," he replied. "There is no high caste or low. You are a man like I am."

Another said, "We believe in self-respect. And in making others respect us."

Chellappa liked the answers. Something powerful fluttered open in his heart and his mind, struggling to be born. In the weeks that followed, he spent more and more time with the young men, listening as they planned with others the non-violent campaign to break the terrible laws about who could walk where. He watched as they, paired low caste and high caste, walked down the road to the sign barring passage to those regarded as low-caste people. He watched as they were arrested. Kovalu went to the toddy shop every night. Chellappa did not go with him.

One day, his share of the money stolen from the Muslim trader, tucked into his waistcloth at the hip, felt so heavy he gave it all away to Kovalu. He found then that he had given away a burden that was weighing him down not just at his hip. His heart, too, felt lighter. Weeks later, the young men he had joined, those who were not in jail, returned to Erode. With hardly any hesitation Chellappa went with them, for he found that what the men said and did, how they thought about the world, satisfied something deep within him. Kovalu begged him to stay, but he told him he could not. He did not part on good terms with Kovalu, whose notorious anger flared at what he thought of as Chellappa's traitorous departure.

Chellappa was not in Erode long, just enough for the startling thoughts and feelings that had awoken within him to grow stronger. He learned names beyond those of Gandhi and Nehru and Rajaji: Lenin, Mussolini, Ataturk. Socialism, capitalism, nationalism. The men with whom he had fallen in spoke with ease about grand topics. Chellappa did not speak. He listened and learned. He learned to call himself Adi Dravidar, rather than Paraiyar. He determined to read for himself, borrowing books and newspapers whenever he could and struggling with them with his rudimentary knowledge of the Tamil script. The most exciting of all the men he read was one whose name was Iyothee Thass, an Adi Dravidar like him, but one who had learned several languages and had protested vehemently against the appalling conditions of Adi Dravidars. Iyothee Thass had denounced the bigotry of caste and converted to Buddhism. Chellappa read everything he could by this man who had earned the title Pandithar because of his learning. If Pandithar Iyothee Thass had still been alive (he had died some ten years before), Chellappa would surely have gone to pay his respects to him.

While Chellappa was still in Erode, EVR broke with Gandhi over Gandhi's refusal to condemn caste outright. EVR did not think, as Gandhi did, that you could separate the system of caste from caste discrimination, and so he left Gandhi's Congress Party to start what he called the Self-Respect Movement. And what was the Self-Respect Movement? As far as Chellappa could tell it was a blur of activity. He too was drawn into the blur. He earned what he could through the trades he had learned in Travancore with Kovalu and the rest of the time he spent with the young men, learning through doing. He did not mind if all he did was carry messages, set out chairs for meetings, or spend interminable hours waiting to be sent on an errand. He listened and he learned. The thoughts within him—those powerful thoughts—grew, and he would no doubt have continued in this fashion with EVR were it not that his blood was young and Madras beckoned. He left for the storied city by the sea, the capital of the province, on his own, but with introductions to men who had similar ideas about caste and Gandhi and the British—men who thought the British were bad, Gandhi was weak, and caste was the worst.

In Madras, Chellappa found a job at the railway coach factory in Perambur as a mechanic and was still working there three years later during the great South Indian Railway strike of 1928. In fact, he was one of the strike leaders. The strike, against the closing of railway workshops and the retrenchment of workers, started off as a non-violent action. It began with railway workers all across the province absenting themselves from work and taking over the railway tracks, blocking the normal running of trains. In response, the police were unleashed. A rain of sticks ensued. Strikers were manhandled. There were even police firings and bayonet charges, resulting in the death of workers. The colonial government was determined to keep trains running, at any cost. Their control of the country depended on the trains. Aroused by the violence against them, the erstwhile peaceful strikers—or rather, mostly peaceful, for who could deny that there had been stray incidents of violence from the workers' side earlier?—stoned trains and set railway stores on fire. Passengers were killed. Four days into the strike, Chellappa was arrested along with dozens of other strike leaders. By the time he was released weeks later, the strike had been stamped out by the harsh boot of the colonial police. His job at the South Indian

Railway coach factory was gone. Friends warned that there was now a file on him in the offices of the Intelligence Bureau. Henceforth, he would be a watched man. They advised him to disappear for a while, go somewhere far away. And that was how, at twenty-three years of age, he returned to Paavalampatti after a long absence. He meant in all sincerity to lie low in the village of his birth. Little did he know that the six years he had been gone had left their indelible mark on him.

Chellappa was warmly welcomed home to Paavalampatti by Murugappa. Murugappa's family had grown. Forty years old now, he had had more children. His last child, a daughter, Ponni, had just been born. Their first meeting after the years of separation was by the hut under the coconut trees. Chellappa was calm, collected, but Murugappa's eyes were moist with tears of joy. Murugappa was not a man to bury his emotions deep within himself.

Quietly, Chellappa slipped into life in the village. He became part of Murugappa's family, one more member alongside Murugappa's wife and six children, two of whom were to die later. He could have worked in the fields as he had done before, but refused to do so—nothing in the whole wide world could induce him to return to a life of bondage for the family of Kumaraswamy Iyer.

Murugappa grumbled good-naturedly about his refusal, but did not compel him. Murugappa could recognize the enormous changes that had taken place in Chellappa, though he could not understand them. There was in him even a certain secret pride about these changes. Murugappa was not yet the drunkard he was to decline into in later years, after the deaths of his wife and two children.

Instead of working in the fields, Chellappa went away for two or three days at a time to Thirunelveli Town. There he was not known and so was able to use the trades he had picked up during the years he was gone to earn some money, enough to amount to a reasonable contribution to Murugappa as head of the family.

Chellappa became something of a curiosity in Paavalampatti, despite the fact that he stayed out of sight and said little. He shared with no one the life he had led since his departure from the village like a thief in the night—a thief whose theft had been himself. He made no attempt to pick up old friendships or make new ones. The months passed, but he stayed for the most part close to the hut under the coconut trees, except for his trips to Thirunelveli Town. It was thought that he had returned because of some great disappointment in love, and he did nothing to dispel the rumor. Whenever he returned from Thirunelveli Town, it was always with a book or two hidden in a bag. The books—literature and political treatises in Tamil—kept him occupied. They often included *Kudi Arasu,* the journal of EVR's Self-Respect Movement, which he picked up at a barber's shop in Thirunelveli Town. He studied the books as if for an examination, though secretly, for he knew what a dangerous thing reading could be for someone like him in a village like Paavalampatti. In the pages of *Kudi Arasu,* he sometimes saw an opinion by someone he actually knew, which made him think longingly of Madras and his life there in the political thick of things. In the evenings, when it had grown too dark to read, he was regularly seen at the spot by the river reserved for the Adi Dravidars to bathe and wash their clothes. He sat silently on the rocks with head bowed, as if scrutinizing the flowing waters of the Tamarabarani for mysterious clues. He was polite but uncommunicative, leading many to speak darkly of the superior airs that some who had traveled a little put on. He did not let himself be bothered by these criticisms. What did those who criticized know of the life he had led and the experiences he had had since his departure years before? He was lying low, biding his time until he would be able to return to Madras. That was all.

If only. Chellappa had arrived when the season was cool and the Tamarabarani River full. Now, when the incident at the village well that precipitously drove him from Paavalampatti happened, it was summer and the river had shrunk almost to nothing. The summer was unusually severe and water accordingly became more and more scarce as the summer wore on. For weeks, the well customarily used by the Adi Dravidars for drinking water had been dry, as was the anicut that took water from the river to some of the fields. The river, reduced to a narrow and muddy channel, or else another well open to Adi Dravidars more than a mile away: in this period of searing heat, these were the only alternatives when it came to water for drinking, and of them the river could hardly be considered a feasible option.

Imagine, then, the murmur of a clay pot in the brown and muddied waters of the river late one night in this season of heat and heartlessness. Chellappa heard the gurgling sound with alarm. It was unusual for him to be at the river so late, but such was the heat that he could not bear to return to Murugappa's hut. He was at his customary place by the river. The dry season had made the river retreat quite some distance from the rocks on which he was seated; still, the river offered relief. The little clearing under the coconut trees, on the other hand, was stifling. It was at this time that Aathaayi arrived at the river with her pot.

The murmur of Aathaayi's clay pot filling with the muddy water of the river aroused Chellappa from his reverie. He called out, "Who is there? What are you doing?"

Aathaayi replied, "My child is sick." Aathaayi's six-year-old son was burning up with fever.

Chellappa recognized Aathaayi's voice. "I hope you are not taking this water to him."

"Where else am I to go for water? How can I walk all the way to the other well at this time of the night when my child is so sick? In this killing heat, how can I ask someone else for what little water they have?"

Anger, sudden and uncontrolled, exploded inside Chellappa. Perhaps it was the heat, perhaps a growing restlessness at being stuck in Paavalampatti when his work, his important work, waited for him in Madras. He sprang up from his seat on the rocks and ran over to Aathaayi. He snatched the pot from her hand and said, "This water is filthy. Go back home! I'll bring you clean water."

That was how Chellappa came to be caught drawing water from the well at the very center of Paavalampatti, where the streets of the high-caste Pillaimars and Chettiars met. He was drawing water up in the metal bucket as quickly and quietly as possible, a shadow at the wall of this well forbidden to Adi Dravidars, when a Naicker man passing down the street noticed him. Despite the darkness, the man recognized Chellappa, whose fame had spread rather more widely than Chellappa would have wished during the months of his return to the village. With a yell, the Naicker man, a well-known hothead, rushed onto the mud platform skirting the well. He grabbed Chellappa by the shoulder and sharply spun him around. The rope slipped from Chellappa's hands and the bucket went hurtling back into the well, down to the little water at the very bottom. Noticing Aathaayi's clay pot, which Chellappa had placed on the ground by the well, the Naicker man sent it crashing into the street with a kick. It shattered into a thousand pieces. He turned then and slapped Chellappa hard across his face, yelling, "How dare you! Snake! How dare you come here like a thief in the night? Have you forgotten who you are?"

Chellappa had not forgotten who he was. He sprang up from where he had fallen and threw himself on the Naicker man, grabbing him by the throat. The two men wrestled there on the mud platform of the well, raising a commotion as they did so. Eventually the Naicker man would have overpowered Chellappa, for he was the stronger of the two. But before he could, doors were thrown up and men emerged cautiously into the street, wondering what all the scuffling and yelling was about.

"Look what this ruffian is doing!" the Naicker man yelled out to them. Two of the men quickly grasped what was happening. They rushed forward. Fear gave Chellappa strength. With a desperate lunge, he threw off the Naicker man's grasp and sprang away, escaping down the street and fleeing into the night. He knew there was no time to lose. There was no telling what would happen next. Adi Dravidar men had been killed for less. He could not return to the hut under the coconut trees. The men knew who he was. That was the first place to which they would go. There was nothing in that hut that he absolutely needed. What little money he had he was happy to leave for Murugappa, who would now be left to face the consequences of his action. There was one place, however, that he could not avoid before fleeing the village. He ran straight to Aathaayi's hut in the Adi Dravidar settlement outside the village proper. Doing so was risky, but he could not put Aaathaayi's sick child out of his mind. He owed it to Aathaayi to explain to her what had happened and why he was not bringing her water.

Aathaayi was waiting for him outside her hut. When he rushed up, panting and in terror, she immediately understood something had gone wrong, terribly wrong. "I'll find the water for my child," she said. "Go. Go before they catch you."

Chellappa ran, and when he came to the Muniappan shrine marking the boundary of the village he kept running, making his way through the fields for the mountains just as he had with Kovalu all those years before. He did not stop running until he had left the rice fields behind and disappeared into the jungle of the foothills. Beyond the mountains was Travancore. From Travancore, he made straight for Madras. It was only when he was safely in that faraway city by the sea that he was able to reflect on what had happened with some calmness.

Back in Paavalampatti, he knew, his brother Murugappa would have to mend what he, Chellappa, had broken. Murugappa it was who would have to prostrate himself at the feet of the angry young men who would come looking for the arrogant brother. He would be protected by Gomati Ammal, but he would still have to plead and beg and crave forgiveness for the insolence of his brother. Quite possibly the consequences would be felt by other Adi Dravidars, too, who might be punished in big ways and small for the temerity shown by one of theirs. Chellappa felt terrible at the thought. Though he was confident that no one would come to too much harm now that he had been run out of the village, he felt a raw anger every time he thought of the injustice of it all. And the irony—that, too, was not lost on him: it was a Naicker man, EVR himself, who had taught him to reject caste, and it was another Naicker man who had now driven him from his own village because of caste. If EVR could forget his caste, why could not that man at the well?

Years later the Brahmin boy Ramu came to the hut under the coconut trees to ask Chellappa why he had been forced to leave the village. Chellappa gave him a short and cryptic answer, something about drawing water from a well, and left it at that. He spoke nothing about how he had arrived at that moment at that well or the effect the terrifying struggle at the well had had on him. He said nothing about irony, or about any of the subtler things that make up a lifetime of experience. How could he? Where would he have found the words? Or the time? He would have had to write a novel to explain himself—a novel with someone like himself as the unlikely hero. A most peculiar and unprecedented novel it would be, for as far as Chellappa knew no such novel existed.

ॐ

RAMU LAY THINKING ON HIS mat in the dark. As usual, he had spread out his mat in the verandah skirting the central courtyard of the house. Through the iron grille above, the fresh night air drifted down. It was late, probably past midnight. He had come awake quite suddenly. The cool air felt wonderful, but he had drawn a light sheet over himself as protection from mosquitoes. Mosquitoes buzzed in his ears. He waved at them with an impatient hand and the buzzing disappeared, only to return shortly. Gomati Paati had reminded him to rub crushed neem leaves over his face before lying down, but he had been too lazy. And now he was paying the price for his laziness. Already, two itchy swellings had sprouted on his cheeks—probably the reason for his coming awake. Ramu moved restlessly on his mat. In the distance a dog barked. He wondered if it was Insect. It sounded like Insect, mean and excitable.

Ramu lay in the dark thinking of Murugappa's daughter. He thought of the way her hair curled against her neck. He thought of the flash of her brown arms in the sun as she repeatedly threw the wet cloth into the air to snap the water out of it.

Ponni. Her name was Ponni. He knew that.

He felt restless thinking of Ponni. He turned onto his side, pulled his sheet all the way over his head as protection against the mosquitoes, and tried to think of other things. Like this white man who would soon be arriving in the village. Douglas Robinson. He had never before seen a white man in his life. That was surely something to look forward to. He had asked Gomati Paati about white people, and she had said, "I don't understand why they are called *white.* They are not white. They are red." She had seen a red person only once, a long time ago, from a distance. She had gone to Thirunelveli Town and there he was in the middle of the street, standing bare-headed in the sun. She had stared at him. Some would say that passing him would pollute her. She did not care about that, but he was nevertheless in the way. Finally, he had noticed her and stared back. She had held his gaze. She had refused to lower her eyes until he had stepped aside and let her pass.

How the drops of water had glistened along the curve of Ponni's neck.

And Ponni's eyes. Yes, her eyes. Ramu felt mortified when he remembered how they had flashed with amusement at him. Indignantly, he turned over, throwing himself onto his other side. The sheet slid away, uncovering his head. Immediately, the mosquitoes returned. The dog that had stopped barking started up again. He was certain it was Insect. It sounded very much like Insect. What a name for a dog! You might as well name a cow Peacock, or a man Stone. Why would anyone deliberately misname something?

If he ever saw Ponni again, he would demand that she explain herself. He had said he could go wherever he wanted and no one could stop him. That had been greeted with amusement both by Chellappa and Ponni. What was so funny about that? He would ask Ponni when—not if!—he saw her again.

Ramu wanted to go looking for Ponni, but when he met her again it was because she came looking for him. It was a few days after that night of restlessness. He was down by the Tamarabarani. He had wandered aimlessly past the bend in the river, away from the village. Really, what he wanted was to return to the hut under the coconut trees, but he felt an inexplicable misgiving every time he thought of doing so—an apprehension he had not felt when he had gone to the hut the first time to see Chellappa. He had a vague thought in his head that he might go for a swim where the bend made the river flow more slowly. It was a good place for a swim. The village was hidden behind the bend, and few people came this far up the river. Farther along the trail, up on the mound, was the ruined fort built by Paavalappa Naicker, the chieftain who had established the village centuries before and for whom the village was named. If he felt energetic enough after the swim, Ramu thought, he might go up the hill to the broken remains of the modest little fort. From there, much of the village and the surrounding fields were visible. He had been there many times. He and Subbu went there to pretend being Veera Paandiya Kattabomman fighting the British. They had not done that in a while, though. Today, Subbu had refused to come out to play. He still had pages of homework to finish. Ramu did too but he was not in the mood to be studying. He was back at school—had been for a few days—but still felt himself on holiday. So it was that he found himself wandering along the river by himself.

Suddenly Ponni was on the path in front of him, blocking his way. Her thick, curly hair was pulled back in a knot at the top of her head, accentuating her broad cheekbones and her large, expressive eyes. Her mouth, the lips pressed together firmly, looked determined, but her eyes belied that determination and suggested something contrary, something more fragile.

Without preamble, Ponni said, "Tell me about the tamarind tree."

Ramu understood what she meant. "I don't want to talk about it."

"I want to know."

"What would you gain by knowing?" Ramu remembered his thoughtlessness a few days earlier at the hut under the coconut trees. He was determined not to repeat it.

"He was my father."

"I know," said Ramu, feeling something he had never before felt in his life: a great desire to be gentle in the way he spoke. He felt as if he wanted to reach out across the little space that separated him from Ponni and touch her, this girl who had had her father taken from her in such a brutal fashion.

"Tell me, then," Ponni insisted.

Ramu did not reply. He stood with head bent and stared at his bare toes in the dirt path. Across from his toes were her toes, similarly bare. A little dirt separated them. Two steps—no, just one long one—that was all.

"What were you doing there?" Ponni demanded. Her tone was accusatory.

"I will not tell you anything about it," Ramu insisted, without lifting his head. He felt calm. He knew he was doing the right thing.

A low sobbing sound startled him, made him look up hurriedly. Ponni's chest was heaving uncontrollably. She was weeping. Without tears. Ramu had never seen such tearless weeping before. When she noticed him observing, a bitter look crossed her face. She turned abruptly and ran. Without thinking, Ramu ran after her. Ponni's faded yellow cotton paavaadai, torn and mended in many places, billowed out behind her as she ran. Beside them the Tamarabarani River flowed in the opposite direction, toward the village. From the sky, the late afternoon sun poured down on them. They passed the spot where Ramu had meant to swim. Ponni did not turn to look back at him. He did not call out to her. He did not know why he was pursuing her. She was not running fast. If he had wanted to, he could easily have caught her. He did not catch her. She ran. And he ran after her.

They ran up the hill to the ruined fort of Paavalappa Naicker. It was not a high hill and it did not take much effort to run up it. Ponni clambered over the shattered stones of the outer wall, through the remnants of what had perhaps been a narrow passageway, and into the weed-choked central yard. She stopped there, in the middle, amidst the weeds. He stopped just inside the yard. Fallen stones and broken walls surrounded them. Above, the faded blue sky patched up the holes that time and neglect had punched into the walls of the fort. She turned to confront him. She was still panting from her running, and so was he. The running had made her hair come loose. It fell in thick curls around her face. Her tearless sobbing had stopped. She glowered at him, her eyes hard and defiant now. The abrupt change in her made him feel helpless.

When his breath had calmed down, he said, "Why do you want to know? You know what I saw was terrible." He knew Murugappa's body had long since been buried according to the customs of her community. He wondered whether Ponni had seen her father's body before the burial.

Ponni's shoulders sagged. Just as abruptly as it had appeared, the defiance seemed to fade out of her. She said nothing. She did not press him to say more. He saw a look very much like fear on her face. It dawned on Ramu, then, that Ponni did not really want to know about her father. Or perhaps that she both wanted to and did not want to at the same time. Simultaneously. Strange to think people could have such opposite desires ground up together! Was that really possible? He again felt an overpowering gentleness toward Ponni. He looked at her with what felt like new understanding and adjusted the way he spoke. Trying to reach out to her without saying anything substantive, he mumbled, "I was playing a silly game."

She looked at him blankly.

"I was pretending to be King Vikramaditya when . . . when . . ." He faltered, then said, "Do you know that story?"

She shook her head.

"It's the one where King Vikramaditya has to bring an undead corpse from a tamarind tree that stands in a cremation ground."

"I don't know it."

"It's great. If King Vikramaditya speaks as he is carrying the vetal, the vetal will be able to escape and return to its perch on the branches of the tree. So the vetal tells him a story with a riddle in it. If the king knows the answer to the riddle, he has to speak it—otherwise his head will explode. But the moment he speaks the answer, the vetal flies back to its perch on the tamarind tree. And then King Vikram, who refuses to give up, has to go back to get it. In this way, the vetal keeps escaping and King Vikram keeps going back until the end, when it turns out the vetal is not really evil. It's the Brahmin sage who had sent Vikram on this mission who is really evil. It's one of my favorite stories. I have a book about it. I was pretending to be King Vikramaditya on that day." Ramu paused and added, "If you like I can show you the book."

They would have to meet again if she wanted to see the book. Ramu felt it would be very fine if they met again.

"I'd like to read it," Ponni replied. She no longer seemed intent on finding out about her father under the tamarind tree.

"It's in English," Ramu said, doubtfully. When he had said

that he could show it to her, he had meant exactly that. He did not think Ponni could read English or Tamil.

"I know how to read English!" Irritation showed on Ponni's face.

"Where did you learn?"

"My uncle taught me."

Chellappa had taught her.

"I can get the book for you tomorrow."

"I'll be here. Same time."

And then Ponni was gone, clambering over the stones and disappearing down the hill in the direction of the hut under the coconut trees.

Returning home, Ramu thought again of how Ponni had both wanted and not wanted to know about her father. Was he too like that sometimes? Did he too sometimes want something even as he did not want it? And his father? Or Gomati Paati? Were they like that too? Hard to think that they could be! People were strange. He had never thought of people that way before, but it was true. People were strange.

The next day Ramu refused Subbu's invitation to play and sneaked off to Pavallappa Naicker's ruined fort at the appointed time with the promised book in hand. Ponni was already there, standing on some fallen stones and looking out across the rice fields in the direction of the river. The expression on her face suggested tumultuous thoughts and roiling emotions barely restrained. In the distance, high above the green foothills of the mountains, two white birds darted after each other across the pale blue sky. Ponni's blouse was stained with sweat at the armpits. A light wind stirred the thick hair off the nape of her neck. Her paavaadai, certainly too short for her, also stirred in the wind, revealing the skin, so smooth, at the back of her thighs.

When Ramu looked at Ponni, he was reminded of Chellappa. Not that she resembled Chellappa in her looks—it was more the way she carried herself. So unlike her father Murugappa, who would wander across the fields with a dirty cloth tied unceremoniously around his waist. If you got too close to him, the smell of his unwashed body could be an awful assault on your nose. Ponni was nothing like her father. Looking at Ponni, you knew you could get close to her. Her clothes were faded and mended, but clean. She was always tidy and composed. Just like Chellappa. How did Chellappa and Ponni do it? Was it because they did not themselves labor in the fields like Murugappa? Was that what it was? Ramu thought guiltily of himself and wished he had washed his face and grabbed a fresh shirt. He could almost feel the dark line of dirt along the rim of his white shirt collar. He knew a faint odor hung around him despite his bath that morning. What was the difference between him and Murugappa, then? Would he not smell even more than Murugappa if he toiled all day in the fields?

Ponni sensed his presence and turned. "You are here," she observed, frowning.

Ramu held out the book in response, but Ponni only looked at him distrustfully. She made no attempt to take the book from him. "I did not think you would come," she said. "I did not think you would bring the book."

"Why?" he asked, surprised.

"Just a thought."

"You thought I wouldn't come because of who you are."

"My uncle says we should call ourselves Adi Dravidar."

"Adi Dravidar . . .?"

"Yes."

"Not Harijan?"

"No." She made a dismissive clucking sound. "That's Gandhi's term."

Ramu placed the book on the low broken wall near Ponni. She looked at it for a long moment and then, reluctantly, picked it up and flipped its pages. A musty book smell lifted into the air, bringing a sudden smile of pleasure to her face. She bent her head and breathed in the smell in one long breath as if it were exotic perfume from distant Arabia, Ramu thought. His story books were full of such phrases. Ponni reminded him of them.

On the title page of the book was a black line illustration of King Vikramaditya with the vetal over his shoulder. The vetal had long fingernails, long thin hair and a sharp, deceitful face. The king was strong and handsome, his thick hair flowing down onto his shoulders from under his crown. Ramu's crown—the crown he had lost on that terrible day he had found the murdered Murugappa—had been modeled on this very crown. Ponni studied the illustration with a look of distaste and then turned the page. The story began, "Once upon a time . . ." Ponni frowned at the words, her lips struggling silently to form them: "On-ce up-on a ti-me . . ." And then she remembered Ramu's presence and sharply shut the book.

"Where did you learn to read English?" Ramu asked.

"My uncle taught me when I was with him in Madras." Ramu understood that Ponni meant Chellappa.

"In Madras?" Ponni had been all the way to Madras and he, Ramu, had never gone anywhere further than Thirunelveli Town!

"When my mother died, my uncle took me to be with him."

Here was something that connected Ponni and him. "My mother too is dead," Ramu noted. "She died when I was born. I never even saw her."

"Mine died when I was eight years old. I don't remember much of her. I was with my uncle for many years. I came back to Paavalampatti only last year. When I was in Madras, I went to school and my uncle taught me English at home. He taught me many other things too."

"What else did your uncle teach you?"

Ponni said, as if in answer to his question, "Did you know that the Buddha did not believe in God?"

Ramu was confused. "What do you mean? The Buddha was a god himself," he said.

Ponni shook her head. "He was a man who was turned into a god later. My uncle says if you read what the Buddha has to say carefully you will see he did not believe in God." Ramu looked startled at her words. Ponni was pleased at the effect she was having on him. "Another thing," she added. "My uncle does not believe in God."

"No!"

"Yes," Ponni insisted. "My uncle says there is no God. It is all just stories. Religion is just a lot of stories."

Ramu thought of Gomati Paati praying in the puja room. He had never before encountered anyone who did not believe in God. "Your uncle does not go to the temple at all?" he asked, incredulously. He could not imagine anyone not going to the temple with its cool stone walls and gay bells and comforting incense smells. Of course, he had the Meenakshisundareswarar Temple in the Brahmin quarter of the village in mind when he thought of these things. People like Chellappa and Ponni didn't come to that temple. They had their own little shrine to Mariattha in the cheri where the . . . the Adi Dravidars . . . lived. Ramu had never been to that shrine. He had no idea what it was like.

Ponni did not answer Ramu's question. Already her mind had moved on. She clutched the book in her hand, looked out again across rice fields and river, and said in a quiet voice, "Yesterday I asked my uncle what happened when you died if there was no God."

"What did he say?"

Ponni turned to look at Ramu, sudden tears in her eyes threatening to spill over at any moment. "He said he didn't know. He said perhaps nothing happens. Perhaps you die and that is it. That is all. Nothing comes afterwards." She lifted a hand and waved it at the distance as if the nothingness of death lay there, in that sky above the river where the two white birds still chased each other back and forth.

Ramu followed her waving into the blue distance where the void of death lay. He felt a disquieting stir of dread. After death, nothing. His mother. Dead. Nothing. But then the dread was quickly succeeded by anger—anger at Chellappa. Ponni's father was dead, recently murdered in the most horrible fashion. Her mother also was dead. How could Chellappa say such things to her? "Your uncle is wrong," he blurted out. At the back of his mind was anger for his own dead mother, too.

Ponni nodded as if in agreement, but then said, "My uncle knows many things. He has thought about these things a lot."

"That doesn't mean he knows everything!"

The moment the words left his mouth Ramu felt embarrassed. The words had come out all wrong, in a whine—like a child's shrill and petulant plaint. Not at all the way he had meant to speak.

A quick smile sprang to Ponni's lips. Ramu had seen that very smile days earlier by the hut under the coconut trees. Now, the smile seemed to release something in Ponni. She jumped off the stones on which she was standing. "I'll bring the book back soon," she said, and then was gone, without saying when exactly she meant by *soon*.

Over the next few days, Ramu often found himself thinking of Ponni suddenly, unexpectedly. Walking home from school with Subbu, for example, Ponni popped into his mind when he passed the trail that went up to the ruined fort. Of course, he did not tell Subbu anything about Ponni. He knew he could not. Subbu was his friend but he would not understand. Ponni was an Adi Dravidar—he savored on his tongue the term she had used for herself—girl. He, Ramu, like Subbu, was a Brahmin. Brahmins didn't mix with Adi Dravidars. They didn't even mix with other non-Brahmins! Subbu was his best friend but he would be aghast if he knew Ramu had become friends with Ponni.

Friends with Ponni.

Novel thought.

Was it true?

Was it right that he, Ramu, had become friends with Ponni? Curious idea, even terrifying. There would be consequences if people found out he was meeting Ponni, had lent her a book. Maybe, just maybe, his father would understand, but even Gomati Paati, who doted on him (yes, she did, he knew she did), would be dismayed. And Uncle Siva? Uncle Siva's reaction did not even bear thinking about. No, he would have to keep his trysts with Ponni secret. Not even Subbu could know. All Subbu would do was tell him he was breaking taboos, doing things forbidden by custom and religion since time immemorial. Subbu would insist that he immediately stop seeing Ponni. Subbu might even tell someone. He could not run that risk. Forbidden or not, dangerous or not, he could not stop. He *would* not stop. Why should anyone tell him what he could and could not do? What right did anyone have to decide who could be his friend? Besides, a special bond linked him to Ponni. He had found her father murdered under the demon tree. In a sense, he was an important link to her father. When she came looking for him by the river, then, how could he just ignore her? If she wanted him to be her friend, how could he refuse? He could not stop meeting her. He would not stop meeting her.

During the days when such thoughts filled his mind, Ramu returned to the ruined fort many times. Christmas, barely registered as a festive occasion in the village which had no Christians, came and went. When Subbu asked to play, Ramu made an excuse so that he could go up to the fort. Or else he disappeared even before Subbu or Hari came looking for him. Always he went up to the fort at roughly the time that he had met Ponni there to give her the book. He sat on the broken stones and looked idly out over the river, the fields, and the village, hoping Ponni would appear. He waited without knowing when she would return with his book. He could have gone looking for Ponni at the hut under the coconut trees, but the vague apprehension he had felt earlier about being seen there had by now deepened into an abundant caution about his meetings with Ponni. He felt certain she would appear sooner or later. No point taking risks. So he resisted the temptation to go to the hut.

He did, however, sometimes watch the hut from the back door to the house where Gomati Paati sat in her wooden chair. One time she noticed him doing this and said irritably, "What are you staring at? You'll go blind if you stare like that!"

Ramu hurriedly looked away. That figure moving about around the hut—had that been Ponni? He could not tell. The distance was too great for him to be certain.

It was a whole week and more before Ponni turned up again at the ruined fort.

Late one afternoon, Ramu arrived at the fort and there she was, sitting on a low broken wall, the borrowed book beside her.

"I came yesterday," she said. "You were not here."

"I couldn't come. Too much homework. My father is back from his tour. My grandmother makes him review my homework when he is here. She would do it herself if she could. I came almost every day before yesterday. *You* were not here then."

Ponni held up her hands so that he could see their calluses and stains. "I was working. Beedis."

"You roll beedis?"

"Yes. Instead of working in the fields. When I came back from Madras, I begged my father not to have me working in the fields. But I had to do something to bring in money. My father couldn't just feed me while I sat idly at home. So I started rolling beedis. I get the tobacco and tendu leaves and thread from the sait who has his shop in Ambasamudram. Muhammad Basheer Sait. He lives in this village." She slowly flexed her fingers and then rubbed hard at the blemishes made by the beedis as if to erase them. The ugly brown blotches had stained large parts of her fingers and even her fingernails. "It's hard work. Maybe it would have been better to work in the fields." She added wistfully, "In Madras, I didn't have to roll beedis. I could go to school."

Ramu stole a quick look at his own fingers. All he had was a little swelling on the middle finger of his right hand from pressing too hard while holding a pencil. He felt guilty. Even though her father had just been murdered, Ponni had had no rest, no time to grieve properly. Embarrassed, he said, "Why did you go to Madras?"

"I told you. I went when my mother died. My uncle offered to take me to live with him so it would be easier for my father."

"Why did you come back, then?"

"My father wanted me to. He missed me. He hadn't seen me for a long time. He was afraid I would forget him."

"You must have been in Madras for many years."

Ponni counted the years in her head. "Three. But that was not the only time. Once before, when my mother was sick, I was there for more than a year. I was only five then."

"How old are you now?"

"Twelve."

"I am too! We are the same age!" It came to Ramu that though they were the same age, Ponni had already spent many years away in Madras, while he had been in Paavalampatti all his life except for occasional trips to Thirunelveli Town. "What is Madras like?"

"Big city. Enormous. Thousands of people. No, hundreds of thousands. We lived in Perambur, where my uncle used to work in the railway machine shops a long time ago. One room for my uncle and me in a big house. The other people in the house were all men who still worked in the railway factories. Three in one room, sometimes even four. They all looked up to my uncle because he no longer worked in the factories and he was such a well-read man. Not just in Tamil, but even in English. Important men were always coming by to see him."

She did not say that the rooms were small and dark and grimy. Or that the floors of the common bathrooms were covered with slime and that the toilets out behind the house stank so abominably that she dreaded using them. She did not mention all the days she and her uncle Chellappa, trying to eke out a living now as a writer and a journalist while also involving himself in a variety of political activities, had gone to bed still hungry. Nor did she bring up the fight that her uncle had had with another of the tenants in that house because of that neighbor's lewd behavior toward her. That was the reason her uncle had agreed so readily when her father had wanted her to return to Paavalampatti. She was turning into a woman. It would not be the same anymore. How could she continue to live there in that house with all those single men as she became a woman?

"In the backyard, there was a mango tree," Ponni said. "Only the landlord was allowed to pick the mangos. Sometimes I would steal a few."

"Were they any good?"

"Delicious."

"Better than our mangos here in Paavalampatti?"

"Much better."

Ramu thought of the way he always imagined Madras: white towers among palm trees. "Did you see tall white towers in Madras?" he wanted to know.

"Tall white towers?" Ponni asked, looking at him doubtfully. "In Madras? Are there such towers there? I've been to Mount Road and Marina Beach, where many of the important buildings are. I didn't see any tall white towers."

Ramu felt disappointed.

"No towers," Ponni continued. "But there are lots of buildings and many cars."

"Nothing like this village." Ramu gestured toward the village that lay invisible below and behind them.

"No, nothing like it at all."

Ramu perched himself on the wall next to Ponni and reflected on Madras, which did not have tall white towers but still was nothing like Paavalampatti. They sat side by side in the shadow cast by another, taller wall. In front of them the little hill fell away to the river. Beyond the river, a green and still land, steaming in the golden late afternoon light, spread before them up to the mountains. Madras was nothing like this land that sprawled before them. Satisfied, Ramu laid a hand on the book lying on the wall between Ponni and him. "Did you read it?"

"My uncle helped me," Ponni admitted.

"I like King Vikramaditya. How he fights his way through the forest to the tamarind tree repeatedly! All so that he can bring the undead vetal back to the holy man who needs it for his magic ritual."

"Yes, all that magic . . ."

Ramu hardly heard her. He was getting excited thinking about the adventures of Vikram, which were indeed among his favorite stories. Not only did he have this book about them, but he had heard them recounted by Gomati Paati many times. Gomati Paati was a terrific storyteller. "And the vetal is great too," he said. "So devious in telling Vikram stories with riddles in them. Of course, Vikram knows the answers to the riddles. He is not only strong but also wise. But the moment he speaks—boom!—the vetal escapes back to the tree! Poor king. How he struggles through the forest again and again. Very brave."

"I was confused, though. Why does the vetal go about escaping in such a roundabout way? Why doesn't he just fly away the moment the king cuts him down from the tree?"

"The vetal was testing the king. Vikramaditya was supposed to be the wisest king in all the world. The vetal was trying to find out if he really was."

"I didn't like some of the answers that the king gave to the vetal. I could think of other answers that would have made as much sense. The riddles weren't much good as riddles."

"You didn't like the book."

"I liked reading it. The stories were fun. But they were all about Brahmins and kings and beautiful princesses."

"That's true. I hadn't thought about that."

Chellappa had pointed this out to Ponni. Her uncle had also pointed out that nothing was as it seemed in these stories of Vikram and the vetal. The Brahmin holy man who had asked King Vikramaditya to bring back the vetal meant to kill him at the end. The holy man was not really a good person. He lusted for power that he meant to attain through a sacrifice of the king and the vetal in a fiendish ritual of dark sorcery. And the vetal was not really evil—at the end it was the vetal that saved the king by telling him what the holy man meant to do. It was the holy man who was the demon, not the vetal. When Ponni repeated all this to Ramu, he looked at her with new respect.

The sun had gone down as they talked. Ramu had not realized how late it was. The light was fading. The mountains were dim and distant outlines. In the gathering dusk, the river and the rice fields and the palm trees seemed to grow into gray and ominous otherworldly versions of themselves. The light wind blowing across the river made the ruined fort rustle with the noises of unseen things. It was a time of day when it was easy to believe in magicians and demons and mortals of superhuman valor and wisdom.

"It's late," Ramu cried, jumping up from his seat on the broken wall, his book in his hand. "Gomati Paati will be furious."

"Will you bring me another?" Ponni said quickly, before Ramu could depart. "An English book?"

"Yes. Tomorrow. Same time."

Gomati Paati was waiting for Ramu outside their house. Her very manner of standing bespoke anxiety and annoyance. She stood at the very edge of the thinnai to their house, leaning against one of the pillars with one hand and peering up and down the street. The gas street lamps spread a very inadequate light into the street. The moment she saw him approaching she called, "Where have you been? I went to Subbu's house to look for you. You were not there."

"I've finished my homework," Ramu said, bounding up the steps past his grandmother. He wanted to put away the book in his hand before she caught sight of it. No need to arouse more suspicion than absolutely necessary. By the time Gomati Paati followed him to the shelf that stood in the room he shared with his cousins, and on which he left his things in complete disorder, he had managed to tuck the book away between two other slim volumes. He then pretended to busy himself with his schoolbag.

"What are you doing?" Gomati Paati asked.

"Getting ready for school tomorrow."

"It's almost time to eat. Where were you all this time? Subbu had no idea where you had gone."

"I was down by the river with Mahesh and Sundar," Ramu lied. Mahesh and Sundar lived at the other end of the street. They hardly ever came looking for him at home. He felt safe lying about them.

"Twice in the last week Subbu has come looking for you. I hardly see you at home. Where do you disappear day after day?"

It was *not* day after day. But Ramu knew better than to point that out to his grandmother. Instead, deliberately raising his voice and injecting a note of irritation into it, he said, "Look, Paati. You are the one who keeps telling me I should have many friends. So now I'm spending time with Mahesh and Sundar."

Ramu's loud voice brought his father from his room, where he was reading the newspaper under the new electric light. "What's the matter?" he asked, the newspaper dangling from his long fingers.

"Ask your son where he has been all this time," Gomati Paati said.

"Why? Where has he been?"

"Down by the river. With Mahesh and Sundar."

"Is there anything wrong with that?"

"He came home a moment ago. Is this the time to come back home?"

"He has already done his homework. I checked."

"Still, this is no time to come home."

"He's growing up, Amma. He's not a child anymore."

"You are one to talk! You didn't even know he was gone all this time. If I don't look out for this motherless child, nobody will."

In a resigned tone, Ramu's father addressed him: "Look, Ramu. See how worried you've made your grandmother. Can't you come back before it gets dark?"

Ramu finished with his schoolbag and turned around. His grandmother stood a few steps in front of his father. They both looked changed in the flickering light of the oil lamps illuminating the room. With her white widow's sari tightly wrapped around her slight frame and over her small head, Gomati Paati was a diminutive apparition. His father looked equally spectral in the half-light of the lamps, thin and tall and hollow-cheeked, his face shadowed as usual by an expression of absence and reverie. Ramu considered them both with fresh and avid interest.

༄

Douglas Robinson leaned back in his chair and regarded the two men before him. To the left was the elder brother, named Vishwanathan, who worked it seemed as health inspector for the sanitation department; to the right was Sivaraman, who looked after the considerable fields and gardens the family owned. They were Brahmins. He could tell. Fine specimens of that noble caste. Especially the younger one, who was a handsome chap. Robinson liked the look of him particularly. He had wide, intelligent eyes and a firm, honest chin. You could tell his fine lineage just by looking at him. As he pondered the men, Robinson remained leaning back in his chair. He rested his right hand with deliberate authority on the worn wooden surface of the portable camp table in front of him and let Sub-Inspector Chandran do the talking. He had learned the hard way that you had to do little things like this to show Indians who was in charge. Otherwise, intelligent fellows like these Brahmins would run circles around you. Also, he felt slightly nauseated. Under the front of his khaki shirt, his stomach had been making worrying noises. It had been upset three days in a row. Mild diarrhea. Leaning back and letting Chandran take over for a bit would give his stomach a moment to settle.

It was pleasant in the shade of the huge banyan tree by the

pitted road that made its way eventually to Tinneveli and Palamcottah, where the district headquarters were located. The village of Pavampaty—the natives had another name for it Robinson could not remember or pronounce—was on the other side of the narrow road, across from the tree with its many impressive hanging roots. This was Robinson's first visit to Pavampaty. He had had no reason to come before. It was a quiet village, equally divided between Muhammadans and Hindoos, but no trouble at all. At least not until now.

A short distance down the road, in the shade of a pipal tree, stood Robinson's Austin with its bonnet raised to let the engine cool. The driver, Sami, had gone off to the village to fetch water for the radiator. Venkaiah and Aravindan, constables from the Armed Police, stood alertly against the car, clutching their Enfield rifles in both hands as if still on the parade ground. The constables and the rifles were routine precautions, especially appropriate now given how tense India had grown in the months since the provincial Congress ministries had resigned. The resignations were in protest against what the Congress Party said was the forcible entry of India into the war in Europe. Gandhi's Congress said the war had nothing to do with India and they were against the British rulers forcing Indians to fight in it. Ridiculous notion; even treasonous in a time of war, if one were to think about it. Robinson had drummed it into his Armed Police guard how vital it was to be vigilant in these times. His own pistol, which he kept loaded these days, weighed comfortingly against his hip.

A mild breeze found its way under the pillared canopy of the banyan tree and rustled the leaves above. The green mountains in the distance, the paddy fields in the sun, the coconut trees with their slim gray trunks—all made for a picturesque scene. Very different from the wolds and dales of Robinson's native Yorkshire, but picturesque nonetheless. Next to Robinson at the table sat Sub-Inspector Chandran, principal Investigating Officer for the division into which Pavampaty fell. Behind him, Robinson could feel the patient presence of his bearer Vijayan. And some distance away stood a group of villagers waiting for an audience with him when he had concluded his present business with the two brothers, masters of the murdered Paraiyar man Murugappa. Also present were two boys, one apparently the son of the elder of the brothers, seated cross-legged in the dirt against one of the many trunks of the banyan tree. The boys were staring steadfastly at Robinson in a most disconcerting fashion. Their unwavering attention was unnerving. Robinson wondered briefly whether he should ask Vijayan to shoo the boys away. That, however, might be taken as a sign of anxiety, of weakness. Better to ignore the boys.

Robinson had set out on tour a little less than two weeks before, right after New Year's Day. Everywhere the villagers were busy with the harvest and the impending festivities of Pongal. It was a short tour. One more day and it would be over. And then, he thought with relief, he would be back at home in Palamcottah just before the villages were taken over by the riotous celebrations of Pongal.

Ann waited in Palamcottah. Ann, whom Robinson had visited at tea time on numerous occasions. Ann, about whom he could not make up his mind. He would have to decide about her soon, though. He couldn't very well carry on like this indefinitely. It just wasn't done, was it? He wished somebody would advise him about women. He was no good—didn't he know it?—when it came to the fairer sex. Ann was quiet, kind, and passably pretty. The problem was that she was Anglo-Indian. Old missionary family, distinguished in its own way. But there was Indian blood in there too. You couldn't really tell by looking at Ann. Her eyes were the clearest blue. Even out of doors, in the bright unforgiving sunlight of India, you would not notice anything different about her, except perhaps for the darkness, almost Indian, of her hair. Nevertheless, he had it on the best authority—from the Anglo-Indian wife of a railway officer, who made it her business to know everybody else's business—that somehow, somewhere, a little India had gotten mixed up in Ann.

It was all very frustrating. Sometimes Robinson felt quite exasperated with himself for the feelings set loose within him by Ann. Love, marriage, family. What did they all matter, anyhow? The world was rapidly descending into chaos. Every week the war in Europe against Hitler crept closer and closer to home. It could go badly, so badly. There had been news of British ships sunk, even of talk of rationing in Britain. Rationing! In England, in Yorkshire! What if England itself fell, and London was occupied by the Nazis? He imagined German soldiers at the gates of Buckingham Palace and marching through Trafalgar Square. He contemplated with dread the possibility of returning home to be ordered about by Krauts. Young though he was, he felt keenly the weight of momentous times.

Four years before, on the P & O boat bringing him out to India, Robinson had had a conversation he had never forgotten. He was twenty-one years old then. (How much younger and greener he had been!) One day, shortly before reaching Bombay, he was up on deck having a smoke when he was joined at the railing of the ship by an Indian Civil Service man many years his senior. For some time, they had silently stood side by side leaning against the railing, while beneath them the waters of the Arabian Sea rose and fell with an oily, gray heaviness. Robinson was only a young recruit into the Indian Police Service and for much of the trip out from Southampton the ICS man, returning to India after home leave, had treated him with the most perfunctory politeness. Now, however, he spoke suddenly in a different tone: "It won't last much longer, you know."

Robinson, not expecting to be spoken to, asked in confusion, "What won't?" He hurriedly pitched his cigarette into the sea below.

"The Empire. I mean the Empire."

Robinson noted the touch of gray in the neatly clipped mustache. *The Empire, which he was coming out to serve, wouldn't last?* Glumly, he nodded his head.

"They are making a mess of it out there," the man continued.

"Who are?"

"The Indian politicians, of course. The Gandhis and the Nehrus and all the others. Fools, all of them." The voice was mildly irritated at Robinson's obtuseness.

"Yes, of course."

"Where would the buggers be without us? My family's been coming out for a hundred years. Since before the Mutiny. Great-grandfather was killed in the Relief of Lucknow. Is buried there. Won't last a day if we leave, I can tell you that. Take my bearer, Ghulam Ali. Decent fellow, on the whole, but a child, a complete child. Won't do a thing unless I tell him to."

"What do you think will happen, sir?"

"I'm afraid the powers that be in London will muck it all up. Men who know nothing about India, have never come out, have no idea what we've done for the old place. India's just something on a map to them. What do they know about Empire?" The man grew more animated. "This 1935 Act. Power sharing with the babus. Big mistake, if you ask me. Best way to deal with non-cooperation, civil disobedience, and all that foolishness is with a firm hand. Knew a man once, fine administrator, who would pick up anybody engaging in political nonsense in his district, strip him naked, and dump him in the streets. Soon he had no trouble at all, trust me. A firm hand, that's what Indians need." The man fell silent for a moment and then added, more quietly, "Of course, the way Hitler is going, there may be war in Europe soon. If that happens, we won't get out of India. No chance at all." He turned and looked at Robinson directly for the first time, giving him a piercing look. "Indian Police Service, aren't you?"

"Yes, sir." Robinson was surprised the ICS man knew that much about him.

"Where are you headed?"

"Madras."

"Bloody hot place. Mosquitoes like elephants. Like the whole damned country, actually. But worse. I take it you are going by train to Madras from Bombay? Have the coolies put a block of ice in your compartment. Makes all the difference at this time of the year." He prepared to return below decks.

"Thanks for the advice, sir."

"Remember, at the end of the day, they are all just blackies," the man said, as he turned away. Startled at the awkward choice of word, Robinson directed his gaze at the heaving waters of the Arabian Sea below. He did not wish his embarrassment to be noticed. He was grateful that the senior man had taken the time to share his thoughts with him. Robinson would need such advice from more knowledgeable officers if he was to survive India. He did not want to spoil the moment by showing how taken aback he was at the ICS man's crude reference to Indians. The ICS man, however, was oblivious to Robinson's discomfort. He repeated, "Just blackies. Keep that straight, my boy, and you'll do fine."

For the rest of the trip, the ICS man had resumed his distance from Robinson, who, unlike him, did not come from a family with generations of Indian connections. True, one of Robinson's ancestors had come out to India during Queen Victoria's reign and had died and was buried in India, but he had left no subsequent family legacy of service to Empire. Not until Robinson did Empire intrude once again into the family in such a personal way.

Robinson had been led to serve India and the Empire by necessity. Orphaned at an early age, he had grown up on a Yorkshire farm with his uncle and his family. His early life had been mud and drystone walls and the bitterness of winter winds whistling down from the wolds on farmer and farm animal alike. School was an escape from the tedium and drudgery of working on the farm. In books, he found visions of a larger world he ached to enter. Against all odds, he did well in school—not so well as to consider university, but enough to dream of escape. There was an added incentive. His uncle and aunt were as kind as they could be given their own straitened circumstances, but it was understood that he should think of moving on as soon as he was done with school. With the completion of school, the pressure of planning his future grew more urgent. One day, he came across a civil service book for India, and at once everything became clear in his mind. What other place could take him farther from his present condition than exotic India? What land could be more distant from the provincialism and miserable dependency he had come to associate with Yorkshire? He found from consulting the book that if he worked hard he might have a chance of qualifying for the Indian Police Service, which had an adventurous ring he liked. The Indian Civil Service was certainly beyond him.

A year later he was on that P & O Boat, having a conversation with the ICS man about the future of the Empire that left him in equal measure embarrassed and dismayed—embarrassed because he preferred not to use words like "blackie" when referring to the natives he was coming out to serve, and dismayed because he did not want to think that the solution he had found in escaping to India might prove abortive.

In India, after two years in the Police Training College, Robinson found himself posted to the upcountry station of Tinneveli far in the south of Madras Presidency. He did not have the right connections to ensure a posting in a less remote part. As assistant superintendent of police, at the tender age of twenty-three, he had responsibility for a vast tract of land from Tinneveli and its adjacent town of Palamcottah to the mountains to the west.

Robinson's superior, the Superintendent of Police of Tinneveli District, was Percy Maitland. Small and wiry and with round glasses that gave him an owlish look, Maitland was a stickler for detail and discipline. It was Maitland's job to take the novice colonial officer, straight out of training college and with hardly a smattering of Tamil still, and mold him into a useful servant of India and Empire.

Maitland was, Robinson soon decided, a strange fish. He was a very private man. Robinson had shared a large bungalow in Palamcottah with him for years (they were the only unattached British men in the Tinneveli police department), and yet he could not say he knew Maitland well. There hung around Maitland always, all the time that Robinson had known him, an air of separateness, of aloofness. He had been in his post a long time, much longer than was normal, for he had turned down promotions and postings to other districts to stay in Tinneveli. It was rumored that he had done so because of the love of a native woman, now dead of tuberculosis, whom he had kept in style in a large house with a garden a few miles out of Tinneveli Town. Some said he still continued his dalliances with native women, although more discreetly.

Because he had been in his post so long, Maitland knew his district well. He had arrived before the motor car had become common for administrative purposes. He had toured the district on horseback and by bullock cart, making his way at a leisurely pace that allowed him, he always said, to get to know the villages and towns under his supervision in a manner you never could in a motor car. Even now, he preferred to travel by horseback whenever he could. He was a man who understood India. He spoke Tamil fluently and had an avid interest in the religion and culture of the people. He was a great admirer of the temple architecture of the region and had even written brief articles on the topic, including one on the thousand-pillared hall of the temple of Tinneveli. Ignorance about India, especially among British officials, enraged him. "If you are going to rule a country, learn the country," was one of his favorite pronouncements. Once Robinson saw him supervise—albeit reluctantly—the savage caning of a reticent informant and then an hour later, over gin and tonic on the verandah of the bungalow, launch a vehement denunciation of the ignorance of India's British rulers.

As far as Robinson could tell there was no irony. Exasperated, and no doubt emboldened by the gin he too had imbibed, Robinson blurted out, "Why stay, then? Why not throw the whole thing up and go back home?"

The moment the words left his mouth he regretted them. But instead of infuriating Maitland, the words had the opposite effect. Maitland grew quiet, shook the glass in his hand so that the gin and tonic swirled round and round, and said, "Home? I don't have a home." Behind the words, Robinson sensed profound experiences left unshared. He thought involuntarily of the rumors of Maitand's predilection for native women. Maitland continued, "Call me a karma yogi, if you like. One does what one has to. One is not free to do whatever one wants, you understand. The Hindoos call this idea karma."

"Yes, yes, of course." Robinson was eager to make amends for his outburst.

Maitland carried on as if he had not heard him. "It is an imperfect world. The job of us British is to prepare the Indians to rule themselves and then leave. We don't do that by being petty tyrants. We should teach them the best part of ourselves—our love of freedom and democracy. In the meantime, we keep order. We keep the Hindoos and the Muhammadans from killing one another."

Imperfect world? Karma yogi? Maitland was a peculiar fish indeed.

Robinson could not understand Maitland, but neither could he deny that he was a very good superintendent of police. He knew from his own visits to the Inspector General's office in Madras that Maitland was a known quantity there. His eccentricities were found exasperating, but his record was well understood. It was appreciated that he had a tight grip over his domain. Tinneveli was a district with a history of radicalism. Long ago, Veera Pandiya Kattaboman, a local chieftain, had fought bitterly against the British as they had tried to establish their control over this part of India. More recently, in 1911, District Collector Ashe had been murdered here by the terrorist Vanchi Iyer. V. O. Chidambaram Pillai, who had challenged the British monopoly in shipping and was imprisoned for seditious activities, was from Tinneveli, as was Subramania Bharathi, the nationalist Tamil poet who had spent years in exile in the French colony of Pondicherry for his anti-British activities. The long memory of the Empire still remembered all these people and events. As long as Maitland was able to keep such a district quiet, especially in a time of war and burgeoning anti-British sentiment in India, he was indulged.

It was this redoubtable Maitland who had sent Robinson to Pavampaty. Robinson brought his attention back to the present—his upset stomach and the ostensible inquiry into the murder of the Paraiyar man Murugappa (who had actually been dead for several weeks). While his mind had been wandering, Sub-Inspector Chandran had been interrogating the two Brahmin brothers of Pavampaty. In point of fact, this case of the murdered Paraiyar man was not worthy of Robinson's close attention. No doubt the murder had happened because of some petty quarrel—apparently the murdered man had the reputation of being a drunkard. Robinson was present not on account of the murder of a lowly Paraiyar laborer, but rather because of the murdered man's brother, one Chellappa, a notorious agitator with a thick file on him in the Intelligence Bureau office in Madras. Chellappa had been seen in the area soon after Murugappa's death was discovered, and Maitland had thought it judicious that Robinson make a stop at Pavampaty under the circumstances. Robinson had to pass through the area on the return leg of his tour anyway: if he stopped for a couple of hours and made inquiries into the case, it would help. Even if he was not able to bring Chellappa himself in for questioning, Maitland felt, an appropriate message would be conveyed to him and any associates he might have in the area. That is why they had made sure the village was aware of Robinson's impending visit well in advance. Maitland was one for nipping things in the bud. The sooner Chellappa could be encouraged to leave the district and return to Madras, where he would be more effectively watched and would be somebody else's problem, the better.

Now Robinson waited until Sivaraman—the younger brother, the one who was clearly the more able of the two—began to say something in response to Sub-Inspector Chandran and then deliberately interrupted to ask, "The killed masculinity. You knew his brother?" He spoke in Tamil, as they all had been doing.

Sivaraman took a moment to comprehend what Robinson knew had come out mangled, and then asked, "Chellappa?"

"Yes, yes, that same thing."

"Very well. He worked for us many years ago, long before he was thrown out of the village for making trouble."

"What did?"

"He deliberately insulted the well-established families. He was run out of the village for his impudence."

"What kind of masculinity he is?"

This time Sivaraman had no trouble understanding. "Very troublesome, sir. Just the other day he came to my house and started yelling at my mother. A man with no respect for anyone. I think he lives in Madras." Sivaraman paused as if something had occurred to him. "Do you think he had something to do with his brother's murder?"

"Does he have . . . ? What do you say . . . ? With him, he has something?"

Sivaraman stared at Robinson in bafflement. Chandran, too, looked bewildered. Viswanathan said in English, "What do you mean, sir?"

Ignoring him, Robinson turned to Chandran and asked, also in English, "Does this Chellappa have friends, comrades, in the village, do you know?"

Chandran understood that Robinson wanted him to translate and did so.

"No. No friends," said Sivaraman, whose opinion was the one Robinson, it was clear to everyone, wanted to hear. "This is a peace-loving village. We don't like trouble here."

Robinson reverted to Tamil—it was important to learn and speak in the vernacular, he had been taught in the training college—and continued to quiz Sivaraman about Chellappa, for whom his men had searched the village without success. Even if Chellappa eluded them, Robinson meant to send him a firm message that he was being watched. He would not himself go looking for Chellappa. It would not at all do for him—a white man—to enter the low-caste Paraiyar cheri of the village. Instead, he would interrogate a cross-section of the village about the vicious malcontent and no doubt news would find its way back to him. It was probable, of course, that Chellappa had appeared in Pavampaty only because of his brother's murder. Nevertheless, as Maitland said, it did not hurt to head off trouble before it occurred. It was good to encourage a professional agitator like this Chellappa to move on out of the district just as soon as possible. Robinson settled back in his chair under the banyan tree and proceeded to set about the task.

A few days later, back in Palamcottah, Robinson found himself discussing Chellappa with Maitland. It was after dinner and they were in the verandah of the bungalow they shared, each with the customary gin and tonic by his side. Maitland was in his favorite chair, under the light of an electric lamp, a book in his hand. Robinson was leafing through the *Illustrated London News,* weeks old because of the time it had taken for it to make its way from England to Tinneveli. Since it was still only late January, the evening was cool. The bamboo thatai blinds that blocked out the afternoon sun had been rolled up by the house servant. The bungalow was located on the outskirts of the small European quarter of the town, facing toward the countryside, so that the mild breeze that blew had a fine freshness to it.

Before dinner, Robinson had managed to fit in a vigorous game of tennis at the European Club. The tennis had taken the place of an invitation to tea with Ann, which he had after much thought politely declined. He had finally, reluctantly, decided that it would be best to snuff out any suggestion of a romantic interest on his part toward Ann. A part of him—a big part of him—regretted the decision, but under the circumstances he did not feel comfortable continuing to visit her in a social way. To do so at this point was tantamount to a declaration of serious intent with regard to her, and he was not prepared to do that. Instead he had fled to the tennis court, from which he had returned feeling tired in a relaxed, pleasurable sort of way. It was this mood of languorous satisfaction that Maitland broke by speaking.

"Ah, yes, Robinson," Maitland said, putting his book down. "I read your report for the Intelligence Bureau on that fellow Chellappa. Nicely done. Thought you'd like to know Chellappa is back in Madras. He's been sighted there."

"Good thing I showed my face in Pavampaty."

"Good thing, indeed."

"Nasty piece of work, is he, this Chellappa?"

"So it seems. Involved in all kinds of bad business. Worker agitations. Anti-Brahmin, anti-caste agitations. That kind of radical stuff."

"Damned nuisance."

"Useful chaps, actually, as long as they don't get out of hand. They hate Gandhi and the Congress, you know. You can always trust them to criticize the Congress and keep them in check. As far as I'm concerned, it's all fine as long as it doesn't go too far. All part of learning to be a democracy, in my opinion. But this Chellappa fellow is more sinister."

"Sinister? Not a terrorist, you say?" As the uprisings against British rule intensified, there had been much discussion in official circles of the dangers of terrorism. Before his recent departure to Palestine, India's foremost expert on terrorism, Sir Charles Tegart, on whose life a cowardly attempt had been made years before, had been very vocal in advising that the government should prepare urgently for this menace.

"Almost as bad. Labor agitator. And very anti-British to boot. One of the leaders in that big railway strike many years ago. Long before your time in India."

"I've heard about that."

"Terrible what happened. I was Deputy Superintendent of Police in Trichy then. As you can imagine, I saw things up close. A lot of vandalism and rioting. Many innocent people died. Bunch of ruffians, the strikers. The worst kind. It seems Chellappa was picked up then and put in jail."

"Must have been very young."

"Probably younger than you are now. Little good jail did him."

"One of the men I talked to in Pavampaty said he was always a real troublemaker. He was run out of the village. Apparently went sneaking into the upper-caste part of the village to steal and got caught."

"Yes, I read that in your report. You can never trust these Paraiyars. They'll bow and scrape in front of you, and then they'll rob you blind when you are not there. Had to employ one as a constable one time. The Brahmin and other caste officers didn't like it, not one bit. They warned me against doing it. But I had to. Got a lot of pressure from Madras to bring more low-caste types into the police. The warnings were right, though. After a few months, I let him go."

"No good at his job?"

"Not at all. And corrupt into the bargain. He was taking money under the table from day one. I don't have any patience for that nonsense. When it comes to employing Indians, I'll take Brahmins every time. Dependable types."

"In Pavampaty, I met this young Brahmin. Fine fellow. Intelligent."

"That's Brahmins for you—sharp. I have many Brahmin friends. I know them well. To tell you the truth, I trust some of them more than a white man."

Robinson did not know what to say in reply to this observation. He himself had come to have an admiration for the Brahmins he had met; but to consider them more trustworthy than white people? He had a feeling Maitland was being deliberately scandalous. Maitland was always testing him in this way. When he remained silent, Maitland glanced over at him challengingly from behind his spectacles, as if to say, *What do you have to say to that?* Robinson took a sip from his gin and tonic and pretended not to have seen the glance. He returned to his magazine, turning over the pages. With a quiet smirk that Robinson did not miss, Maitland too returned to his book.

Perusing the *Illustrated London News,* Robinson thought of what Maitland had said. Robinson had a grudging respect for Percy Maitland, but he had to admit he was a character. He remembered again the whispered stories of Maitland's love of native women. Not his own taste when it came to feminine beauty, but then again it was none of his business, really. He was amused to consider what the ICS man he had met on the P & O boat would make of Maitland. Or, for that matter, what old Percy would make of the ICS man. Maitland had broken so many taboos, crossed so many lines of separation he was supposed to respect. The ICS man would certainly disapprove of such behavior, and Robinson could not say he was wrong to do so. For his part, Maitland would probably object to the ICS man's use of words like "blackie." And he was right to do so too. What was the point of words like that? Prejudice was a terrible thing. And ignorant. Robinson felt he had enough experience of India now to make that judgment. Nehru, for example, was a Brahmin, and Brahmins, as was well known, were Aryans, just like the British and the Germans. All Indo-Europeans. You could tell that by just looking at a picture of Nehru. How was Nehru a blackie? Nonsense!

And, yet, that didn't mean Robinson was entirely in Maitland's corner on this topic. There were differences between the British and the natives too, differences that you couldn't ignore. You couldn't just pretend many Brahmins were not quite dark-skinned—black, actually, unlike Nehru. And all the other things that separated Brahmins and Europeans—religion, for example—you couldn't just wish them out of existence, either. What was the use of doing that? It was foolishness to think you could. Brahmins worshipped cows. How could any self-respecting Christian—or any decent, reasonable human being, for that matter—accept such pagan superstition? Brahmins were no doubt the finest types of Indians, intelligent and cultured even, but they were not Europeans, not at all. Of course, it was also true . . .

On the verandah of the bungalow in Tinneveli, far from his native Yorkshire, Douglas Robinson sat and ruminated in this fashion. He went round and round in his head thinking about India and Indians. Round and round he went with his gin and tonic in his hand, while around him in the dark of night India moved and breathed and whispered with a restless mystery that was in equal measure intoxicating and frightening.

ঌ

"I SAW THE DURAI."

"Durai?"

"Yes, the police durai. The white man."

"Hmm."

"Under the banyan tree. I went to see him with Subbu."

"Who is Subbu?"

"My friend. He and I are in the same class at school."

"What was the durai like?"

"Tall and thin. He had this big, round hat on his head, so I couldn't see his face clearly. Sola topee, I think they call it. He spoke a funny Tamil. Made me laugh. He kept glaring at me. But I wasn't frightened. What can he do to me?"

"Why should he want to do anything to you?"

"I'm just saying . . ."

"Hmm."

"Sub-Inspector Chandran was there too. He is the one who came and spoke to me after . . ." Ramu came to an abrupt halt, realizing he was about to mention Ponni's murdered father to her. Wordlessly, he berated himself. Why had he started talking about the durai? He cast his mind back to all that had been said under the banyan tree. He could not imagine repeating to Ponni Uncle Siva's observations about Chellappa and Murugappa. Ramu and Ponni had already met many times at the ruined fort, and yet they had never discussed Murugappa's murder directly. That was one topic that was avoided as if by unspoken mutual consent. Ponni's earlier desire to quiz Ramu about how he had found Murugappa's body seemed to have vanished. At least, she no longer made any attempt to bring up the subject.

When they met, late in the afternoon invariably, Ramu and Ponni spoke mostly of the books that Ponni continued to borrow. Chellappa of course knew of their encounters and that Ponni was borrowing books from him, but no one else did. Chellappa did not like it that Ponni was meeting Ramu. He feared the consequences of their encounters: unusual boy though he was, Ramu was still a Brahmin. He realized the dangers, especially to Ponni, in what Ponni and Ramu were doing. Had he not directly experienced similar perils himself? The times had changed, but not that much. Nevertheless, a part of him was secretly pleased to witness Ponni's love of books and reading. He could not—the defiant part of him would not let him—prohibit her from going up to the ruined fort. He understood that in a way she *had* to. Otherwise, where would she find books in Paavalampatti, this village so unforgiving of Adi Dravidars? Many were the risks he himself had taken in his journey out of Paavalampatti, and he could not refuse Ponni the right to run similar risks. All he could do was make certain his niece understood exactly what the dangers were and exactly how real. Scandal, abuse, social ostracism, even violence—all were possible. Caution was not a luxury.

Ponni understood. *Be careful.* That was the mantra. It meant Ponni tried to keep her conversations with Ramu as much as possible about the books she borrowed. Even so, more recently, Ramu and Ponni had occasionally begun to probe beyond superficialities. The reasons were not complicated. Once begun, who can predict or control the twists and turns of human colloquy? Ponni might, because of her avid curiosity, ask Ramu about school, and he with equal interest about her stay in Madras. Or else they would speak of

Paavalampatti, home to both of them, and when they did they would realize how separate their lives really were. The Brahmin neighbors and friends of Meenakshisundareswarar Temple Street, who played such an important role in Ramu's life, were largely unknown to Ponni. She knew by sight and had heard of the more important of these people—the grander landholders and men of influence—but beyond this cursory knowledge she knew nothing of them. For his part, Ramu could not claim even such a distant knowledge of Ponni's world. With a few exceptions (mostly the workers who toiled in his family's fields), the men and women of the Adi Dravidar cheri of the village were a great undifferentiated mass of humanity to him. The two of them lived, Ramu and Ponni realized, in different villages that only happened to have the same name and to occupy the same extent of dirt on the face of the earth.

Even as, despite Chellappa's warnings, their innocent dialogue led Ponni and Ramu to each other, they came to appreciate more and more keenly the great distance between them—a distance not to be measured by the quarter mile or so that lay between his house and her hut. That quarter of a mile could easily be run across on their own two legs, but what legs could cross the truer distance that separated them, the distance that mattered, the one wrought by custom and law and religion? The mystery of this question, vaguely glimpsed and unarticulated, deepened with every meeting of theirs in the ruined fort. Because of it, there remained a terrible awkwardness in the midst of the burgeoning personal familiarity between them. Even as they came to know each other as Ramu and Ponni, boy and girl—no, young man and young woman—they also understood better what it meant to be Brahmin and Adi Dravidar.

The weight of this understanding was often unbearable, making silence the only refuge. Sitting side by side, as the sun set and the gloom drew closer all around, they would stop talking. If only briefly, they managed to isolate themselves in a little world of their own of fallen walls and broken stones—no Brahmin, nor Adi Dravidar, here. In silence, they would find a freedom not to be found in words. Alas, eventually the silence too would fail; it too would begin to feel a burden. The temporarily exiled world would come crashing back to spoil everything once again with its divisions and distances. Was there no escaping the iron grasp of the world?

Breaking just such a silence that had befallen them after Ramu's report on the white durai's visit, Ponni said, "My uncle has gone back to Madras."

Ramu was surprised. "When did this happen?"

"Several days ago."

They had not met for a few days. Ramu had been busy with the three days of festivities for Pongal that had just ended. Before that there had been the preparations. The harvest had been brought in—Uncle Siva had complained ceaselessly about how cruel it was that Murugappa had chosen this time to be murdered—and the village and the temple had been taken over by gaiety. The cattle had been brightly decorated with flowers and colorful dyes. The house had been cleaned and new clothes donned. Rice had been boiled into different kinds of pongal—white, made with cane sugar, or brown, made with molasses. There was much visiting back and forth, amidst shouts of "Pongal O Pongal!" In the midst of all this revelry, how could Ramu get away to the ruined fort? And yet Chellappa had chosen this very time to leave for Madras.

"Why did he go?"

"It was time for him to return to Madras, I suppose. After he had grieved for my father and made sure we were all right, what else was there for him to do here? He had already been here for so many weeks." She paused as if there was more to say about her uncle's departure and then, seeming to change her mind, said, "Did you bring an English book for me?"

"Yes. Will you still borrow books from me now that your uncle is gone?"

"If you will lend them to me. I want to."

"I have many exciting books," Ramu said eagerly.

"The stories all seem the same to me. But I want to improve my English." She looked determined. It was a look Ramu had come to recognize.

"I can help you with words you don't understand now that your uncle is not here."

"Hmm."

"If you like."

"Hmm."

Ramu changed the topic. "What did your uncle say before he left?"

"Nothing."

"Nothing?"

"He left in a hurry. In the middle of the night. He woke my brother and me up and said he had to go. He said he would be in touch when he got to Madras. That was it." She did not add that before leaving her uncle had strictly warned her to stop seeing Ramu and that she was now breaking this injunction because she craved the books and the meetings with Ramu and could not bear to think of her life reduced to beedis and the hut. Her uncle had issued his warning out of earshot of her older brother Manickam, for Manickam knew nothing about the borrowed books or about the meetings at the ruined fort and it was better that things stayed that way.

With Murugappa dead and Chellappa back in Madras, now only Ponni and Manickam were left in the hut under the coconut trees. Ponni's family had dissolved, almost vanished from Paavalampatti. Even Ramu could remember a time not so long ago when there had been—he counted quickly—as many as eight people sharing the hut under the coconut trees. Murugappa, his wife Nagamma, Ponni, Manickam, two older sisters who had married and moved away, and two brothers who had died. Eight altogether. How long would it be before Manickam too was gone? And if he went, could Ponni stay? Young though he was, Manickam had already worked in the fields alongside his father Murugappa for many years. Would he now take Murugappa's place as overseer? Murugappa, despite his drunken ways, had commanded the respect of the workers. Manickam was young, only a few years older than Ramu. Ramu found it hard to imagine him in charge of the other Adi Dravidar workers. The workers would not give him the obedience that Murugappa had commanded.

Another thought suggested itself to Ramu: would Uncle Siva allow Manickam and Ponni to stay in their hut if Manickam did not step into Murugappa's position? He was always saying it was a mistake to have an Adi Dravidar overseer. Preferable to have the higher-caste Padaiyatchi if possible, he said. That was the way things had generally been done. That was the way the other landlords—Pillai or Brahmin, it did not matter—did it. Why should this one family be different? That is what Uncle Siva liked to say, though Gomati Paati disagreed. Where would Ponni and Manickam go if Uncle Siva threw them out of their hut despite Gomati Paati? To the Adi Dravidar cheri, which lay all the way on the other side of the village? The proliferating questions troubled Ramu. He reduced them to a single, short query: "What will you do now?"

"What do you mean?"

"I mean, what will happen to you now?" The question was blunt.

Ponni was silent for a long moment, and then she said, "I will make beedis. I will get married. I heard my uncle and my brother talking about it. My brother wants me to. I'm the right age to be married. If I am married, I'll belong to my husband like my sisters. And then my brother will not be responsible for me anymore."

"What did your uncle say to that?"

"Nothing much. He said it was something to think about. Immediately, my brother began complaining about how, because I've been to school and know how to read and write, no boy will want to marry me. He blamed my uncle for that and so they started arguing."

"Do you want to get married?"

"No!"

The response was emphatic. The evening gloom had gathered around them and so Ramu could not see Ponni's face clearly, but he could sense the resentment in her voice. He looked away from her and out from the little hill into the deepening dark. He was surprised to find he himself felt that resentment. Married? He could not imagine Ponni married.

Chellappa's departure had consequences that became clearer as the weeks went by. Ponni's appearances at the ruined fort at the top of the hill became more frequent despite the dire warnings she had been given. Her uncle's strict instructions could not stop her. It was as if she *needed* the meetings on the hilltop. They were her escape from Manickam.

Manickam worked all day in the fields—Ramu saw him there, noticing him in a fresh way now—and when he returned to the hut he was tired and covered with dirt and indignant that he was stuck with the responsibility of a sister who had been gone for long years, whom he knew little, and who made him feel stupid because of the schooling she had had and he had not. Every opportunity he got, Manickam fought with Ponni. If the evening koozhu, accompanied by green chillies, was not ready—few were the days now that they were lucky enough to have vegetables or a piece of meat or even rice—there would be yelling. If her hands had been aching and she had not been able to put in too many hours rolling beedis, there would be yet more yelling. Perhaps not unreasonably, Manickam would glower at her and ask what she thought would happen if he were to forego his work in the fields every time he felt a little unwell. If she made the slightest answer, the impudence might be met with a blow, and so Ponni learned to say little, keep her peace, and do her best not to rile Manickam, who was after all her older brother though hardly a full-grown man himself yet.

Every opportunity she got, Ponni fled the hut under the trees, for this minimized their interaction and their quarreling. She hated to be there when Manickam returned drunk from cheap toddy bought at the Nadar's shop. His drinking had increased greatly after their father's death. Ponni recognized easily the powerful, sour reek of the fermented sap of the palm tree even from a distance, for it was that same smell that had hung night after night around their father after their mother's death. It seemed men—and some women too; she could think of a few over in the Adi Dravidar settlement—were feckless and needed the succor of an intoxicant to numb them to death and the myriad difficulties of life. But they were not all feckless in the same way. Toddy called forth a deeper nature, which differed from man to man. While her father would get maudlin and full of self-recriminations when drunk, Manickam became reproachful and belligerent. Deep down, Ponni could not blame

Manickam. After all, she herself felt reproach and anger and a host of other emotions at her own circumstances, had cried on her mat many a night since her father's death. How could she condemn Manickam, then? But neither did she wish to offer herself up on the altar of Manickam's discontent. So, when evening came, she escaped to the ruined fort on the hill. Now, often, it was she who waited for Ramu to appear with a book. What toddy was to Manickam, books were to her. She read them secretly during the day when Manickam was gone (a little between beedi rolling), or else by the faint light of a precious oil lamp when Manickam had gone to sleep, more often than not passed out from the toddy.

It was not difficult to live this secret life—to escape from Manickam and the hut, and to keep her reading from him. For all the resentment and the quarreling, Manickam did not care very much what Ponni did with herself, as long as she had rolled an appropriate number of beedis for the day and was there to give him his koozhu when he wanted it. Beyond that, why should he trouble himself with what she did? In his drunken state, he hardly noticed she was gone, and when he did he did not mind that she was. Was she sneaking away to an amorous tryst with a boy? So what if she was? He did not care. In fact, if she ran away with some man, it would make his life easier, now that his uncle had so cruelly absconded to Madras and left him responsible for her. Or so Manickam thought. He could not have imagined even in his wildest dreams that Ponni was secretly meeting the master's son, Ramu, to borrow books. If he had known, no doubt his response would have been far different.

And so books continued to be borrowed. Sometimes Ramu lent Ponni Tamil books, though she always insisted that he also bring her books that were in English. Ramu wondered how much of the English books she could actually understand. She never asked him for help and he was reluctant to offer it without being asked. Who knew how she would respond?

Ponni was moody and unpredictable now. Ramu saw startling changes in her as the weeks went by. She grew haggard. She had a cough that would not go away. She began to look—Ramu hated to admit it—a little slovenly. Her paavaadai was often dirty and her blouse smelly with stale sweat. Sometimes, from the way she held her hands, he could tell they were hurting from rolling beedis. He wanted to take her stained and callused hands in his own, then, but did not dare. The change was not just physical. She made valiant attempts to keep her old curious and engaged self on display, to act as if she did not feel a desperation inside, but he could sense the falsity of the act. Even he, unschooled as he was in the ways of the world, could understand that she was plunging deeper and deeper into a forest of despair.

Once, Ramu arrived at the fort to find Ponni weeping. Concerned, he said, "What is it?" She gave him a fierce look, shook her head, and then abruptly got up and went away. The next day, it was as if the weeping had not happened at all, except that she was unusually talkative and lively. Ramu could easily recognize the forced nature of her jollity but could do nothing about it. He knew Ponni well enough by now to recognize the look in her eyes—the warning to him not to presume that he could mention what had happened the previous evening. He felt apprehension when he looked at Ponni. He felt a terrible foreboding.

There were many reasons for the foreboding that grew day by day deep within Ramu. Ponni's behavior was one. Another was the much subtler changes he had begun to notice in Gomati Paati. Did she know about his secret meetings with Ponni? Had she begun to suspect something? Small things—the way she looked at him when he returned home, or the nagging way she questioned him about his day—made him feel that perhaps she did. And sure enough, when he got home one day from a tryst with Ponni, Gomati Paati was waiting to confront him. She was standing on the thinnai to the house, as she often anxiously did when he did not return home at an appropriate time, except that this time her small and slender body was stiff with something more than suppressed worry.

"Where have you been?" she said, before he could enter the house. It was past dusk. Evening sounds emanated from the neighboring houses. In the distance, at the end of the street, the bells of Meenakshisundareswarar Temple sounded repeatedly from devotees reaching up and ringing them so that the gods might pay attention to their many worshipful entreaties. Under the giant flickering oil lamp by the wooden doors of the temple, a group of young women stood talking. Ramu had just passed them on his way home from the ruined fort on the hill. No one was in the street in the immediate vicinity. Still Gomati Paati spoke softly, as if of unmentionable things best kept hidden.

"Out with friends," Ramu replied.

"Where?"

"I don't have to tell you." He spoke with a feigned calmness. He felt a premonition of what was to come.

"You don't have to. I know where you have been."

"Then, why do you ask?"

"You go out to see that Paraiyatchi girl. You take books to her."

"No." Ramu was surprised to note that he too was whispering now.

"Don't lie to me."

Unaccountably, Ramu began crying—great, dry sobs, like the desperate wheezing of a dying man. Like the way Ponni had cried the day he had pursued her up to the ruined fort. Was it fear? Guilt? Shame? Relief? What was it? From the moment he had left Ponni sitting by herself at the ruined fort, lost in her unreachable loneliness, he had felt a tremendous sadness within, and now all of it was coming out. Gomati Paati's face softened. She came over to him and stroked his back in the gentle way she had. He looked at her—he was now the same height as she was—and saw the familiar love and trust glowing forth from her face. She was his grandmother. No, she was the mother he had never had. Even more, she was the center of his world and he of hers. "Yes," he said. The word was enough. She understood.

"I want you to stop."

He did not say anything.

"Promise me." Her voice was tender, compassionate, but resolute. "You have no idea what you are doing."

"How did you find out?"

"I have my ways. Don't think I'm an old woman without means."

Gomati Paati old and without means? Ramu would never have thought such a thing about his grandmother. He knew her only too well. "Does Appa know?"

"No. And Uncle Siva doesn't either. There is no need for either to know. But first you have to promise me you will stop."

He nodded. "I will," he said. He felt his treachery even as he spoke.

Gomati Paati kept stroking his back. He was again aware of the overpowering love emanating from her touch, but could not look her in the face. She said, speaking with profound sympathy and a lifetime of experience behind her, "I understand. Don't think I don't. I do. When you are older, you will too. Sometimes you do what the world wants and sometimes you don't." Ramu felt he already understood what Gomati Paati was saying. He felt a great burden settle on his shoulders as she spoke.

"Now, we will not speak of this anymore," Gomati Paati continued. "I want you to go around to the back of the house and have a bath at the well before you enter. In this situation, I'm sure people would say this ritual is needed and that ritual is needed. There is no end to the rituals of the world. I say a bath is sufficient. What is important is what is in your heart. But have your bath quietly, so no one notices."

Ramu understood this too. He had been with an untouchable Adi Dravidar girl. He had to cleanse himself, purify himself, though he had never yet touched Ponni, nor she him, despite the books that had gone back and forth between them. He knew he had not because touch, the possibility of it—would they touch? should they touch?—was a ghostly presence every moment of the time he spent with Ponni. It was always there among the unspoken, awkward questions lurking like shameful sinners in the shadows of the ruined fort when they were there. If they had touched, he would know. It would have been an electric thing between them. His skin, his body, his mind would remember forever. No, they had not touched, but they had been so close to each other and had exchanged objects. He had to exonerate himself. Redeem himself. Return to the fold. This is what the world decreed. He went around to the back of the house to do as he had been told.

In the dark courtyard at the back, Ramu raised up, hand over hand, a bucket of cold water from the bottom of the well. He drew slowly and steadily on the rough coir rope to keep the creaking of the pulley as soft as possible. Inside the house, he could hear Gomati Paati's well-loved voice speaking to his cousins. Behind him were the cattle sheds, where the animals moved restlessly in the night, and beyond were the fields, harvested and bare for many weeks now. Beyond the fields was the demon tree in one direction and Ponni's hut in another; he could sense their presence in the night. Above, the glittering stars bore brilliant witness from the immense black night sky. As he poured the cold, purifying water over his head, Ramu found he was again weeping great, dry sobs. Despite Gomati Paati, he could not stop thinking of Ponni. He felt himself a traitor as the water went cascading down his shuddering shoulders and his chest and his legs.

Traitor.

He was a traitor.

But who was he betraying?

ॐ

SOMETIMES THE DEAD DO NOT stay dead.

One day, Sub-Inspector Chandran took Murugappa to Assistant Superintendent Douglas Robinson at the district police headquarters in Thirunelveli. Chandran bringing Murugappa in this manner to the ASP was unusual. Chandran did not report directly to ASP Robinson; but since the ASP had taken such an interest in the murder of a lowly Paraiyar man, he thought perhaps the ASP would want to know what he had found out. Inspector Venugopalan was Chandran's immediate superior, and he would not appreciate Chandran going directly to the ASP. However, Venugopalan had shown no interest in the Murugappa case—he had not even been present during the ASP's visit to Paavalampatti. Given these circumstances, if Chandran had an opportunity to update the ASP about the details of the case, why should he not take it? Who could blame him for doing so? Reasoning in this fashion, Chandran stepped briskly down the yellow-walled verandah toward ASP Robinson's office to update him on the Murugappa case. As he did so, the metal buttons of his khaki shirt gleamed in the morning light flooding the verandah. Chandran was ever attentive to the way he looked. He knew a good impression was as important to advancement as making use of every opportunity that presented itself.

Fortunately, ASP Robinson was in his office and the doors of his room stood ajar. He was alone, sitting at a desk placed at the very center of the room. He was reviewing some papers in a file. A newly installed electric ceiling fan turned above. Such fans were just becoming common fixtures. Chandran knocked respectfully, marveling at the metal blades swinging slowly in a circle above—what a wonder the British were at technology! The ASP looked up from his file, frowning and taking a moment to recognize Chandran against the glare of the sun from the outside. "What is it, Chandran?" he asked, impatiently.

Chandran entered the room and said, "It's about the murder of the Paraiyar man in Paavalampatti, sir."

"Yes?"

"My inquiries have turned up interesting information. I thought you would want to know. It seems there might have been trouble between Murugappa and the man he worked for."

"Murugappa?"

"The murdered man, sir."

"Of course. And you say something was going on between him and the Brahmin brothers for whom he worked?"

"Actually, just the younger brother, sir. Sivaraman Iyer is the name."

Robinson remembered the younger brother well. "What kind of trouble?"

"It seems Sivaraman has a . . . How shall I say it, sir? It seems he likes low-caste women."

"Likes?"

"He visits certain women from time to time. Very discreetly, of course. It is not well known."

"What does that have to do with the murder, Chandran?"

"You can imagine the scandal if people came to know of Sivaraman's behavior with low-caste women, sir. He is a Brahmin from one of the most prominent families in the village. A married man with children. Sivaraman likes to keep his—what is the word?—activities quiet. It seems Murugappa was talking too freely."

"Why would he do that?"

"Toddy problem, sir. Murugappa was a big drunkard. The problem had become worse recently. My informant in the village says it's possible Sivaraman had Murugappa killed to shut him up."

"It's possible, you say? You mean there is no hard evidence?"

Douglas Robinson had been about to ask Chandran to sit down. Now he decided to keep him standing. Before Chandran's interruption, Robinson had been reviewing reports from informants about political operations in the district by Congress Party organizers. In a short while, he had an important meeting with Maitland about this matter. He felt irritated that Chandran had interrupted him with this tawdry business in Pavampaty.

"No, sir. But I will look into it more, sir," Chandran replied eagerly. "I'm sure I'll be able to find out something important."

Robinson considered what he had been told and came to a swift decision. Nobody cared about the death of a Paraiyar man. At a time of war and growing social unrest, precious police resources could not be diverted to this case. "No, Chandran, you will not," Robinson said firmly. "I will talk to Venugopalan about this case but, really, there is more urgent work to be done. Please wait for instructions from Inspector Venugopalan. That will be all, Chandran. Thank you." Feeling not a little annoyed, Robinson flipped over the sheet of paper in his folder to indicate to Chandran that he was dismissed and continued with his reading for the meeting with Maitland.

Later, after a conversation with Venugopalan, Robinson felt confident he had come to the right decision regarding the Pavampaty murder case. Once Venugopalan had got past his annoyance at Chandran for bothering the ASP, they both agreed there were more urgent matters at hand than the murder of a Paraiyar man. As it was, the resources of the police force were stretched thin. Weeks had gone by since the murder, since the body had been buried. It was unlikely they would ever get to the bottom of the case.

Might this Brahmin Sivaraman be truly involved in the murder? Young though he was, Robinson had been a policeman long enough to know anything was possible; however, if he was any judge of character, Robinson would wager that he was not. What Chandran had reported was probably idle rumor. Venugopalan certainly seemed to think so—none of his informants had related any similar suspicion of this Sivaraman. You couldn't very well throw away valuable police resources pursuing rumors in trying to solve the murder of a Paraiyar serf, now, could you? Probably, the murdered man had quarreled with another Paraiyar coolie when drunk and had come to this terrible end. That was usually what had happened in such cases. That was probably what had happened here too. The dead man was deep in the ground. Best to leave him buried there, Robinson reckoned.

Despite Robinson's re-burial of him in this fashion, Murugappa visited the widow Gomati Paati's house one afternoon. Gomati Paati and her two sons Siva and Vishu were gathered in the portico of the inner courtyard in their customary way. Vishu stood leaning against a pillar, and Siva sat on the floor busy with his wooden tray of betel leaves, areca nuts and chunamb. Gomati Paati was rocking back and forth on her swing at a comfortable pace. Ruminatively, she asked of no one in particular, "I wonder who could have murdered poor Murugappa. Whatever became of the police inquiry?"

Looking up from his tray, Siva frowned and said, "Why do you want to rake all that up again? It's all over and done with. Let it be now." He passed his mother areca nut and chunamb wrapped in betel leaf from the tray in his lap.

Vishu said, "I saw Inspector Venugopalan when I was in Thirunelveli Town the other day. I asked him about Murugappa."

"Why did you do that?" exclaimed Siva. "You don't know how to leave well enough alone. Both of you! I have no interest in this topic."

"What did he say?" Gomati Paati asked, ignoring Siva and speaking through the betel and nut in her mouth.

"Not much. The police don't care about the murder of a Paraiyar man."

"It's true," Gomati Paati agreed.

"As I was talking to him, Venugopalan behaved strangely."

"Strangely? What do you mean?" Gomati Paati asked.

"Venugopalan took me aside, put his arm over my shoulders, and told me not to worry, that the inquiry was more or less over. I was confused at the way he spoke. I told him I hoped they would not abandon the inquiry until they found Murugappa's murderer. When I said that, he gave me this surprised look."

There was a loud clatter. The tray had fallen to the floor from Siva's lap. He busied himself in picking up the fallen contents of the tray, bending low over the scattered leaves and nuts and chunamb. He asked, "Why did you say that, Vishu? What do you care how that Paraiyar dog got himself killed? What is it to you?" He did not look at his mother or his brother as he spoke.

Gomati Paati said, "When will you learn common decency, Siva? It's time you learned to speak civilly. I am tired of hearing you speak this way." And then she added, "He worked for us all his life. If we don't try to get the poor man justice, who will?"

The tray assembled once again in his lap, Siva said, "I don't like to get sentimental about these things. Yes, Murugappa worked for us all his life, but it is not as if we did nothing for him. We took care of him and his family better than any Paraiyar could hope for. And how did he repay us? By drinking and wandering all over the village with all kinds of people, saying all kinds of things. I have made my own inquiries. Do you want to know what I think happened to Murugappa? He was at the toddy shop with Kovalu the night he was murdered. You know how he hated Kovalu because he was the one with whom that rogue brother of his, Chellappa, ran away. Murugappa always blamed Kovalu for taking Chellappa away from him. I was told they had a fight that night. From the toddy shop, they were seen wandering off into the night shouting at each other. Perhaps that is when something happened."

"Really? I did not know any of this," Vishu said, sheepishly.

"You never know anything, Vishu," Siva said, his disgust plain. "What do you know about Murugappa even though he worked here all his life? Just because he was murdered doesn't make him a saint. I've told you what a problem his drinking had become. When he was drunk, he could talk very loosely. He could say just about anything without thinking. Who cares if he was killed? The only thing I can say is that that Paraiyar snake should have died some other time. How I had to work to bring the harvest in! I had to stand in the sun like some low-caste peasant to make sure the workers didn't steal half the harvest. Who will respect me now?"

Gomati Paati spoke in the measured voice she reserved for when she was really angry. She said, "You make me ashamed when you talk like that, Siva. Murugappa might have been a Paraiyar but he was still a human being. As for your standing in the sun, don't exaggerate. I found someone else to take Murugappa's place, didn't I? Your honor—it is safe."

"I make you ashamed?" Siva asked belligerently. Then he looked at his mother in confusion and said, "After all, a Paraiyar. Because of him you say such harsh things to me?"

Gomati Paati heard the confusion in Siva's voice. Her relationship with Siva was profound, for it was he who cared for the land she had preserved so assiduously through the years; but now she looked at him with an implacable expression. Mother and son stared at each other wordlessly, while Vishu, still leaning against the pillar, watched the scene before him in consternation. It was a familiar scene. The way they were standing or sitting, the sun in the courtyard, the creaking of the swing—all of it was familiar, known, a repetition of the past. And yet there was something alien there too—something new, invisible as a ghost, but most definitely there. Vishu felt disturbed, afraid at the newness.

Finally, he said, "None of this matters anyway. The police are not going to pursue the murder of a Paraiyar man. They have other things to worry about because of the war and all the trouble the nationalists are making. I'm sorry I brought up the conversation I had with Venugopalan about Murugappa. You are right, Siva: I should not have said anything to Venugopalan. What is the point of dragging trouble into our lives? Let's just forget this whole Murugappa matter. He is dead. There is nothing to be done about that."

But forgetting is not always easy. In Madras, too, Murugappa refused to stay quietly buried. He came to Chellappa often in the guise of a troubling visitor. Chellappa felt the full weight of his love for his older brother only with his death. For Chellappa, Murugappa had stood all his life as an example of everything he himself wished never to be—the obedient and resigned Adi Dravidar menial, drowning his sorrows in drink, grateful for every little scrap of munificence his masters chose to throw his way. It was a frightening destiny and Chellappa had run away from Paavalampatti precisely to escape it. In the many years of his running—could it be said that he had stopped even now?—he had often thought uncharitably of his brother. Murugappa had brought out in him a mixture of anger, contempt, and pity. Cruel words these, but Chellappa, looking back over the years and ever the ruthless speaker of truth, could not deny they were accurate names for what he had felt so frequently. Of course, he had felt love too, but alas he had never been able to hold on to that feeling for long.

Murugappa had had to die—indeed, be murdered brutally—for Chellappa to reassess his most cherished notions about his brother, and consequently about himself. Was Murugappa a drunkard full of passive resignation? He was. A man foolishly grateful for the meager leavings the world had tossed his way? Surely. And yet to stop with this assessment, Chellappa now realized too late, was to turn his brother into a convenient parody against which he could selfishly define his own vision of himself as a stronger and nobler man. A revolutionary Adi Dravidar—that is what he, Chellappa, took delight in being; and how could he be that without reducing his brother Murugappa, born of the same womb, to the sum of his negative traits? To be what he wanted to be, he had had to make Murugappa into something he was not. He had made himself forget all the admirable qualities Murugappa had—his loyalty as a friend; his lovingness as father and husband and, yes, brother; his ability as a farmer whose knowledge about the ways of the land was matchless. How difficult Chellappa had found it to honor Murugappa's best qualities! Even at times when it should not have been so difficult, such as when he had gone to see the Brahmin overlords of his brother in Paavalampatti. He had been angry then, and because of his anger had not been able to find a way to speak that dignified Murugappa in front of the very people for whom he lacked all dignity. Kumaraswamy Iyer and Gomati Ammal liked to brag about how unusual they were for placing an Adi Dravidar in the position that Murugappa had held. Unusual it certainly was—who had ever heard of an Adi Dravidar working as an overseer for a Brahmin landlord?—but they never mentioned all the advantages they gained from this arrangement. They had the eager gratitude of Murugappa, who knew everything there was to know about the land—and thus they were able to exploit his labor and knowledge that much more effectively. Chellappa should have been able to confront them with this elementary truth during that visit; instead, he himself had demeaned his brother in the way he had spoken. He himself had compared his brother, who had indeed been like a father to him when he was growing up, to a dog. He felt his betrayal now as a matter for utter shame.

Chellappa grieved the manner of Murugappa's death with especial sadness. Blow to the head, throat cut, left to die all alone under a tamarind tree. Death comes to all, but a violent and lonely death only to the most unfortunate. Chellappa thought of the Muslim trader he had robbed all those years before in Travancore. He remembered the stone in his hand thudding against the trader's skull and how the shock of the blow had shuddered through his arm. The man had dropped so quickly and quietly to the ground. Murugappa, who had tried all his life to live by the rules, did not merit the grisly end he had received. It was, perhaps, the kind of end that he, Chellappa, deserved, not Murugappa. That is what Chellappa told himself.

And, after Murugappa's death, Chellappa had once again failed his brother. He had spent his life fleeing Paavalampatti, and he had fled it again without being able to bring Murugappa's murderer to justice as he had wanted to. At the time, it had seemed the right thing to do. Manickam had buried Murugappa before Chellappa had arrived in Paavalampatti. In the village, even other Adi Dravidars treated Chellappa with suspicion. Many remembered still the trouble he had caused by drawing water from the well forbidden to Adi Dravidars. Others resented the very fact of his escape from the village. Those who did neither were afraid to talk to him because of the suspicion that might come to be directed toward them by association.

Despite many inquiries, he could find out nothing about Murugappa's murder. Even Kovalu, with whom he had fled the village for the first time, avoided him in the strangest way. Then had come news of the white assistant superintendent of police wanting to bring him in for questioning. Two constables came looking for him one day when, by pure luck, he was not in the hut under the coconut trees. These were difficult times. He knew he was generally under surveillance in Madras, but there he also had many friends and comrades, some even among the police. In Thirunelveli he was alone. While the police really had nothing they could hold him on, it was foolish to take chances. There was important work waiting to be done in Madras. Plans to which he was crucial were afoot in the Nizam of Hyderabad's territories and in the Malabar region. It would not do to be jailed, taken out of circulation, for any length of time.

So, Chellappa had fled the night before ASP Robinson was to visit the village. He had tried to delay his departure as much as he could, but the sudden visits from the constables had become more and more worrying. Once, Sub-Inspector Chandran had come to speak to him. He feared being taken into custody for questioning any day. He had run away, unable to countenance the idea of being locked up as he had been once before, and that too for a quest that he was now convinced was futile. Not until he was back in Madras and Murugappa began to haunt him did Chellappa feel he had perhaps been hasty in rushing away from Paavalampatti. He who prided himself on his keen sense of justice had abandoned his brother without getting him any. This too was a betrayal and a matter for shame. Too late now to do right by Murugappa; but was there not another way to make amends? The more Murugappa visited him, refusing to stay safely buried, the more the question began to preoccupy Chellappa.

Finally, Chellappa found an answer to his urgent question. The answer involved Ponni.

~

MURUGAPPA WAS INVISIBLE BUT PRESENT the last time Ramu and Ponni met at the ruined fort up on the hill. Ponni said, "Where were you all these days? I have been coming here every day, looking for you. I have books to return to you." She had in her hands two books, one Tamil and the other English. For the first time since Ramu had met her, Ponni seemed truly happy.

Ponni was right to rebuke him. It was days since he had returned to the ruined fort—not since Gomati Paati had confronted him about Ponni had he returned. At first, he had stayed away because of the promise he had made his beloved grandmother. How could he go against the word he had given her? However, try as he might he could not stop thinking about Ponni. At last, he had thought, *I will meet Ponni once, only so I can explain to her that I can't meet her anymore. That is what I will do. To not do this would be rude.* He had screwed up his courage and sneaked away at an opportune moment. It was only as he was making his way back to the abandoned fort up on the hill that he admitted to himself that he was not returning to explain anything to Ponni. Not at all. He was returning because he wanted to. That was the simple truth.

Now, Ponni was speaking to him, babbling excitedly. Before he could respond to her, she said, "I am leaving for Madras. My uncle wants me to join him there. Manickam will take me tomorrow, or maybe the day after. It's good you finally showed up. Otherwise you would not have got your books back."

Ramu stood, stunned, taking in the news. No wonder Ponni was happy! She was leaving for Madras to be with Chellappa.

Ponni took in Ramu's dazed silence. She did not know what to make of it. She looked down at the books in her hands and said, "I enjoyed the books you let me borrow."

Ramu said, "I won't see you again, will I?"

Ponni shook her head and held out his books to him. Ramu

took the books quietly. Suddenly, Ponni reached out and touched him, holding him gently by his chin. The touch was soft, tender. Ramu smiled. He had imagined the touching many times and it was everything he had expected. He too touched Ponni, then, with his free hand. He reached out and boldly trailed his fingers down her face from her forehead, over her lovely eyes, over the gentle upward angle of her nose, over the moist tenderness of her lips. He stopped abruptly at her chin, embarrassed, all his daring gone just as suddenly as it had appeared. Inexplicably, there were tears in Ponni's eyes. She reached out and did the same to his face now, letting her fingers lightly follow the firm curve of an eyebrow down to his soft cheek and chin. For a long moment in the fading light of evening, Ramu and Ponni stayed and looked at each other wordlessly. What was there left to say? Nothing. They turned and made their separate ways down the hill, one toward the village and the other toward the hut under the coconut trees.

When Ramu returned home from the ruined fort on the hill, Gomati Paati was not waiting for him. Ramu did not have a bath at the well at the back of the house. He did not wash his face where Ponni had touched him. He went straight into the house and put the books away. He quietly ate his dinner, spread out his mat in his usual corner, and lay down with his face to the wall with a sheet pulled over his head. He did not fall asleep for a long time. Late at night, when everybody had gone to bed and the whole village was still, he heard a dog barking in the distance and thought, *That sounds like Insect.* And then he tried not to think of anything else at all.

Part Two

Love in the World

AT EIGHTEEN, RAMU DEPARTED PAAVALAMPATTI to read economics at Loyola College in Madras. By the time he left, the great war for planetary dominion had ended with the world in ruins. The British war effort had caused famine in Bengal and severe price inflation everywhere else in India. The dire outcomes of the war left one significant mark on Ramu's family, which had been otherwise more or less protected from the calamity: a few months prior to Ramu's departure, his father, disgusted at the British, resigned from his job with the Sanitation Department. He could no longer stand the idea of working for the colonial masters.

Ramu's father did not make a great drama out of this momentous decision, not even when Uncle Siva insinuated that the real reason for his resignation was office politics—trivial trouble with his colleagues. He nodded at Uncle Siva's suggestion and replied mildly, "Fine, Siva, as you please. It is just as you say." The sardonic tone was too subtle to register on Uncle Siva.

Unlike Uncle Siva, Ramu's father abhorred histrionics. The truth of the matter was that something had changed in him the day he had been interrogated by ASP Douglas Robinson about Murugappa's murder. On that day, he had realized his smallness in the colonial scheme of things. He was not a vain man, but the treatment he had received from Robinson rankled. It had taken years and the atrocities associated with a world war to finally move him to rebel, though in typical fashion he preferred to keep his rebellion private. Quietly, he sent in his letter of resignation and stayed home, pretending to help Uncle Siva in his work. Rather than the fields, however, he was generally to be found in his easy chair, reading.

Of course, Uncle Siva complained, but not too much and not too loudly, for as a matter of fact he wanted Ramu's father out of the way. Gomati Paati, who was almost sixty now, was more and more turning over control of the family lands to him, and that was just the way he liked it. Every day Ramu's father performed one or two small tasks as instructed by Uncle Siva—as if he were the younger of the two brothers rather than the elder—and then disappeared to his room to read. More often than not, Uncle Siva muttered something insulting as he departed. "Ah, yes," he might say as he watched his older brother go, "great scholar that he is, Vishu is plowing the field of his mind in the comfort of the room, leaving others to drive the plow in the hot sun." Uncle Siva himself would be standing in the shade of a tree watching his workers toiling in the field as he made this observation. His remarks were never so vehement as to require a response. If Ramu's father should out of guilt return to dawdle in the fields, Uncle Siva would studiously ignore him until he disappeared once again.

Really, Uncle Siva's pointed remarks were meant more for Gomati Paati than for Ramu's father. The constant theme of Uncle Siva's life was that Gomati Paati did not appreciate him, though she certainly felt sympathy for him. Who could deny that Uncle Siva had justice on his side with regard to Ramu's father? Gomati Paati hated laziness and was exasperated by her elder son's behavior. The family fortune could bear the loss of his salary; money was not the issue. Ramu's father's love of books also was not the issue. She understood the value of reading, of book knowledge, though she herself had very little of that. The matter, rather, was *purpose.* Life had to have a *purpose.* Whatever could be the purpose in Ramu's father's endless reading? She could discern none.

Purpose did not much concern Ramu's father. He was not a scholar, great or otherwise. Though he read voraciously, there was no design to his reading. He read out of a curiously passive longing, rather than purpose, devouring newspapers and magazines rather than learned tomes. Often, when going through the newspaper, a brooding expression settled on his face and he muttered under his breath. There, in the newspaper, was a larger world, both inviting and terrifying. How dreadful as well as exhilarating the doings of the world! Ramu's father read with the yearning of a faint-hearted spectator wishing ardently but fearfully to enter an engrossing game of cricket. Of course, he did not think himself a spectator. Had he not resigned from the Sanitation Department? When he thought of that act of rebellion, he felt he too had been a part of the game, if only in a tiny way—if only as a substitute fielder valiantly flinging himself onto the ground to stop four runs. Ramu's father had seen a little of the world beyond Paavalampaati in working for the Sanitation Department. What he had seen had whetted his appetite. There was so much more, so very much more, to see and do than was possible in a village like Paavalampatti! It was too late for him now, though, he felt. No matter. He was determined Ramu would have the opportunities he had not had.

Ramu learned from his father to be a keen follower of unfolding events. He learned to see how tumultuous the times were and how everything was happening out there, not back here in Paavalampatti. The village was isolated from the changing world—so his father taught him. The British, wearied by the war and the million mutinies all over India, were getting ready to leave. When India was in the throes of the Quit India movement against British imperialism, when talk of partition and Pakistan gained ground, when Gandhi was arrested and then released, Ramu discussed the issues with his father. Together, father and son followed Bapu Gandhi's exploits and pronouncements closely, arguing about their different opinions. No one could deny Gandhi's personal courage, but the romance of Bapu was not for Ramu. With easy confidence, Ramu declared himself no Gandhian: Gandhi did not feel like the answer to the urgent questions of the age. Much as he admired Gandhi's sincerity, Ramu insisted his ideas were wanting. The village as self-sufficient republic? The spinning wheel as universal panacea? The capitalist as trustee of society? Was the Mahatma serious? No, when it came to the modern world, Gandhi was too muddleheaded. Periyar E. V. Ramaswami, Ambedkar, Subash Chandra Bose, even Nehru, disciple of Gandhi though he was—these were the men for the world of factories and atomic bombs and airplanes. Not Gandhi.

Discussing the world with his father, Ramu learned to say such things before his departure to Loyola College in Madras at the age of eighteen.

In reality, however, Ramu was mostly ignorant of the world. "You have never been farther than Thirunelveli Town, child," Gomati Pati noted in the days of preparation leading up to his departure for Madras. Feeling as if a son born of her own womb, not her grandson, was leaving home, she kept her voice even, unemotional.

"I'm not a child," Ramu retorted, annoyed.

Ramu remembered with amusement how, years before, he had imagined Madras as a city of tall white towers. He knew better now. He remembered how Ponni—how could he ever forget her?—had dispelled all thoughts of a city of towers long ago. Also, his Aunt Saroja, who had been with his mother Kanchana when she died and was the same age his mother would have been had she survived, lived in Madras with her family. When she visited Paavalampatti, Ramu made her tell him stories about the city. Now Ramu himself was on his way to Madras to study economics, a modern discipline about human wants and material goods and the just way to arrange society in order to match one with the other. It seemed an especially appropriate subject to study: economics was destined to play a central role in a country like India, clearly to become independent soon.

Ramu traveled from Thirunelveli to Madras by himself. The journey by train took most of the day and all of the night. Until night fell, he sat by the window and watched the paddy fields and palm trees and little temples pass. When it was dark, the land turned invisible except for the flash of a village here, a lonely light there. He spread his hold-all on his assigned berth and lay down. He slept only fitfully, coming awake every time the train lurched to a halt to peer through the wooden window slats of the train into cavernous stations sounding with the loud voices of porters and hawkers.

Early in the morning, the train arrived in Egmore Station, the Madras terminus for trains from the south. Egmore was even more cavernous than the stations Ramu had glimpsed in the night. A road ran through it so that horse carriages and motor cars could pull up right alongside the platform. He dismounted from the train with his rolled-up hold-all and green-painted tin trunk, clad in his best trousers and shirt. Lost in wonder at the high arched roof and the tall red walls of the station, it was some time before Ramu heard the honking and turned to see that Aunt Saroja's husband, Uncle Natarajan, had drawn up to the curb in his sleek car. He waved at Ramu without getting out. Ramu ignored the porter offering to help and hurried over with his luggage.

"Is this all you have?" Uncle Natarajan asked, taking in the trunk and the hold-all. He waved airily to the back of the car. "The dicky is not locked. Throw them in there."

The dicky confronted Ramu with a new-fangled handle. In the rear-view mirror, Uncle Natrajan watched with amusement as he struggled with it. When he was finally seated in the car, Uncle Natarajan said, "Never been in a motor car before, Ramu?" Of course, Uncle Natarajan was teasing Ramu. They had ridden together in cars when Uncle Natarajan visited Paavalampatti, but the rented cars of Ambasamudram were nothing like the modern Madras car Ramu was in now. Uncle Natarajan continued proudly, "Packard 110. American. Americans know about cars, you know. Got it almost brand new for a throwaway price from a white man running away to London. With all this independence talk, white people are disappearing as fast as they can."

Uncle Natarajan pulled smoothly out of Egmore Station and asked, "What do you think of this independence business, Ramu?" Without bothering to wait for a reply, he shook his head doubtfully and said, "We Indians are no good at ruling. In five years, we'll be wishing the British had never left."

Uncle Natarajan was high up in the Indian Bank. He and Aunt Saroja lived with their three children in a portion of an old garden house at the far end of Mylapore, near the Basilica of San Thome. The drive home from Egmore Station was through wide and tree-lined streets with many cars and people in them. Uncle Natarajan pointed out important buildings as they passed them. They entered Mount Road at Hotel Connemara and then drove past

Spencer's department store and Thousand Lights Mosque before turning into Cathedral Road.

As they approached San Thome, an unfamiliar smell grew stronger. The air seemed to grow heavier. "The sea?" Ramu guessed excitedly. Uncle Natarajan laughed uproariously in reply. Ramu had not meant to be funny. He had never before in his life seen the sea.

After a few days in San Thome with Aunt Saroja and Uncle Natarajan and his cousins (there were trips to the beach and also to Spencer's for its famous ice cream), on the appointed day Ramu moved to Loyola College in Nungambakkam to prepare for the start of the academic year. A newly built Church of Christ the King with a tall white spire towered over the tree-filled campus of the college, which admitted only male students—so, after all, there was at least one tall white tower in Madras! The college hostel with its canteen was behind the church, far from the main building where classes were held. Ramu had fought a heroic battle with his grandmother over the previous year, with even his father only reluctantly on his side, so that he would not have to take up residence in a private hostel exclusively for Brahmin college students. His room, fruit of this battle, was hard by the outer wall of the college campus, opposite Nungambakkam Railway Station, where city trains thundered in and out. Ramu readily settled into his little room with its cheap metal cot and wooden furniture and attuned himself quickly to classes and hostel life, so different from the rhythms of Paavalampatti.

The director of the hostel and many of Ramu's professors were Jesuit priests, and several Roman Catholic Christians were among the students, including some from so-called low castes. There were students of other backgrounds too, even some from faraway places in the north, for Loyola was a prestigious college. Many students were day scholars from Madras who did not live in the hostel. They tended to look down on mofussil students like Ramu. Ramu tried not to be irritated by their condescension. He had too many fresh and wondrous experiences to digest. He had no time for irritation.

There was so much to do, so much to discover. There was Ponni.

Ponni, as far as Ramu knew, was still in Madras with her uncle Chellappa. Though he had breathed not a word to anyone in Paavalampatti, his intention had always been to search out Ponni in Madras. She was a big part of the reason he had preferred Loyola to St. Joseph's College in Trichy, where also his application to study economics had been accepted. He did not know exactly why he was looking for Ponni, nor what he would do when he found her. But he was certain that he wanted to find her.

The question was: how? How was he to get into touch with Ponni in this far-flung city of multitudes? Where should he start his search? He had no address for her. He had a vague idea of Chellappa's radical activities from unreliable rumors flying through Paavalampatti, but there was no detail of practical use in these sensational reports. He pondered the problem, while unconsciously, instinctively, searching for her everywhere, all the time. As he explored the city (he had bought a second-hand bicycle), a part of him was always on the lookout for Ponni. Cycling under the trees of Pondy Bazaar toward Panagal Park, he found himself scouring the faces of shopkeepers, street-side vendors, and customers, paying special attention to beautiful dark-skinned women about his age. At Gemini Circle's New Woodlands Hotel for coffee and tiffin with friends, he would without thinking turn away from the conversation to let his eyes wander over the faces of young women, earning himself ribald teasing from his friends—"What? Are there no women in Paavalampatti?" "Tchee! Even I would be afraid to be as shameless as this fellow!" and so on. It was foolishness, and he knew it. He had no doubt whatsoever that Ponni, when he found her, would be lovely, but staring at every attractive woman of the right age who crossed his path was certainly no way to find her—and it was likely to get him beaten up.

In the meantime, Ramu had Arokiasamy and Kannan, who were his closest friends. He was the glue that held the threesome together. Without him, the other two would certainly never have become friends. Kannan was a Tamil Brahmin like Ramu, but he had grown up in New Delhi, where his father worked in the Indian Civil Service. He too lived in the hostel. He was fine looking, a dapper dresser, and already, at this young age, weary, so weary of the world. Arokiasamy did not live in the hostel. He was small in size but fierce in spirit. His most prominent features were his smoldering eyes, which belied a gentleness that only those who knew him well experienced. He was a poor, so-called low-caste Christian who had lived all his life in Madras. The three made up an incongruous group, their commonality being that they were all in different ways at odds with the prevailing culture at Loyola.

Kannan felt himself superior to Loyola because he had grown up in New Delhi. He could not dominate the affluent Madras city boys, upper-caste or Christian, who ran the show at Loyola, and he was not ready to join them as an equal. Arokiasamy's quarrel was more directly political. Though a Christian, he despised the zeal of his fellow Christian students. He embarrassed them by telling stories about the hypocrisy of the priests and the better-off Christians. He had been admitted to Loyola on a scholarship, for he was brilliant, but he was not one to hold his tongue out of gratitude. Very quickly, he had alienated nearly everyone, student and staff and priest alike, with his outspokenness—unheard of in a first-year student!—about every topic from the self-righteousness of the Church to the domination of Brahmins in the bureaucracy of Madras Presidency under the British.

Ramu was the tall, thin, and somewhat awkward member of the group, neither wearied by Loyola like Kannan nor enraged by it like Arokiasamy. Loyola was fine. It was a welcome change from Paavalampatti. But he wanted more. Now that he had finally departed from Paavalampatti, there was much to see and learn, and Kannan and Arokiasamy were interesting parts of the world. He was intrigued both by the worldliness of the former and the passion of the latter. Besides, he detested the clubbiness of the city boys. What he did not realize was that his insistence on being friends with the two malcontents would inevitably exact a price. He found himself slowly pushed to the margins of the student culture at Loyola, never entirely accepted, nor rejected. Thus the threesome was formed.

At Arokiasamy's urging, Ramu became a member of the Debating Society. New student though he was, Arokiasamy was already in the midst of yet another campaign against the domination, this time of student debating, by certain city boys. As a mofussil student, Ramu had no love for the supercilious city boys but, as a new student himself, he had misgivings about joining Arokiasamy's campaign. Arokiasamy had to cajole him to get him to go. At the very first meeting Ramu attended, the rich city boys prevailed over Arokiasamy and Ramu in choosing the topic for the next debate—*Love Will Ever Triumph.* When the topic was first mooted, Arokiasamy gave Ramu a look of exasperation. Like Ramu, Arokiasamy preferred a topic more relevant to contemporary events—something related to the momentous changes underway in the world. Since it was clear that India would soon be independent, Arokiasamy asked, shouldn't that prospect be a matter for the Debating Society?

When the senior city boys who ran the Debating Society pooh-poohed the idea, Ramu intervened, blurting out, "What about Periyar?" Perhaps, he suggested, a debate topic touching on the ideas of that iconoclastic thinker would be appropriate. The boys laughed even more uproariously than they had at Arokiasamy. Periyar E. V. Ramaswami? A debate about the rantings of that crazy loudmouth hater of Gandhi and the Congress who had been given the grandiloquent title of Periyar? How absurd! In the end, eternal and transcendent love prevailed, and Arokiasamy and Ramu left the meeting thoroughly disgusted.

Much later, when he was done with his tirade against the city boys and his temper had cooled somewhat, Arokiasamy gave Ramu a peculiar look. "Periyar?" he asked. They had retired to Ramu's hostel room to console each other after the defeat in the battle of the Debating Society.

Ramu said, "We get newspapers in Paavalampatti, you know. And books too. We know how to read and write." He had stretched himself on his narrow cot, while Arokiasamy had taken the wooden chair. Through the window, a light breeze stole into the room.

"You are a Brahmin. Brahmins hate Periyar."

"So? Anyhow, I didn't say I love Periyar. All I said is that we should debate his ideas." And then Ramu added, "I knew someone in Paavalampatti who was rumored to be a follower of Periyar."

"Who was that?"

"His name is Chellappa. He is in Madras now. I'd like to find him if I can." Ramu did not add that he did not *really* know Chellappa, that he had only met him once, briefly. Nor did he say anything about Ponni.

"Don't you have an address for him?"

"No. He is an Adi Dravidar man. I knew him many years ago."

"You were friends with an Adi Dravidar man? You are full of surprises today, Ramu!" There was genuine wonder in Arokiasamy's voice. He said, still marveling, "You even know what term to use. Yes, you are right—Adi Dravidar is the preferred term."

Ramu was pleased at the effect he was having. He said with studied nonchalance, "He was rumored to be a radical, a rebel, a very political man."

"You are a deep one," Arokiasamy said. "Who would have thought you kept such company?" He added, "There are many ways to look for such a man. There are publications and organizations, for example."

Ramu perked up. Would Arokia be able to help him find Chellappa (and thus Ponni)? Could this happen? Confronted with the possibility of really finding Chellappa, Ramu felt constrained to amend the information he had provided. He said sheepishly, "I don't know if he is truly a follower of Periyar. I do think he is involved in all kinds of politics. What exactly I don't know."

"Come now, Ramu. Tell me the truth. Did you really know this Chellappa well?"

Reluctantly, Ramu spoke the truth, "I was actually friends with his niece."

"Friends with an Adi Dravidar girl?!" Arokiasamy's previous astonishment was nothing compared to what was audible in his voice now.

Deliberately, Ramu returned a blank look.

"An Adi Dravidar girl?" Arokiasamy repeated, incredulously.

Ramu gave an annoyed shrug of his shoulders, making clear he was not going to elaborate.

"Ah! Now I understand," Arokiasamy said, nodding. "I'll find a way to ferret out this man for you. What did you say his name is? Chellappa?"

~

DAYS PASSED WITHOUT ANY MENTION of Chellappa by Arokiasamy. Embarrassed at having mentioned Ponni, Ramu did not broach the subject, either. The hope he had allowed himself to feel had begun to ebb when one day Arokiasamy suddenly announced, "This evening we are going to Marina Beach."

Kannan said, "Marina? Why?"

"Not me. It's too far away. I'm not in the mood," said Ramu.

Arokiasamy flung an arm across Ramu's thin shoulders and said, "Hero, how can you not go? All this is for you. We'll look for your Chellappa there." Obligingly, he did not mention Chellappa's niece, of whom Kannan knew nothing.

"At the beach?"

"Yes, it seems political types set up tables there in the evenings. Opposite Madras University."

"Tables?" Kannan asked.

"Tables. You know, to meet people, to propagate their ideas. That kind of thing."

"This we must investigate," Kannan said in an amused voice. "People with ideas here in Madras. Actual ideas. Certainly something to be investigated."

Ramu thought of the Chellappa he had met one time in his life—the Chellappa who had come to the back of the house in Paavalampatti and whom he had then followed to the hut under the coconut trees. Would he recognize him again after all these years on a beach in Madras in the gloom of dusk?

Arokiasamy misunderstood his silence. "Chellappa probably won't be there," he said. "But someone might know about him."

"We'll go and make inquiries," Kannan added. "We will explore what the great intellectuals of Madras are thinking."

They went on their cycles as evening fell and birds fluttered around the dusty tops of trees, calling to one another in loud sociability. They cycled through College Road and Pantheon Road, went single file across the Cooum on the Harris Road bridge, and then crossed Mount Road to Wallajah Road. When they arrived at Marina Beach, the great domed and arched Senate House of Madras University was fading into the darkness, along with Chepauk Palace and Presidency College and the other stately buildings that fronted the sea along South Beach Road. A teasing breeze, redolent of the ocean, blew in over the waves toward them. Far out to sea, the lights of anchored ships waiting to enter Madras Port gleamed, hinting of unseen things. The lights reminded Ramu of puzzles in a coloring book he had had as a child back in Paavalampatti. What unseen promise did the bright dots in the darkness hold? What mysterious figure might connecting the dots reveal? A portentous mood had grown within him during the ride from Loyola.

From the sands of the beach, thronged as it was with people, a great humming rose into the night. Gas and hurricane lamps struggled with the evening gloom. Beneath the lamps were stalls at which myriad things were being sold—popular magazines, strings of flowers for women's hair, nails and bolts and screws and other hardware, and much else. Around the stalls, elderly people walked sedately, children ran, young men and women promenaded in separate groups, couples floated by wrapped in an atmosphere of intimacy. Groups sat on the sand, silent or boisterous as the mood took them. At the sea's ever-shifting, restless edge was much squealing. Feet below demurely lifted sari hems and rolled-up trousers were being wet in the frothing waves. Vendors selling their wares wandered across the sand, imploring whomever would listen, pressing on them roasted peanuts in newspaper cones, toy windmills in many bright colors, slices of spiced and salted guava arrayed on a tray. It was as if all of Madras had arrived at the beach to escape the sticky heat of the city and to while away the evening by the waves.

Ramu, Kannan, and Arokiasamy left their locked bicycles leaning against the roadside tea stall of a vendor Arokiasamy knew and plunged into the crowd. When informed of their purpose by Arokiasamy, the vendor suggested they try the far end of the beach. He pointed out the direction. Kannan led them, saying, "Come.

This way. Let's see what we can find for Ramu among the intellectuals of Madras."

They found a lone elderly balding man with a neat gray mustache. On the table before him were spread out various pamphlets and booklets in Tamil, Telugu, and English decorated with the hammer and sickle emblem. They had titles such as *What Is to Be Done?, Landlordism and Land Reform,* and *The World War and the Coming Revolution.*

No Chellappa. No Ponni. Ramu's disappointment was keen.

Before Arokiasamy could stop him, Kannan strode up to the elderly man at the table and said, "We are looking for someone named Chellappa. Is he here? Do you know where to find him?"

The man smiled and said, "So many Chellappas in this city. Very common name."

No amount of questioning on the part of Kannan could budge him to say more. Finally, Ramu said, "It's no use. Let's go."

By the tea stall where they had left their bicycles, Arokiasamy scolded Kannan for the abruptness of his questioning. "Even if he knew Chellappa, why would he tell us about him?" he asked. "He has never seen us before. He knows nothing about us. Why would he answer our questions? There is a way to do these things, Kanna. Wait here. I'll be back soon." When he returned, he looked pleased. "He doesn't know any Chellappa," he said. "But he said to come back on Sunday. Won't be as quiet as it is today. More people come then to set up their tables and pass out their literature. That is the day to come. We'll have a better chance of finding who we want." He laughed and said to Ramu in a conspiratorial voice, "It is Chellappa we are looking for, isn't it?" He was clearly delighted that the mysterious Chellappa's niece was a secret between the two of them. Kannan looked from one to the other in bemusement.

On Sunday, Ramu went with Arokiasamy. Kannan could not join them because his father was visiting from Delhi. The old man they had met on the previous visit was nowhere to be seen. His table, attended now by a young man with glasses, had been joined by three others, similarly burdened with political pamphlets and dimly illuminated by hissing hurricane lamps. Around the tables a little crowd was gathered. An animated discussion, evidently about recent events in China, was underway at one of them. Ramu cast a quick eye over the scene. No Chellappa. No Ponni. Again his face showed his disappointment.

"No matter," Arokiasamy said. "Let's go talk to them. Don't mention Chellappa. Just chat." He did not need to add that Ramu should avoid mention of the niece too.

Communists, Dravidianist followers of Periyar, Congress Socialists, the Rational Progressive Association—these were the organizations and viewpoints displaying their literature on the tables. The animated conversation about China—Ramu heard the name Mao several times—was at the table of the Rational Progressive Association. Ramu and Arokiasamy listened in on the discussion, leafed through pamphlets and brochures at all the tables, and made small talk with the men—there were only two women in the crowd.

On the ride back to Loyola, Arokiasamy exhorted, "Go back next week, Ramu. You will find her sooner or later." Finding Ponni for his friend seemed to have become a mission for Arokiasamy.

Ramu went back, again and again, sometimes by himself, sometimes with Kannan and Arokiasamy, sometimes with just one of them. He went back so often that he came to know the men and women at the tables and they him. There was Comrade Grandfather, the Communist they had met on the first day, who generally did not say much, but who suddenly opened up to Ramu once and spoke at great length about the terrible conditions in the textile factories of Bombay and his experiences working and organizing there, and how the only hope for the world was an international workers' movement. There was Palani the Dravidianist, full of rhetoric about the beauty of the Tamil language and the venality of the Aryan caste system. He would expound to any who would listen on how the Dravidians of South India were truly a distinct racial, cultural, and linguistic group.

And then there was Muthu of the Rational Progressive Association, handsome and silver-tongued, the enemy of caste and of British imperialism and of the oppression of the poor. "We are not

Dravidianists," he explained to Ramu. "We don't believe in separating North Indians from South Indians. But we share the Dravidianists' hatred of caste—in fact we hate caste even more than they do. We are not Communist. We think they are too soft toward the British. But we share their hatred of working-class exploitation. That's us. The Rational Progressive Association."

Not all the groups set up tables every Sunday, but the Communists were always there and so were the Dravidianists, who had the most lively, popular table of them all. Occasionally, a fifth or even sixth table appeared. Soon Ramu's hostel room was filled with the literature of all the groups. Many an afternoon, after classes, he lay atop the steel cot in his room and read through the pamphlets carefully, with great interest in the many ideas expressed in them. He made notes to himself, especially when he found some idea persuasive, worth pondering. He found announcements of meetings and lectures, some of which he attended. He wrote about the lectures and about the groups on the beach in letters home to his father, testing his opinions about them for himself. In wistful replies, his father gravely shared his own thoughts about what Ramu had written.

Ramu did not find Ponni at Marina Beach. But one evening, when he had almost completed his first year in college and it was approaching time to return to Paavalampatti for the summer vacation, he attended a lecture by a somewhat well-known author of plays and movie scripts of a political nature. The announcement on the table of the Rational Progressive Association had said the lecture would touch on the state of contemporary Tamil literature and films. And there at the lecture, quite by chance, was Ponni. The lecture was held in the large hall of an imposing but dilapidated private house in Kodambakkam, just off Arcot Road, close to where the new film studios were coming up now that the war had ended and movies were being made in large numbers again. A desk had been placed at the head of the hall for the speaker, an earnest middle-aged man with a mustache and slightly protruding teeth in a veshti and a plain white shirt. A few chairs had been arranged along the walls. On the floor, cotton jamakaalams had been spread for people to sit on. Ramu arrived early enough to snag a chair. Ponni came in a little later with two other women and found a place on the floor toward the front.

Ramu noticed Ponni the moment she entered. He knew immediately it was Ponni. It had to be, because his breath caught in his chest, and the walls and the meaningless buzzing of the people in the hall fell precipitously away. It had to be.

And it was. It was Ponni. How well he remembered her! The broad face had changed, of course, matured. It was no longer the face of a girl, but rather of a woman. A striking woman. Exactly as he had predicted. From across the room, Ponni reminded Ramu of stone statues on temple walls—her face had the same fine proportions and firm, unsullied lines. The lips were full and lovely curves. The skin of her face, bare of any mark, was smooth as polished stone. But the limpid eyes were vibrantly alive, and the thick, curly hair was pulled back in a loose braid—it was hair such as this, Ramu was certain, that ancient poets had compared to dark rain clouds. Ponni was beautiful. No doubt about it. She had a solemn expression on her face and was dressed rather plainly in a cotton sari. She wore no jewelry, not even rings in her ears. But the seriousness, the studied plainness, were of no avail—they could do nothing to detract from the luminous loveliness that seemed to Ramu to light up the entire room.

Ramu hardly heard the erudite lecture. Instead, he watched Ponni from across the room and wondered at himself and what he was feeling. Such churning within! Why? True, he had been searching for Ponni for months and had now finally found her. Hardly surprising that he was excited. But such a storm of feeling? He could not understand it.

Or perhaps he would not understand it.

Ramu slipped out of the hall just before the lecture ended. In the unruly, neglected front garden of the house, now dark because it was late in the evening, he waited under the low branches of a lime tree, trying to calm himself. In a little while, the lecture over, the audience began to leave. Through the barred yellow rectangle of a window, Ramu saw Ponni speak at length to the man who had delivered the lecture. Soon Muthu, whom Ramu knew from the

Rational Progressive Association table on the beach, came up to join the conversation, his hand brushing momentarily against Ponni's arm in a familiar way. It seemed to Ramu from the way the three of them spoke that they knew one another well.

Ramu waited patiently until Ponni came out of the house. She was alone, the two women with whom she had arrived having long since disappeared. She walked briskly down the path through the garden to the front gate, passing close enough for him to touch. He looked her full in the face in the little light cast into the garden from the windows of the house. It seemed to him that she noticed him too, but she said nothing. Before he could speak a word, she had passed. Quickly, Ramu followed her. It took him a moment to collect his locked bicycle, parked just inside the front gate to the house. Wheeling it, he rushed into the lane after Ponni.

"Ponni!" he cried to get her attention when he caught up with her where the lane connected to Arcot Road. In one direction, Arcot Road led to Nungambakkam and Loyola College; in the other to the new film studios.

Ponni turned, frowning. "Yes?" When she saw the thin tall man confronting her on a poorly lit, notorious stretch of Arcot Road, the frown on her face deepened. Many hapless young aspiring actresses had been teased and even molested here late at night.

"I saw you at the lecture," Ramu blurted out quickly when he saw the expression on her face.

Ponni looked at him doubtfully. "I am in a hurry." She indicated the bus stop a short distance away, adding in a perplexed voice, "How do you know my name?"

"Don't you remember me, Ponni?"

Ponni looked back blankly at Ramu.

"Paavalampatti!"

"Paavalampatti?"

And then, simultaneously, they both cried, "Ramu!" Even as he spoke Ponni remembered. She looked at him in amazement.

"Is it really you?" Ponni asked.

"Yes, it is," Ramu replied happily, very much pleased at the wonder in Ponni's voice now that he had finally found her.

"You are in Madras now?"

"Yes."

"You go to college here," Ponni guessed.

"Yes. Loyola."

Ponni nodded—of course. "How did you know about the lecture?"

"I saw it announced at the table that the Rational Progressive Association sets up on the beach."

"That's our group."

"Your group?"

"I mean my uncle is one of the people who started it."

Ramu asked, "Your uncle. How is he?"

"He's well. He—" But Ponni could not continue, for down the dark stretch of Arcot Road a bus approached. Ponni indicated the bus stop again and said, "I'd better hurry. I don't want to miss the bus. Who knows when the next one will appear at this time of the evening?"

Ramu said, "How do I contact you?" In a rush, he added, "I have been looking for you for months. Ever since I arrived in Madras." He wanted to convey to her his sense of urgency, his fear she would disappear again.

Ponni gave him a peculiar look, which made Ramu regret his words, for he could not know she was not thinking the same thoughts as him. Ponni was thinking how perturbing, how unsettling, it was to have a fragment of her past life, a life that she had worked so hard to leave behind, intrude so unexpectedly upon her. Nevertheless, also speaking rapidly, she replied, "There's a printing press in Perambur called New Age Press. A small one. Not far from the loco works. It's on Lower Naidu Street. Not really a street, more an alley. The press belongs to my uncle. You can always contact me there. Not for a while, though. It will have to be after a couple of weeks. I'm leaving Madras on a trip tomorrow."

"Trip? When exactly will you be back? I too . . ." He was rushing to tell her that he didn't have two weeks, that the academic year was almost over, that in just a few days he would be back in Paavalampatti for the summer vacation.

But Ponni was gone, her plain brown cotton sari billowing behind her as she ran to catch her bus. Ramu waited for the bus to lumber past before climbing onto his bicycle. Then, exultant at having finally found Ponni, he pedaled madly back to his hostel. He had neglected to obtain permission from the Father Director of the hostel for his evening out. If he was lucky, he would arrive before the second bell, signal for all hostellers to be in their rooms or else in possession of a chit permitting them to return late. Ramu raced against the clock through the dark streets, elated and at the same time feeling forlorn that the timing of his encounter with Ponni had turned out so wrong, so unfavorable, because of her impending trip.

The next day, Ramu confided his breakthrough to Arokiasamy. Arokiasamy congratulated him and then said, "Ramu, do you remember when you first mentioned Ponni to me?"

Ramu looked at him in confusion.

"It was after that Debating Society meeting many months ago. The first one that you came to. You started talking about her uncle. And then it came out that you were really interested in the niece. You were so shy about Ponni!" With a sly glance at his friend, he added, "Ramu, do you remember the topic the fools that run debating at Loyola chose at that meeting?"

"No."

"No? You should. I haven't forgotten it. It stuck in my mind when you mentioned the niece. *Love Will Ever Triumph.* That was the topic. And it has. You have proven the case for the resolution. You have found your Ponni!"

Ramu gave Arokiasamy a look of annoyance. "What does love have to do with any of this? Ponni is my friend from childhood. I used to lend her books, that's all. Don't be silly!"

"Good. I'm happy, then. It is much better for me that she is just a friend."

"Why?"

"Don't you know what happens when a woman enters the story, Ramu? You will have no time for me. I will lose you as a friend!"

⸙

Ponni had been found, but not really. Ramu rued his luck. He had succeeded in his quest, yes, but only then to be frustrated and placed in a wretched suspense. By the time he had stumbled into her at the lecture off Arcot Road, the annual year-end exams were already upon him. Much like everyone else, he had neglected his studies during the year and now was forced to cram day and night to prepare for the all-important final exams. Nevertheless, he would have somehow, anyhow, made the time to go to the New Age Press in Perambur in search of Ponni; but there wasn't any point, for Ponni was not in Madras. And right after the exams, he would have to leave for Paavalampatti for the summer vacation. The train ticket had been bought long before. Such was the rush for trains during this season that there could be no question of changing the day of travel. Alas, it would be months before Ramu could finally seek out Ponni again.

During the exams, Ramu and Kannan broke hostel rules and studied together well past midnight in Kannan's room. Exams were a time when such infringements were overlooked. Nevertheless, they were discreet, using candles and blocking the window with sheets. Unlike Ramu, Kannan's subject was physics. His ambition was to be an engineer, a profession his father deemed to have a bright future in the new, independent India that was imminent; he was to apply to engineering college soon. Few of the exam subjects therefore were shared between Ramu and Kannan. They studied together mainly out of a desire to keep each other awake. During the day, Arokiasamy, in economics like Ramu, joined them. Ramu's every waking hour was consumed by preparations for the exams. By the time the exams ended, he was exhausted. He had one day before he was to leave for Paavalampatti for the vacation. That day he spent clearing out his hostel room and moving the few things he had accumulated in his time in Madras to his aunt's house in San Thome. Such was his weariness that he slept away the entire train journey to Paavalampatti.

Back in the village of his birth, Ramu made startling discoveries. He found he had changed in unimaginable ways. He looked around and felt like Gulliver in Lilliput. (He had read an excerpt from Swift's *Gulliver's Travels* in the mandatory General English class.) The village had shrunk in the time he had been gone. He looked at old and familiar things with fresh eyes. He looked at his father and saw not a giant of lively intelligence, wise in the ways of the world, but a small man unsure of himself. He thought a terrible thought—perhaps what he had previously admired in his father was not so admirable. What was the use of reading up on the world if all you did was hide out in a small village? He found himself withdrawing, impatient when his father wanted him to talk yet again of his experiences in Madras. Similarly, he looked at Uncle Siva and saw clearly his small-minded and obstinate prejudices. He contemplated Gomati Paati and saw not her enormous will and vast generosity but her small caution and her stolid defense of an old world deserving to be swept away.

One thing alone seemed to Ramu exempt from the contraction to which all things in Paavalampatti were now, suddenly, subject. Unlike the rest of the village, the tamarind tree had burgeoned instead of shrinking. The tree stood out behind the house more enormous than ever. From the very first moment of his arrival back home, Ramu felt it calling, beckoning him. One morning, before the sun had climbed high into the sky, he walked out to it. The air was motionless all around him as he made his way past the fields and the irrigation well and the gardens. From a distance, the tree—inert, sullen, brooding—lifted into the sky as if made of iron. But the moment he stepped under its branches, the iron stirred, came awake, filled with ominous swaying and whispering. He stood at the very spot where he had found Murugappa's body (no terrible, accusing blood stain in the dirt now) and felt himself shrink, Gulliver no longer, even as the tree grew before his very eyes. He looked up and saw the menacing branches reach down, down, for him. Fearfully—he was embarrassed about it afterwards—he searched the thick foliage for . . . for . . . He knew not what. He stood there feeling the full, terrible weight of the tree upon him until he could stand it no more. He stepped quickly away, fleeing as he had once before from the tree.

That was the demon tree, terrible and terrifying as ever. Aside from it, though, everything and everyone had faded, become

Lilliputian. The finding troubled Ramu. He had certainly not ceased to love his family in the year (almost) he had been gone; but he could no longer overlook their terrible smallness, the terrible smallness of the village—the words thrust themselves insistently upon him when he cast his unsparing eye over Paavalampatti. *Terrible smallness.* He remembered how he had refused to be ashamed of Paavalampatti when confronted by the city boys in Loyola. Now he wondered. He had not found a new love for those city boys. No, that was not it. Nevertheless, his attitude to Paavalampatti had changed. He knew by now that he hated inherited privilege—whether of class, or caste, or of any other kind—and it was clear to him that Paavalampatti was a small place built on terrible privilege. At the end of his summer vacation, he headed back to Madras for the second year of college with relief—desperate Gulliver escaping Lilliput.

On the first day in Madras, Ramu moved his things back into his room in the Loyola hostel, trading vacation stories with Kannan and Arokiasamy but really thinking all the time of Ponni, whom he was determined to search out the first chance he got. Kannan had gone to Delhi, while Arokiasamy had stayed in Madras. They discussed how they had fared in the final exams. Arokiasamy had excelled. Ramu and Kannan had done reasonably well, although Kannan's father had warned him he needed to do better if he wished to get into a good engineering college.

In between setting up Ramu's room, they inspected with appropriate hauteur the entering class of first-year students. Whenever they spotted one, they called out and subjected him to merciless questioning (as indeed they themselves had been the previous year). The inspection confirmed to them their own new standing. They were seasoned members of Loyola now. The realization sparked Arokiasamy's imagination. Indulgently, Ramu and Kannan listened to his schemes to recruit first-year students into his campaign against the many foolishnesses of Loyola, on all of which he had ruminated amply—much too amply—during the long summer vacation.

Through all this, though, Ramu's mind was secretly on the following day, when he would be able to go to Lower Naidu Street in Perambur after classes ended. Accordingly, late in the afternoon the next day, he climbed onto his bicycle and set off. He told no one—not even Arokiasamy—he was going. Lower Naidu was not easy to find. He located it eventually not too far from the railway workshops. The misconceived street was an obscure afterthought to Naidu Street. Surrounded by a refuse-strewn cheri of huts and open drains, it was so narrow and short that he cycled right past it at least twice. It led to nothing important—at its end was an empty lot choked with weeds and rubbish. A modest pharmacy, a kerosene shop, and a scrap paper dealer were on one side of the street. Opposite was a poor little store selling a meager supply of oil, rice, lentils, flour, matchboxes, and a handful of other home provisions still in their sacks on rough wooden shelves. Ramu cycled through the mixed-up aromas of the street, the smell of kerosene and paper and gunny sack all tumbling together in open comradeship in the city air. He found New Age Press humming between the provision store and the weed-choked lot.

Despite the battered and faded sign above its front, New Age Press was more substantial than its neighboring stores. Its interior was illuminated by three overhead lamps with green shades. The walls too were a dingy green. Under the lamps, machinery about which Ramu could only speculate was visible; at one clanking and wheezing device—a printing press surely, what else could it be?—a short man stood working a foot pedal. Simultaneously, his hands moved rapidly, placing and removing sheets of paper between two flat plates in a rhythm matching his machine. Farther inside, another contrivance idled, a flat table with a hinged top, attached to a wheel with a lever. Against one of the green walls stood wooden frames with—again, Ramu surmised—the moveable type for the presses. Opposite were cluttered shelves with cans of ink and reels of paper and sundry other items. Ramu leaned against his bicycle in the falling dusk and watched with wonder. Homo faber—that was what the scene said to the college student in him. Man doing, making things—it was a concept he had studied in his economics class. The short man picked up a can with a brush stuck in it and with a practiced hand smeared black ink over one of the flat surfaces of his machine. At the press of the pedal with a foot, a roller swept first over the freshly inked surface and then over the type. Then paper and type pressed together and a printed handbill was produced, which the man deftly picked up and placed on the growing stack by his side. As Ramu watched from the gathering gloom of the street, man and machine seemed to become one in the yellow light falling from the overhead lamps. It took Ramu a moment to realize this was Chellappa—this short man was Chellappa!

Seven years, and still Ramu recognized him. His memory of the brief encounter in Paavalampatti had not faded—not at all. Chellappa seemed smaller. His unruly hair was gray now, though he could not be that old. Unlike the last time Ramu had seen him (so vivid the picture in his head), he was dressed in an ink-stained veshti and vest. He looked tired. Still, there was a sureness in his demeanor, an air of compact and purposeful energy as he worked his machine, that conformed to the memory Ramu had of him.

"What is it?"

Chellappa had paused in his exertions. He had noticed the scrutiny of the man in the street with the bicycle. He leaned on his machine and peered into the darkening street. He grabbed a towel from his shoulder and vigorously wiped the sweat off his face.

"What do you want? We are very busy right now. Can't take on any more work for two or three days at least." He spoke impatiently, probing the rapidly deepening gloom of the street with his tired eyes.

"No," Ramu hurriedly replied. "I'm not a customer." He hesitated, wondering whether he should say who he really was, and then rushed on. "I'm looking for Ponni."

"The back."

"The back?"

"Yes, go around to the back."

Chellappa abruptly returned his attention to his machine. He seemed not at all interested in this young man who had come looking for his niece. The machine started up again in its gasping and clamoring. Ramu vacillated in the street, balking at springing himself on Ponni without so much as an announcement.

Chellappa called out over the noise as he whipped sheets of paper in and out of the press, "Go on. Go around to the back of the building. You'll find Ponni there."

With reluctant steps, Ramu did as instructed. The side of the dilapidated building abutted the vacant, rubbish-filled lot, but at the back, beyond a fence with a gate, was a well-kept little yard with a well in it. Into this yard, light and voices poured out from an open door and a window. Ramu leaned his bicycle against the wall of the building and climbed the three steps to the door. He called out, in English, "Hello," and waited.

Soon a young woman appeared and asked, "Are you here for the meeting? Why announce yourself? Just come on in. But you should know you are very late. The meeting is almost over."

"Meeting?" Ramu replied. "I'm not here for that. I'm looking for Ponni."

"Yes, this is Ponni's home. But she is busy with the meeting. What do you want with her?"

Ramu felt annoyed. If Ponni's uncle himself had not bothered, who was this woman to ask such questions? Still, he replied, "My name is Ramu. I am a friend. I knew Ponni in Paavalampatti, the village in which she was born."

"Oh yes," the woman said readily. "The Brahmin boy." She looked at him with fresh interest. "My name is Meena."

Meena was fat and short and dressed in a sari and blouse of bright colors that clashed with shocking disregard for each other. She gave off an indubitable air of bossiness. Ramu stood silently at the door, irritated and also unsure how to respond, while Meena boldly looked him up and down. She made no move to get Ponni. Finally, Ramu stepped past her into the short and narrow corridor of the house, saying, "May I look for Ponni?"

"Ponni!" Meena shouted in response. "The Brahmin boy you told us about is here to see you."

Announced in this rather exasperating way, Ramu moved into Ponni's tiny home. To the left of the corridor was a room, dark and silent. Opposite was another, dimly lit by a naked light bulb dangling by its wire from the ceiling. Standing at the door to this room (there were no others), Ramu saw beaten-up wooden shelves sagging with books and, in a corner, a desk and a chair. Bedding was rolled up and stacked against a wall. The floor was rough cement. In the little space in the center of the room, five young men and women were gathered on mats spread out on the floor. Among them, Ramu recognized Muthu from the table on the beach, debonair as ever, and next to him Ponni, who was now looking up at Ramu, clearly surprised. Even as he watched, the meeting ended and the gathered people rose to their feet, bumping and jostling one another in the little space. Ponni, busying herself with a notebook and sheets of paper over which the group had been poring, was the last to stand up.

Muthu pushed himself forward, forcing Ramu to step back from the doorway to make room. Recognition dawned in Muthu's eyes. "So this is the Ramu you told us about. I remember now. I've seen him at the beach at our table."

Clearly, Ponni had spoken freely of Ramu to her friends. What had she said? How had she described him? Ramu did not know whether to be pleased or annoyed.

Muthu faced Ramu in the narrow corridor. "What do you want?" he asked. His manner was blunt, suspicious, not at all friendly.

Before Ramu could reply, Ponni said, "Go on home now, Muthu. I'll see you tomorrow."

"But what does he want here?" Muthu persisted.

"I'll see you tomorrow as planned. Go home now." Ponni's tone was firm.

Muthu complied, but not before darting another stern glance at Ramu.

When he was gone, Meena said, "Don't mind Muthu. That's just the way he is. Always suspicious of everyone."

Ponni said, "I didn't think you would come."

"I was away in Paavalampatti for the holidays," Ramu explained. "I returned yesterday."

"Paavalampatti?" Ponni said. There was marvel in her voice, as if Paavalampatti were a distant planet.

"Yes. Paavalampatti."

"I have not been back since I left."

"No?" But of course Ramu knew she had not. How could she have returned without his knowing? It was unthinkable.

"No."

"Your brother left too," Ramu remembered. "You have no one left there."

"Yes. My brother is in Madurai. At least that is what I think. I have lost touch with him."

"Just as well," Ramu said, meaning Ponni's not returning. "There is nothing in Paavalampatti worth going back for." Thinking of his own return there over the summer, he spoke with great sincerity. He added, so that she would not misunderstand, "I'm sorry you are no longer in touch with your brother."

Except for Meena, everyone had gone. Ponni said, "My uncle will close up the shop and come back here soon." She went into the room across the corridor. Her manner did not say go away; it did not say stay. Feeling bold, Ramu followed her and Meena into the room, which also had a naked electric light bulb hanging from the ceiling. One wall had two shelves with jars and pots and pans. In one corner, a basket with vegetables hung from the ceiling by a metal chain; in another, on a wooden plank resting on bricks, was a kerosene stove next to pots with rice and kuzhambu. Ramu recognized a smell he had encountered only after leaving home. Chicken. Beef. Something like that. No such smell had ever filled his home in Paavalampatti.

"Meena brought the chicken kuzhambu. She is going to eat with us. Will you?" Ponni asked. She pumped the kerosene stove to prime it as she spoke. Her face was in the dark, but Meena's was not. Was that amusement in Meena's face? Did she expect him, a Brahmin, to be discomfited by the invitation? In the dim corner of the room, the flame of the kerosene stove suddenly leapt up, casting unreal hues of blue into Ponni's face.

"No," Ramu said, because he had to get back to his hostel. The moment he spoke, he felt ashamed. He added, "Some water would be good."

Ponni indicated a pot. "Help yourself."

Ramu took the tin tumbler by the pot and dipped it into the cool water. He drank as he had always been taught, pouring the water down his throat without touching the tumbler to his lips. Ponni was busy at the stove. She put a pot of water to heat on it. Then she put ginger in it to soak. She began to chop onions on a wooden cutting board. The water with ginger slowly turned yellow. Ponni reached in and kneaded the pulp with deft fingers so that more juice was squeezed out. She worked with practiced ease. The smell of ginger spread faintly through the room. She said nothing to Ramu. Her back was turned to him. Her thick hair had come loose from its knot to fall down her back in a torrent of curls. Ramu looked away and then, suddenly feeling a great need to break the tense silence, said, "What was the meeting about?"

Meena answered, "We are staging a play."

"A play?"

"Yes. Based on the Ramayana."

Ramu knew the Ramayana well, of course. The exile of Prince Rama, the kidnapping of his wife Sita, the defeat of the great abductor Raavanan—who did not know the story? Ramu was unimpressed. For thousands of years the story had been told and retold. Weren't Valmiki and Kamban and Tulsidas enough? Was there really a need for a play about it?

Meena saw the skepticism in Ramu's face. She said, "It is not what you think. We are staging the Ramayana in a new way. In our play, Raavanan will be the hero and Rama the villain."

"How is that possible?"

"Why not? The Ramayana is basically a bunch of lies to make the lower castes look bad and the upper castes look good. In our version of the play, Raavanan is an outcaste. He does not believe in caste. He is for the working class. He does not abduct Sita. She leaves with him willingly, disgusted with Rama's cowardice and brutality toward Soorpanaka." She described the many shocking changes they had made to the well-known, even sacred, story.

When Ramu understood, he laughed delightedly. "How clever! I'd like to see such a play."

"We are still working on the script. But we will start rehearsing soon."

Ponni turned from the stove and said, "What are you prattling on about, Meena? He is not interested in our play."

"That's not true. I'd like to help."

"What do you know about the Ramayana or what we are doing?" Ponni demanded.

Ramu did not respond that he knew the Ramayana very well. Gomati Paati had told him the stories of the epic a million times. Nor did he say that the previous year he and Arokiasamy had read Periyar's incendiary little book attacking the Brahminical values of the Ramayana. He did not point out that he recognized some of Periyar's ideas in the play Ponni and her group were writing. Instead, he said, rather tersely, "I didn't say I know anything. All I asked is whether I could help."

"Stop it, Ponni," Meena said. "He should help if he wants to. He can give us the Brahmin perspective." She laughed at her own little joke. Clearly, her sense of humor could be blunt.

"Yes," Ramu agreed, also laughing in a good-natured way. "I can do that."

"Next week, same day," Meena said, before Ponni could speak. "And don't come so late."

After Ramu was gone, Ponni said in exasperation to Meena, "Now you've given him a reason to keep coming back!"

"What's wrong with that?"

"He'll want to talk about Paavalampatti. I'd rather not talk about that part of my life. It was long ago and I don't have good memories of that time."

"I thought you liked him," Meena said in a mollifying voice. "Your Brahmin friend from Paavalampatti who lent you books."

And who found my father's ripped and broken body, Ponni silently added to herself, not daring to share the dreadful image with Meena.

↝

THAT WAS HOW RAMU CAME to be involved with Ponni and her comrades in Madras. They called their play *The Ramayana: The True Story.* Ramu came to all the meetings; he wanted to be near Ponni. That was the main reason he came. But he had not lied. The play truly intrigued him. He listened with rapt attention to the discussions.

It was not long before Muthu noticed that Ramu was Rama's namesake. Much joking followed—"Rama himself has arrived to sabotage us"; "Rama, where is your Sita? Lost her again, have you?"; and so on. Ramu did not mind the jokes except when Muthu made them, for in Muthu's mouth they sounded spiteful.

Arokiasamy had begun to attend as well, soon becoming one of the group, just like Ramu. He, too, noticed the meanness. "That Muthu doesn't like you," Arokiasamy observed after one meeting as they headed back to Loyola on their bicycles. "What did you do to him?"

Ramu had no answer. In addition to his political inclinations, Muthu was a striving actor who had already been in important plays and even had had brief roles in movies—the face in the background, the man in the crowd given one line to shout out. There was little that Ramu and Muthu shared. Why would Muthu take a dislike toward him? Ramu could think of no reason at all for Muthu's antagonism, and did his utmost not to tangle with him. He mostly sat quietly and listened as Muthu, Ponni, Meena, Arokiasamy—who had effortlessly made himself one of the prime drafters of the play—and the others turned the great story of Rama upside down. Raavanan became the handsome, accomplished hero and Rama the whining, sneaky villain. This was propaganda, not art. In one concise hour, they took the story to its scandalous conclusion. They began with Sita's horrified witnessing of Rama's cruelty to Soorpanaka (how savagely Rama made his brother Lakshmana slash off Soorpanaka's ears and nose for no greater offense than declaring her love for Rama!). Then came the disgusted Sita's encounter with Raavanan in the hut in the forest. Their love ensued, followed by Rama's bloodthirsty quest for revenge and, finally, the unforgettable tragic murder of Raavanan by Rama. There was nothing subtle about the play: it was a wild, powerful transgression of a revered age-old story.

When the script was ready, actors were assigned and roles were chosen. There was little doubt who would play Raavanan and Sita. Muthu had already laid claim to the role of Raavanan as if it was his birthright, and only Ponni could match him in beauty. Muthu overcame Ponni's reluctance with his persuasion. But who would play Rama, the most reviled character in the play? Arokiasamy wanted the role; but before he could volunteer, Muthu, looking at Ramu meaningfully, said, "When Rama himself has graced us with his presence, how could anyone else aspire to play the role?" The tone was taunting. Muthu was confident that Ramu would not have the courage to step up for the role.

Ponni said sharply, "Muthu, stop playing the fool! You are always making fun of Ramu. He doesn't want to play Rama in our silly little play." Muthu's bullying scorn for guileless Ramu upset her, but she was thinking too of herself and the consequences for her of Ramu playing such a central role in the play, one in which he and she would have to work together closely. She had been ruminating over Ramu in the days that he had been coming to her home in Perambur. How could she not? He had been a part of her life during a short but unbearably dark chapter. He had been a big part, without a doubt; even so, she did not trust herself to remember him rightly as he had been then or—even more vexingly—relate as she properly should to the man he was now.

Ponni's remark made Ramu irate. True, he had no desire to play Rama. He could have easily laughed off Muthu's comment as he had so many times before. But now Ponni had spoken, and the seeming kindness in her voice cut him like a knife. Why had she inserted herself into his business like that? "I'll do it," he blurted out, speaking as sharply as she had and surprising Muthu. "I'll play Rama."

Ponni skillfully covered up her dismay at Ramu's unexpected response. She felt exasperation at Muthu, but also a grudging respect for Ramu—and she wanted neither of those two emotions to be made evident in that setting. Muthu was proud—it was one of the things she liked about him—but she saw that Ramu also was proud in his own way. His willfulness surprised her a little. Ramu was usually mild-mannered, even shy, though she did sometimes feel the shyness might simply be around her, for he was always a little awkward in her presence.

For Ramu, this episode provided just one more example of Ponni's generally maddening behavior. Just thinking of her made him feel exhausted. His sense of grievance had been growing even before he found himself memorizing the lines of cowardly Rama for the play: he had been coming to Perambur for weeks and still had hardly spoken to Ponni. Was she avoiding him? He tried to linger after meetings so that he could talk to her alone, but she always seemed to find a way to have Meena stay back as well. She *was* staying aloof from him; but why? Was it because he had discovered Murugappa's body? Was he unbearable because he reminded her of her father's violent death? Or was he unforgivable because her family had worked for his back in the village? Was it because he was a Brahmin? The questions gnawed at Ramu like . . . like . . . like vultures, or some other cruel birds of prey. He felt helpless before them. What could *he* do about the fact that he had stumbled on her father's body? Or that her family had worked—no, he should name it for what it was: had been serfs—for his? Or that he had been born into a Brahmin family? How could he change these actualities that went far beyond him?

Yes, all these facts were true—but Ramu cared nothing for them. He yearned for other truths. He wanted to know if Ponni remembered their meetings at the ruined fort in Paavalampatti as vividly as he did. The shared books. Their conversations among the ruined stones. The last day when they had touched each other so tenderly. Had all that made as lasting an impression on her as on him? He wanted to ask her that. He wanted to tell her how much he enjoyed coming to her home and sharing in the brave and brilliant conversations of the men and women—of every caste, for Muthu was a Mudaliar and Meena was a Gounder, and he did not even know the castes of the others—he found there. Even Muthu was part of that bravery and brilliance. He felt desperate to tell her how he had felt in Paavalampatti this past summer when he had returned to the village in which they both had been born.

And perhaps most importantly of all, he wanted to share with her something quite amazing: the alienation he had felt in Paavalampatti disappeared in this room in Perambur! He did not know why. He only knew it did. He had realized it one day cycling home from Perambur. Just that morning a letter had arrived from Paavalampatti, and it had made him feel irritated and small in all the ways he had felt when he had visited over the summer. And then he had come to the meeting and by the time it ended he could not bother to be annoyed at all the nagging news his father had written in his letter. He longed to tell Ponni this. But he could not because Ponni would not let him.

In his frustration, Ramu came to contemplate Ponni with the assiduousness of a logician. Logic was his refuge from the confusion he felt at her treatment of him. It helped him see that he had a special, undeniable bond to her that she, maddeningly, refused to acknowledge. Logic told him that she was wrong in this matter and he was right. Had he not realized the specialness of their bond even all those years ago in Paavalampatti? What did it matter if Ponni did not behave with proper awareness of the link that bound them together? Logic told him their link was deep, strong. Unbreakable. Forever.

Ramu systematically laid out his reasoning to his confidant Arokiasamy one morning in his Loyola hostel room. He was missing a class, and he was making Arokiasamy miss it too.

Point (Ramu the logician ticked off the first piece of evidence for Arokiasamy): He—Ramu—and Ponni came from the same place, not some big city, but a village. Some might say the circumstances of their families had been very different. So what? He had known her when they were both little more than barefoot children in that remote village of their birth.

Point: He had known Ponni longer than anyone else in that group that met in her home in Perambur. What was her so-called friendship with Muthu in comparison? If only she thought about it, she would quickly realize that the nature of her bond with Muthu, such as it was, was nothing compared to her bond with him.

Point: He had discovered her father's murdered body. Some might think that was a reason for her to avoid him. Not at all. Terrible as it was, that fact alone linked them forever.

Conclusion: The matter was simple. Chellappa was the only person in Madras who had known Ponni longer than Ramu, and Chellappa was her uncle, linked to her by blood. The bond between Ponni and Ramu could not be disputed. Why, then, was Ponni so intent on doing so by her behavior? Ramu ended his analysis plaintively and waited for Arokiasamy's response.

Arokiasamy looked at him solemnly and said, "Quite a little Socrates you have become."

Ramu was impatient. "What do you think? Am I not right? Is there not a special bond between me and her? Why will she deny it? Tell me what you think."

"Point:" Arokiasamy said sadly, "Your logic is flawless. Point: Logic has nothing to do with it. Conclusion: You are in love with Ponni, friend."

Love? Was that it? Arokiasamy had brought up that word again and now Ramu was forced to admit the thing he had named. He was in love with Ponni!

Love. A word. That was all it had been to Ramu. Now, though, it was a thing in his body—a part of his flesh, another organ within him, like his lungs or his heart or his stomach. It was a hurt, an ache, a restless snake twitching and twisting in the middle of his stomach. Strange thing: Ramu wanted the snake there. He would not have dreamed of giving it up. He hugged the snake to himself with a fierce possessiveness.

Baffling was the only way to describe the snake called love. Its power was strange. The snake made strange things happen. First, it took him away from Ponni. He found that once he had named his love, he could not bear to be in Ponni's presence. He stopped going to the gatherings in her house. When Arokiasamy asked why, he replied, "Ponni and Muthu are lovers." Arokiasamy nodded and did not question him further. How did Ramu know they were lovers? The magical, powerful snake within him told him so. It revealed to him that which had been hidden before. He was shocked at himself for not having realized such an elementary fact about Ponni and Muthu. Of course. It was obvious—he could see it in the way they looked at each other, in the sudden and soft way they touched, in the way they seemed always set apart. Ponni and Muthu were intimates. *Lovers.* When he was alone, he spoke it out loud: *Ponni loves Muthu.* Admitting it made the snake within him throb and lash back and forth as if in pain, but it was true. Ramu could not deny it.

The snake was nothing if not capricious. First, it had made Ramu hang back; now, it forced him to return to the meetings in Perambur. He could not stay away from Ponni. He had told Arokiasamy he had no intention of returning, that Arokiasamy should tell the others to find someone else to play Rama in the play; and then, before Arokiasamy could do as instructed, he turned up at Perambur. This happened two or three times, until Arokiasamy said in an irked but not unkind voice, "You want to go to Perambur, go to Perambur. What is the use of all this pretending? Don't ask me to carry any more messages to Ponni and the others. Whatever you want to say, say it yourself." He knew Ramu had no intention of dropping out of the group that met in Perambur. It was Ramu's link to Ponni. It was his excuse to be near her.

೫

RAMU'S ERRATIC ATTENDANCE AT REHEARSALS, his fickle behavior, did not go unnoticed by Muthu. "That Brahmin is in love with you," he said to Ponni one day, looking at her intently with hooded, jealous eyes. They were alone, lying in each other's arms in Muthu's room in an Elephant Gate lodge. Ponni sat up and looked away. She did not care for Muthu's jealousy, which felt to her more like an intolerable claim than heartfelt anguish. But she could not deny the veracity of his observation.

It was true—Ramu loved her. Whatever might that mean? Ponni felt the full weight of the question as only someone who had been raised by Chellappa could. Always reflect consciously on the world and your place in it, her uncle had taught her, by word and by example. This was supposed to be a powerful way to master a hostile world eager to break you. And so, ever since Ramu had re-entered her life, Ponni had been reflecting on him and the world and his place in the world relative to her. Now she weighed what Muthu had said: "That *Brahmin* is in love with you." Was it not enough to say *man?* Ramu was a Brahmin and a man, but what part of him was which? And which part of him loved her? Was it the Brahmin, or the man? She did not want the love of the Brahmin. She was sure of that. And of the man? No, she did not want that either—it was enough that she had Muthu's love. She surely felt respect, appreciation, even fondness, for the Ramu who was a man. But his love? She did not want it. Or did she?

⁓

THE TIME TO STAGE *THE RAMAYANA: The True Story* arrived. Ramu moved through the performances in a daze. The play required him to touch Ponni twice, once softly and lovingly on the shoulder and the other time by harshly grabbing her arm. During some performances, he was so fierce and unrelenting toward Ponni as Sita that she looked at him with surprise and appreciation. During others, he was listless and spoke his lines with little conviction. There was a part in the play when Rama said to Sita, "Who betrays whom? I am your husband, more than your husband, linked to you since the beginning of time. How can you, my wife, turn your back on me?" To this Sita replied, "Husband? That is all you are—my husband. You never loved me. You loved what I stood for, not me. You married me because the world said you should, because the gods said you should. I have felt Raavanan's love and I know you are incapable of loving me. You make me your wife. Raavanan's love makes me Sita." Ramu dreaded this moment during every performance of the play. He hated Sita's lines, for it made him want to say, "I'm not Rama, I'm Raavanan. I love you like Raavanan loves you, against all the taboos of the world." But those were not his lines in the play.

The performances, held in little auditoriums and makeshift stages around the city without any sets, ended after several weeks. Such had been the play's success that there was talk of perhaps touring to interior towns and villages during the summer college vacation. There were politically minded organizations willing to pay for the travel. But there was a problem. A new Raavanan would have to be found, for Muthu could no longer play the role. An amazing thing had happened—Muthu had had a breakthrough: he had been given a prominent role in a movie. He was to play the best friend of the hero in a social drama. If the film did well, he would be noticed. There was no telling how far he could go from here, for the film was being made by a prominent studio, and the director was someone sympathetic to Muthu's political thinking. In fact, dialogue had specially been written for him that would expose the plight of the poorest of the poor. Muthu glowed with joy at his good fortune. Ponni glowed with him. She spoke with pride about all that he meant to do for their cause with his newfound visibility. Muthu basked in Ponni's excited pleasure at his impending success, though he also felt he had to make clear that as his career took off he would have to be cautious in how he went about supporting their political principles, the principles that they all cared about above all else.

Ramu could not bear to be near Muthu and Ponni, to see how joyful they were at Muthu's career taking off. He was secretly happy when the plans to tour with the play fell through. He felt he had done a good job of hiding his true feelings from Ponni and especially Muthu, but going on tour—spending day after day in one another's constant company—would surely have tested his powers of deception.

Ramu sought out Chellappa so as not to find himself drifting out of Ponni's orbit now that the play had ended. He could not endure the sight of Ponni with Muthu, but neither could he give up going to Perambur. Chellappa was the answer to Ramu's predicament. When he learned who Ramu was, Chellappa had not reacted as Ramu expected. Ramu had thought Chellappa would be hostile. He remembered the altercation between Uncle Siva and Chellappa all those years ago in Paavalampatti. He sensed that Chellappa felt Ramu's family had much to answer for. And who could deny the justice of Chellappa's feelings?

Still, Chellappa did not seem to harbor ill will toward him. He said only, "You are the boy who found Murugappa." It was his sole reference to Ramu's prior history. Ramu was grateful to him for the careful reticence, but found it surprising coming from the man he remembered as fiery. He saw now that he had understood very little, that the events that had transpired behind his house in Paavalampatti all those years ago had been beyond the ken of a child.

Chellappa was always busy in his shop, or so it seemed to Ramu. He had an older man named Mohan who worked with him, and Ponni helped as well. She had managed to finish school, a free school run by the Labor Department for students like her from the Scheduled Castes, as they were now officially known, and was very well-read in Tamil and in English. But she was not in college. Chellappa could not afford to send her.

Ramu began to do one or two small things in the shop whenever he could. Chellappa was grateful for the extra set of hands. Ramu liked working with the machines. He liked the atmosphere of industry and urgency in the shop. Sometimes, when Mohan brought steaming glass tumblers of sweet tea from the shop on Naidu Street, Ramu and Chellappa sat together companionably at the ramshackle table, while Chellappa discussed some book or essay he was reading, making Ramu marvel at the fierce intelligence of this diminutive man without any formal education whatsoever. At other times, grave men and women who spoke in low voices came to the shop to meet Chellappa; then the machines fell silent and Chellappa and the visitors sat around the little table, whispering over the tea. Occasionally, Ponni joined them. The mood grew conspiratorial.

The first time the mysterious visitors came, Ramu entered the shop thoughtlessly and there was immediate silence. Chellappa spoke with unaccustomed sharpness: "What do you want?" Ramu shook his head weakly and retreated. Ramu learned to leave the shop whenever the visitors appeared, feeling the deepening communion between Chellappa and himself interrupted at these enigmatic moments.

What could Chellappa and the visitors be discussing? Ramu had no doubt: the cataclysmic events overtaking India, the events about which Chellappa and he sometimes spoke. As rebellions exploded, the British had suddenly announced that their huge colony was to be partitioned into the two independent nations of India and Pakistan in August—in less than three months! They were running away much sooner than previously announced. India would be free before 1947 ended. No doubt, this was what was being discussed in Chellappa's shop. When, one day, Ramu saw a stern khaki-clad police officer with a flourishing mustache on his upper lip seated across the table from Chellappa in the shop he felt more certain than ever. He wished ardently to be a part of the discussions. If Ponni could participate, why not he? Perhaps Chellappa and the others were preparing grand schemes, laying the groundwork for reform in independent India, plotting to conquer power. It did occur to him that these might be tasks far beyond these men and women. No matter. Small or great, these members of the working class were the future of India. He wished desperately to join them. It galled him that he was not invited and also that he lacked the boldness to invite himself.

When they were in the shop together, Ramu watched Ponni covertly. He loved the intense expression on her face as she worked at a press. As days passed into weeks and weeks into months, he learned to adore the way she bit her lower lip as she concentrated over the moveable type. Her dark face would flush with her exertions and her thick hair would escape from the knot to fall around her face. He yearned to run his fingers through that hair. He imagined its soft feel between his fingers. He imagined its incomparable aroma—of course it was without peer!—as he pushed his face into it. He wanted to hold her and comfort her—yes, comfort her, for Ponni was not happy. Disappointment was making itself at home in her life.

Muthu and Ponni were not doing well. Muthu was wrapped up in his movie and hardly came by to see her. He was frequently away shooting on location; the movie was big-budget and the director insisted on realistic locations rather than studio sets. Muthu had moved up in the world. He had been signed on to other movies that were to begin production soon. When he dropped by, he complained casually of his make-up man and mentioned well-known Bombay artistes. One day, Ramu read in a newspaper that Muthu had been seen rather too often in the company of a famous Bombay actress. He immediately thought of Ponni, her air of sadness. He understood.

But he knew he could never bring Muthu up with her. She would not let him. Muthu was another taboo subject—another topic never to be broached between them.

Ramu was certainly the last person in the world with whom Ponni would have discussed Muthu. Ponni was moved by Ramu's commitment to her uncle's shop, and by what she had come to recognize as his thoughtfulness and quiet intelligence; but there was always the matter of how Ramu felt about her—his love for her, which remained a powerful, confusing, vexatious force before which she felt helpless. She could not help comparing Muthu and Ramu. They were both much higher in caste than she was—whatever that meant. But the differences between them were immense. Muthu was handsome; Ramu was awkward—not bad-looking but without Muthu's charisma. Muthu was silver tongued, a great orator; Ramu was more often tongue-tied than not. Muthu loved attention; Ramu liked to remain in the background . . . Ponni stopped when she realized that the comparisons she was making were turning out, perhaps unfairly, very much to Muthu's advantage.

In Loyola, Ramu discussed the intolerable situation with Arokiasamy, who felt helpless at his friend's predicament. Kannan, too worldly to tolerate his companions' earnest new Perambur friends, had long since dropped away from their company. The threesome was no more. Arokiasamy was Ramu's sole refuge, and Arokiasamy was hardly an experienced man when it came to matters of love. He listened, and tried, unsuccessfully, to hide his pessimism: the social differences between Ponni and Ramu were vast. It was quixotic of Ramu to think that they could be bridged. A Brahmin boy and an Adi Dravidar girl? Life was not a movie. And then there was Muthu. Whatever the ups and downs of their relationship, Ponni and Muthu had been lovers for a while and, whatever the troubles between them, he did not think they were ready to go their separate ways. Why would Ramu want to put himself in the middle of that mess? Arokiasamy's wise counsel was that of a true friend. It was also that of a man who had never been in love himself. It was a poor substitute for what Ramu truly yearned to do—speak freely with Ponni.

Ramu and Ponni did speak, of course, but instead of discussing Muthu or Ramu's feelings, they spoke seemingly of every other topic under the sun, usually in the company of Meena and Arokiasamy. The group that had produced the play had shrunk to the four of them. They gathered in Ponni's home behind New Age Press and discussed the world, or else discussed nothing, which to Ramu seemed the same, for what he really wanted to discuss was how he felt about Ponni. Mostly they spoke of India's impending independence, of how Ambedkar, who called "untouchables" Dalits, was fighting frenetically to ensure maximum rights for them. They also discussed the Muslims. What would partition do to the Muslims left behind in India? They had rousing debates about that question, and about the princely states, nominally independent from the British, which would have to be integrated into the new nation. Nationalists, feudalists, communists, loyalists, communalists, casteists, atheists, socialists—they and the votaries of a myriad other isms like them would be part of the new nation. How would it all hang together? There was no dearth of topics to bicker over.

They had spirited discussions of such worldly questions, while Ramu hankered to have a more private conversation with Ponni. Very rarely, Muthu visited in his finely tailored shirts and smoothed back hair. When he came, he sat on the floor like them and was openly affectionate to Ponni, draping a familiar arm over her shoulders. This was new and Ramu thought it rather ostentatious—film-world ostentatious. Ponni did not object but Ramu could sense a slow anger beginning to burn inside her. He saw it in the way Ponni stiffened her shoulders under Muthu's arm. He noticed it in the way there was no longer that softness in Ponni's eyes when she looked at Muthu. Once he and Arokiasamy interrupted a fierce argument between Ponni and Muthu as they arrived at Ponni's home. He could not say that he was unhappy to see the trouble brewing between Ponni and Muthu. Ponni was, he knew, nothing if not proud. He waited patiently to see what would happen.

What happened was quite unexpected, so unforeseen that not even Ramu could have predicted it in one of his moments of wild imagination. One hot and humid evening, when Ponni, Meena,

Arokiasamy, and Ramu were gathered in Ponni's home, Ramu's life took a turn that first lifted him to great heights of happiness and then just as quickly flung him down into the dark depths of despondency. Ponni, lying on a mat with face averted from the others, had been distant and sullen all evening. More trouble with Muthu—trouble, clearly, of an extreme kind, so miserable did she seem. Perhaps because of the heat the others too were gathered around her in varying degrees of listlessness.

Arokiasamy, who was browsing a newspaper, said to no one in particular, "Did you read this story here about intercaste marriage?"

Meena said, "What story?"

It was about Periyar and public weddings between men and women of different castes. Periyar thought intercaste marriage was the surest way to break the hold of caste prejudice. The morning of the next day there was to be one such wedding on Marina Beach.

"Four couples from different castes will break the untouchability taboo in the most basic way. They will be married without any mention of God or any kind of ritual," Arokiasamy read from the newspaper.

"That is how these Self-Respect Movement weddings are done. They are atheist weddings. No priests or sacred chants. In fact, they choose a time that is considered inauspicious by orthodox Hindus and deliberately hold the weddings then. Isn't that amazing?" Meena said. She added, "I know a couple who went through a Self-Respect marriage."

"Really? Who were they?" Ramu asked.

"A couple in Erode. They did not really know each other well but they were very political, very involved in the movement. They came from different castes and wanted to make a point and so they went through a Self-Respect wedding."

"What happened to them afterward?" Ramu asked.

"I don't really know. I think they just went their separate ways. After all, they had successfully made their point to the world."

"What an idea this Self-Respect marriage is! It strikes at the very heart of the caste system," Arokiasamy marveled.

Ramu spoke excitedly. “Let’s go to the beach tomorrow! I have never seen a Self-Respect wedding. I’d like to. It might be fun.”

At this, Ponni, who had been silent and aloof all this while, roused herself and glared at Ramu. She said, “What a way to talk! It’s not a show, Ramu. These are not animals in a zoo. They are revolutionaries. They are challenging society. I’m not a Dravidianist. I don’t agree with all of Periyar’s ideas. But I can respect what they are doing . . .” She felt unreasonably surly, irate at the whole world, but especially Ramu.

Ramu was taken aback. “I didn’t mean to . . .” he began.

Ponni was not to be interrupted. “You could never do anything like the couple in Erode Meena mentioned. At least respect those who have the courage to confront the world.”

“You are misunderstanding . . .” Ramu began again, trying to defend himself.

“I’m tired of people who do nothing but talk,” said Ponni, making no attempt whatsoever to disguise her spiteful mood. She felt unsettled and reckless.

“I’m not afraid of the world! I too can confront it if I want to,” Ramu said, stung by the accusation.

Ponni was dismissive, “That’s right. You confront the world by coming to drink tea here with us. That’s your bravery.”

A cruel jibe. It startled Ramu into hurt silence, and shocked Arokiasamy and Meena too, for the cruelty was so unlike Ponni, who could be fierce and uncompromising but was never cruel. Arokiasamy, trying to intervene, playfully slapped his newspaper at Ponni and said, “Ponni, what’s wrong with you? Why are you taking out your bad mood on Ramu?”

Ponni ignored him and said to Ramu, “When it is time, you will marry a little Brahmin girl from Paavalampatti. We all know that.”

“No, I won’t,” Ramu mumbled.

“Just talk,” Ponni retorted. “I’ll believe it when I see it. Why don’t you marry someone from a different caste, then? Instead of treating tomorrow like a circus for your entertainment, perhaps you should think of participating!”

It was a dire challenge, sharp, to the point, an argument closer. Ramu was silent, unsure of what to say. Arokiasamy gave Ponni an incensed look—what had happened to her? What possessed her to behave like this?

Meena, who was nothing if not loyal, caught the look. Feeling protective of Ponni, she blurted out, rather thoughtlessly, "So, Ponni, do you have a nice Adi Dravidar girl from Paavalampatti in mind for our brave Ramu?" The question was mean, and Meena realized it as soon as the words had left her mouth. She laughed loudly to cover up, to try and turn her question into a joke.

Ponni turned her face away and covered her eyes with her arm. She looked exhausted. To Ramu, her manner—the way the shoulders were hunched against the world and the lips quivered—conveyed fatigue and a woman on the verge of tears. Rather than anger, Ramu felt an enormous surge of love. "I'll marry *you* tomorrow," he blurted out. "How about that?" He was as surprised as his companions at his words. The words had tumbled from his lips without deliberation, but now that they had he had no regrets.

Meena abruptly stopped laughing and looked at Ramu in shock. Arokiasamy's face too showed his amazement. Ponni did not move her arm from her eyes, but her breathing grew quieter.

Ramu pressed his advantage: "Let's do it. I'll marry you tomorrow on the beach." He did not say, *You are anyhow not happy with Muthu.* When Ponni did not reply, he said triumphantly, "There. You see, I am not the one who's afraid."

Ponni abruptly sat up on her mat. Her hair tumbled madly around her face. Tears trembled in her eyes, ready to spill over. She said fiercely, "You are just talking!"

"No, I'm not," Ramu said, pleased to have taken the initiative. "I'll marry you tomorrow on Marina Beach. At the most inauspicious time. When all the stars are misaligned and every misfortune possible is meant to befall us. I don't believe in any of it. I will marry you at that time. No priests, no family, nothing. I don't need any of them. I can be like that Erode couple Meena mentioned. I am not afraid to challenge society or the stars. Are you, Ponni?"

Ponni glared at him through her tears. "Be careful what you say!"

Ramu glared back. "I know very well what I'm saying. Do *you* have the courage to marry someone like me?"

Meena and Arokiasamy looked from one to the other in consternation.

"Stop it you two," Arokiasamy said sharply. "Stop behaving like children."

Meena said, "Whether it's a Self-Respect marriage or not, a marriage is a marriage. It means *something*. How can you get married? You don't love each other." She felt frantic at what her offhand question had caused to happen.

"Love?" Ponni said. "Love has nothing to do with it! Isn't that what you said about the Erode couple?"

Was Ponni seriously considering Ramu's proposal? She couldn't be! "How can you get married if you don't really want to be married?" Meena insisted, reproaching herself rather belatedly for having mentioned the Erode couple about whom, in truth, she knew very little. Her thoughtlessness really had started something terrible, hadn't it?

"Listen to Meena," Arokiasamy pleaded with Ponni. "If you won't listen to me, at least consider what she's saying."

Ramu and Ponni both ignored Meena and Arokiasamy. Their eyes were locked on each other; they were suddenly alone, secluded behind an invisible wall that had sprung up around them. Arokiasamy, Meena, the cluttered room, the city around them—all had melted away. The world had disappeared.

Time had bent. So it seemed to Ramu. Ramu and Ponni were back in the ruined fort on the hillock in Paavalampatti. At last. Ramu had waited so long to return there with Ponni.

"Don't test me," Ponni said in a proud but soft voice, the words meant only for Ramu. "You will regret it." Her face was stony now, more beautiful than ever. Unlike Ramu, she had not been transported back to Paavalampatti. She was right there, right in that moment, tired and angry, but grateful to be able to lean on the immovable strength of her convictions as she locked herself in this peculiar, unforeseen, and unforeseeable struggle with Ramu, and with herself.

"I won't," Ramu replied, equally softly. He added boldly, with a crafty intuition that came from he knew not where, "If you have the courage of your own words, marry me tomorrow on the beach." He did not stop to consider what he was doing—what his words might do to Ponni at a moment when she was at her most vulnerable.

"Okay," Ponni said, "I will marry you. Tomorrow on the beach."

Ramu felt a jubilation that he tried not to reveal. "Very good. Tomorrow. On the beach."

Meena spoke urgently, forcing her way into the intimate scene unfolding before her eyes. "What are you saying, Ponni? Your uncle. Muthu. Think about them."

"They don't own me. I am my own woman." With an emphatic thrust of her chin she added, "It's only a show marriage. Like that Erode couple. To make a point. To see if Ramu here will do what he says he will."

"Muthu, Ponni. What about Muthu?" Meena insisted. Surely Ponni could see how awful she was being to Muthu?

Arokiasamy said quietly, "Don't do this, Ponni. Ramu is being foolish. You at least should show some sense. Think of Ramu and Muthu if you won't think of yourself." He thought to himself: *Love is blinding Ramu and making him do this crazy, terrible thing to himself and to Ponni. What is forcing Ponni?* And then he thought of Ponni's recent troubles with Muthu.

"Ramu's an adult. He knows what he is doing," Ponni said. She looked at Ramu, "I'll be at the beach tomorrow. Be there if you want to marry me and show the world what you think of it."

Meena said, "You can't just show up and say you want to get married. Why would the Self-Respecters include you in their ceremony? These things are planned. You have to be part of the movement." She was desperate to atone, to discourage Ramu and Ponni from going through with their insane plan.

"No matter," Ponni said. "I'll be there."

Ramu said confidently, "We too are a part of the movement. In our own way. Who is to say we are not? We don't have to agree with every single thing the Self-Respecters say. I'm sure they will let us participate." He added in a challenging manner, "I too will be there, Ponni."

That made Arokiasamy want to shout many angry things at both Ramu and Ponni for their dangerous heedlessness, but he saw his words would be futile, and it was not until later, when he and Ramu were on their bicycles returning to Loyola, that Arokiasamy voiced to him what he had wanted to say, but in a much kinder manner, "Ponni is unhappy with Muthu. Have you considered that she is agreeing to this madness to get back at him?"

Ramu said, "I don't care."

Arokiasamy gave up trying to hide his annoyance. "It's just as they say—love is blind. Your love has turned you mad! You are doing a foolish thing. And Ponni is doing a foolish thing too. You are both going to hurt yourselves and Muthu and a lot of other people."

"Are you telling me that Ponni doesn't love me and that she loves Muthu? I know that already. What is the worst that can happen? I will have taken a stand against the world. I will have shown what I think of caste and all that nonsense in the most effective way possible. That is reason enough to marry Ponni tomorrow." He did not voice his faint hope that Ponni did not love Muthu anymore.

"You are talking very rationally, as if you are doing something very sensible. But I don't believe you. I think your love for Ponni has made you lose your mind."

"Sometimes losing your mind is not a bad thing."

Arokiasamy saw that this line of reasoning was of no use. "Your father. Your grandmother in Paavalampatti. Your uncle and aunt. What about them?"

"I am my own man," Ramu responded, unwittingly echoing Ponni's words. Then he added, "Why so insistent, Arokia? One would think you would do anything to stop Ponni and me. Is that what it is? Perhaps you really don't believe people like Ponni and me should marry. Is that what it is?"

"What a thing to say, Ramu! Why would you make such an accusation?"

"Your attitude is confusing. It makes me wonder."

"I want you to make the right decision for the right reason. I want you to be happy, Ramu. That is all."

"Then let it go, Arokia," Ramu said angrily. "This is what will make me happy. In fact, if you are truly my friend, you will help me tomorrow when I marry Ponni."

It was futile, completely futile, to talk to Ramu. Arokiasamy saw that. He tried not to be hurt at Ramu's unfair accusations of him. He knew Ramu loved Ponni, and that was an explanation of a kind for his behavior. But Ponni? Could she not see that Ramu loved her? Could Ponni not see the trouble she was creating for herself and Ramu, that she was going to hurt him and Muthu, who still deserved better even if he was a cad? Could she not see that you don't fight pain with more pain? Arokiasamy did not really care about Muthu but he did care about Ramu and Ponni. He reflected helplessly on how they were both being reckless and foolish, though in their own different ways.

↜

RAMU DID NOT SLEEP THAT night. He lay on his narrow cot in his hostel room and felt himself at the threshold of something. He was not a child—after a few hours of lying in the dark, the enormity of what he was doing dawned on him. *It's not too late to change your mind*, a voice deep within him said to him. *You shouldn't playact at marriage!* But then, despite everything that that reasonable voice insisted on bringing to his attention, another part of him, the more dominant part of him, took over. *Too late to change your mind? Let it be too late*, it said, *let it be much too late.* When this voice spoke, he felt restless for the morning to arrive so that he could go to the beach and marry Ponni and bind her to him forever and ever as marriage was supposed to. If it was too late, he could not change his mind, could he? The thought was a strange comfort to him.

In Perambur, Ponni too did not sleep. She too lay wide-awake in the dark. She could hear her uncle's shallow breathing from the other room. She had not let slip a word to her uncle about what she had planned for the next day. There was no need to. After all, she and Ramu were not really getting married. The knowledge that Ramu loved her had inserted itself into her thoughts; but she resolutely put it out of her mind. Ramu's love did not have anything to do with what they were proposing. At best, what they were engaging in the next day was a political marriage, a marriage to make a point, not a marriage of love. And who better to do this with than Ramu, whom she had known from when they were still children, who got her (yes, she knew he did), and for whom she had learned great respect? She had been very clear to Ramu about what the marriage really meant. She trusted Ramu to understand. And hadn't Ramu been very clear that he too was approaching the next day in exactly the same spirit as she was? Indeed, wasn't the very idea of marrying to make a political point his? She refused to allow ideas of love to get in the way of politics. Tomorrow she and Ramu would make a statement, an important statement, to the world and to themselves, and then be on their separate ways. He would go back to Loyola and to his life there, and she would go to Muthu, who was returning to Madras tomorrow from shooting on location. She would go to Muthu directly after the wedding. She would tell him what she and Ramu had done. She wanted to see how Muthu would respond—would he understand the courage of her convictions? Would he understand that this was how change came into the world? Or would he be jealous and unreasonable? She wanted to know.

EARLY IN THE MORNING, RAMU bathed and took out his best shirt from his tin trunk. He was about to put the shirt on when he realized that he was still wearing the sacred thread that marked him as a Brahmin. He slipped the thread off his shoulder and threw it on his bed. He remembered the ceremony in Paavalampatti several years before when the thread had been conferred upon him as a sign of his impending manhood, his readiness to leave childhood behind and enter the world. The sacred thread marked him as twice-born—born once of his mother and then a second time through the ceremony of the sacred thread into the adult world. That ceremony had been full of priests and sacrificial fires and sacred chants. But that had not been his true entry into the world, Ramu realized now. Really, he would enter the world today on the beach, through his marriage to Ponni, when there would be neither priests nor family present. Ramu exited his room without a second thought for the sacred thread abandoned on his bed.

Ramu reached Marina Beach well before the appointed, inauspicious time. Arokiasamy accompanied him. However foolish Ramu might be, however unfair in his harsh accusations, Arokiasamy could not abandon his friend. Should the Self-Respecters consent to include Ramu and Ponni in the ceremony on the beach, he wanted to be there. He could not let Ramu go through this preposterous marriage on his own!

A crowd had already gathered on the beach, by the surging waves of the Bay of Bengal. The four couples stood to one side, looking around awkwardly, and around them milled political activists and gawking spectators. The sky was overcast. Though Madras was steaming hot, the monsoon had set in over Kerala many weeks before. It looked as if it might rain in the city later in the day. The air was sticky and clung thirstily to the skin. Ramu searched the crowd for Ponni. Had she changed her mind? Had she taken fright? He examined faces anxiously. He was relieved when he saw Meena making her way toward him through the crowd. Behind her came Ponni, head lowered.

"I see you decided to go through with it," Meena said to him by way of greeting. She seemed not at all happy to see him. Ponni did not say anything. She had made no attempt to dress up for the occasion. If anything, she had made less effort with her appearance than usual. Her thick, curly hair was pulled back in a careless knot. She was wearing one of her most ordinary cotton saris. But such was her beauty that it made no difference to Ramu. He looked at her and saw only her loveliness.

"I thought you would not come," Ramu said. Hope filled his heart that perhaps she did really want to marry him.

"It's still not too late," Meena pleaded with Ponni.

Ponni said, "I am not one to back down from what I said I would do. Ask Ramu whether he has changed his mind and no longer wants to go through with this."

Ramu said, "I am ready. I haven't changed my mind."

"Perhaps the Self-Respecters won't agree to marry you. I wouldn't if I were in their place," Meena muttered irritably.

Meena's words made Ramu stir himself. There was no time to be lost. He persuaded a reluctant Arokiasamy to go with him to a makeshift awning set up on the beach sands. Under the awning, officious men who were in charge of the event sat at two tables bearing registers and legal paper. To his satisfaction and Arokiasamy's secret disappointment, one of the men was a slight acquaintance of Arokiasamy. The man also knew Ponni's uncle Chellappa well by repute. And he had attended a performance of *The Ramayana: The True Story!* When Ramu explained that he intended to marry Ponni, the man was delighted—after all, wasn't the point of the wedding precisely to make the kind of public statement Ramu had indicated he and Ponni were interested in making? He conferred with the other men and, as soon as consent had been obtained to include Ramu and Ponni in the ceremony, conveyed to them what needed to be done and when.

Between the awning and the churning gray waves, the four couples originally scheduled to marry faced each other, the brides on one side and the bridegrooms on the other. Ponni and Ramu joined the lines, each holding a garland of flowers in which Ramu recognized the bright yellow of marigold and the sweet fragrance of jasmine. Ramu had no interest in the men who stood to either side of him or in the women who flanked Ponni. He looked at Ponni. She did not look back at him. The ceremony was short. A few words were read out that Ramu was to repeat. He had trouble paying attention. He repeated with half a mind the words that registered and pretended to mumble the rest: ". . . Today our conjugal life based on love begins. From today I accept you, my dear and beloved comrade, as my spouse, so that I may consecrate my love and cooperation for the cause of social progress, in such a manner as would not contradict your desires . . ." He heard and repeated that he and Ponni were to take each other as "life-partners." The exact inauspicious moment—chosen astrologically for its supreme misfortune—arrived, marked by a burst of drums and woodwinds and shouts for the brides and bridegrooms to exchange garlands. Ramu stepped boldly forward and placed his garland around Ponni's neck. Then he bent his head to receive hers. Almost before it began, the wedding was over. Ramu felt a rush of emotion. He was married now. And to Ponni!

Ramu and Ponni rejoined Meena and Arokiasamy, neither one of whom could find it within themselves to congratulate the newlywed couple. Still elated, Ramu thought, *I should take Ponni's hand.* He did not. He could not. He looked at Ponni and saw immediately that he could not. In the general air of gaiety, the four of them formed a peculiar group. Ramu did not feel somber, but he was the exception. Ponni, Arokiasamy, and Meena looked up at the overcast sky, looked down at the beach sand, looked around at the other joyful newlyweds and their companions—they looked anywhere but at him or at one another. Ponni and Ramu were called to have their marriage registered. The registration was not official: it had no legal force, but still it was a way of solemnizing what had just occurred. Meena and Arokiasamy served as witnesses.

Then all the newlyweds and gathered witnesses were asked to sit on the sand to listen to fiery speeches condemning caste, Brahmins, and superstition. The policemen monitoring the event stood to one side and listened. One of the speeches was by a woman who praised the ceremony and contrasted it to the traditional Brahminical ritual, which she said was full of superstitions and contained no talk of love or equality between the married couple. The speeches made Ramu restless. He wanted to leave, but Ponni said severely, "This is the main thing. This is the only important part." They were the first words she had spoken since their exchange of garlands. They stayed.

Afterward, Ramu, finally impatient of how the others were behaving, said, "What should we do now? We should celebrate. Let's go to Bukhari's." Bukhari's was a famous restaurant on the beach, not far from where the ceremony had been held. It seemed to Ramu an appropriate place to commemorate his newly married state.

Just for a moment there was softness in Ponni's eyes. She said, suddenly gentle in a way that contrasted with her previous manner, "I have some work. I have to go back to Perambur." She did not say she was going to Muthu. She turned abruptly and set off toward the road that ran along the beach, Meena trailing behind her. Before she reached the road, she removed the garland Ramu had placed around her neck and gave it to Meena.

"Are you happy now?" Arokiasamy asked. Without waiting for an answer, he too turned and briskly followed Ponni and Meena to the road. Ramu ran to catch up with him. Arokiasamy said with a sigh, "I wish you the best, Ramu. I really do."

Ramu was not listening. He thought, *Tomorrow I'll go to Ponni. To my wife.* Wife. He was determined to have a frank conversation with Ponni first thing the next day about that word—and about their meetings at the ruined fort in Paavalamapatti years ago, and about Muthu, and about how he had discovered her father Murugappa's body, and about everything else they had studiously avoided since they had reconnected in Madras.

But early the next morning, before he could go to her, Ponni came to Ramu. The watchman who manned the gate to the Loyola College hostel knocked on his door to let him know she was there. The watchman was doing him a favor, for it was not acceptable to receive female visitors at the hostel, especially at such an early hour, when it was barely light. The watchman had no idea how she had managed to get past the college's main gates on Sterling Road. Ramu hurriedly threw on shirt and trousers and stopped only to wash his face.

Ponni was waiting outside the gates of the hostel. Ramu went up to her and said, "Come." He led her away from the prying eyes of the watchman, toward the Church of Christ the King, gleaming white in the gray dawn. It had rained lightly in the night and the dirt crunched under their feet. The doors of the church were open even at this early hour, so he led Ponni around to the secluded side facing away from the hostel. Here the church adjoined ancient gravestones under trees; beyond the gravestones was the field where he sometimes kicked around a ball with friends. They stopped under one of the arched windows of the church.

Ponni looked disheveled, as if she had not slept all night. She looked like a ghost. She said, speaking abruptly, "I wanted to make something clear."

Ramu looked at the pools of rainwater on the field. He felt a wrenching within at Ponni's ominous tone. He knew what was coming. Some part of him had always known. Still, he feared it. As if to preempt her and whatever she wanted to say, he spoke quickly. "I was planning to come to you today. I too wanted to talk to you."

Ponni nodded as if in affirmation, but then said, "Muthu came to see me yesterday. After the ceremony on the beach." She did not say what had really happened, that she had gone to Muthu.

Ramu felt again the wrenching within, only deeper, stronger, more unbearable.

Ponni spoke gently. "You know he and I are lovers."

Ramu did not say anything. He could not say anything. He felt like crying. A grown man crying!

"You know our marriage does not mean anything. It's not that I don't believe in what we did yesterday. I am proud of you. I am proud of what I did. I am proud of what *we* did. But we are not really married. I explained that to Muthu. He understands it too. He is waiting for me at home." She smiled a sad smile, for she was not sharing with Ramu the truth about how her conversation had gone. She and Muthu had fought first and then had fallen into each other's arms and made desperate love, which felt as if it meant something, as if it *had* to mean something. "He wants me to go away with him. I can't really leave my uncle. But I might for just a bit."

Ramu felt the tears on his face. He wanted to wipe them away, but he felt too proud to draw Ponni's attention to them. Then he saw that she was crying too. She said in a low, low voice, "I'm sorry."

Ramu wanted to speak. He wanted to say he was not sorry, he wanted to say he felt betrayed, he wanted to say he understood, he wanted to say he did not understand, he wanted to say many things. The words would not come. His throat felt dry. His thoughts had shattered into a million pieces and he could not pull them together again. He knew nothing he said would be any use. He knew Ponni was right. Arokiasamy was right. He had let his love blind him and imagined something he had no right to imagine.

"I'm sorry," Ponni repeated, her cheeks wet with tears.

Why was she crying? Ramu felt a burst of anger. The ceremony yesterday on the beach had spoken of love. He knew he felt love for Ponni. What did Ponni feel for him? Where was the love she was to feel for him? What right did she have to cry?

"I don't think we should meet any more," Ponni said. "I'm sorry, but I don't think you should come to Perambur anymore." Her voice was gentle, sad, as she spoke. "I'll miss you but I really don't want you to come. It's best for you and for me. You have to promise me."

Ramu nodded mutely.

Ponni turned and walked away along the wall of the church. She had not stopped crying. She turned the corner and then was gone.

LATER THAT DAY, PONNI TOLD her uncle Chellappa everything that had happened. Her uncle's face grew grave as he heard her. When she was done, he said bluntly, "What you did was not right, Ponni. And Ramu, he was wrong too. Both of you have behaved terribly foolishly."

She nodded in dejected agreement.

"I'm not saying you shouldn't have gone through a Self-Respect marriage with a man like Ramu. I'm not even saying that you could not have done exactly what you did with someone else. But a man is not a pawn on a chessboard. A pawn does not have feelings. A man does. Ramu loves you, but you don't love him."

Surprising her uncle and herself, Ponni blurted out, "Maybe I do." And then she hastened to add, "But not in that way."

"What way is that?"

Why was her uncle being so dense? Ponni said impatiently, "I don't want to be married to him. I don't love him that way."

"Then what you did was not right."

"I know." It tore her up to confess it.

"And as for Ramu—I cannot forgive him for putting his feelings before yours in this rash way."

That made Ponni feel strangely protective of Ramu. She said, "Don't blame him. He too was making a political statement . . ." And then her voice trailed off, for she did not sound convincing even to herself.

"And Muthu? What about him?"

"You know how it has been with Muthu. I've told him about what happened with Ramu. And how it happened. He wasn't happy but he and I are going to try and fix things."

Chellappa saw how troubled and confused Ponni was. He felt immense love mixed in with worry for this girl he had raised into womanhood with very little knowledge of how such a thing was to be done. He had been young once himself, like Ponni and Ramu, and had done foolish and desperate things. He had struggled to figure out how to balance the demands of the heart against the demands of the larger world—indeed, he was struggling to figure it out even now. He could not judge her (or even Ramu, for that matter). He knew how passionate, idealistic, loving, and brave Ponni was—but she had had hardly any training for the challenges of life. He had never been one to lay down the law and he was not about to start. He said simply, "What you did with Ramu is done. It can't be undone. You both are young and you were foolish. There is no point in revisiting what happened. You were right to tell him he cannot come back here. You will only hurt him again and again. As for Muthu, I will say just one thing. Muthu loves no one more than himself."

Ponni lowered her eyes and asked, "So you think I should stop seeing Muthu."

Ponni's uncle heard how her voice caught in her throat as she spoke. He replied, "That is for you to decide. I can't decide that for you." It was the only answer he could make. Muthu was suave, handsome, dazzlingly successful, passionate in his own way. He could tell she was not ready to give him up. Not yet, anyway.

꩜

When Ramu told his father and Gomati Paati about his marriage to Ponni, two years had already passed and he was living in Calcutta. He had spent the last year at Loyola miserable and withdrawn. The world was in turmoil—India had become independent, riots and insurgencies had torn through the land, Gandhi had been assassinated by a Hindu fanatic. The old Ramu would have followed all the events with avid interest; he would have felt the urgent need to do *something.* The new one paid little attention. He fell sick several times and barely got through the final exams to complete his degree. Indeed, if Arokiasamy had not shepherded him through the revisions he might very well have failed. Afterward, his course of study at Loyola completed, he returned to Paavalampatti and to his old life, except that he was a new person. How could he behave as if nothing had changed when he had accumulated so many experiences in the three years he had been gone, when he had the deadly secret of his marriage to Ponni buried in his heart? Yes, *buried* was certainly the right word, for he felt as if his heart was nothing less than a desolate grave. He moped and was so surly that one day he came to blows with Uncle Siva over a remark.

Uncle Siva's generally impolitic attitude had grown with his years. The provocation was some contemptible comment Uncle Siva loudly made about Paraiyatchis. Since Ramu loved an Adi Dravidar woman and was indeed married to one, he took the remark very personally and grabbed Uncle Siva by the throat without warning. Uncle Siva was strong, and he flung Ramu off easily, like a bull flings an errant crow off its back. Then, standing over Ramu as he lay helpless on the floor, Uncle Siva said with a smirk, "I see you have tasted a Paraiyatchi." He smacked his lips lewdly as he said this. "That is it, isn't it? Is that why you no longer wear your sacred thread like any good Brahmin should?" Uncle Siva had never shared the indulgence with which Ramu's discarding of the sacred thread had been treated by Ramu's father and grandmother, who regarded it as a typical and temporary act on the part of a young man naively enamored of modern ways.

For Ramu, the incident with Uncle Siva was just one more indication of the intolerable nature of his narrow, cruel, caste-ridden village life. This life needed to be left behind. He determined to escape. He searched and took the first job he found that would take him away, far away. The job was managing the accounts of a Tamil company based in Calcutta that traded in timber from Burma. It was not much of a job—he would do a slightly glorified version of the job the Kanaku Pillai did for them. His father did not understand why he would take such work when there was no urgent need—surely their lands provided enough for them. Ramu's heart too was not in the job, such as it was. But Calcutta was sufficiently distant from Paavalampatti and Uncle Siva. And also from Madras and Ponni. As he had before in his life, he decided to escape into the larger world, only now he would go farther even than Madras.

So it was that several months after Ramu started his job, Gomati Paati and his father came to Calcutta. The apparent reason was to visit Ramu in his new home, but really they came to persuade him to marry. So grave did they consider this mission that Gomati Paati had chosen to ignore several injunctions pertaining to her condition as a widow to undertake the long journey by train to Calcutta. They had identified a girl, the only child of one of the most respected and affluent Brahmin landlords of a village not too far from Paavalampatti. The two families corresponded in status. Ramu's horoscope matched the girl's very well. The girl was attractive in appearance and had finished school.

It was not the first time Gomati Paati and his father had brought up the question of marriage with Ramu. Ever since he had finished at Loyola, Ramu had been subjected to their pressure on the topic. Now that a perfect alliance had been identified, Ramu found himself without excuses. He had no choice but to confess the truth that he was already married. He made a clean breast of things. He told his father and grandmother about Ponni and how his marriage had come about and where things stood now. He declared defiantly that even if he could, even if the law permitted (for Self-Respect marriages did not have legal force), he had no intention of marrying again. In Calcutta, he laid bare his heart to his stunned and uncomprehending father and grandmother.

"Murugappa's daughter? You married our Murugappa's daughter?" Ramu's father asked incredulously.

Gomati Paati said, "A Paraiyar girl. What were you thinking?"

"A Paraiyar girl!" Ramu's father repeated. "Our Murugappa's girl."

"Yes," Ramu said proudly. "Murugappa's daughter. An *Adi Dravidar* girl." He pointedly emphasized the different term he had used.

Gomati Paati recalled her suspicions from years before when Murugappa's daughter still lived in Paavalampatti. She recollected how she had confronted Ramu one evening when he had slunk back home from meeting Ponni. She had feared some terrible outcome. Her fear had made her strict with Ramu, but even she could not have predicted what had actually come to pass. She said, "You found Murugappa's body. Does the girl know that?"

"Yes," Ramu replied. He had not discussed Murugappa's death and his role in it with Ponni in Madras. It was a topic that he carefully avoided. But of course Ponni remembered. He was confident she did. How could it be otherwise?

"This will never work," Gomati Paati said.

"What do you mean?" Ramu asked.

Gomati Paati said, "We are different people, a different kind, with a different place in the world. That is why we marry our own kind and they marry theirs."

"I don't believe in any of that nonsense!" Ramu declared hotly, hating Gomati Paati's cowardly way of expressing her opposition to his marriage to Ponni. His suspicions regarding Uncle Siva's furtive liaisons—he had made use of his new eyes, his new way of looking at the world, during the time he had spent in Paavalampatti before fleeing to Calcutta—trembled on his lips, eager to burst out, but he contained himself. What would be the point of complicating matters with all that?

"This is the way it has been from the beginning," Gomati Paati insisted. "They have their place in the world. We have ours."

"Do you understand what you have done?" Ramu's father asked, love mixed with fear in his voice. "Everyone will shun you.

The world will turn against you. It won't matter what you think. You can't just recklessly go against the world. You will have no community. You have thrown away your sacred thread, but really you have thrown away more than that."

Ramu felt his father's fear. It awoke his own. He looked into his future. Surely it was dark. He felt alone, utterly alone, though not for the reasons his father thought. His reasons were in fact exactly the opposite of his father's. He felt keenly Ponni's absence from his life. He hid his despair and made himself say, "I don't care for the world. I did what I believe in." He did not say he loved Ponni and that was why he had married her. To use the word *love* in that instant he felt would be to sully it.

"You did not stop for a moment to think that you were doing this great thing without consulting me?" Ramu's father asked. "You were *marrying* and you did not think to tell me, *your father?*" His voice sounded injured, betrayed. Ramu remained silent, for he knew there was some justice in his father's complaint.

Their arguments went back and forth, by turns angry, conciliatory, rebuking, fearful, loving, though Ramu did not feel the love, such as it was. At one point Gomati Paati observed, "You are not really married. You yourself say you have never been husband-and-wife with this Paraiyar girl. You say you two have no intention of behaving like a married couple. She is in Madras and you are here in Calcutta, far away. You have made whatever statement you wanted to make to the world. Why should you not get on with your life now?" She went on to note the ways in which he could be freed to do so. There were rituals that would scrub away the stain of his reckless deed. If one were to spend the money, anything could be set right. There were penances that would dilute and deflect the karmic force of Ramu's thoughtless act. Ramu had only to say the word and Gomati Paati would make inquiries.

Ramu glowered through Gomati Paati's speech, thinking of the bath she had made him take all those years ago in Paavalampatti when she had discovered his secret meetings with Ponni. When she was done, he replied with a finality he did not feel, "You don't understand. I *am* married." Was he? Was he married? Ponni did not think so. Nevertheless, he knew that he could not imagine a life without Ponni. Ponni had sent him away but he could not leave her behind.

After a while, the heated arguments died away; everything that could be said had been said. Neither Gomati Paati, who feared the wantonness with which he had broken immemorial laws, nor his father, who worried about the cruelty of an uncomprehending world, could persuade Ramu to renounce his marriage. Ramu was especially perplexed by his father's stance. Where was the man who had discussed with him the absurdities and injustices of caste in days gone by—who had extolled the virtues of science? Where was the man who had encouraged him to question the world he lived in, the man who he had felt had understood him? Ramu was baffled by the paradox of his father. Had his father really held the opinions that he had in the past? Maybe he had. Maybe he still did. Yet, those opinions did not prevent his opposition to his marriage to Ponni. What, then, was the difference between his father and Uncle Siva? Wasn't his father a hypocrite? Vexing questions to answer. Ramu could not deny his love for his father, but suddenly the love felt cheap and tawdry. Suddenly it felt like a burden rather than a comfort. He secretly began to look forward to the departure of his father and grandmother.

The final days of the visit were filled with awkward silences. Ramu's loss of caste and his limbo status with regard to marriage were no longer mentioned. Things could have been worse—it was Gomati Paati's love that kept his father from advancing the date of departure, that ruled out of bounds any discussion of the consequences of Ramu's loss of caste for the family as a whole. When Ramu returned at the end of the day from poring over the account books of the timber depot, he and his father exchanged the most perfunctory of greetings.

At last came the day that Gomati Paati and Ramu's father were to leave. In Howrah railway station, Gomati Paati lifted her two hands and cupped Ramu's face in them and said, "Child, write regularly. Take care of yourself. What has happened is over. What is the use of worrying about it now? If you are happy, that's enough for me." At that moment of leave-taking, her worries about immemorial laws seemed suddenly to vanish.

They were waiting for the train to arrive at the platform. Ramu's father looked away along the shimmering railway tracks in the direction the train was expected and did not speak. Ramu felt his own eyes fill with tears. He remembered how his father had sat by his bed when he fell sick after finding Murugappa's body. He remembered how he would read from the newspaper and conjure up for him a larger world in which people behaved differently than in Paavalampatti. Where was that father now? He felt sad as well as bitter. These—his father and his grandmother—were his family, his only family in the world, but still he was glad they were leaving. He felt distant from them. The train arrived; they boarded it; it carried them far away from him. He returned to his life in Calcutta, feeling betrayed.

Ramu had come to Calcutta to escape into a larger world. In that great, alien city thronging with people and overrun with refugees of the partition, he surely had every chance of escape, did he not? His life was filled with people with whom, into whom, he endeavored mightily to flee, not stopping to consider why it was that he continued to feel alone, or why he could not bear to spend a lot of time with any single person. He lived in a tenement building of single rooms with shared bathrooms down the hall. He knew most people in the building, which was in the Lake Market area, where many Tamils lived. Most of his neighbors were single Tamil men like him, but there was also the Gujarati trader with his young wife and the Malayalee mechanic come to try his luck in India's premier city. Ramu spoke to his neighbors even when language was a barrier and even if they showed no interest in being spoken to. His room was unadorned and barely adequate—Gomati Paati and his father had managed in it only with difficulty during the three weeks of their visit. The walls were a morose gray and marked by the water that had seeped into them in monsoons past. There was a cot and a desk and a chair. There were mats on which he and his father had slept during the visit, leaving the cot for Gomati Paati. It was the room of a man afraid to spend time by himself.

He ate his meals at a Tamil mess down the street from the building in which he lived, dawdling over his meal so that he could talk to the other customers, again mostly single men like him. He filled his life with their lives. He took the tram down Rash Behari Avenue to the timber depot in Ballyganj every morning and back again in the evenings. He watched the people on the tram and in the streets and wondered. The well-proportioned bahu with keychain tucked into her sari at the waist, the garrulous men in white dhotis and kurtas around a teashop: what dreams and worries filled their heads and hearts? He struck up conversations in English with his fellow passengers on the tram, eager to replace his thoughts with their stories. Once he felt an overpowering desire to touch the thin shoulder of a rickshaw puller running alongside the tram with his load behind him. To the great consternation of the rickshaw puller, he did so, reaching through the window and feeling for a moment the bony shoulder.

At the timber depot he counted up the money, made entries in the enormous leather-bound ledger, helped the owner, a Chettiar originally from Thanjavur, with his correspondence, and visited the bank or business partners with him. The work had little connection to the economics he had read at Loyola. It was dull and unfulfilling, but his office was at the very entrance to the depot, so that the clamorous sounds and smells of the street entered at will. He annoyed the Chettiar by inviting in passersby and by talking at length to the customers who visited. Sometimes he unshackled himself from the green pages of his ledger and escaped into the dark interior of the depot to watch the workers unload the fresh timber. He loved listening to their loud chatter as they stacked all manner of wood all the way up to the ceiling, though he understood virtually nothing of what they said. He loved the smell of their sweaty bodies mingling with the scent of sawdust. When the workers were done, he would run his fingers over a smoothly planed plank and try to imagine the rustling beauty of the living tree from which it had been wrought. He felt keenly the changeability of the restless world.

Into this protean world in which Ramu was trying desperately to drown himself, the monsoons came in a torrent. The incessant rain—gray and formless and all-encompassing—washed away the sharp edges of the alien city. New feelings stirred in Ramu. He found himself a lover. Her name was Munmun. She sold mishti dohi in little clay pots in a shack at the corner of the street in which Ramu lived. Ramu, who had developed a liking for the sweetened yogurt, had taken to stopping at the shack almost every day on his way home from work. If there was no other customer, the rain falling in sheets from the black sky became an excuse for him to linger under the canvas awning of the wooden lean-to; for, along with the mishti dohi, he had formed a taste for its seller, who had large soft eyes and shiny hair either tied in a tight knot at the back of the head or else left loose on her shoulders when wet from a bath.

For several months now, Ramu had felt the desperate need for a lover. He had felt the need to escape into love, to be touched by it, or if not by love (he had little hope of finding it again), then lust. Lust too would suffice. Munmun had a son but no man by her side. Unattached just like him (though, really, he was still attached to Ponni), she filled him with desire. Ramu stood under the awning, scooped the mishti dohi out of the clay pot with his fingers, and boldly stared at Munmun. He knew his lust smoldered plainly in his eyes even in the weak light of the hurricane lamp swinging back and forth from a bamboo pole in the wind. He refused to feel embarrassed by the force of his twisting, cutting need for this complete stranger who squatted beside her pots of mishti dohi and looked up at him with such innocent eyes.

One evening Ramu deliberately let his fingers brush against Munmun's arm as she handed him a clay pot of mishti dohi. The gesture, he realized with a shameless thrill at the very moment he made it, was borrowed. Had he not seen Muthu brush Ponni's arm in just such a way that evening years before when he had finally found Ponni in Madras? He had now unwittingly reproduced the same gesture with Munmun, who sat back on her haunches, her breasts straining against her tight blouse. She answered by glancing up at him quizzically but not uninvitingly. He touched her lightly on her cheek.

She rose and took him by the hand. She led him to a room (really a hole in the wall) behind the shack, saying, "Esho, esho," which Ramu by now knew meant *come* in Bengali. Inside, she drew

Ramu to herself in the inky dark. He felt the softness of her flesh against his and breathed in her smell—a mustard oil smell—deeply. Sensing his awkwardness, she dropped her sari and guided his hands to all the right places. He found the softness of her breasts and the trembling smoothness of her lips and the bony thrust of her hips. And then he was on a mat on the floor and her fingers were on his nipples and her tongue was in his mouth. First, he kissed her back softly and then harder, desperately. He thrust himself inside her and felt her shudder under him and press herself against him so that his face was in her smooth hair. When they were done, he got up from the mat and dressed himself silently and went back to his room down the street in the pouring rain. He lay down wet on his cot with his face to the wall. He thought of Ponni and felt ashamed. Then he thought of Ponni with Muthu (probably together at that very moment) and he was not ashamed any more. Then he thought of Ponni again.

In the days that followed, Ramu went to Munmun regularly. With his limited Bengali, he discovered she was a refugee from East Bengal—a piece of humanity torn up and thrown into the world by the partition of two years before. Nineteen forty-seven had been the year both of independence and of the violent heaving of hapless millions of lives from one part of the earth to another. Ramu tried to imagine the terrified flights and bold gambles that had brought Munmun from Dhaka to Calcutta. Even as Ramu had spent 1947 far away in peaceful Madras moping over Ponni and desultorily reading newspaper accounts of the birth of India and Pakistan, Munmun had been caught up in the maelstrom of the partition. When Munmun's son, perhaps eight years of age, looked at Ramu with eyes of unnatural emptiness, of black nothingness, Ramu could not help wondering. His imagination fired by what he had read and heard, Ramu pictured merciless knives, raging fires, and bloody sticks driving Munmun and her son from place to place until they had ended up in this hole near Rash Behari Avenue in Calcutta. What had happened to the boy's father? Had he been lost to a stab from a knife or a blow from a stick? Munmun did not say and Ramu could not ask.

The hole in the wall was Munmun's home. Ramu and Munmun made love in it while her boy lay outside on a mat under the awning. Ramu learned when he should kiss her gently and when she liked his hands to be rough on her breasts and between her legs. He learned the endless pleasures of her hands and her tongue and her teeth on his body. He learned what would make her moan and bring the alien words tumbling over her lips. The second time that they were together, he took out some money and left it under the mat on which they had made love. She did not protest. She only looked silently at him out of her enormous eyes in the dim light seeping in from the hurricane lamp outside. A few days later, he gave her some more. She herself never asked him for money, or said of the money he left that it was too much or too little. He came, they made love, he went away. Sometimes they spoke a little, restricted by his broken Bengali. Sometimes he left her money. This was the extent of their interaction, though Ramu certainly sensed a deepening of feeling within himself for her. Once he arrived to find her weeping silently in the darkness of her hole. Then he took her in his arms and held her until she stopped. He did not ask her why she was weeping, for he knew he would understand little of any answer she might make. They did not make love that night. When he left, he gently slid the money that he had brought under her mat as usual.

Letters arrived from Gomati Paati in Paavalampatti and from Arokiasamy in Madras. Ramu's father did not write. The letters from Paavalampatti were sometimes accompanied by money. Ramu kept the money and threw away the letters without replying. Arokiasamy's letters were full of news. He had found a job in an elite school in Madras. It was the last place he wanted to work but his father had compelled him and he had consented for the time being because he did not want to leave the city. He missed Ramu and implored him to return so that he could free Arokiasamy from his bourgeois existence teaching the children of bourgeois Indians. Arokiasamy's letters were filled with schemes for them to pursue together—they would become radical publishers of Tamil political tracts and experimental novels; they would start a fishermen's cooperative (of course he was aware that neither knew anything about fishing, but fishermen were sorely oppressed); they would set up a commune for writers and artists with a social conscience on the coast road leading south from Madras to Mahabalipuram.

His letters also mentioned friends and acquaintances. Meena was getting married (in fact, Meena had asked him to invite Ramu to the small, simple wedding). Kannan had at last succeeded in entering a reputed engineering college in the north as his father had desired. Muthu was rapidly rising to stardom in the Tamil film world. His last two films had done exceptionally well (as even Ramu in Calcutta might have heard) and he was being offered lead roles now. Despite his growing success, he remained committed to his political views.

Of Ponni, Arokiasamy's letters said little, only that she was well. Ramu understood Arokiasamy's reticence. Unlike the letters from Paavalampatti, he put Arokiasamy's letters away carefully in his desk to reread. Ponni was not to be found in them. Still they were a link to her.

The days passed. The monsoons ended. He made love to Munmun. He gave her money. He went to his dull job in Ballyganj. The weather grew cooler. He made love to Munmun. He lay in his cot, his face to the wall, and thought of Ponni. The days passed.

Finally, a telegram broke the round of days. It brought terrible news and abruptly ended Ramu's time in Calcutta. Arokiasamy sent the telegram care of the Chettiar's timber depot. It read, "Return urgently. Chellappa-Sir dead. Ponni doing badly." Ramu went immediately to the Chettiar and said, "I have to make a trip to Madras. There has been a death in the family." Then, still in a state of shock, he went back to his room and packed up his few belongings in the green tin trunk that had been his companion in his travels since he had first gone to Loyola from Paavalampatti.

On his way to the tram that would take him to Howrah railway station, Ramu stopped at Munmun's shop. Munmun sat under her canvas awning, waving flies away from her pots of mishti dohi. It was January and she had a worn blanket around her shoulders to protect her from the chill in the air. She saw the trunk in Ramu's hand and at once understood. Ramu handed her an envelope.

He had taken all the money he had to spare and put it in that envelope. He said in the little Bengali he knew, "Ami Madras choley jaachey, ami firothey ashbey na," which he knew meant *I am going to Madras, I will not be coming back.* It was only when the words were out of his mouth that Ramu himself realized he was leaving Calcutta for good.

As always, Munmun's boy lay on his mat and stared up at Ramu with big vacant eyes. Munmun took the envelope silently and nodded. Ramu walked away without looking back. On the tram to Howrah, it occurred to Ramu that he had never learned the name of Munmun's son. He thought, *Whatever it was that happened between Munmun and me, it was not bad.* He looked out the window at the passing streets of Calcutta and again reassured himself, *What happened happened the only way it could. No harm was done to anyone.* He looked out the window and told himself that again and again.

Then a sense of anticipation began to gather itself within him. Arokiasamy's telegram had made it seem that Ponni needed him. Ponni. Soon he would see her again. Very soon. But before he could savor the pleasure of that thought, it was chased out by the rest of the telegram: Ponni's uncle was *dead.* Chellappa dead. That man of unbounded industry. Dead, well before his time—he could not have been more than in his mid-forties at most. He remembered the time he had spent with Chellappa surrounded by the machines in New Age Press. He had not seen him after the abrupt break with Ponni—how could he?—and now that Chellappa was dead he regretted deeply that he hadn't. He felt that his return to Madras would be a kind of honoring of that remarkable man.

At Howrah Station, Ramu sent Arokiasamy a telegram from the post office, apprising him of his arrival. Because of the unplanned nature of his departure, he had to travel to Madras by the appallingly crowded unreserved coach. He jostled for scant space with his fellow passengers for a journey exceeding three days. He found a spot in the corridor where he had to ignore the curses of passengers stepping over him on their way to the filthy toilet or the exit. There he sat on his trunk and brooded on Arokiasamy's telegram. *Chellappa-Sar was dead. Ponni needed him.* Ponni. He was returning for her, then. Whatever that meant. He knew now that Arokia had been right, Meena had been right: he should not have gone through with that Self-Respect marriage on the beach. He had taken advantage of Ponni when she was miserable—true, because he loved her, but still his selfishness in what had happened could not be denied. All that was in the past, though. He was older and, hopefully, wiser. What would happen with Ponni now, when he got back to Madras? And what of her relationship with Muthu? No answers, but in a way, it did not matter, for he was done with Calcutta. He thought back on his time in that vast city of millions, where he had been a refugee. Like Munmun. Like her boy. The moment the comparison occurred to him, he had a vision of the boy with empty eyes and felt ashamed. He himself a refugee? Hardly—at most he had run away to Calcutta because of disappointment in affairs of the heart. He was a love refugee. What kind of a victim was that when compared to Munmun and her boy?

In this fashion, while he sat perched on his upright trunk, Ramu's mind went round and round over the previous years like the wheels of the swaying train racing toward Madras down the east coast of India. He arrived tired and dirty at Madras Central, where Arokiasamy met him looking rested and smelling of fresh talcum powder. Despite his begrimed condition, Arokiasamy gave him a great hug. It was the hug that finally revived Ramu's spirits. Ramu and Arokiasamy held each other for a long, emotional moment. It was good to be back after three years away.

Ramu had arrived in Madras on a beautiful January morning, washed clean by the rain the previous night. He marveled that he was actually back in Madras. After the hug, Arokiasamy held him at arm's length and said, with concern in his voice, "You have grown very thin, Ramu, even thinner than usual," and then he blurted out, "Ponni is doing very badly. Ever since Chellappa-Sar died, she's been in a terrible way."

"Chellappa-Sar is dead! It seems impossible. What happened?"

"Heart attack. He was working at a press in his shop and just keeled over. It was a while before he was found. He had fallen forward on the press as if he was hugging it. Imagine that! His chest was stained with printer's ink. He had somehow knocked a can over. Even his lips were black with the ink."

"It's hard to take in. No one was more alive than Chellappa-Sar. Always busy with something or the other. In all the time I knew him, I don't think I saw him sitting idle once."

"He was working like a maniac for months before he died. Not just at the press but on something else. He was very hush-hush about it. He went on several trips to Telengana. Even Ponni knew very little about what he was doing. He said it was too dangerous. He said he would tell her when the time was right. And then he was dead. Yesterday men came from Kerala and took away boxes of things."

"What things?"

Arokiasamy shook his head to indicate ignorance. "I don't think even Ponni knows. Or if she does she won't say. But you know the peasants in Telengana have been in revolt for years. Perhaps it was something to do with that."

They reached the jutka Arokiasamy had hired to take them to Ponni's home in Perambur. They threw Ramu's tin trunk into the front of the carriage and sat with their legs dangling out the back. As the horse—a scrawny brown nag, really—clip-clopped through the familiar streets of Madras, weaving its way between trams and cars and hand rickshaws, Ramu bounced up and down in the carriage and wondered why they were going to Perambur. There had been that confusing part of the telegram implying he needed to return to Madras immediately for Ponni. And now they were on their way to Perambur straight from the station. What did it all mean? Did Ponni know they were coming? What would Muthu think?

As if reading his mind, Arokiasamy said, "Muthu and Ponni are not together anymore."

Ramu tried to hide his joy. He assumed a calm demeanor and said, "Why? What happened?"

"Muthu turned out a fraud. He cheated on Ponni. Ponni warned him. He just kept lying to her. Finally, she ended it."

"The newspapers were full of stories about Muthu and different women from the film world. I did not know what to think of them. After all, newspapers often make up gossip."

"Unfortunately, enough of the stories were true. You know Ponni. She is not one to put up with that kind of behavior." He deliberately left out the twists and turns, Muthu's wheedling ways and inveterate lies, all the terrible scenes. He had seen Ponni through all of it. He had watched her grow painfully into a new person.

Suddenly, Ramu felt anxious about his appearance. He felt soiled from the train journey. He wished he had freshened up at the station. Too late now.

Arokiasamy continued, "Be careful with Ponni, Ramu. She has had a hard year. I did not mention all the trouble with Muthu in my letters because Ponni did not want me to. And now it's hardly been four days since her uncle died. It's a lot. She's brave, but it's a lot. Don't be surprised at how you find her." There was concern and fondness for Ponni in his voice.

"Has she said anything about me? About how she feels about me?"

"She and I have talked. She knows she did not behave properly. The marriage. The way it happened. She realizes now you might have been hurt by it. She's told me many times that she regrets her behavior and that she appreciates yours through the whole thing. But you know, Ramu, she's not being fair to herself. She feels horrible for what she did and so wants to take all the responsibility herself. You have to admit you too have a share in the blame."

"I do, Arokia. I have spent a long time thinking about this. Believe me, I know I do."

"I am glad to hear you say that," Arokiasamy said, with affection in his voice.

"How long has it been since Ponni and Muthu separated?"

"About six months, I think. I'm sorry, Ramu, but Ponni insisted I should not write to you about this matter. I think she was afraid of doing something stupid again, something that would hurt you. It's only now with her uncle's death that she seems to have shifted a little. She knows I sent you a telegram. She wants to see you again, but after everything that has happened she herself would never ask you to come back from Calcutta for her. At least that is my interpretation of the situation."

"I'm not going back to Calcutta," Ramu stated matter-of-factly. "It has nothing to do with her. It doesn't matter how things turn out between Ponni and me. I'm not going back."

Arokiasamy nodded his understanding. His pleasure was clearly evident on his face.

The jutka drew up in front of the worn sign of New Age Press. The secured wooden doors of the shop were an unmistakable indication of the catastrophe that had befallen the proprietor. Never before had Ramu seen the doors shut during the daytime. After he had paid for the jutka, he and Arokiasamy made their way around to the back of the building. Ramu remembered Ponni's home filled with lively voices raised in loud and good-natured argument. Now only silence welled out of the open door to greet their arrival. Arokiasamy entered without knocking and Ramu followed him sadly into the familiar corridor, his tin trunk in his hand. Here, in this very house, their temporary theater group had planned their scandalous play about Rama, Raavanan, and Sita. He remembered how every time he as Rama betrayed Ponni as Sita, the words had stuck in his throat. He had had to force them out. How keenly he had felt the weight of the fictional dialogues in his own life during those months of rehearsal and performance!

Ponni and Meena were in the room with the bookshelves and the desk. They were dumping books into wooden crates that stood in the middle of the room. They worked together in a silence that spoke more than words, for Meena was not a woman to lightly abjure speech. The grim diligence with which they were clearing the shelves made the somber mood in the room palpable. Instinctively, Ramu and Arokiasamy halted at the room's entrance, as if afraid to intrude.

Ramu's eyes went immediately to Ponni, who was reaching for a book high on a shelf. He saw she had let her hair grow. Thick and curly, it tumbled now over a shoulder almost to her waist. The lovely hair framed her upturned face, whose contemplative expression as she read the spine of the book was caught in the sunlight entering from the far window. As always, she wore no jewelry—no nose ring, no earring, not even the plainest chain around her neck. Ramu looked at her and felt inside the sharp throb of love and desire. He recognized both—the two were not the same, he now knew. How magnificent she was! More beautiful than ever. Her enthralling face—countless were the times he had imagined himself gently tracing its features with his fingers—was the same, and yet not the same. The years had molded her beauty—the pure lines as if chiseled out of stone—into an even greater loveliness. In the sunlight falling across her face, he saw that it had acquired fresh depths and layers. The subtle mark of life was upon her visage and it only made her more beguiling than ever to Ramu.

"Yes," Arokiasamy agreed softly so that only Ramu could hear. "She is beautiful." Pride and affection mixed in his voice. Ramu sensed with satisfaction how the friendship between Arokiasamy and Ponni had deepened in the intervening years.

At just that moment, Ponni turned, her hand still on the spine of the book. Seeing Ramu and Arokiasamy at the door, she stepped away from the shelf and, with a deft gesture, gathered up her hair in a knot. "You have arrived," she observed. "I hope the journey from Calcutta was comfortable?"

"I am so sorry about your uncle," Ramu replied. "I can still hardly believe he is gone." Even as the words left his mouth, he felt their banality.

Ponni nodded. For a moment, it seemed she was going to say something that would break the false formality of the moment. And then she looked away and simply nodded again.

Meena came forward and said, without her usual jovial manner, "I am glad you could come. It is very good of you."

"How could I not?" Ramu cried in reply. "The moment I got the telegram I left for Madras." He wanted to rush forward and gather Ponni in his arms, so lost did she seem despite her brave manner, so unlike her usual commanding self.

They, all four of them, stood looking at each other awkwardly in that little cluttered room, until Arokiasamy said, "Ramu probably wants to have a bath. I'm sure he wants to wash away the grime of the journey. Is there a towel for him?"

Meena got soap and a towel while Ramu drew up a bucket of water from the well at the back of the building. Ramu carried the water to the adjoining bathroom, which was three tin walls and a wooden door, open to the bright blue January sky. He poured the cold water over his head directly from the bucket and scrubbed himself with the soap. And then he poured more water to wash away the soap. He thought of Ponni as he did so. How was he to behave toward her? She was no longer with Muthu. He, Ramu, was married to her and yet not married. How should he behave in these circumstances? The situation was vexing.

When Ramu returned to the house feeling refreshed from his bath, Ponni was lying down. Arokiasamy and Meena had retreated to the kitchen and were speaking in whispers. They stopped abruptly when Ramu appeared, but not before Ramu felt he had heard his name and Ponni's mentioned.

Meena said to him, "Ponni is resting. She hardly slept all night. Ever since the funeral she's been like this—full of energy one minute, sad and quiet the next."

Arokiasamy glanced at his watch, made a face, and said, "It's late. I should go to my school. Can you stay here until I come back, Ramu?"

Ramu nodded.

Then Meena said, "I should leave too. I should go home. I have been here since the day before yesterday. My husband must think I have run away!" She laughed in a manner that hinted of the old Meena, the Meena Ramu knew so well.

Meena and Arokiasamy left, promising to return in the evening. After they had gone, Ramu peeked into the other room. Ponni had her face to the wall. He could not tell whether she was asleep or pretending to be. He decided to go to the shop on Naidu Street to get the day's *Hindu.* On his return, he sat on the rough pocked surface of the washing stone by the well and read about Prime Minister Nehru's doings in the newspaper until he heard sounds emanating from the house. He went back inside to find Ponni once again at work on the bookshelves. He said to her, "Arokiasamy and Meena have left. They said they would be back later today. I think they expect me to stay until they return." It was his way of broaching the subject of his presence in her home. He had rehearsed the words outside by the well.

At first a look of irritation passed over Ponni's face. "I'm not a child," she said grumpily. And then her face softened and she said, "They mean well." She looked at Ramu and added, "Thank you for coming. My uncle liked you. Did you know that?"

Ramu shook his head.

Ponni continued, "He remembered you as a boy. He said he still saw that boy in you." Just to be clear, she added, "He meant that in a good way."

"I'm glad," Ramu said sincerely. "I had a lot of respect for your uncle. He was an amazing man. He did brave things in his life."

"He was certainly amazing to me," Ponni said, tears filling her eyes. "Without him I have no idea where I would be today. He was my only family. I have lost touch with everybody else—my brothers, sisters." She gathered herself and said, "Do you want to help me with the books?"

"What am I to do?"

"Put them in the boxes. The English go in this box and the Tamil in the other. If the book is in a really bad condition, leave it here on the floor."

"But why? Are you giving these books away?"

"I've found someone who will buy them. I need the money. Badly. Or else I would not be selling them. I know how much my uncle loved these books."

"What about the shop? Isn't there money there?"

"No, not at all. Nothing in the shop was my uncle's. Everything is owed to someone or other. I can't be sentimental about these books." Ponni pursed her lips and pulled another book off a shelf.

Ramu began to help Ponni. They worked silently for a while and then Ponni asked, "How was Calcutta?"

Ramu described the timber depot and the building he had lived in, but did not mention Munmun. When he was done, he said, "I am not going back to Calcutta. It's a fine city but it's time for me to come back to Madras."

"Where are you staying in Madras?" Ponni asked, glancing back from the shelf she was clearing.

"I don't know yet."

A peculiar look crossed Ponni's face, one that Ramu could not easily interpret. He could not know that she was thinking her uncle was right—that there was something of the boy, an earnest and sincere boy, still in Ramu. Quite possibly he would never lose that boyishness. She hoped he didn't. It was one of the most endearing things about him.

"You should stay here," Ponni said. She laughed awkwardly and added, "After all, we are married."

Ramu laughed back and said, "True. We are." He felt his heart lurch. What was behind Ponni's remark? Was it bold acknowledgment? Or playful dismissal?

"Yes," Ponni repeated. "You should stay here. But let's not assume anything. Let's see how things go."

~

So Ramu stayed with Ponni on his return from Calcutta. In the days that followed, Ponni slept in the kitchen and Ramu in the room opposite. In the mornings, she cooked while he went to the market on Naidu Street to buy vegetables and other provisions. But they did not eat together. It wasn't because of different diets. Ramu had long since begun to eat meat and had even tried fish in Calcutta. Rather, it was because Ponni continued to be guarded with him. When she sat down to eat, she did not invite him and he definitely felt hesitant to invite himself. Having taken the plunge and asked him to stay, she seemed now to retreat within herself and hold him at a distance. Even though Ramu saw how overwhelmed she was by the task of untangling the web of debts and obligations that was the printing press, he did not feel he could help her. She spent much time in the shop with Mohan, her uncle's assistant, meeting men who came to see her or else overseeing the carts that came to take away the equipment.

For his part, he dawdled through the day or else went through the newspapers for jobs. He spoke to Meena when she came visiting, which was often, such was her concern for Ponni. He wrote to the timber depot Chettiar as well as his landlord in Calcutta, informing them of his decision not to return. The Chettiar owed him unpaid wages but he had little hope that he would get the money. He knew he had left the Chettiar in a bit of a lurch by his sudden departure—he could expect no goodwill from him. Money worried Ramu. The little he had brought from Calcutta—he had given most of his money away to Munmun—would not last long. He discussed looking for a well-paying job in a school with Arokiasamy, but Arokiasamy was discouraging in this regard, for he himself was restless to find alternatives.

Ramu and Arokiasamy met most evenings at Arokiasamy's house in Royapettah. When they were not coming up with fantastic plans for the future, Ramu brought up Ponni. "You know how I feel about her, Arokia," he said, speaking plainly. "What I don't know is how she feels about me."

"Ponni's not the woman she was, Ramu," Arokiasamy replied. "She's been through a lot. Be patient." He wanted desperately to say more, to reassure his friend, but was afraid to in case he was wrong about how he thought Ponni felt.

Patience. That meant weeks passed by while Ramu lived in a continuing fog of uncertainty about his status with regard to Ponni. Certainly, there were times when the fog lifted a little and a moment of real communion between him and Ponni appeared—a moment when Ramu felt let in, when he felt less unsure about what he was doing there in Perambur in Ponni's home. One such moment was provoked by a story about Muthu. Ramu was going through the Tamil newspaper, seated as was his wont on the washing stone in the yard, when he came upon the story, which featured a glamorous picture of Muthu throwing out a dazzling smile. He had a carefully groomed mustache on his upper lip. He had made his eyes soft and alluring for the camera—which was not at all how Ramu remembered Muthu's eyes. The accompanying article lauded Muthu as the hottest new star in the Tamil cinema firmament. The first sentence read, *There may be a thousand established and aspiring stars in the cinema world, but not one of them has the beauty, the seriousness and the freshness of Muthu.*

Ponni surprised Ramu as he was reading and re-reading this article. She wandered out of the house to find him perched on the washing stone. In one hand, she had a notebook and pencil; she had been going through the accounts for her uncle's shop. Before Ramu could turn the page, she had noticed the article about Muthu and taken the newspaper out of his hands. She looked up from reading the story as Ramu watched with trepidation—how would she react?

Ponni burst out laughing. She waved the newspaper at Ramu. "What a ridiculous piece of nonsense!" she exclaimed. "According to this article, he's an angel. If only they knew. They should have interviewed me. I would have told them what he is really like." Impulsively, she took her pencil and scribbled on Muthu's picture. When she handed the newspaper back to Ramu, he saw that Muthu had sprouted a donkey's ears, a goat's beard, and tentacle eyes. Ramu could not help smiling. He felt a sudden release from the confusion of the preceding days. He grabbed the pencil from Ponni and drew a horn in the middle of Muthu's forehead. And then Ponni grabbed the pencil and newspaper back, scratched out the headline, and wrote in its place, giggling all the time, *Monster Man Terrorizes Tamil Film World.* Ramu burst out with a guffaw. It was his turn now. He wrote below the new headline, *Strange Happenings Reported in Movie Studios.* He was laughing so hard he could barely finish writing the words. As soon as he had, Ponni squeezed into a little bit of space: *Beast Eats Up Every Piece of Cloth in Sight, Actresses Terrified for Their Modesty.*

So they went back and forth, drawing or writing ridiculous things, bursting into peals of laughter every time, until not a bit of blank space was left on the sheet of newspaper. Muthu's picture was entirely obscured by their additions. Headlines and solemn statements on the monster's doings were scribbled into every available space. Ponni was so convulsed by merriment that she could hardly stand. Ramu had to make room so she too could perch on the rough surface of the washing stone. Sitting side by side with their shoulders touching, they would calm down for a moment, but then one or the other would point to something they had drawn or written and convulsions of laughter would follow. They stopped laughing only when Ponni made a ball of the newspaper and threw it over the fence into the adjoining rubbish-filled lot. And then, finally, they sat in quiet companionship on the washing stone, wiping the tears from their eyes, stomachs hurting, finally done.

⁓

January ended, February began, and Ponni's landlady descended promptly on their doorstep to collect the rent. The rent amount was not great, but with Ponni's difficult financial situation in mind Ramu offered to pay. When Ponni did not demur, the landlady threw Ramu a sharp glance and asked curtly, "Who is this?"

Surprising Ramu, Ponni replied, "My husband." The moment the words were out of her mouth, a look of embarrassment passed over her face. Clearly, she had surprised herself too.

The landlady, thin and rather prim-looking, narrowed her eyes to scrutinize Ramu, who stood behind Ponni in the shadowed corridor. She said suspiciously, "Husband? I had no idea you were married. Why is it that I have never seen him before?"

"I was in Calcutta. I returned recently."

"I don't see a wedding necklace around Ponni's neck."

"What is it to you?" Ponni asked hotly, very much annoyed at the interrogation. "I told you we are married. That should be enough for you. We don't believe in superstitions like wedding necklaces." Self-Respect marriages rejected the wedding necklace as an intolerable imposition on the woman.

"Shall I show you the marriage certificate?" Ramu asked, partly in sarcasm. He had the Self-Respect certificate safe in his tin trunk, though he knew it did not convey the status of a legally registered marriage.

"Why should we show her anything, Ramu?" Ponni railed. "Who is she to ask us these questions?"

The landlady said, doubtfully, "He doesn't look like one of you."

"What do you mean?" Ramu asked, himself provoked to greater indignation now. Of course the landlady was referring to their difference in caste. He knew it very well.

"Is that right?" Ponni cut in fiercely. "Why? Doesn't he look human to you? Don't you see that he has two arms, two legs, and a head with two eyes and a mouth?"

The landlady sighed as if at Ponni's childishness. "This is my house," she said. "I can throw you out any time I want. I won't have loose behavior here. Let me tell you that. You can't just bring any man you want into the house." She did not say *now that your uncle's dead* but the accusation was certainly implied. And then she added, "It is time to raise the rent. We'll talk about it the next time I come." She went away, tucking the money Ramu gave her into her blouse and leaving her ominous warning hanging in the air.

Ponni said, "What a shrew! If she tries to raise the rent because of you, I'll tell her a few things about the law."

"I have the marriage certificate," Ramu reassured her. "She can't use that excuse."

Ponni flashed a look of contempt at Ramu and said, "You are always so ready to give in, Ramu. Please stop doing that. People will take you more seriously if you do. That certificate means nothing. You can show it to her if you want. I'll show her nothing."

Taken aback at the vehemence of Ponni's reaction, Ramu retorted angrily, "Really, Ponni! You should watch the way you talk to people!"

Ever since their shared jollity over the Muthu newspaper story, there had been a new though unspoken rapport between them. But now Ponni glowered at Ramu, and then quickly stalked back into the house as if she feared what she might say. That night Ramu slept fitfully because he could not stop being upset at Ponni. A while after he had fallen into a light sleep, something unquiet in the dark woke him. He lay awake for a while until he realized that the restiveness he sensed was in the other room. He got up and went into the kitchen to investigate. A little light entered through the window, softening the gloom in the room. Ponni, reduced to a silhouette in the gray murk that was the kitchen in the night, was sitting up on her mat, staring blankly ahead. In that cinereous light Ponni seemed a ghost, forlorn and alone. She seemed so different from the Ponni Ramu knew in the clear light of day, so frail, so vulnerable, that his anger at her vanished instantly. "What's the matter?" he inquired gently.

A long moment passed before Ponni spoke. "I am sorry," Ponni said, in that plain and straightforward manner he loved. "I had no right to speak to you that way. Especially after how you have been toward me. Right from the beginning."

"What do you mean? I have things to answer for. I am not proud of how I behaved when we got married. I was rash, and selfish."

She nodded. "Both of us. We were both stupid and selfish."

He came closer. "Do you remember how we used to meet as children in the ruined fort in Paavalampatti?" he asked. "I have loved you ever since then, Ponni."

There. He had said it. He was glad. He felt a great relief. Let her make of it what she would.

A quietness followed his words, stepping softly into the gloom of the kitchen like a shy bride at a wedding. Ramu felt the stillness in Ponni, but because of the darkness he could not decipher the expression on her face. He did not wait for her to speak. He said, "I don't know what that means to you, but I felt you should know." And then, abruptly, he returned to his mat in the other room and lay down. He shut his eyes and listened to the silence in the kitchen. He had spoken. What did his speech signify to Ponni? He had no idea. None at all. That is why he was startled when a hand touched his shoulder. It was not expected. He did not know what he had expected.

"Ramu," Ponni said.

Ramu turned urgently and held Ponni. He held her and drew her to the mat on the floor of the room in which Chellappa's bookshelves had stood. She did not resist. She was weeping silently, her body shuddering with her sobs. He held her close but did not speak, suddenly afraid of the treachery of words. Perhaps for the same reason, Ponni too did not speak, letting her tears do the talking for her. Soon, inexplicably, he was weeping like Ponni, quietly. He did not know what Ponni's tears meant to her, but his tears were an enormous relief to him. A great cleansing. A great emptying. A washing away of unspoken, unspeakable things from their pasts. After a while, when they were done with their weeping, they touched each other with wonder and held each other so close that neither could fall asleep for a long time.

The morning after Ponni came to Ramu in the middle of the night, they lay on his mat long after the sun had slid across the wall opposite the window and disappeared into a corner, leaving its glow spread all through the bare little room. Ramu sensed a tranquility in Ponni that had been absent during the night, when he had gone into the kitchen to find her sitting up and staring into the darkness. He lay next to her now, gently stroking her arm with the tips of his fingers, afraid to break the calm. He thought, *I could lie here like this until the end of time* and was both pleased and amused that such a thought had occurred to him. He lifted his head up from the pillow and said, "Do you know what I was thinking just now? I could lie here like this until all time ends."

Ponni had her eyes closed. She did not open them. She laughed and said, "That's a very long time."

"I don't care. It would be nothing to me."

"We would just lie here? We would not get up for anything?"

"No. Not for anything."

"We would start smelling soon. In Madras weather, I give it two days at the most."

"I might. You never could." He poked theatrically at her nose. "Your fragrance is unfading."

"That's silly. You are very silly."

"No, I'm not." He grabbed the sheet that they had flung off during their night of tenderness and drew it over them as if to shut the world out. "The world itself will have to wait until we are ready to get back to it. It would not dare to disturb us with its smells and sounds and other nonsense."

Ponni's eyes flew open. In the translucent light beneath the thin sheet with which he had so grandly insulated them against the world, Ramu saw how very lovely her eyes were. They were lovelier than ever because he saw something new in them he had never seen before. "You are quite the lover," she said, laughing again. "And a poet. I didn't know."

"You make me one," Ramu replied very sincerely. He thought how wonderful it was to see Ponni at peace like this.

Ponni hugged him and said, "I'm glad you came back from Calcutta."

EVERYTHING WAS NOW NEW, THOUGH Ponni and Ramu kept mostly to their old routine, allowing Arokiasamy and Meena to understand what had happened only through inference and deduction. Ramu was kind and loving, but nevertheless Ponni felt odd in her altered relationship with him and so nothing was announced. Their reborn relationship was allowed simply to slide into view. Why did Ponni feel so peculiar in her relationship with her old husband who had now become her new lover? Was it because she could not help comparing him to Muthu? Muthu had been moody and unpredictable; Ramu was steady, generous. She loved Ramu's reluctance to judge, his almost unconditional support of her; nevertheless, she just could not bring herself to voice her love openly, freely, to him or indeed to Arokia and Meena. What was it that held her back? Was it that she had become used to the tempestuousness that had characterized her relationship with Muthu and found Ramu's steadiness somehow lacking? Or were the immense social differences between them—caste and class and all the rest of it—the reason? Or—the third and perhaps most disheartening possibility—was it something deeper still, something constitutive of her very nature, that made her hold back despite Ramu's tremendous openness to her? Was she broken in her capacity to love and be loved? Ponni felt this third possibility as the most frightening of them all, the one that gave her the greatest pause, made her the most nervous when she reflected on her developing relationship with Ramu.

One day, she said to Ramu, "I think we should make a new beginning." They were lying on a mat in the room that had held Chellappa's books, spent after an afternoon of lovemaking.

"What do you mean?"

"We should leave Madras. We should go away."

"Where would we go? What would we do?"

"Something meaningful. Something we could do together. So that we could make a new beginning together."

"Yes, but where? What?"

"Somewhere far away. We would leave Madras. We should start anew where what we do matters the most—among ordinary people."

"You are serious?"

"Very."

"Arokia has an idea. He is very excited about it. I am interested in it too."

"What is his idea?"

"He wants to start a school. A school that is the exact opposite of the school at which he works right now. For the really poor. For the children at the bottom of society."

"Where would this school be?"

"Far away from Madras. Exactly as you say."

"Does this faraway place have a name?"

"In Thirunelveli District."

"Near Paavalampatti? Near where we grew up?"

Ramu hastened to reassure Ponni. "No," he said. "On the other side. Closer to Thoothukudi. Somewhere around Ottappidaram. Not at all close to where you and I grew up. A Christian priest Arokia knows told him about that area. It's very arid and filled with stone quarries. Nothing like Paavalampatti. The workers have terrible lives. Arokia thinks the only way to change the atrocious conditions there is to start a school for the workers' children. That way when the children grow up they will have choices. They won't be slaves to the stone quarries, which is where they end up now. He and the priest have talked this idea over many times."

"A school?" Ponni was intrigued.

"Yes, a school! A school to change the world! Imagine if there had been a school in Paavalampatti for children like you."

"My life would have been different if there had been a school for me to go to regularly in Paavalampatti!"

"Arokia is very serious about this idea. I too would like to do it!"

Ponni caught Ramu's enthusiasm. She said excitedly, "Children! Working with them would be wonderful. I would love that."

Ramu said, "Let's do it, then! Arokiasamy will join us. We'll talk to his friend the priest. With the three of us working together, I'm sure the school will be a success."

"It'll be good to get out of Madras and work with children. It's good Arokia will join us. He is a smart man—full of spirit but also sensible. We will need someone like that."

"We can make it a success. I'm sure we can."

Their ardor for the school grew moment by moment. They sprang up from the mat and began planning it, imagining it in vivid detail. They paced the room, stopping only to grab the other by the arm when an especially exciting notion presented itself. Ponni wanted trees so there would be shade for the children. Ramu regretted that they had sold Chellappa's books; they would have made a fine library. So their planning went until Ponni's face suddenly fell.

"Money," she said. "What will we do for money? We can't start a school without money."

Ramu too was stumped for a moment. Then he said, "I'll ask my family."

"Your family? Do you think they'll give money for something like this? Why should they?" Her tone implied that she had no faith at all in his family.

Ramu had no answer. He had spoken impulsively. Ponni was right. His family had no reason to help him, especially after the way he had behaved following the Calcutta visit. *Never mind*, he thought. *All they can say is no.*

That very day he wrote to Gomati Paati—not to his father—explaining all that had happened and asking for financial assistance. He felt embarrassed writing the letter because it was his first since leaving Calcutta. There were several bombshells in it: he had quit his job in Calcutta (unexpected though this news would be, it was not likely to meet with much disapproval); he had returned to Madras and Ponni (this news he was certain would be received badly); and he wanted money (what chance then that this request would be granted?). To his surprise—and even more, to Ponni's—a few days later he received a positive-sounding letter from Gomati Paati (unaccountably he found it disappointing that the letter was not from his father). The letter was brief. She asked him to come to Paavalampatti to discuss his request, which the letter suggested was acceptable.

Ramu went, excitement and reluctance warring in his mind. This return to Paavalampatti was hard for him. He took the overnight express from Egmore to Thirunelveli Junction and then the local to Paavalampatti. He arrived late in the morning and hurried out of the little station. Proceeding up the all-too-familiar Meenakshisundareswarar Temple Street in the direction of the tall red-and-white-painted walls of the temple, he passed several neighbors. He wondered if they knew of his marriage to Ponni. Curious glances were thrown in his direction but Ramu kept his head down. Even with his eyes carefully lowered, however, he recognized his childhood friend Subbu's mother and Doctor Gopalan, who despite his advanced age stood tall and straight and as alert as ever on the thinnai of his house.

As he pushed aside the unlatched front door and stepped into the house in which he had grown up, Ramu heard Doctor Gopalan exhale loudly. The retired doctor had put two and two together to successfully come up with his identity—Ramu, prodigal grandson of the widow Gomati, who had fought with his uncle and fled. Before the morning was out the whole street would know of Ramu's return. Suddenly, Ramu regretted that he had attempted to slink unseen into Paavalampatti, as if he were a thief. Even if they knew of Ponni, and his relationship to her, what of it? Had he done something criminal by marrying Ponni? No! He banged the door shut behind him and yelled, "I'm home!" He would not be made to feel ashamed for the way he had chosen to live his life.

Uncle Siva emerged from within, but instead of coming forward to greet his nephew, returning home after so long, he stopped in the doorway leading further into the house from the enclosed front verandah. Blocking the way in, he said in a deliberately insolent manner, "So, you are here. What do you want? Why have you come?" He filled the frame of the door with his bulk. He was big and powerful and his mouth was red from the betel leaves he was chewing. The way he stood there made it clear he had no intention of letting Ramu pass. His handsome face, only a little thicker around the jowls because of the passing years, sneered at Ramu.

Ramu felt his hatred rise up within. He had no doubt Uncle Siva knew why he had come. He controlled himself and said in an even voice, "How are you, Uncle?" He had come as a supplicant. It would not do to be provoked into a repetition of the fight that had driven him from Paavalampatti the last time.

Before Uncle Siva could respond, Gomati Paati appeared, brushing her way past him to grab Ramu's hand. She pushed the hem of her white sari out of her face so that she could examine him properly. He was after all her third son—the motherless son who had needed her the most while growing up. "Why are you standing here like a stranger?" Gomati Paati cried, when she had finished scrutinizing his face as if for buried secrets.

Reluctantly, Uncle Siva stepped aside and they moved to the verandah around the central courtyard, in which a wind stirred lazily despite the midday heat. Gomati Paati went to her usual place on the swing in the cool, shaded part of the verandah. She made Ramu sit next to her on the swing—just like the old days when Ramu was a child growing up in Paavalampatti. On the train, Ramu had promised himself that he would be very formal and businesslike in Paavalampatti. *No sentiment*, he had said to himself. He saw now that it would not be that simple. It could never be that simple.

Gomati Paati said to Uncle Siva, "Does Vishu know Ramu's here? Go find him, Siva."

Uncle Siva was leaning against a pillar of the verandah. Without moving, he shouted at the top of his voice, "Vishu! Oh, Vishu! Come and take a look at your fine son! He's here now. Oh, Vishu!" He threw mocking glances at Ramu as he did so.

Instead of Ramu's father, Uncle Siva's announcement brought Aunt Malati with his cousin Sharada, almost a grown woman, in tow. Ramu remembered that his other cousin Kumar had gone to Kharagpur in West Bengal as one of the first batch of students to join the elite engineering institute newly established there. Unlike him, Kumar had always been a good student. Aunt Malati said, "He has gone out into the fields." She meant Ramu's father. She added with meaningful emphasis, "He left not even a moment ago," making Ramu wonder whether his father had fled because of him.

It was at least an hour before Ramu's father appeared. By the time he did, Ramu had bathed and was sitting at the new dining table in the verandah around the inner courtyard eating his lunch. Uncle Siva laughed and said, "Usually he has no time to go to the fields. Now suddenly he has all this interest in them." He left the rest of his meaning unstated.

Ramu's father did not respond to Uncle Siva's taunt. He came and stood at the table, tall and angular, and watched Ramu eat, but did not speak. Ramu looked up from his stainless steel plate of rice and sambhar and said, "Are you well, Appa?"

His father nodded, his eyes distant and guarded.

"No, he is not. He is sick all the time," Uncle Siva said.

"It's true," Gomati Paati agreed.

"I am as well as can be expected," Ramu's father said in a soft voice.

The words, so lightly spoken, settled heavily into Ramu's mind. He had no idea what his father meant by them. Shameful though it was to admit it, he was afraid to find out. He asked, "Have you eaten, Appa?" He could feel his father's eyes watching, burning, from deep within their recesses.

"Not yet," Ramu's father replied in the same soft voice, and quickly turned and walked away as if he was afraid Ramu would ask him to join in the meal.

Later, with the afternoon sun beginning to decline, Gomati Paati and Ramu sat side by side on the swing. Ramu's father was napping. Even Uncle Siva, who had tried his utmost not to leave Gomati Paati and Ramu alone, had finally had to abandon the inner courtyard to go into the fields.

The moment Uncle Siva was gone, Gomati Paati said without preamble to Ramu, "Your uncle does not want me to give you the money."

"And Appa?"

"He has expressed no opinion."

"What do you plan to do, then?"

"You are very serious about this school?"

"Yes."

"And about this girl?"

Ramu felt irritated. "Her name is Ponni."

"Ponni. Yes, I know that. Golden. It's a lovely name."

Ramu had never considered the meaning of Ponni's name before. "Yes," he said, "it is."

"It is not a name found among us."

"No. She is not one of us. You know that already." *Not one of us.* He hated the euphemisms.

"And she will be involved in this school?"

"Yes, of course."

"You should know—your father and I have mentioned Ponni to no one. Not even Uncle Siva knows about your marriage to her."

To her. To that girl. Ramu did not say anything. He was shocked by Gomati Paati's revelation. He felt soiled. He wanted to ask why they had kept his marriage secret, but he did not.

"Tell me about the school."

Ramu repeated to her what Arokiasamy had told him and what he had discussed with Ponni. Despite himself, he grew excited as he spoke about the school and about Ponni. He did not tell her how preliminary their plans were still. He made it sound as if they had all but picked out the venue for the school.

When he was done, Gomati Paati said, "You are happy with her, with this . . . with Ponni?"

"Yes."

"Then I'll give you the money."

"Uncle Siva does not want you to."

"That doesn't matter." Gomati Paati's voice was that of the woman who had successfully held the family lands together even though widowed at a young age. "It is my money to give. He knows I will give you the money. He is just trying to make it as difficult as possible for me." She paused and asked, "Do you know why I'm giving you the money?"

"Because you love me." He had burst out with the very first notion that had occurred to him, and it had occurred so easily to him because it was true. Gomati Paati loved him, despite all their disagreements. Her love was as certain as the sun that rose every single day. And his father? His father loved him too; he knew that very well. But his father did not have Gomati Paati's strength. That made all the difference. Almost for the first time in his life, he felt as if he had a clear understanding of Gomati Paati.

Gomati Paati smiled. "Yes, child. I'm giving it to you because I love you. But there is another reason too. Have you considered that perhaps I believe in this school just as you do?" She paused again and continued, "I may advise you against something because I think it will make you unhappy. That doesn't mean I think it's wrong. The world is more complicated than you realize, child."

"I don't understand."

"I know you don't, Ramu. That is why you do the foolish things you do." Her voice was playful, suggesting that perhaps she did not really mean that he was foolish.

ও

THE NEXT DAY RAMU RETURNED to Madras, mission accomplished. Yet during the train journey back he felt his success grimly twinned by failure, his gain by loss. Stretched out on his wooden bunk in the train, he mused on the tornado of emotions that his return to Paavalampatti had aroused in him.

Back home in Perambur, Ramu told Ponni only that they had the money. When Ponni expressed wonder at Gomati Paati's generosity, he gave a careless wave of a hand and said, "Why call it generosity? This money is only a small portion of what my family owes the world."

Ponni heard and did not say anything. It was true. Everything her uncle had taught her confirmed the perspective Ramu had advanced. In fact, one could go further, could one not? One could be more trenchant, name names. Why speak abstractly of the world? It could be said she herself had a special claim on money from

Ramu's family. Ramu had not named her father or her brother or her uncle. But she could: Murugappa, Manickam, Chellappa. Had they not slaved—yes, that was the right word, *slaved*—for his family for years and years? That money with which she would build a free school for children such as she herself had once been—low-caste children, untouchable children, the world called them derisively—was her family's congealed blood. *Congealed blood.* She would not disclaim the melodrama of that phrase—it was not melodrama but truth. And if she chose not to say all this to Ramu, was it not her own act of generosity toward him—her own struggle to make a new beginning in her relationship with him?

⁓

At the very first opportunity after his return, Ponni and Ramu spoke to Arokiasamy, who grew as excited as they were when he heard that they had already procured money for the school. The money Gomati Paati had promised would be enough to rent premises, perhaps even buy land, for land was likely to be cheap in the desolate area where the school would open. There was money too to be deposited in a bank for a fixed term, so that Ramu, Ponni, and Arokiasamy could support themselves and the school on the interest, which would be just enough to make ends meet if they lived frugally. The school was not a business; they were not planning to get rich through it.

Ponni, Ramu, and Arokiasamy went to Athanoor, the village where Pichayya, a contact highly recommended by Arokiasamy's priest friend, lived. Athanoor was the most likely location for their school. It was poor but not small, for it was conveniently located to the stone quarries where many worked. Athanoor had one or two brick structures, but the village was mostly mudwalled huts. There was one great house, painted a brilliant white and sitting on a little hillock at one end of the trail that passed for Athanoor's main street. The house belonged to quarry owner Parthiban Reddy, the richest man in the village and one of the biggest quarry owners and landlords of the region, who was referred to respectfully by the villagers as Reddiar.

While in Athanoor, Ponni, Ramu, and Arokiasamy visited the stone quarries surrounding the village and were thrown into consternation when confronted by incomprehension and disinterest from the workers, parents of the prospective students of their free school. Sobered but not disheartened, they returned to Madras to plan some more in that house behind the shop that had formerly been New Age Press. The sign had been taken down, and a *To Let* sign now hung on the shut doors. In the quarries, they had seen children slaving in the hot sun, covered in dust. The grim sight was etched unforgettably in their minds. It only increased their determination to start the school.

Such was their passion that in only a few months they had wrapped up their affairs in Madras, obtained the necessary license, and moved permanently to Athanoor. The evening before they were to leave Madras, Ponni said to Ramu, "There's something I want to show you." They were still in the rooms Ponni had shared for many tumultuous years with Chellappa; but the rooms were bare now—the next morning they would take the train south from Egmore with Arokiasamy, who was spending his last evening in Madras with his family. Ramu and Ponni had successfully reduced their belongings to two pieces of luggage. Ramu's green trunk stood in a corner next to a faded leather suitcase that had once belonged to Chellappa and into which Ponni had carelessly flung the very few things she wanted to keep from the life she was leaving behind. The landlady was to come by early the next morning before they left for the station.

"What is it? What do you want to show me?"

"Come," Ponni said in reply. "Can't explain. Better that I take you there." She led Ramu silently through the streets of Perambur in the rapidly fading light, through bustling Naidu Street and into a different part of the city where the houses were less mean and the lanes less choked with weeds. They came to the end of one such lane, quiet except for the dun-colored sparrows chirping excitedly into the deepening gray of dusk. Ponni halted under the branches of a jackfruit tree whose twisting roots rose underfoot like the massive tentacles of a monster lurking just beneath the ground.

Opposite was a dimly lit tailor's shop open to the street. Within the shop's gray walls, a woman sat at a sewing machine, working the pedal with a foot as she expertly turned cloth first one way and then another under the needle. The woman was dark and slim and small, with hair neatly knotted into a bun at the top of her head. Ramu and Ponni watched as a man walked up and spoke to the woman, who got up from her machine and found a package wrapped in newspaper. The customer, glancing at his wristwatch, hurried away with the package under an arm.

"Who is that?" Ramu said to Ponni in the shadow of the tree, as the woman went back to the sewing machine.

Ponni leaned closer against him and whispered, "My uncle's lover."

"Chellappa-Sar's lover?"

"Yes."

"I didn't know he had one!"

"He didn't when you knew him. He had given up his relationship with her by the time you came to Madras."

"Amazing!" Ramu said, gratified that even the man he had known as Chellappa-Sar was not immune to love.

"My uncle was very secretive about her. He never introduced us or even told me about her. He used to make up an excuse and meet her here at this shop. I followed him one day. That is how I found out."

Emotion filled Ponni's unsteady voice. Instinctively, Ramu put his arm around her shoulders. She leaned closer still into him. He could feel her chest rise and fall with her breathing. In the darkness beneath the jackfruit tree, she put her arm around his waist and squeezed. She said, "I'm glad you are here with me. I'm glad I'm showing you her."

"Do you know her? Have you ever met her?"

"No. I would come here and stand under this tree and watch her. I would imagine what it would be like if my uncle married her. I very much wanted him to. I think I would have liked her for an aunt."

"But he didn't," Ramu said, stating the obvious.

"No. He couldn't. His life was like a hurricane. Always. He was always consumed with some project or the other. I think he wouldn't see her for months and then he would go to her. That is why he ended it, I think. It was impossible. It wasn't fair to her."

"Did you ever try talking to your uncle about her?"

"No. I couldn't. For some reason, he wanted to keep her separate from the rest of his life. I couldn't take that away from him. I didn't want to."

Something occurred to Ramu. "Does she know about your uncle's death, Ponni?"

Ponni hesitated. "Yes. I think so. Maybe." She added helplessly, "I can't go to her. I can't confront her with something that both she and my uncle wanted to keep quiet. I just can't. Especially now, when he is dead. What is the use of that?"

Ramu thought, *She loves but does not know the first thing about love.* He felt his own love for her within him like a palpable thing.

Ponni said, "I have never brought anyone here. You are the first person, Ramu. I have told no one about her. Not even Muthu." Ponni's voice was powerful with emotion but Ramu did not notice. He was thinking with great pleasure, *Not even Muthu!* Ponni looked at Ramu's face in the darkness and repeated, "I'm glad you are here with me now, Ramu. I'm really glad you know about her. It means everything to me that you do."

That was their last evening in Madras. The next day they and Arokiasamy were on their way to Athanoor.

꩜

BY THE TIME THEY ARRIVED in Athanoor, Pichayya, the respected if enigmatic elder of the village, had helped them buy land from Parthiban Reddy. Pichayya was not from Athanoor, though he might as well have been because he had lived there for a long time. In bits and pieces, Ramu, Ponni, and Arokiasamy learned his mysterious story—whatever was known of it—over the first few weeks of their taking up residence in Athanoor.

By some accounts, Pichayya had appeared with his donkey

twenty years before; by others, forty. Pichayya did not know his own age, and it was hard for anyone to guess, for he had aged in his own unique way. He might be fifty, or else he might be eighty. Whether twenty years before or forty, all the villagers agreed Pichayya had arrived one morning when the unaccustomed sound of a donkey's braying woke up the village and led several of the more curious men to the village pond. They followed the "Eeyah! Eeeyah! Eeeeyah!" of the donkey, sawing into tiny pieces the easeful silence of the morning, to find Pichayya sitting on his haunches on the huge rock that stuck out over the pond. He was waiting for them, his donkey braying away without a care for the sleeping world while gazing up at him from the water's edge with almond eyes.

"Who are you?" one of the men demanded.

Pichayya replied with his name.

The man felt aggrieved at the intruder and his donkey. "What do you want? And why is your donkey making such a ruckus so early in the morning?"

"Do you have a washerman in the village? I am a washerman by trade." Pichayya spoke with an unmistakable dignity that immediately impressed the man, who had become spokesman of the village by virtue of his initiative in speaking to the stranger.

The man calmed down and said doubtfully, "We are mostly untouchables here. You will not be able to wash our clothes." The village consisted largely of Adi Dravidars who worked in the stone quarries in the adjoining areas. It was clear to the men who had wandered out of the collection of huts to investigate the braying that this man who called himself Pichayya was higher in caste than they were. If he was a washerman, then it was to high-caste folk, not people like them.

Pichayya said, "No matter. Clothes have no caste. I don't care what caste you are."

"We are poor. We don't have the money to pay someone to wash our clothes."

"Then give me food to eat. Whenever you can is fine. My needs are few. I'll make myself a hut by this rock and live here with my donkey."

"Why do you want to live in Athanoor? There is nothing but stone and sun and hardship here. There is no farming. Nothing can survive in Athanoor. Only we Pallars and Paraiyars can. We keep skin and bone together by working in the stone quarries for the Reddiar. Anyone who can runs away."

"It is the perfect place for me, then," Pichayya replied. "I am a wanderer. I am one without a home. In this desert that is not my home I can wander without leaving."

"You are a funny one. How strangely you talk. Like a poet. If the Reddiar gives you permission, wander in this desert all you want. I doubt anyone will object to your foolishness."

That, Ramu, Ponni, and Arokiasamy learned, was how Pichayya came to Athanoor. He lived in a hut by the pond. He plied his trade on the rock, scrubbing and slapping clothes on its rough surface, though if truth be told there was little work for him. Mostly he was busy on festival days, weddings, and funerals. If there was a grave sickness in a family, he boiled the family's clothes in a pot that stood over charred stones by his hut. He also knew about herbal cures for ailments, for which he was much in demand. The donkey was Pichayya's closest companion. The donkey was for collecting and delivering clothes, though like Pichayya it was in semi-retirement since the load of clothes to be carried was never very great.

Ramu, Ponni, and Arokiasamy learned also the wild rumors that circulated about Pichayya's past before his arrival in Athanoor. Like his age, Pichayya's past was indeterminate. Some said he had murdered his wife's lover and was hiding in Athanoor from the law. Others said that he had loved and lost a woman of higher caste, and heartbreak had driven him to Athanoor. Yet another rumor insisted he was once a terrifying brigand like Angulimala, who murdered until the Buddha converted him to the right path. Unlike Angulimala, though, Pichayya did not wear a garland of his victims' fingers. Whatever the truth, Pichayya had a serene disposition and over the years had become a revered elder. His calm was a resource to all the villagers in their petty quarrels. In return for his diverse services, the villagers fed him and his donkey. Whenever it occurred to the woman cooking, a child was sent to Pichayya with a portion.

Pichayya ate most days in this fashion. He demanded nothing from the villagers for himself or for his donkey, which like him was of indefinite age though certainly old, but there was no hut in the village that would turn Pichayya away.

This was the Pichayya who helped Ramu, Ponni, and Arokiasamy buy their land from quarry owner Parthiban Reddy. Reddiar seemed amused at these young outsiders from faraway Madras intent on starting a school for the children of his workers; nevertheless, he sold them a barren piece of land in *his* village, in the village in which *his* workers lived—he made sure they understood he owned the village and its inhabitants.

After Reddiar had made this clear, Pichayya looked steadily back at him and said, "The world is water, Reddiar. You think you hold it in your hand, but before you know it, it has flowed away." Later, he said to the outsiders he had helped buy land, "The only things worth holding are those which are in the heart and in the mind. That is why I am for your school." This was the first encounter Ramu, Ponni, and Arokiasamy had with the riddling ways of Pichayya, who was from the beginning one of the greatest friends of the school.

Soon after their arrival, Ramu, Ponni, and Arokiasamy divined that the Reddiar expected them to be gone within a year, at most two. A school for the children of the ignorant, low-caste buffaloes who were his workers? The idea was laughable! The school was sure to fail. In the meantime, he could make a little bit of money from land that could not be put to any other use. So the Reddiar had reasoned to himself as he sold them the piece of land. But he was to be proven wrong. In his calculations, the Reddiar had failed to account for the outsiders' youthful passion, which, ignorant of all the hurdles that could prove insurmountable, made a way even where common sense said no way was possible. He had neglected to consider that sometimes naiveté is an asset because it is a shield against disillusionment.

The outsiders did not fail. The school grew steadily. With Pichayya's help, Ramu, Ponni, and Arokiasamy recruited their first students. Such was the bond between the three of them that to the villagers it seemed they were a single family, that Arokiasamy was a brother to both Ramu and Ponni. Month by month, year by year, the free school grew. Reddiar realized that the success of the outsiders could, after all, be useful to him—the school could be a place where the youngest, the most tender, of the children could go while the parents worked in his quarries. From a mean temporary shed with a handful of children who went in the evenings for a few hours, the school became a small hedged compound with a modest office building of rough brick and two classrooms with thatched roofs where nearly ninety students studied until they turned twelve.

The children came from all the villages nearby. By the time they left the school, the students who came regularly (not all did, alas) could read and write fluently. They could do simple math and had studied geography, history, and science. They learned about discoveries like the number zero in ancient India and enterprising inventions like the airplane little more than fifty years before in America. They learned about the Buddha and Karl Marx and Tiruvalluvar, for whom the school was named—*Tiruvalluvar School, Athanoor.* They learned the motto of the school, the great couplet #972 from Tiruvalluvar, which they were taught means *All Life Is One at Birth, Deeds Make the Difference.* They had an idea of the world that went beyond stone quarries and goat-herding and coolie work in Thoothukudi and Thirunelveli Town.

Ramu started a library in the school, and Ponni planted trees just as she had wanted to. Against all odds, the trees took root in that barren patch of land—the mango tree began bearing fruit about three years after their move to Athanoor. Even a rudimentary playground came into existence for the younger children, the result of Arokiasamy's efforts. Because of Ponni's tireless advocacy, several of the best students received scholarships to residential schools in Thirunelveli, Nagercoil, and Madurai. Encouragingly, one such student, Karuppan, returned to Athanoor to work with the school. When Karuppan joined them, Ramu, Ponni, and Arokiasamy felt an immense sense of fulfillment. Soon another student, Devi, too joined them. Now the school was not just a noble scheme of outsiders; it was a part of the community it served. Sweet success! They had not dared to imagine such sweetness when they had started years before.

Barren as Athanoor was, there were other kinds of sweetness to life there. There was Selvam. Selvam was born to Ramu and Ponni three years after they moved to Athanoor. He came into the world just about the time they harvested the first lusciously sweet mangos from Ponni's tree. When he was yet an infant, Ponni liked to carry Selvam out to the tree in her arms. She would stand under the abundant foliage of the stately tree, now in its prime, breathe in the pungent smells of sap and bark and fruit ripening in the heat, and remark, "Look, Selvam. Look at this great tree. You and the tree are growing up together. This tree is your brother." It was a bit of whimsy. Selvam brought out the whimsical in Ponni, who was otherwise so serious.

Soon after the decision to try for a baby, Ramu and Ponni had moved into a mudwalled hut abandoned years before. Until then, like Arokiasamy, they had simply slept in the school. This clearly would not do if they were to have a child. But before they could move into the hut that was to be their new home, it had to be fixed. The hut was in a terrible condition; one of the walls was badly damaged. They cleaned the hut out and then, with the help of the father of a child who went to their school, repaired the damaged wall. At the same time, they widened the two doorways, back and front, so that the inside of the windowless hut became light and airy. Cheery cotton curtains with multicolored parrots on them (bought in Thirunelveli Town with no thought at all for how quickly they would get filthy, requiring much too frequent washing) were hung in the doorways so that the glare of the sun, now suddenly increased because of the widened doorways, was mitigated.

Inside they painted the walls a gay yellow and placed a wobbly self-built shelf of discarded wooden planks along one wall so that they could arrange precious as well as pretty things for view—a black-and-white studio photograph of Chellappa as a young and handsome man, a papier mâché doll of a potbellied merchant who bobbed his head in assent when nudged, a coconut shell carved with intricate designs that they had picked up on a trip to Kanya Kumari, colorful drawings that the schoolchildren had made with crayons. In one corner of the single room, they set up the kitchen. They bought a Primus kerosene stove and new aluminum pots and pans (expensive indulgences). When they were done, their neighbors the villagers stopped by to see the amazing and fanciful way in which they had transformed the humble hut into a cheerful home.

Here, in this hut, Ramu and Ponni spent many happy years, before the trouble with Parthiban Reddy began. The hut was not far from the school—you went down the trail that was the village's unofficial main street, rounded a bend, and there it was, the third hut on the left. Hardly two minutes from the school. Though Arokiasamy came and went freely from the hut (neither Ponni nor Ramu would have had it any differently), they had more privacy than before. Arokiasamy was a man of immense discretion and knew when to keep away and when to make his appearance. Ramu and Ponni learned, not without some guilt, to savor their private time together. Sometimes, just to be alone in each other's company, they worked at home sitting side by side on a mat on the floor, leaning against a wall that left fine yellow dust on their clothes (the paint, they discovered, did not take so well on the mud wall).

At such times, Ramu found it much harder to concentrate than Ponni. Ponni could easily shut him out as she bent frowning over a book she was reading to cull out (for example) interesting folktales from all over India to tell the six-, seven- and eight-year-old children the next day. He, on the other hand, would stare like an illiterate at the elementary long division sums he might be reviewing, unable to make the slightest sense of them. He might as well have been reading Hebrew or Chinese. He would grip his pencil and concentrate, but the numbers could not be stopped from floating free of the paper on which they were written and rearranging themselves into Ponni's face. "Ponni," he would say plaintively, "what are you doing in my students' math problems?"

Ponni would reply, suppressing a smile, "Seeing whether you can add me up properly." There would be mischief in Ponni when she said this, but still she could not be distracted from her work and Ramu would have to return, groaning, to the dancing numbers in front of him. It was a game between them—a game in which Ponni played the serious storyteller and Ramu the playful mathematician.

Now that they had their own home, they could lie on the mat on mornings when there was no school and talk with the curtains drawn across the doorways. Murugappa came boldly visiting on one such morning soon after they had moved into their hut, when they lay side by side on the mat, fingers interlocked, at peace with each other and with the world while the sounds of the village floated in through the drawn curtains. Ramu said suddenly, "You know, we haven't talked about how I found your father." Ponni's fingers stiffened in his. Ramu tightened his grip so that she could not withdraw them. He said, "I know. It's hard for you. I just want you to know something. What happened is always in my mind."

Ponni murmured, almost as if to herself, "What is the use of that? What is the use of always having that in your mind?"

"Don't you think about it?"

"I used to. A lot. Then it faded away and now I hardly do."

"They never found out who did it." *It.* The murder.

"There were rumors. But the British police officer had no interest in finding out the truth."

"I think a lot about finding him under the tamarind tree. I used to have nightmares about it." *Him.* Ponni's father.

Ponni stirred. She said, "I don't want to talk about it."

But Ramu could not stop. He said in a rush, "So many nightmares! But if I had not found him you would not have come looking for me all those years ago in Paavalampatti, and I would not have come looking for you later in Madras, and we would not be lying here like this today. Being here like this with you is worth all the nightmares I suffered." The moment he had spoken he realized the possibility for misunderstanding and rushed on. "Of course, best would have been to have nothing for me to find. That would have been best of all. I would give up being here with you for that."

Was that true? Would he have? Would he have returned life to the father in exchange for his own life with the daughter as her husband, her lover? He did not know. Still, he felt the need to say that he would. It was a way to express his love for Ponni.

Ponni withdrew her fingers from his. "Why, Ramu? Why talk about all this?"

Ramu did not try to take her hand again. He smiled a false little smile in an attempt to lighten the moment and said in a joking tone, "So that you know I can add you up properly." When it was clear his attempt at humor had failed, he sat up so that he could see her more clearly and said with great seriousness, great urgency, "Do you remember how you searched me out after your father died? Then you wanted to talk about it and I didn't. What is different now, Ponni?"

"I didn't really want to talk about it even then. I only thought I did."

"I suppose I too understood that at that time," Ramu acknowledged. "But isn't it different now? I just think we should talk at least one time about it. So you know how I feel. I don't want there to be anything between us. I am afraid this could be one of the things that keep us apart."

"There will be . . . There is nothing between us." Ponni's face was as calm as stone.

"That is what I want."

"That is what I want, too."

"You know I love you."

"Yes, I know." Ponni did not say *I love you too,* and if Ramu had noticed he did not show it.

Perhaps Ponni did not need to say *I love you* because she was looking at Ramu with such sad but gentle eyes that Ramu could not help leaning over and kissing her softly on her lips. He kissed her once, twice. He felt his tongue touch hers. When he boldly pressed his tongue against hers, she did not withdraw. Between kisses, he said, "I love you" again, making her sigh, as if giving in. Her lips were moist and yielding. Every time he said *I love you* she kissed him more urgently still. So then he said quite sincerely, "You are utterly and completely beautiful," making something flash brightly but briefly in Ponni's eyes that was gone before he could catch it. What was it? Was it gratitude? Forgiveness? Love? He could not tell, and he could not even be sure that he had actually seen what he thought he had. He only knew what he himself felt—an immense desire for her that made him selfish and selfless at one and the same time. He wanted to drink and drink and drink endlessly and ruthlessly of what he was feeling, and he wanted to share all of it with Ponni too.

Ponni was running her fingers through his hair. She stroked him along his spine and over his back, stopping at all the places of delight she knew he had. His veshti had come loose. She slid it off and slid off her sari and undergarments too. They were naked now, filled with a thousand sensations from skin touching skin, kissing skin, becoming one with skin. There was nothing between them. Add it all up and it was zero. Add them up and they were one. She stroked the inside of his thighs gently, gently, and then she gripped him between his legs and stroked him there also, letting her fingers linger over the most intimate parts of him, the tender flesh beneath the foreskin and in the soft buried fold of his anus. He kissed her beautiful, firm breasts, tenderly, running his teeth lightly over her nipples. He licked and breathed in the sweat of her. He buried his face in the soft wetness between her legs and kissed her where he had never kissed her before. His tongue found its way into all her hidden places, and then hers did the same to his. At last they were kissing and licking and touching each other as if in harmony, as if there was nothing between them, as if they were one, skin dissolving into skin, mind into mind, heart into heart. That is how it felt. And then, in one luminous instant, they had moved beyond touching. They *were* one, and it was touching that had made them so.

Months later, when Selvam was born, Ramu and Ponni counted back and decided with great assurance that this wondrous morning of lovemaking was when he was conceived.

Part Three

Heart and Stone

THE WAY THE COACH SWAYS, leans to one side as the train takes the bend, is familiar to him. His body understands that almost imperceptible signal. Instinctively, he bends his head to look out the barred window of the train, searching up ahead for the bridge, surest indicator of impending arrival. Soot from the engine gently stings his face as he does so. He squints, looks through slit eyes. He sees the dip in the ground—the Tamarabarani River—and straddling the dip, sure enough, the white-painted bridge. Beyond, the familiar coconut palms huddle together with their green heads leaning against one another, as if gravely conferring on some matter of great import. He scans their shaggy tops, searching again. There—the gopuram of the temple rises above the tops of the trees. In the bright afternoon sun, bridge, river, trees, and gopuram make up a vivid scene. Just as he remembers it.

How long has it been since his last return? He casts his mind back as the train crosses the bridge and slows for its approach to the station.

Two years. And still everything is as always. Has anything changed? At all? Does anything *ever* affect the tranquility of the village?

He feels a hand on his shoulder.

Selvam.

Consider, on the other hand, *his* life. Ever changing. Never tranquil.

"Are we there, Appa?" Selvam asks, leaning across him and trying to peer out the window.

Ramu turns away from the window, his eyes stinging. The soot. It's the soot. The soot is making his eyes water. He wipes his eyes with quick fingertips so Selvam does not misunderstand.

It's going to be hard enough without misunderstanding.

He forces a smile onto his face and nods in reply to Selvam. "The train won't stop for long," he says. "Let's go."

Ramu grabs the cloth bag and the small battered tin trunk from under the bench. The fellow passengers of their cubicle, seated on the two facing wooden benches, observe their departure with keen interest. The big quiet woman in the bright blue sari who has sat next to them for most of the two-hour journey, insulating them from the other passengers. The lanky eater of peanuts, who has inconsiderately scattered the floor with discarded shells. The family of four on the opposite bench—a tableau of father and mother, son and daughter, as if from one of the Family Planning posters beginning to appear everywhere. Now that he and Selvam are ready to leave, Ramu flashes them all a smile. Quickly, he helps Selvam pick his way over their legs and out into the corridor. At one end of the swaying coach, alighting passengers crowd the open doorway through which a hot wind swirls. The sky outside is shimmering white, bright and hurtful to the eyes. In the heat, the sharp smell of stale urine, too strong to be dispelled by the wind, emanates from behind the closed door of the toilet. Ramu quickly scrutinizes the waiting passengers. He does not know any of them. Not that it would be of any consequence if he did. Not at all.

The black-on-yellow sign board of the station flashes into view in the open door of the coach, and then passes. *Paavalampatti* is written in Tamil, English, and Hindi; but the Hindi letters are barely visible, for someone has slashed black paint across them. Ramu does not recall noticing the disfiguring marks on his last visit. The most recent wave of language politics convulsing Tamil India has arrived in Paavalampatti. The hands of the anti-Hindi agitators have reached this far. Change has come, after all. He will have to amend his earlier thought. Suddenly he is exceedingly annoyed with himself. How silly of him to think change could pass by Paavalampatti!

The slowing train finally comes to a shuddering halt at the station. Selvam has never before been to Paavalampatti, but he knows of the village. He has heard many stories about it. He knows both Appa and Amma are from this village. When they alight, he looks around with curiosity. The platform onto which they have descended from the train is packed dirt. Midway down the platform is a small building with yellow walls to which the other passengers are making their way. His father hurries in the same direction, dragging him along. At the far end of the platform, the station master stands talking to the engine driver, a green flag furled under his arm. Casuarina trees line the platform's edge, veiling the station from the village. Across the railway tracks is another platform, similarly made of dirt and similarly fringed by trees.

No sooner have Ramu and Selvam reached the exit from the station than the station master waves his green flag to send the train onward on its journey. Selvam pulls away from his father to watch the train clatter past. Ramu lets him. He knows the station master. His name is Sundaram. He lives in Meenakshisundareshwarar Temple Street. Ramu would rather not talk to him. Now is not a good time for questions. Never is it a good time for the kind of mischievous questions that would be asked. But he will not be furtive; he will not slink. By now, he knows, everyone is aware of his scandalous story. Nevertheless, he will not creep back into Paavalampatti like a criminal, as he once did, much to his later regret.

Sundaram approaches briskly, curious no doubt about the familiar-looking figure with an unknown boy, perhaps ten, by his side. Ramu looks boldly in Station Master Sundaram's direction, refusing to avert his face. He will not deliberately avoid an encounter in which he would have to introduce Selvam to Sundaram, but before Sundaram reaches them, Selvam of his own accord turns away from the departed train. Ramu follows him out of the station feeling vaguely cheated.

When they are in the street, Selvam says to his father, "Gomati Paati did not meet us at the train."

"She does not know when exactly we will be arriving," Ramu replies. He had sent her an urgent telegram only the day before.

"What is she like?" Selvam has never met Gomati Paati. But he has heard many stories about her. Like his father, he calls her Paati, even though she is really his great-grandmother.

"She is very old now."

"How old?"

"I'm not sure." Ramu tries to add up the years in his head. "About seventy-five, I think."

Ramu and Selvam are in Station Road with the relentless sun beating down on them. When they come to Meenakshisundareshwarar Temple Street, they turn into it. The street. *His* street.

Hurrying along with Selvam, the cloth bag under one arm and the tin trunk held securely on the opposite shoulder, Ramu feels his childhood stir awake all around him. Here is the spot where he fell and severely scraped the palms of his hands. And there, that is where he and his friends scratched lines for wickets into the wall of a neighbor's house. It is a good spot for a game of cricket. He wonders if the lines are still there, etched into the brick. With a mixture of nostalgia and dread, Ramu considers the houses arrayed on each side of the street, wall against wall. The thinnais, the rounded pillars, the tiled roofs, the barred windows. He is about to say to himself that the dignified Brahmin houses are exactly as always and then catches himself, remembering his earlier error. Some houses—Postmaster Mani's, for example—have come down in the world; others have gone up. Outside his childhood friend Subbu's house, he notices a brand-new Enfield motorcycle leaning majestically on its kickstand under a thatched shelter built specifically for it. Subbu has done well for himself. He practices law, while also lecturing at the law college in Thirunelveli Town. He is among the few Brahmin landlords of Paavalampatti who have managed to keep their lands intact. Most others have sold and moved away to salaried jobs in Madras or Bombay or Delhi. The door to Subbu's house is open. Through it, an indistinct figure is visible in the dim interior. Subbu? Perhaps. Ramu does not stop to find out. Other than a distant childhood, they share nothing now. Their lives have diverged utterly.

"A temple!" Selvam cries, pointing ahead to the red-and-white walls of Meenakshisundareshwarar Temple rising up where the street branches into two. The imposing wooden doors of the temple are shut because it is afternoon.

"Yes, a temple," Ramu says. "Maybe we will go there later." He comes to a halt. "Here we are," he announces to Selvam. They have arrived—the moment has arrived.

At once, Selvam falls silent. He understands what their arrival means.

The house is as immaculate as always. The paint is fresh. The heavy wooden front door with its ornamental decorations, left slightly ajar as if just for their arrival, is well polished. The broad red floor of the thinnai shines. On it, two fine wooden chairs, new additions, have been placed facing each other. Ramu climbs the steps with Selvam and pushes the door open all the way. They leave their rubber slippers outside and enter. Ramu's feet are rough and bony and callused—not feet that have known leisure and luxury. They pass through the enclosed outer verandah and into the cool dimness of the front room where a Rexene-covered sofa set is arranged around the imposing wooden cabinet of a radio. This is the room in which the Kanaku Pillai, long gone now, once had his desk. Ramu gratefully unburdens himself, placing the cloth bag and the trunk on the sofa. On the radio cabinet stands a plain vase with plastic flowers in it. On opposite walls of the room, garlanded black-and-white photographs of Ramu's father Vishu and his aunt Malati hang. The décor of the room is Uncle Siva's.

Selvam points to the picture of Ramu's father and says, "Thatha."

"Yes," Ramu replies.

Selvam has never met his grandfather Vishu, but the exact same portrait, similarly garlanded, is in the hut in Athanoor that is home. His grandfather is dead now. He knows that is why the portrait is garlanded. Why did he never meet his grandfather when he was still alive? His grandfather is such a vague notion to Selvam that the question has barely even occurred to him. Selvam follows his father deeper into the house, into a room with two beds in it and sundry other pieces of furniture, including an almirah. Overhead is a wooden loft to store things. A window opens into an inner courtyard, bright with the fierce sun. The sound of a swing creaking back and forth enters the room through the window. He follows his father toward that sound, into the verandah skirting the courtyard.

On the swing, an old woman in a white sari sits reading a book, gently moving herself back and forth by the toes of one outstretched foot. Her shaved head is covered with spiky white hair. When she sees Ramu and Selvam, she drops the book onto the broad wooden plank of the swing with a delighted cry. She halts the swing, springs to her feet. For a woman her age, she is surprisingly vigorous. Her expressive eyes, lovely still, spill her warm joy into the verandah. Every time Ramu meets his grandmother, he realizes anew what he has always known—beauty such as hers has no age. She was beautiful when young and she is beautiful now, if in a different way. He touches her feet and gestures to Selvam, saying, "Come, greet Gomati Paati."

But Selvam does not come forward. He remains where he is, just inside the verandah. He remembers now. He remembers many things. He remembers why he is here. He remembers why he has never met Gomati Paati before in his life. He does not want to come forward to greet her. He wants nothing to do with her. He wants to go back home to Athanoor.

Ramu repeats, "Come, Selvam, come greet your great-grandmother."

Selvam stands and glowers in reply.

Gomati Paati says, "Let it be. It's hard for him."

"Selvam!" Ramu says. He means to be sharp, but there is no sharpness in his voice.

Gomati Paati gives Ramu a warning look that Selvam does not miss. She says, "You must both be tired from the trip. Go on into the kitchen now. Drink some water. Straight from the clay pot. It will be nice and cold. Then, Ramu, show Selvam the well in the back. Have a wash. That will freshen you up."

Ramu looks helplessly at his son.

Gomati Paati continues, "In the meantime I'll make you idlies. I have everything ready. I knew you would come today, just not by which train. Or else I would have had hot idlies for you even as you arrived. Wouldn't that have been something? You like idlies, don't you, Selvam? With fresh coconut chutney that has just a hint of coriander leaves in it. I know you do. Your father has told me." She takes a step forward in Selvam's direction. Selvam takes a step back. She stops. She is right, though. Selvam does indeed like idlies with coconut chutney.

In the kitchen, Ramu and Selvam dip their stainless steel tumblers into the glistening moist clay pot and drink thirstily of the cool water. As the water pours down his parched throat, Ramu again acknowledges change. Here he stands with his son drinking water in his grandmother's kitchen. Unthinkable! He knows it is his grandmother who has made it thinkable. He will never understand his grandmother. He has not forgotten how she made him wash the night she confronted him about his secret meetings with Ponni up on Paavalappa Naicker's hill. Yet here he stands with Selvam in his grandmother's kitchen. No, he will never really understand his grandmother.

While Gomati Paati steams idlies, they wash at the well. Ramu uses the coir rope to draw up the water in a bucket. Because it is the dry season, the water is far down, at the very bottom of the well. But it is clean and cool. They wash feet and hands and faces, pouring out the water for each other and scrubbing away the grime of travel. First they had to take the bus from Athanoor to Thirunelveli Junction, and then the train to Paavalampatti. They have been traveling many hours.

After they are done at the well, Ramu takes Selvam out back to show him—and really to see for himself—the memory-soaked landscape of his childhood. They stand in the shade of the neem tree and look out over the fields and the gardens, wilting in the fierce sun but still able to convey a sense of gentle welcome. It is a fertile land, delightful, full of promise. Even in this season, the marks of centuries—no, millennia—of industrious toil are clearly visible all around on the land. In the distance, the green mountains shimmer in the hazy yellow heat with an allure all their own. The little hill on which Paavalappa Naicker's fort once stood rises up closer to the village. And *there* is the tree. The tamarind tree. Demon tree. Ramu looks at it. Dark and terrible are the secrets it hides under its twisting branches. He says nothing to Selvam of the hideous truth of the tree. There it is—the terrible, beautiful world of his childhood. Seemingly as it ever was, but in truth changed utterly. Most of the family lands, preserved so carefully through the decades by Gomati Paati, are gone, sold off by Uncle Siva for this unavoidable thing for his son Kumar, or that necessity for his daughter Sharada, or else for mysterious expenses beyond explanation. Only a small portion of the lands remain. There is no hut in the coconut grove now. *Ponni's hut.* Gone.

By the time they return to the house, Ramu and Selvam are covered in sweat again. Such is the terrible heat. They eat the idlies sitting silently at the dining table in the verandah of the inner courtyard. The dining table is a novelty for Selvam, but he refuses to be distracted by it. They eat off washed banana leaves from the garden out back. The leaves still have a green smell of sap where the stalk was broken. The idlies are soft enough to melt in the mouth. The chutney is fresh and tart in just the right way. Selvam is clearly hungry, for he gulps the idlies down one after the other, without pause. When Gomati Paati replenishes his leaf with chutney or idli, he neither looks up nor says anything. Gomati Paati makes one or two trivial observations, but neither Ramu nor Selvam responds.

After he is done, Selvam asks abruptly, "When will you leave?"

"Tomorrow morning," Ramu replies.

Ramu knows Selvam is on the verge of tears. Selvam gets up from the table and goes to the back of the house to wash his hands. When he comes back he says, "I want to sleep."

Gomati Paati gestures toward the room across the courtyard, the room with two cots in it, the room in which Ramu lay sick after finding Murugappa's murdered body, and says, "You can lie down in there, child."

Selvam does not move. He does not respond to her or even look at her. He stands glaring at his father. He is small and thin for his size, with hair that flops into his eyes. He has Ponni's broad features but Ramu's build.

Ramu says, "Yes, go lie down in there. You can switch on the fan if you like." For there is now an electric ceiling fan in that room.

All the rooms in the house now have electricity, a common feature of the more affluent houses in the village.

Ramu watches Selvam disappear into the room.

Tomorrow Ramu will go back without Selvam. Back to Athanoor. And to Ponni. That is why he speaks now so urgently to Gomati Paati about Selvam. He says, as if in apology, "It is hard for him."

"Of course it is," replies Gomati Paati. "He is a child. He has never been away from the two of you. He hardly knows anything about me. How could it not be hard?"

"I don't know what else to do, where else to take him."

"You did the right thing bringing him here. He is always welcome. You know that. I have told you that many times."

Ramu feels anger flare within. "No, I don't know that," he says, unable to keep the bitterness out of his voice. "I don't know if even *I* am welcome here."

The hurt shows on Gomati Paati's face, but she does not say anything.

Ramu says in a softer voice, "I shouldn't have spoken like that. I'm afraid. That is why I spoke as I did. You should know I trust you. Why else would I bring Selvam here? Whatever you think of the choices I've made in my life, I know you will do right by him."

Suddenly, there are tears in Gomati Paati's eyes. Ramu is startled. He has never seen Gomati Paati weep. She is not one for weeping. Now she says, in a faltering voice that mortifies Ramu, "If I have done wrong in the past, forgive me."

Ramu knows she has done wrong. He cannot forget the words she spoke in Calcutta when first he told her and his father about his marriage to Ponni. Still, he feels shame for the way he spoke, for she has also done right. Did she not give them the money for the school? Suddenly, he cannot bear to stay there in the verandah of the inner courtyard of the house. He cannot keep sitting there in front of Gomati Paati. He stands up quickly to go to the back of the house to wash his hands. And then he wanders over to the outhouse farther back. He stands in the shadow of the outhouse's walls, breathing in the faint, familiar smell of human refuse emanating from it. He tries not to think of the scavenger, of a caste even lower than Ponni's, who comes every morning to clear the night soil. Such thinking would make him very angry. Instead he looks once more over the beguiling landscape of his childhood and listens to the quiet murmur of the village in the afternoon, supine under the force of the sun. When he goes back inside, he is calmer. He has made himself calmer. He and Gomati Paati resume their conversation in the inner courtyard, speaking softly because they both know Selvam is not really asleep. It is not because he is tired and wishes to sleep that Selvam has disappeared to the refuge of the cot in the room. It would be terrible if he were to overhear their words.

"When does Uncle Siva return from Bombay?" Ramu asks, sitting cross-legged on the floor in such a way that he can lean against the wall.

From her usual perch on the swing, Gomati Paati notices how thin and haggard Ramu has become. Not yet forty, he looks older. His hair is liberally dusted with white. His lean face would be handsome were it not for the lines that worry and struggle have etched into it. His deep-set eyes look hollowed out now. She remembers his bright eyes from when he was still a child, from before he found Murugappa's body and everything changed. The brightness is still there—it flashes forth now and then from the hollows—but it is buried deep inside now. Or so it seems to her. She is shocked at his appearance. He has aged since his last visit two years ago. Clearly it has been a hard two years for him. She notices the frayed collar of his shirt and the much-washed, much-used veshti around his waist. It breaks her heart to see his clothes. Of course, these clothes are nothing unusual. It is the way it has been with Ramu. She, who has known poverty herself, will never get used to his. Never. She made her own choices, different from Ramu's. In her young age, before her marriage. It hurts her now to see her grandson—son of her eldest—as poor . . . no, poorer still, than she once was.

Gomati Paati says, "I think Siva will be in Bombay for another two weeks at least. Maybe longer." Kumar works in Bombay as an engineer for a big industrial house. His wife is pregnant again for the third time—they have two girls and the quest for a boy continues—and Uncle Siva has gone to help out. The baby is due any time. After the baby is born, he might stop to visit Sharada in Madras on his way back to Paavalampatti, because she too is planning to move to Bombay. If he did that, he might be gone even longer than two weeks.

"I'll certainly be back by then to get Selvam," Ramu says. His relief that Uncle Siva is not expected back for at least two weeks is palpable.

Gomati Paati speaks dismissively. "Don't concern yourself about Siva," she says. "He can shout and misbehave all he likes, but I still have a say in this house."

"Even so," Ramu insists. "I will be back in a week. That is all it will take for things to quiet down. As soon as it is safe, I'll be here to take Selvam back to Athanoor."

"Things are bad?"

"Bad enough." He adds hastily, "Of course, I don't think anything will actually happen. We've been through this once before. We'll survive it again."

"But it's worse this time, isn't it?"

Reluctantly, Ramu says, "Yes." He cannot lie about the situation in Athanoor. But he dispenses with the frightening details, the nasty caste angle that has been introduced. He says nothing about the accusation of rape, of a woman of a higher caste, that has been concocted against Karuppan as a way of getting at the school. Nor does he mention that the hut in which Ramu and Ponni live has been vandalized by people claiming to look for Karuppan. And he most definitely does not say anything about how the crisis in Athanoor has badly affected his relationship with Ponni—how they have fought and disagreed about the school in a manner they never have before.

"Why don't you yourself stay a few days, just until you are sure things are calm?"

"I can't. I have to be back as soon as possible."

"Ask Ponni to come here. She too can be here until the situation in Athanoor improves."

Is there a slight hesitation before Gomati Paati makes the invitation? Neighbors would disapprove, and perhaps more than disapprove—some things, Ramu is sure, haven't changed. But if there is hesitation, he cannot detect it. "No," he says. "That is exactly what our enemies want us to do. We both have to be there. How can we just run? We will lose everything we worked for."

Gomati Paati does not argue. She knows it is no use. Instead, she says, "Selvam is a handsome boy. He looks just as you did when you were a child."

For the first time since his arrival, Ramu laughs. At her grandmotherly indulgence. He says, "You know that's not true. Everybody agrees Selvam looks like Ponni. His hair. His face. Just like hers."

"But his eyes and the way he stands," Gomati Paati insists. "Say whatever you like, I see you in him."

Ramu cannot stop chuckling. "Okay. His eyes and legs are mine. His face and hair are Ponni's. The rest of him belongs to all humanity! Can we stop parceling him out now?"

Gomati Paati too laughs. It makes her happy to see Ramu this way. Excited. Witty. Grand. *So* grand. Full of big words and ideas. *Humanity.* The words and ideas had caused him plenty of trouble in his life. Of course, *he* wouldn't consider any of it trouble, probably. And, truth be told, she has come to accept him the way he is. He would not be Ramu if he were any different, would he? She feels her love for him as the permanent dull ache it has become within her.

Before it gets too dark, as a distraction, Ramu goes down with Selvam to the river, and then to the temple. There is of course neither such a lovely river, nor such a fine temple, in Athanoor. He lets Selvam splash to his heart's content in the river, in which water still flows despite the parched season. And then, wet and dripping but drying fast in the heat, they go to the temple, stepping past the high and ancient wooden doors to walk between the stone pillars blackened by time and soot from oil lamps. They go at a time when no one Ramu recognizes is in the temple, though Ramu is quite prepared to outstare anyone they encounter should the need arise. They stand on the stone floor and peer at the idol of Meenakshi on one side and the black stone lingam on the other, each within its own gloomy shrine. Ramu refuses to bring his hands together in obeisance, or to prostrate himself in worship, and so neither does Selvam. Afterward, Ramu contemplates going up to the ruined fort on the hill and then decides against it. Too many memories. Of Ponni and himself during what feels to him now a more innocent time. Not true, of course. Whatever that time was, it was not innocent, any more than the present is.

After dinner, he takes Selvam aside for a talk. They go into the room with the two cots, where Selvam is to sleep during his time in Paavalampatti. Ramu has brought the battered green tin trunk into the room. It is the same trunk he took with him nearly twenty years ago when he left Paavalampatti for college in Madras. It is the trunk that went with him to Calcutta, and then to Athanoor. Now the trunk has returned to Paavalampatti filled with his son's things. Ramu opens the trunk and shows Selvam the three shirts and two pairs of shorts Ponni has placed in there for him. They are his best shirts and shorts, faded and a little small for him, but nevertheless in good condition. He makes sure Selvam knows where his spinning top and marbles are. He shows him the two books Ponni has included—one has brief biographical essays on famous men and women, the other retellings of Panchatantra stories. And then he remembers that his own books from when he was a boy are still here in Paavalampatti. He will ask Gomati Paati to show Selvam where they are, especially the storybooks of Vikram and the Vetal that he loved as a boy. Selvam knows the stories. Ponni has told them to him. But it will be good for him to read them himself. For his age, Selvam is a great reader. Finally, keeping it for the last, Ramu shows Selvam a brand-new toy, bought at Thirunelveli Junction railway station during the trip without Selvam noticing. It is a plastic toy camera, with an eyehole and a little wheel on top that can be turned with a finger to make famous places appear in a window—the Taj Mahal, the Eiffel Tower, the Great Wall of China, the Pyramids of Giza, Niagara Falls, and so on. All the places he would have liked to see. All the places Selvam might still be able to. The toy is to remind Selvam of the world that waits for him. It was not cheap. They cannot really afford it. Ramu has been indulgent. Selvam takes up the camera and looks at it without much interest. He is old enough to know a bribe when he sees it.

Sitting on the cot with the open trunk between them, Ramu says to Selvam, "I'll be leaving by the nine o'clock train tomorrow morning."

Selvam says, "I want to go with you."

Ramu feels impatient. After all, Selvam is only going to be in Paavalampatti for a week, give or take a day or two. What is so terrible about that? "We've already talked about this, Sela," he says, using the private name he alone sometimes uses for Selvam. "It is better for you to be here."

"Why?"

"Because of the bad people in Athanoor."

"What will they do?"

"Probably nothing. But it is better to be safe." Selvam does not know about what has been done to their hut back in Athanoor. Ramu and Ponni have kept the mayhem from him. Ramu had sent someone to Keelpaarai to transmit a telegram to Gomati Paati as soon as the devastated hut was discovered, as soon as they had decided it would be best to send Selvam away. In the meantime, Ponni made up a story for Selvam and all three of them spent the night at the school. This was not so strange to Selvam because Arokiasamy and Karuppan usually slept at the school anyway. In the morning, Ponni went back to the hut to pack a few of Selvam's things and Ramu and Selvam were gone before the sun was too high in the sky. Selvam knew of the trouble brewing in the village, of course, but he did not know the worst of it.

"What about you and Amma, then? How will you be safe?" Selvam says, asking the obvious question.

This is what Ramu has been afraid of—that Selvam would begin to worry about Ponni and him. Ramu is not really too concerned about their safety in Athanoor. It is Karuppan who is in real danger. Ramu has brought Selvam to Paavalampatti because managing a volatile situation will be that much easier with Selvam out of the way. How can he make Selvam understand that? He tries.

"Don't worry about us," he says. "You know Uncle Arokia is there with us. And also Brother Karuppan, Sister Devi, and Uncle Pichayya. I don't think anything bad is going to happen. It is just that Amma and I want to make sure you are safe. That is the most important thing—that you be safe."

Selvam nods, but it is clear he is not persuaded. Ramu tries something else. "There is another reason too."

"What reason is that?"

"Gomati Paati. This is a way for you to get to know your great-grandmother. How do you like her?"

Selvam says fiercely, "I hate her!"

"Don't be silly," Ramu says. "You can't hate her. You barely even know her."

"She hates Amma."

"Not true."

"It is true!"

"Hate is a very big word for a very small boy like you."

"I don't care what you say. She hates Amma. And she hates me."

Ramu grips Selvam's shoulder hard, urgently. "Listen to me," he says, his voice harsher than he intends it to be. "Gomati Paati does not hate you or Amma. I was wrong not to have brought you here before. Then you would have known what Gomati Paati is really like. It is very important that you understand why you are here. You have to listen to Gomati Paati when I am gone. She'll take good care of you. But you have to listen to her."

Suddenly Selvam's resistance crumbles. His body sags, as if deflated, as if he is a balloon from which all the air has been let out. Ramu lets go of his shoulder. "You know my mother died when I was born," he says to Selvam. "I never knew her. Do you know who raised me?"

Selvam shakes his head.

"Gomati Paati."

Selvam remains silent, but Ramu feels something shift within him.

"It is only for a week, Sela," Ramu says, trying not to sound pleading. "You will be here for a week and then I'll come and get you. You'll see. The time will pass just like that." He snaps finger and thumb to indicate just how quickly. "Okay?" He is insistent on getting a positive answer.

Selvam nods in reply. It is something. It will have to suffice.

The next morning Ramu gets up in a leisurely way and is ready to leave after a quick bath at the well at the back and a hot tumbler of coffee. Gomati Paati has wrapped freshly made dosas in banana leaves for him to take on the journey. He leaves for the station at a quarter to nine, just enough time to buy a ticket and board the train. He and Gomati Paati have agreed that it would not be a good idea for Selvam to come to the station to see him off. When he sets off briskly down Meenakshisundareshwarar Temple Street, Selvam is still in bed despite the lateness of the hour; but at the end of the street Ramu glances back and sees Gomati Paati standing on the thinnai with Sela by her side. They are watching his departure. Gomati Paati is only a little taller than Sela. In her white widow's sari, she looks old, frail. Her face with its strong and determined features is not visible at this distance. Sela is bare bodied, the way he has slept, for the heat persisted through the night. His hair, grown long because Ponni hasn't had the time to wield her scissors, is tousled from sleep. In one hand, he holds the brand-new toy camera. Gomati Paati's right hand rests protectively on his shoulder. Ramu is reassured that Sela has not flung it off. One week, at most two, and then he'll be back. Ramu raises a quick hand in farewell to his grandmother and his son, and then turns the corner into Station Road.

To Athanoor now. To Ponni. And to the resurgent trouble that confronts their school and them.

~

THE TRAIN FROM PAAVALAMPATTI TAKES Ramu to Thirunelveli Junction Railway Station. In the train, he shuts his eyes, but cannot help listening to his fellow passengers, men on their way to Thirunelveli Town for work. Their conversation this morning is full of Nehru, patrician Brahmin leader of the freedom struggle, Prime Minister of India. He has died. Ramu takes in the news. Nehru is dead. Caught up in his own crisis, he has not been following current events. He knows of Nehru's recent return to Delhi from convalescence in Kashmir, but little more. His fellow passengers discuss Nehru's legacy. The conversation grows heated. The debacle of the border war between India and China! The attempted imposition of Hindi on South India! The decline of the Indian National Congress as a political party! The men are clamorous in their opinions. After Nehru, whither India? After Nehru, who will be prime minister? Will a Tamil ever become prime minister? Why not? They buzz with questions and counter-questions, opinions and counter-opinions. Ramu does not buzz. There was a time when he might have—no, *would* have. He would have jumped headlong into the discussion. Now, he feels detached from it all. He knows Nehru's death is an important and uncertain event for the country. But he can think only of his own crisis—the crisis in Athanoor. The second crisis. There was one before and now this is the second one in Athanoor. Obscure though the village may be, his work there is *his* legacy. People in far corners of the country may not be talking about it; still, it is his. His and Ponni's and Arokiasamy's. After all, they have kept the school going for more than ten years against all the odds.

At Thirunelveli, Ramu switches to a bus. The bus to Thoothukudi on the coast makes a stop at the little roadside Mariamman temple by the neem tree. From there, it is only a half hour's walk to Athanoor. Ramu makes his way from the railway station to the bus terminus to find that his bus is only half full. It will not leave until more passengers arrive. On the wall behind the bus is a film poster—for a Muthu starrer, he notices. Muthu, as agelessly handsome as ever, is riding a horse across a desert landscape while a cape streams behind him from his shoulders. The film is called *Robin Hood*—the words are spelled out in Tamil. It is typical of the movies Muthu makes now: a dashing hero saving the hapless masses in completely incredible ways. A mix of populism and fantasy. Ramu regards the poster with detached amusement, a feeling that would have been quite impossible in days gone by.

Before climbing into his bus, Ramu goes to the water tap under the jackfruit tree in a corner of the terminus. He washes his hands and then returns to his bus to take a seat toward the front. He unwraps the dosas that Gomati Paati has prepared for him. The dosas are still fresh and crisp. When he's done eating, he's thirsty, and he would like to wash his hands. He should have thought of that before climbing into the bus to eat. He dismounts, leaving an old Tamil magazine from his cloth bag on his seat to indicate that it is taken. It is only mid-morning and already the air feels hot, sticky—palpably hotter than Paavalampatti, which is closer to the mountains. Above the water tap, the thick and waxy leaves of the jackfruit tree hang limp and still. A bus, heat shimmering off its metal body, passes, making for the exit from the terminus. He splashes water on his face and returns to his bus to find, alas, a big woman, fat enough to spill from the seat into the aisle in fold upon fold of quivering flesh, has commandeered his seat. She has his magazine in her hands. At his approach, she silently holds it out to him but makes no effort to get up. He takes the magazine and retreats. He does not try to repossess his seat. Ponni would have. He does not. The bus has filled. The only seats remaining are at the very back, where he will be rattled and tossed by every bump and pothole in the road. No matter. No choice. He takes a hard wooden seat, places his cloth bag between his feet, and promptly dozes off.

He comes awake with the coughing and spluttering of the bus engine. The bus is finally departing. It leaves the terminus and heads east, in the opposite direction to Paavalampatti. The bus conductor makes his way down the aisle collecting money and handing out tickets to passengers, an assortment of villagers and townspeople, laughing children and grave grandfathers, loud-voiced women returning home from the market with empty baskets, and impoverished listless young men with a dull anger in their eyes. Ramu looks at the young men with a sense of recognition. He knows many such young men. He knows well the boys they once were.

The bus passes the tall, thin spire of the Holy Trinity Cathedral in Paalayamkottai, and then the town is behind and it is the open road to Thoothukudi. Ramu buys his ticket from the conductor and watches the country passing outside his window in the fiery sun. The paddy fields ringing Thirunelveli Town, fed by the

Tamarabarani river, are fallow now because it is the dry season. But there are trees and gardens all along the road. When they leave the river well behind, the land changes, grows more arid. Scrub jungle replaces cultivated land as the bus rattles east along the narrow road. The farther east they go, the fewer and meaner the villages become. Lone obstinate palm trees dot the land. Hardy goats nose at wild bushes, watched by half-naked children leaning on sticks, looking like ancient dwarves. They pass wide expanses where there is no jungle, no goats, no dwarves, only dirt and rock. Muted green gives way to barren brown. Ramu is familiar with this dirt and rock. After all, Athanoor is surrounded by just such desolation, and he has made it his home now for quite a few years.

The bus lets him off at the Mariamman temple, a modest little shrine protected by a rough low wall. The bus flings a great, generous cloud of exhaust and dust on him as a parting gift and moves down the shimmering black ribbon of the road toward Thoothukudi. He is the only passenger to alight here. It is past one in the afternoon. The sun above is white and fierce. The sickly neem tree by the shrine casts a paltry shade, the only refuge in any direction. The three palm trees in the distance will surely provide no shade. Beyond the palms is a rocky ridge, and some distance beyond that, invisible from the road, Athanoor. A faint trail in the dirt indicates the way. Cloth bag under his arm, Ramu trudges along the trail. He passes the palm trees and toils up the ridge. His rubber slippers are worn. His feet ache from the stones on the trail. He should have bought a new pair of slippers in Thirunelveli Town. Maybe he'll have time when he goes next week to bring Sela back. By the time he reaches the top of the ridge, he has developed a dull ache in his head. He has walked the trail countless times, but it feels especially difficult today.

From the top of the ridge, Athanoor is visible as a raggedy collection of huts. Ramu pauses to rest, shades his eyes with one hand, and squints in its direction. The village has grown in the years he has been there but it has not become more prosperous. The huts still have only thatch roofs. The few houses are still mostly of rude brick, little better than the huts. There is still only one imposing building in the village—the mansion belonging to quarry owner Parthiban Reddy. At the other end of the village from the mansion is their school—his and Ponni's and Arokia's. The huts are strung out along the trail that runs through the village. The pond, hidden behind a little cluster of trees to one side of the village, is now almost entirely dry. The rains are still weeks away.

He begins his descent from the ridge. He walks more briskly now because he is almost home. He makes for the side of the village closer to the pond. This is the end of the village where his own hut is. It is where the school is. He passes the slender black trunk of the headless coconut tree, standing like an ominous sentinel at the entrance to Athanoor. The dead tree has been there ever since he has been in Athanoor. He passes a boy, torn shorts slipping low below his hips, driving his goats into the shade of the faded, sickly trees around the pond. The goats have been grazing on the weeds growing in the pond bed around the shrunken muddy pool right at the center. He does not know the boy. The boy has never attended his school. If he had, he would surely know him.

He sees the school now—*his* school. It is small, but it has trees in it, for Ponni believes every school should have trees, even ones that struggle in the rough soil. Under the trees are the two sheds with thatch roofs and the more solid construction of brick that is the office, such as it is. A wire fence buttressed by scrub bushes encloses the school. Inside each of the two sheds, three walls have blackboards. Bright paintings made by the children over the years decorate the outer walls of the sheds and the office building. The rudimentary, but clean and inviting, playground with slide, see-saw, and swing is in one corner of the compound. Next to the metal gate to the school is the sign in Tamil, faded now—*Tiruvalluvar School, Athanoor.* A judicious name, he and Ponni and Arokiasamy had felt. Who could voice any objection to a school named after the great Tamil saint and scholar?

Ramu arrives at the gate of the school. The gate is locked. Not surprising, but still Ramu is saddened. What is the use of a locked school? A school should be open always, with children running in and out, with laughter ringing from every corner.

Ramu gets sentimental when he thinks of his school. He peers through the bars of the gate. The door to the office is open. He can hear voices within. He shouts loudly, "Who's there? I'm back from Paavalampatti. Open the gate!"

Even the shouting exhausts Ramu and makes his headache worse. It is late in the afternoon by now. He hasn't had lunch. He is hungry. Karuppan appears from the brick office building, carrying a long, stout stick. When he sees Ramu, he removes a key from the waist fold of his veshti and opens the gate. Ramu steps through and Karuppan locks the gate behind them again. He gives the lock a good tug to make sure it's secure. The school compound is tidy if small. Most of the space within the fence is taken up by the two thatch-roofed classrooms with mud walls, the rough brick office structure, and the playground. The playground has a small sandbox that Ponni uses to teach the youngest children the alphabet the old-fashioned way, by drawing figures in the sand with a twig and having the children trace them—அ, ஆ, இ, ஈ, and so on. The vowels first, then the consonants. A mango tree casts welcome shade over the playground. In one corner of the school compound, two coconut trees lean against a sky bleached white by a fiery sun.

"This stick," Ramu says, gesturing to the stout weapon in Karuppan's hands. "Is it necessary?"

"You don't know, Teacher-Sar," Karuppan replies. "Anything is possible. You have to be prepared for anything." Because Karuppan was once a student at the school, when he calls Ramu Teacher-Sar and Ponni Teacher-Amma, he's not using the terms only as honorifics as most villagers do. After all, he really was a student of theirs, and of Arokiasamy too. Ramu remembers well the wide-eyed boy with knobbly knees and a restless hunger for learning. It enrages him to see the jackals in human clothing circling now, plotting to bring him down so as to get at the school.

Ramu shakes his head doubtfully. "Just be careful what you do with it," he warns. "You can kill someone with that thing."

Karuppan grins and gives the stick a gay twirl. His knobbly knees are a thing of the past. He has perfect teeth despite the beedis he smokes. Ramu has reached an age when he has a keen appreciation of the resplendence of youth. *Long may Karuppan enjoy his youth*, he thinks. Ramu has plenty of life left in him, but he feels older than his age in the dazzle of Karuppan's smile.

Ramu and Karuppan go into the office building, a single room with a wooden desk, a beaten-up old chair, a shelf of books, and a Godrej cabinet. Arokiasamy is sitting at the desk, fanning himself with a tattered notebook. Ramu looks at him with fond relief. It is good to be back in Athanoor. He knows there is nothing that Arokiasamy would not do for him, or he for Arokiasamy. Time has been kinder to Arokiasamy than to Ramu. His hair is still black and he is without the lines that life is known to thoughtlessly trace on faces. He has grown in the opposite direction from Ramu—though small in stature, he is rotund, not fat exactly, but given to fatness. It is not because he is any less poor than Ramu, nor because he has grown less intense over the years—not at all: he is still as energetic as ever. Arokiasamy's fleshliness is a mystery. Ramu and Ponni have constructed an elaborate joke around it. They accuse him of having a lover in an adjoining village who shamelessly plies him with sweet things made of ghee. Arokiasamy plays along and sighs sheepishly at the accusations. But there is no lover. There have been lovers in the past, but there is none now. Arokiasamy's affairs of the heart never last. He has neither the time nor the patience to make them last. His life is consumed by his passion for the school and his deep friendship with Ramu and Ponni.

"How was Paavalampatti?" Arokiasamy asks, speaking in English. "How did Selvam take it when you left?" Ramu, Ponni, and Arokiasamy have promised to speak English to one another as much as possible so as not to lose touch with the language. Whenever they go away to a likely town, they return with English books that they share among themselves. The books are then added to the Tamil and English books on the shelf in the school office. This shelf, Ramu's responsibility, is the school's library. The books are neatly numbered according to the order in which they were acquired and also noted in a register that also sits on the shelf.

Ramu remembers when they started the library with just eight books bought with pooled money, after much heated argument over the final list, from the used books shop in Palayamkottai. The numbers are marked on the book spines:

No. 1: *The Tirukural* of Tiruvalluvar (Tamil original accompanied by the English translation of G. U. Pope).
No. 2: a selection of Sangam poetry.
No. 3: a collection of essays and speeches by Dr. Ambedkar.
No. 4: selected poems of Subramania Bharathi.
No. 5: a collection of Romantic poetry by Wordsworth, Shelley, and Byron.
No. 6: Leo Tolstoy's *Anna Karenina.*
No. 7: Nehru's *Discovery of India.*
No. 8: a collection of speeches by Periyar.

It was not until they came home to Athanoor and arranged the books on a shelf that they realized that these were books meant for them, not the children of their budding school. Never mind, they said shamefacedly to one another. These would be good reference books, useful in devising lessons. (Imagine teaching Indian history out of Nehru, but of course only after having supplemented him and corrected his more terrible opinions with the help of Ambedkar and Periyar!) After that they took more care in acquiring books. From eight books, there are now almost eighty, including books specifically written for children. As the school has evolved, so has the library—both have grown in a lurching, learn-as-you-go way. Ramu likes looking at the bookshelf, for it is a reminder of how far they have come.

"Paavalampatti was fine," Ramu says in reply to Arokiasamy, also speaking in English. "I left Selvam with my grandmother. Uncle Siva is away in Bombay."

"When does that . . . that . . ." Arokiasamy searches for the right English word; there are a few choice Tamil ones he can think of, ". . . scoundrel get back?" He has never met Uncle Siva but has heard enough to dislike him without reservation.

"Not for a week at least. Hopefully by then I will be able to bring Selvam back."

Arokiasamy nods but does not say anything. His face has a gloomy expression on it. "I hope so, Ramu," he says.

Ramu is surprised. Arokiasamy was not in favor of taking Selvam to Paavalampatti. Why has he changed his mind in the little time that Ramu has been gone? "Tell me. What has happened? Where's Ponni?"

"She has gone with Devi to see Reddiar."

Devi and Karuppan. Former students who have turned into helpers at the school. What would they do without them? Neither Devi nor Karuppan gets paid, any more than Ramu or Arokiasamy does. Karuppan is happy to sleep at the school like Arokiasamy, while Devi sleeps at Cinema Crazy Susi's hut. They all share in the food—anyone who is able cooks in the hut that is Ramu and Ponni's home.

Ramu frowns to hear that Ponni and Devi have gone to Reddiar's house.

Karuppan notices and says, "I said I go also. Teacher-Amma said no." When it comes to English, he is better at reading than speaking.

"It would have been a very bad idea for you to go, Karuppan," Arokiasamy admonishes.

"Yes. What were you thinking, Karuppa?" Ramu asks. "It would have been terrible if you had gone." The very idea is incredible. Exactly the kind of thing Karuppan would impulsively suggest. "It is bad enough that Ponni and Devi have gone. Reddiar is not the kind of man to treat them with respect."

"We are trying to reduce the trouble, not add to it," Arokiasamy observes. He is aware of Ramu's worry. "I tried to stop them from going, Ramu," he says. "You know how Ponni is."

"I'll say one thing," Karuppan interjects boldly. "Reddy is not big man. Not even little afraid I have."

Ramu silently swallows his exasperation. This is not the right moment to educate Karuppan in the dangerous ways of the world. "Tell me what's happened," he asks again. He has switched to Tamil.

Arokiasamy says, "We sent Karuppan away to Keelpaarai last night. Pichayya and I slept here at the school. Ponni and Devi slept at Cinema Crazy Susi's hut. We didn't think it was safe for Ponni to be alone after the way Reddiar's men ransacked your home. Ponni wasn't too happy about going to Susi's but she did. It's good we took these precautions. Reddiar's men came to the school in the middle of the night and made a huge ruckus. They stood at the gate and demanded we turn Karuppan over to them. We said we didn't know where he was. They knew we were lying. I saw two of the men had guns—like long rifles. The others had knives and scythes. I thought things would get bad, really bad, but then Pichayya spoke to them. He still has influence with them, you know. They left but said would be back in the morning. They haven't been back, though."

The mention of guns and knives worries Ramu. It is the first time such weapons have made their appearance. Day by day the situation grows more critical. He says to Karuppan, "Why did you come back here? You should have remained in hiding for a few days, at least until we told you it's safe to come back."

Ramu's words anger Karuppan. "I've done nothing wrong," he says, resentfully. "Why should I be in hiding? It's that Reddy bastard who should be in hiding."

"He is right, Ramu," Arokiasamy says. "It makes sense for him to go away at night to be safe. But if he disappears completely, it will be like Reddiar has won. Karuppan hasn't done anything wrong."

Ramu decides not to argue the point. "What happened this morning?" he asks.

"First thing in the morning Ponni went to the police station in Keelpaarai to register a complaint about the ransacking," Arokiasamy says. "The police laughed at her. You know they are in Reddiar's pocket. They wrote down her complaint but made it clear they were not going to do anything about it."

"Did she say anything about the rape accusation?"

"No, just that her home had been attacked."

"Just as well."

"It was afternoon by the time she got back. When she heard what had happened at night, she was very angry. We were still discussing what to do when she rushed off to Reddiar's. I tried to stop her. I said she should wait for you to come back, but she wouldn't listen. I sent Devi with her. I thought I should stay here because of Karuppan."

"Where's Pichayya?"

"Gone to Cinema Crazy Susi to get some food," Karuppan says. "He should be back soon."

Ramu says, "I should go to Reddiar's."

"Wait for Pichayya to come back," Arokiasamy says. "You must be hungry. None of us has eaten yet. Have some food before you go. Who knows? By then Ponni and Devi may be back. I don't think Reddiar will try anything with them during the daytime with the whole village watching."

Ramu says to Karuppan, "Do Reddiar's men know you are here?"

"Probably," Arokiasamy replies on Karuppan's behalf. "But I don't think they will do anything as long as it's daylight."

"This is bad," Ramu observes gloomily.

"Yes," Arokiasamy agrees. "It's not like the other times. This is more serious."

"They want to shut the school down," Karuppan says. "I'm just an excuse. Even if I go away, they will find another reason to attack the school. That is why I'm not afraid. They don't really want to catch me. If they do, how will they continue to target the school? That's why they haven't gone to the police to report this so-called rape."

Ramu looks at Karuppan with new respect. He hadn't thought of that. It's true. Reddiar shows no hurry to go to the police. "Don't worry," he says, bravely. "We won't let them do anything to you or the school." But how is he to protect both Karuppan and the school? He knows Reddiar has them cornered. Give up Karuppan or let the school be destroyed. That is the impossible choice with which Reddiar has confronted them. Reddiar knows perfectly well that they will never give Karuppan up. Then must the school be destroyed? The thought is unbearable. There must be a way out!

A shout interrupts his worrying. "Pichayya," Arokiasamy says. Karuppan goes to open the gate. Soon he and Pichayya return carrying packets of food and a roll of banana leaves. Pichayya's donkey ambles across the rectangle of the door toward the back of the compound, heading for the shade under the mango tree where it usually lies. When Pichayya sees Ramu, he acknowledges him with a gesture of the head. He is a man of few words. Over the years, he has lost more of his teeth. His wispy hair is entirely white now and there is a faded quality to him, as if time has washed all the brighter colors out of the washerman.

The smell of food awakens Ramu's hunger. He takes the roll of banana leaves from Pichayya to wash at the cement water trough behind the office structure. Pichayya's donkey is slaking its thirst at the water pooled around the edges of the trough. When he appears, it steps away considerately. From the shade of the mango tree, it watches as he pours from the little water left in the trough with a battered tin cup. First Ramu washes his feet, thick with calluses, rubbing them against each other, then splashes water on his face and neck. Finally, he washes the banana leaves, dangling each by its spine under the cascading water as the donkey and the coconut trees watch him gravely.

When he returns to the office, the packets of food are open and waiting on a mat on the floor. The four of them range themselves around the food. There is parboiled rice mixed with salt and buttermilk, lime pickle, and a vegetable stew in a battered old pot. Ramu puts some of the rice on his banana leaf, pours some stew on top of it out of the pot, and then mashes it all together with his fingers. He eats ravenously, taking large handfuls to the accompaniment of the fiery lime pickle. He feels his spirits revive as the food fills his stomach. They end the meal with mangos from their own tree. Fine Neelam mangos, so called because of the light bluish tinge they often have. They bite into the thick mango skin, peeling it off with their teeth. The pulp beneath is sweet as nectar and soft, so soft that it melts in the mouth. At the end is the contrary pleasure of sucking on the fibrous tart mango seed as yellow juice drips off the hand and onto the banana leaf.

Karuppan is the first to finish. He folds his banana leaf over and says contentedly, "Cinema Crazy Susi knows how to cook."

Cinema Crazy Susi runs Athanoor's sole shop. The shop leans against her mud-walled hut and is no more than a plank and a shelf with a tarpaulin over both. It carries small quantities of the necessities of life, whatever Susi is able to acquire on her many trips to the tent cinema in Keelpaarai. The nearest proper store is at least a half hour away in a neighboring village. Susi supplements the income from the shop by cooking dosas on an enormous pan. She will also cook meals on request. Of course, when she cooks for Teacher-Amma she charges no more than cost.

Ponni has done much for Cinema Crazy Susi. She gave her the money to start her little shop. When Susi's daughter ran away from home, Ponni went with Susi all the way to Thoothukudi to look for the thirteen-year-old girl. They found her in a tough part of town close to the port. She was in a house full of girls who had either run away or had been forcibly taken. It was not easy getting the girl out of the house, but Ponni knew men in the Thoothukudi Port workers union, men who are not to be crossed lightly. Now the girl is married and has two children, but who can tell what might have come to pass if they had not found her in time?

After the used banana leaves have been offered to Pichayya's donkey and the food put away for Ponni and Devi, Ramu, Arokiasamy, Karuppan, and Pichayya gather in the office. Arokiasamy takes up his old place in the ramshackle chair behind the desk. He shares use of the chair with Ponni. One of his jobs in the school is general administration. Ponni uses the chair and desk to confer with the parents of the children and to correspond with the schools in Thirunelveli, Nagercoil, and Madurai to which a few of the better students go on scholarships after their start here in Athanoor. She is the indefatigable champion of these children not only with the distant schools but also with their parents, who will have to forego an income, however meager, if the children continue with their schooling. Now Arokiasamy sits in the chair and Ramu sits cross-legged on the mat on the floor opposite him. Pichayya squats on his haunches with his back to the wall, while Karuppan stands in the doorway leaning on his stick.

Ramu says to Pichayya and the others gathered in the school office, "What should I say to Reddiar when I see him?"

Karuppan hisses, "Tell the bastard Kunti is lying. I had nothing to do with that woman. I did not touch her, let alone rape her."

"Reddiar knows that," Arokiasamy says. "He is the one who is behind this accusation. He is plotting to discredit the school and to turn the villagers against us. You are just a small piece of a bigger plan, Karuppa. You know that."

"But it's my life that is being destroyed," Karuppan says angrily. "How will I show my face around the village again?"

"We will fight Reddiar," Arokiasamy reassures Karuppan. "We will clear your name." He injects a confidence into his voice that he does not feel. Kunti is of a different, somewhat higher, caste than Karuppan and this has allowed Reddiar to foment trouble among the men of her caste. The matter is grave.

"Poor Kunti," Ramu says. "Her life is being destroyed too."

"That scrawny piece of flesh," Karuppan says impetuously. "I wouldn't touch her even if someone paid me to!"

"She has little choice," Arokiasamy chastises Karuppan. "She is in hock to the Reddiar. Some say she is the Reddiar's keep. She goes to him whenever he wants her. I understand the terrible thing she is accusing you of, but what else can she do? She is completely in the power of Quarry Owner Reddy."

Ramu cannot bear thinking of Quarry Owner Reddy, enemy of the school that takes away potential workers from his quarry, and indeed from every other quarry in the area. Ramu knows that every Pallar boy or girl who looks out into the larger world through the school is a worker lost to the quarries. True, Reddy sold them the land to start the school, and even had supported it for the first few years when the true scope of the school had not yet become clear, but there had been nothing noble in those actions. He had thought then only of the money he could make by getting rid of a piece of dirt in the middle of nowhere to foolish outsiders; and he had calculated that he could control the school, keep it functioning simply as a place to store children until they were old enough to work in his quarries as was their destiny. He could not have imagined that the outsiders would not only actually *educate* children but grow from strength to strength, year after year, until now, when classes are offered up to the seventh year. Or that the school would draw students from more and more of the adjoining villages. The children are actually learning to read and write and to count. Imagine how dangerous that could be! Ramu knows Quarry Owner Reddy had not thought outsiders could show such resolve, or that they could escape his control so completely, but Ramu, Ponni, and Arokiasamy have been single-minded in their work with the school. Ramu knows just how single-minded. That is why Quarry Owner Reddy wants to destroy them. He tried once before and failed, and now he is trying again.

"What if the Reddiar's men don't stop at the gate next time?" Ramu wonders. "What if they tear down the gate and attack the school when Karuppan is here?"

Karuppan lowers his voice. "I have gelatin sticks hidden away. If that Reddy bastard attacks the school, we will attack him too." He does not tell them that he has a homemade pistol too—a metal tube attached by a crude mechanism to a piece of wood by someone who knows about such things.

"What will you do with gelatin sticks?" Ramu demands.

"I will blow up the quarry office. Or else Reddy's stone grinder!"

"What if somebody is hurt in the explosion?"

"No one will be hurt. I'll be careful."

"How did you get the sticks?" Arokiasamy asks.

"I have friends. Some of them work in Reddy's quarry. The gelatin sticks are Reddy's." He laughs at the irony.

Ramu wonders which of Reddy's workers are Karuppan's allies. Ramu has been to Reddy's quarry, during a time when he still could go. He has been there when the quarry resounds with voices and with the sharp clatter and dull thud of pickaxes and sledgehammers. He has seen the dust rise in a great cloud in the wake of a loaded truck rumbling by to the grinder on the rocky dirt trail that dips into the quarry. The grinder is a recent innovation, meant to speed up the stripping of the open stone quarry, already made wondrously deep by generations of bare hands and crude tools. He has seen how the dust in the quarry coats hair, eyebrows, arms, cheeks. Down on the quarry floor the air can be so thick with dust that breathing is difficult and eyes become red and swollen. Men, women, and children are metamorphosed into gray ghosts by the dust. He has seen the ghosts gather at the end of the day to receive their meager pay from Reddy's minion seated behind a wooden table by the little shack that guards the entrance to the quarry. Which of these ghosts, some of whom have children in his school, stole the gelatin sticks for Karuppan?

"This rape accusation has no substance to it," Ramu says. He speaks firmly. "We will clear your name. But I don't want anything violent happening in the meantime.

"Neither do I," Karuppan agrees. "I don't intend to start anything. You see how patient I am being, Teacher-Sar. Even after being falsely accused of rape I have not lifted a finger against Reddy or his men." Then he adds fiercely, "But if that bloodsucking Reddy attacks me or the school, I won't stand by quietly."

"Ayya," Ramu says to Pichayya, who has been silent all this while. "Can you talk some sense into this boy? I don't want him jeopardizing the school."

Finally, Pichayya speaks up. He says to Karuppan, "Violence solves nothing. Don't do anything foolish." But he does not stop there. He goes on speaking, saying to no one in particular, "There is something you learn as a washerman. In the old days, before I came here, I used to dye clothes as part of my trade. You learn something very quickly in dyeing—if you want to dye a piece of cloth, you first have to make sure it is clean. If there is any blemish or stain on the cloth and you dip it in the dye—blue or yellow or red or pink; it does not matter—the cloth will look poorly dyed and the color will not come out properly. But if you dip a clean, stainless cloth in a vat of dye, the color will come out bright, pure. Think of it this way. Your every action is a piece of cloth."

For a long silent moment Ramu, Arokiasamy, and Karuppan ponder Pichayya's wisdom.

"Ayya," Karuppan says finally, expressing what Arokiasamy and Ramu are too timid or else too proud to say, "I don't understand. Why don't you explain what you mean?"

"I have. If I explain it any more, you still won't understand," Pichayya says, calmly. "Think on your own and you will." He pauses and then adds, "Don't take any action until you have figured it out."

But Ramu knows they do not have the time to ruminate at leisure on Pichayya's gnomic utterance. The world presses in upon them. Reddiar is coming down hard on them, determined to destroy their school. Unstained cloth or not, Ramu is intent on saving it. The time to do something is *now.* He respects Pichayya and knows him well enough to take what he says seriously, but he cannot tarry. He cannot wait to solve Pichayya's riddle before acting. He thinks morosely, *Perhaps this is how it has always been—when the time to act is upon you, the knowledge of what to do is missing; and by the time the knowledge arrives, the time to act is past.*

Is this the secret history of the world?

The question cannot be answered, not now at any rate. Feeling keenly the urgency of the moment, Ramu stands up. Time to go to Reddiar's mansion, to which Ponni has stormed off with Devi. He is afraid to think of what has already transpired there. He must go immediately; but before he can there is a shout at the gate to the school. Have Ponni and Devi returned from Reddiar's? Ramu pauses to find out.

↝

Even as Ramu waits to see who is at the gate to the school, across the village Quarry Owner Reddy sits in the mansion his father built when he first grew rich from quarrying. The imposing white-painted mansion, with a broad verandah along its front, is perched up on a small rise overlooking the village, at the foot of which is an ancient tamarind tree. Reddiar is in his wooden reclining chair, looking out over Athanoor from this fine verandah. Not even ten minutes have passed since he dismissed Ponni and Devi from his presence. He feels pleased with the way he made the two whores wait for a long time in the hot sun at the foot of the steps leading up to the verandah before giving them an earful. He taught the teachers words they did not know. Not for the rest of their lives would they forget the choice words he made them learn! Reddiar leans back, satisfied, and looks out across the village at the trees in the distance that hide the school from view. All drooping, except for the mango tree. He considers his position in his war on the school—yes, it has become a war. It was not so at the beginning. Now it is most definitely a war and he is determined to win it.

Despite the school's success, he had left the school alone during its early years; it had not worried him then. It was harmless enough, he had thought. When the school did not fail miserably and fold up as per his expectation, he had still perceived its utility as a place where his workers could leave their youngest children when they came to work. If the children, too small and tender yet to work in his quarries, had a place where they were safe, he had reasoned, his workers would be less distracted. There had been one or two unnecessary incidents (in one a child had almost been killed by falling rocks) that could have been avoided if there had been a place for the smaller children to be left. With such a school, he had felt, he would get more out of his workers.

The school had certainly fulfilled this expectation during the early years, when only the smallest of the children went there. Reddiar had felt supportive enough during this time to give money for a playground at the request of one of the three outsiders running the school, the Christian Arokiasamy. Then the children grew older, and Reddiar began to notice that many stayed on in the school even though they should have been working in his quarries breaking stone alongside their parents. He began too to hear about what older children were being taught in the school—about caste and untouchability and the oppressiveness of religion. Atheistic things! Trying to be reasonable, he ordered Ramu and Arokiasamy brought to him, to this very verandah where he sat now. Treating them well, not at all eager to chastise them, he had offered them chairs to sit on and explained to them what he expected of the school. The two outsiders listened politely. They went away. Nothing changed. Reddiar felt sorely betrayed, personally disrespected. He had tried to be tolerant, indeed had helped the school in its inception, but what had the outsiders done? They had turned around and struck at their very patron!

Belatedly, Reddiar had discovered that the hypocritical outsiders did not appreciate him as their patron. Nor, as he found out when he finally set about turning people against the school, were the outsiders outsiders anymore. Some villagers opposed the school. Some were indifferent. And some, in the years gone by since the school's founding, had become supporters. Children from many villages had gone through the school. Many parents said they valued what the school had taught their sons and even their daughters. Equally vexing, the school had the support of Pichayya, who had an uncanny hold over the villagers. Reddy's rage had grown along with the threat to his authority in Athanoor—in *his* village. When he met his fellow landlords and quarry owners, he felt ashamed that he had permitted such a school to grow in his own village. When they questioned him irritably because their affairs too were affected by the upstart school, which was becoming a bad example in the whole area, he assured them that he would take care of the situation.

First, Reddiar had called in workers who had children in the school and explained the ways of the world to them. Speaking to these clueless breakers of stone in their own simple language, he said, "You fools, you idiots. You are smashing your own foot with a sledgehammer. Think about it. You are buffaloes. You are illiterate, ignorant. If your children go to school, won't they learn to look down on you? Do you want your children to feel superior to you? Do you want them to hate you? If they go to school, will they want to work in the quarries and help you with their earnings? Of course not!"

This line of argument shook some workers. They looked at him with terror-stricken eyes and said, "Ayya! Swami! You are like a god to us. Tell us what we should do!"

Reddiar was unsparing in his advice. "Pull your children out of the school. Bring them to the quarries. If they refuse, beat them and drag them there. What boy has ever become a man without a good whipping now and then?" Such was Reddiar's exhortation, for he believed in plain speaking.

With other workers unmoved by this line of reasoning, however, Reddiar had become tougher. He told them bluntly that he wanted their children. "Your children belong to me," he said. "That is how it was in the past. That is how it will be in the future. Tomorrow I want to see your children in the quarries with tools in their hands, or else you, the parents, will lose your jobs. That is it. Simple as that." Many panicked workers took their children out of the school, but too few, not enough, so he did fire one or two workers on a pretext, to make an example.

Unfortunately, there were limits to this form of intimidation. Firing workers hurt him as much as it hurt the workers. He couldn't afford to keep firing workers to punish them. He needed workers in his quarries! He needed as many hands breaking his stones and loading his trucks as possible. His stone was distributed to construction sites all over the district, and even as far as Madurai. He couldn't afford an interruption in supply. To make matters worse, the workers he fired defied him by switching to coolie work in Thoothukudi rather than pull their children out of the school. The school shrank but did not shut down.

What could Reddiar do? The workers had left him with no choice. He could not permit defiance. One night he had his ruffians beat up one of the more outspoken workers, who had gone around boldly saying that come what may he would not pull his daughter out of the school. Now when Reddiar considered the matter, he realized that the assault was a mistake. It had set back his campaign against the school by years. Reddiar had thought, "This will put real fear in the workers." But the strategy backfired. He was the first to admit it—he had not read the situation correctly. Suddenly he—the hunter—had become the hunted. All attention turned to him. Questions began to be asked. Not by the police. No, the police were not his problem. They could never be his problem. He had been paying them off for years. This wasn't the first time he had had to deal with troublesome workers in his quarries. It was always useful to have the police on your side. No, the police were safely in his control.

The problem was a foolish journalist who, instigated by that whore Ponni—that, that . . . Reddiar couldn't find the words to properly describe that woman!—had managed to sneak an article into a local newspaper. Once the story appeared, it took great nimbleness on Reddiar's part to keep it from blowing up into a full-scale scandal. It was just the kind of story that some national dailies liked—*Bloodsucking upper-caste oppressor deprives lowly, untouchable children of opportunities to go to school.* Nonsense like that. He could just imagine the damage if the story caught fire. To keep that from happening, he had to retreat. He had to pay off the publisher of the newspaper and abruptly back off from his campaign against the school. The journalist who had written the story, Ponni's friend, was not happy at a second story being killed and had let his displeasure be known. Reddiar was advised to lie low and, indeed, pretend to be the school's friend. He had to watch helplessly as many of the workers who had removed their children from the school began sending them back. The children wanted to go back, the parents said to him when questioned. What kind of inhuman children were these that *wanted* to go to school? Not even his own children had *wanted* to! Unbelievable! Surely the Age of Darkness was at hand if untouchable children who had no business in school begged to go there! Reddiar fumed privately, while the workers laughed at him behind his back. He knew they did. They bowed and scraped and groveled at his feet, but the moment his back was turned they laughed at him as if he were a mangy toothless cur.

The workers, however, had it wrong. Yes, he was a cur. Most definitely a cur. But not toothless. He had underestimated the outsiders and would accordingly have to make adjustments. He had thought a frontal attack would work, but now he saw that he would have to be patient and take a more nuanced approach. The journalist would not stop nosing around, trying to write another story about stone quarrying. Reddiar was forced to bide his time, as months turned into years. He did not doubt that he would finally be able to eject the outsiders and the school they had started with *his* permission for *his* abject low-caste serfs. But he saw that he would need to proceed with caution.

His son, who had gone away to study in Madras, told him that the times were changing and that he should respond to a challenge such as this with subtlety. Heeding his son, Reddiar began to scheme and lay the ground for a more careful attack. He saw now that he first had to discredit the school, throw mud on it, smear its name with the foulest-smelling shit, so that not even the hardiest of supporters would want to go near it. And then, once the strength had drained away from the school, one sharp blow, right to the heart! That would be enough. He would show them who was toothless!

And so, when the troublesome journalist was gone and the time seemed finally right, Reddiar had his ruffians quietly start little rumors—about Arokiasamy and the many women he screwed in every village; about that defiled casteless Brahmin ass Ramu who was not really a man, not a real one (if he was, would he tie himself to the sari hem of a slut like Ponni?). But mostly he started rumors about Ponni—about her loose character and her unspeakable family. Reddiar found out about Ponni's dead uncle Chellappa and had his ruffians diligently spread the word that Chellappa was wanted by the police when he died. He was, he let it be known, a criminal, a dacoit, a murderer of innocent travelers on dark and lonely roads (it did not hurt to embellish a little). This campaign of rumor-mongering was in full swing when Karuppan returned to join the school.

Karuppan, unlike the outsiders, was a native dog who had gone to the very school under attack. Afterward, he had left Athanoor to go to a residential school in Madurai on a scholarship and then had returned with his head filled with foolishness. Reddiar had to admit he was earnest and passionate about the school and its children and fiercely loyal to the outsiders. At the same time, he was young and hotheaded. He had grown up in the village but his parents had died during the time he was gone. Diplomacy did not sit well with him. When Reddiar's ruffians picked a fight, he fought back. When he heard the rumors Reddiar was spreading, he did not hold his tongue, badmouthing Reddiar himself! It was not easy to get to him, to intimidate him by threats to family.

Such was the man whom Fortune, ever mysterious, chose as its weapon in aiding Reddiar. The opportunity when it presented itself to Reddiar was delicious and fit in perfectly with his campaign of rumors already underway. A young woman who worked in Reddiar's quarries—a girl who had never been to the school, a hot little hussy who loved her arrack and whom Reddiar had in fact mounted once or twice himself; in short, a girl completely in his power—was seen walking late in the evening with Karuppan. Best of all was that she was of a different caste than Karuppan, somewhat higher than him in social status. Later that night, the woman was heard moaning and groaning about Karuppan in a drunken rage. She was heard calling him the foulest of names in front of several witnesses (including one of Reddiar's men). Probably the woman had made an advance on Karuppan, who had declined. The woman was well known for her drunken misbehavior, and nothing would have come of the incident except that Reddiar, learning what had happened, hatched a plan. He eagerly accepted the ripe fruit of mischief Fortune had flung so graciously into his lap—and that too without any scheming on his part whatsoever! It would be, he felt, a sin to refuse such a gift, freely bestowed on him, by Fortune. He promptly had the girl brought to his mansion. There, under the tamarind tree where he generally received his workers, he declared his heartfelt sympathy for her and told her he was going to investigate her accusation against the ruffian Karuppan—how dare he rape an innocent woman, especially a woman higher than him in status?

The girl, now all sobered up, looked at him in confusion and asked, "Rape?"

Reddiar said, "Yes, rape."

"But . . ."

Reddiar, his ruffians arrayed behind him in menacing fashion, raised an admonitory index finger to interrupt her.

Slowly, understanding dawned in the girl's eyes. "But, Ayya . . ." she began again.

Reddiar wasted no time in reaching across and slapping her hard. "Yes," he said, making sure to load the words with menace. "Rape."

"Ayya," the girl said, weeping, "I beg you. Don't make me do this. Rape is a terrible word. If I say I've been raped who will come near me again?"

"I will," Reddiar said readily, looking at the girl with great pleasure. *What would the world come to without women like this?* he thought with satisfaction. And then that slut Ponni came inexplicably to mind and caused his growing sense of gratification and well-being to deflate. No matter. He would take care of Ponni and her companions. He would waste no time in turning the attack on Karuppan into an attack on the school that taught him and now employed him. He knew how to get the men of Kunti's caste riled up about the honor of their women. He would have his men go around the village linking the rape charge against Karuppan to the morals of the school.

Reddiar caused a meeting to be held under the tamarind tree in front of his house, to which Ramu and Arokiasamy were invited. "Is this what the school teaches?" Reddiar asked at that meeting. "A violated woman's honor is at stake," he thundered to the gathering which, aside from Ramu and Arokiasamy, who were there to defend Karuppan and the school, included Pichayya, Reddiar's manager Karthikeyan, and an assortment of the village's older men, whom Reddiar had carefully chosen for their docility and purported respectability. Reddiar surveyed the men gathered under the tree and noted with satisfaction that Ponni was not present. When Reddiar considered the moment right, Kunti, shaking with fear, was trotted out between two of Reddiar's ruffians from where she was being held in a shed behind the mansion. As instructed, she repeated her accusations against Karuppan with eyes lowered, a bruise slowly ripening on one side of her face. Reddiar felt no shame at the sight of the bruise. Such were the things one had to do in life. He knew everyone suspected coercion but none dared accuse him of it. Pichayya alone said in his enigmatic manner, "Everything that appears before the eye need not be the truth."

The moment Pichayya spoke, Reddiar rounded on him (he had previously reflected on how to handle Pichayya) and said, making no attempt to be respectful, "You be quiet. Here this little child has been hurt and her most precious possession forcibly taken from her, and all you can do is speak mumbo-jumbo." Before Pichayya could react, Reddiar pointed in the direction of Ramu and Arokiasamy and yelled, "Where is that wretch Karuppan? Bring him to me!"

Arokiasamy stepped forward and said, "Please listen to us. The accusation cannot be right. Karuppan would never do such a thing."

Enjoying himself immensely, Reddiar had pushed Kunti forward and said, "Are you saying this child is lying?" Kunti hung her head low. Her hands were trembling. Inspired by the sight (he was proud of himself afterward), Reddiar said, "See how agitated she is because of what that brute Karuppan did to her."

Ramu and Arokiasamy looked at each other, wondering how to proceed.

Reddiar hurried on, "Of course you are silent. I am not surprised. Where did Karuppan learn his morals? In your school. And now you defend him. I'm sure you have that Karuppan hiding in your school. Or maybe even in your home. I'll give you until tomorrow to produce Karuppan. After that, I cannot be responsible for what happens."

There. The trap had been set.

Reddiar knew very well that the outsiders would not give up Karuppan. That is why he immediately set about pouring more oil into the fire he had started. A little escalation at the right time could not hurt. On his instructions, a few of his ruffians who were of Kunti's caste swaggered about the village flinging truculent looks in every direction. Tomorrow came and went. Karuppan was not turned over. There were minor fights between Reddiar's men and several of Karuppan's friends. The classes in the school were suspended because of poor attendance amidst the hostile situation. He waited for a couple of days and then had his men, ostensibly looking for Karuppan, ransack the hut in which Ramu and Ponni lived. His men took the couple's meager belongings and threw them outside—the chair and mats were tumbled into the street, rice was spilled into the ditch behind, clothes were flung into the branches of the drumstick tree that grew against the hut. When they found Ponni's underclothes they could not stop themselves from making obscene gestures with them. Reddiar smiled with satisfaction on hearing the report of the attack that was given to him.

Reddiar did not hide from the village the fact that his men had done the ransacking. It was time for naked intimidation under the cover of a hunt for the rapist Karuppan, given refuge by the outsiders who ran the school. After the defeat in his first campaign against the school, he had been forced to waste years when all he could do was spread rumors. He, Reddiar, had been forced to keep quiet like some low-caste serf. No more. Spreading rumors was all very well, but hardly enough to get the job done. It was time to strike. He intended the ransacking to magnify the already deep mood of alarm in Athanoor. He was pleased when he heard that Ramu had taken away his son Selvam because of the gravity of the situation. Inexorably, the crisis was coming to a head, and his crushing victory was at hand.

⁓

So things stand at the moment in Athanoor. Reddiar leans back in his chair on his verandah and reviews his lengthy war against the school, while across the village Ramu waits to find out who calls out at the gate. From the door to the school's office Ramu can see Reddiar's white mansion perched on its mount in the distance. He gazes at it and considers just how much worse the situation has become since he took Selvam to Paavalampatti. Guns and knives! He senses that Reddiar believes he has gained the upper hand. He senses in his enemy, waiting and plotting in his lair across the village, a determination to destroy the school once and for all using the accusation against Karuppan. That is why, as Karuppan says, the police have not been brought in about the alleged rape of Kunti. The police are in Reddiar's pay, but once they are informed he won't be able to control events as he is doing now. He won't be able to attack the school with impunity. Reddiar is deliberately keeping the police out of it. He is not interested in Karuppan. He is interested in the school. Ramu is glad that Selvam is in Paavalampatti. It was hard taking him there. It is not easy to think of Paavalampatti as a place of refuge, but it really is the only convenient place he could have taken Selvam. Despite everything, Selvam will be safe there with Gomati Paati until he can go back and get him.

For the third time that day Karuppan goes to open the gate to the school with key in one hand and stout stick in the other.

He returns with only Devi. Why is Ponni not with her? Did something happen at Reddiar's?

Seeing the anxiety on their faces, Devi quickly says, "Don't worry. Teacher-Amma is fine. She went home."

Home? To the ransacked hut that is their home? Ramu wonders why.

Karuppan repeats what he has just learned from Devi: "Teacher-Amma sent Devi to ask me to meet her. She wants me to do something for her."

Arokiasamy asks, "Does Teacher-Amma know Teacher-Sar is back?"

Devi shakes her head. "We did not think he would be back before evening."

"I hurried back as quickly as I could."

"What happened at Reddiar's mansion?" Arokiasamy queries.

"Reddiar made us wait in the burning sun for a long time, so long I felt the skin on my face would peel off, and then he appeared on his verandah looking cool and rested and said, 'Oh, you are still here? Why have you come? There is nothing I can do for you. The whole village is thirsting for that Karuppan's blood.' Then he abused us and had his men chase us away, while he stood there laughing. He would not listen to a single thing we had to say." A wondering look crosses Devi's face. "Some of the words he used no self-respecting man would own up to knowing. Not even my father in his most drunken rages used such words."

Devi is small, thin, with a delicate sensibility that matches her frail physical frame. Before he died coughing up blood on his mat, her father was an alcoholic. It is a wonder to Ramu that such a man has produced such a daughter as Devi. Encouraged by her mother, Devi has grown into a quiet and sensitive woman, quite the opposite of her father, but Ramu knows there is steel in her. He knows her well. The school has been Devi's refuge from a young age. When other children went home, she stayed back, trailing Ponni wherever she went. From following Ponni around, it was a natural progression for her to begin helping out when she graduated from the school, mainly by assisting Ponni in her teaching just as

Karuppan helps Ramu. Unlike Karuppan, she did not receive a scholarship to a school far away, but Ponni is working with her informally to keep her education going.

Karuppan is preparing to leave, to go to Ponni as she has asked. He is handing over to Devi the key of which he has made himself custodian.

"Is it safe for you to go?" Ramu asks Karuppan doubtfully. He is somewhat persuaded by Karuppan's reasoning that he is in no immediate danger, for to apprehend or otherwise harm him would be counter to Reddiar's real purpose. Still, to wander through the village in broad daylight is to recklessly tempt Reddiar and his ruffians.

"I won't let myself be seen," Karuppan reassures him. "I'll take the back way through the bushes."

"Tell Teacher-Amma that I'm back," Ramu says, unable to keep impatience out of his voice. "Tell her to come here right away. Tell her I and the others are waiting for her so that we can discuss things before I go to Reddiar. There is food too for her here. I'm sure she has not eaten yet." He knows how Ponni can get when she is in the grip of a righteous anger. Feeling aggrieved, Ramu watches Devi let Karuppan out. Why is Ponni summoning Karuppan to her?

Of late, Ramu feels a distance between Ponni and him. He knows the recent assaults on the school have affected her badly. They have affected Arokiasamy and him too, but with Ponni it feels very different. Reddiar's relentless campaign has taken a different kind of toll on her. Something has shifted in Ponni. He senses it. She betrays a bitterness that is new. He and Ponni have had a few excited discussions—no, better to call them what they are: angry arguments—about Reddiar's vicious campaign against the school. It is clear Ponni believes he is underestimating Reddiar and the lengths to which he will go to destroy the school. She has accused him of naivete, whereas Ramu feels he has only advocated caution. Ramu does not mind the accusation, though he does not for a moment think he is being naïve. They can argue about an accusation and they can debate how best to respond to a rogue like Reddiar.

They have done it in the past; they can do it again. But now even the arguments have ceased. What can he do if she will not talk to him? He minds the growing chill between them more than any heated argument. It feels to him as if she is withdrawing, as if she is keeping things from him.

When Devi returns from locking the gate, Pichayya breaks his customary silence to note, "Teacher-Amma is very angry."

Devi nods her assent.

"She has reason to be," Pichayya remarks.

"We all do," Ramu says irritably and settles down on the mat to wait for Ponni, while Arokiasamy indicates to Devi the leftover food from lunch.

From the school gate Karuppan darts quickly into the waist-high scrub that grows in a tangle between the school and the rest of the village. Soon he is at the hut where Ponni waits for him. He pushes aside the pink and blue curtain that hangs limply in the doorway and enters. He remembers a curtain with birds printed on it that hung there once. There have been several such curtains over the years, all cheerful. Ponni is precariously poised on the hut's sole wooden chair, one of whose legs is cracked from the recent vandalism.

"Look what they have done!" she exclaims, sweeping a hand over the shambles. The wooden shelf, always rickety, lies shattered on the floor. The Primus stove has been toppled from its perch on a low stool and the strong smell of kerosene hangs in the air. Lentils and spices and clothes are strewn across the smooth-packed mud floor of the hut.

Ponni sits in her chair holding a black-and-white photograph in her hands. She has thickened a little in her face with age but her beauty is still unmistakable. The picture she holds depicts a young man with a shock of black hair and an intense gaze. Karuppan knows from having been told that the picture is of her beloved uncle Chellappa, long dead now—the same man about whom Reddy has been spreading such terrible rumors. Another picture, of a gaunt man with sunken eyes, is on the floor but carefully propped against a wall. He knows this picture is of Teacher-Sar's father, the one who died a few years before. He frowns at the mess in the hut and says, "There are things lying in the bushes outside." On his way to the hut he passed some of Ponni's undergarments trampled into the dirt. His instinct was to pick them up, but then embarrassment made him leave them there. How could he appear before Teacher-Amma holding her underwear in his hands?

Ponni points to a neat pile of clothes and other objects—a seashell, children's drawings, pens, notebooks—in a corner of the one-room hut. "You should have seen the mess outside yesterday. Susi and I picked up everything we could find and brought it all back in here. The monsters!"

"Teacher-Sar is back," Karuppan announces. "He asked you to come to the school to discuss things. Pichayya and Arokia-Sar are there too."

"I wanted to ask you something," Ponni says, as if she has not heard him at all. "Do you have it?"

Karuppan guesses what she means. "Yes," he says.

"Where is it?"

"Safely hidden near the quarry. Under a rock so that no one can find it."

"We need it."

"I'll get it, then," he says readily. He trusts Teacher-Amma completely. He can imagine why she wants the homemade gun now. After all, didn't Reddy's goondas bring guns with them to the school the previous evening? "What happened at that rogue Reddy's house?"

"That beast will not rest until we are destroyed. He has all his hooligans with him. A little army. We have to be able to protect ourselves."

Karuppan's anger rises. "I have friends," he says. "They are the ones who gave me the gun. They are not afraid of Reddy. I can call on them to help us."

Ponni nods vigorously. "It will begin getting dark soon. We will go then. We will get the gun and go back to the school with it. Later, you will go to find your friends. Let's wait here till the sun begins to set." The time for half measures is over. Reddiar is intent on playing up Kunti's higher status compared to Karuppan. He has no problem lighting the fire of caste hatred to destroy the school.

"There is food for you at the school," Karuppan says.

Ponni makes a dismissive sound at the mention of food. Karuppan can guess why she does not want to return to the school right away, hungry though she must be. She does not want a discussion of what she has planned. He has overheard some of the arguments between Teacher-Sar and Teacher-Amma. The gun will not be greeted with universal welcome at the school. He hunkers down to wait with Teacher-Amma in her home, modest and ravaged as it is. Her broad face has a stony determination that seems oblivious to the world. Neither talks as they wait for the light outside to dim into dusk.

After a while, Ponni gets up from the stool, unable to bear the silence any more. She carefully leans her uncle's picture on the floor next to the picture of Ramu's father and walks around restlessly. She picks up the seashell from the pile in the corner and looks at it. The seashell brings back fond memories. It is from a trip to Tiruchendur that Ponni, Ramu, and Arokiasamy made with Selvam. It was not the famous and beautiful little temple to Murugan that had drawn them there. Rather, the trip was an impromptu holiday, a jaunt to show Selvam the sea, which he had never seen. That was the ostensible reason, but the real one was the mutual contrariness that seemed to have entered her relationship with Ramu. Might a brief change of scene help? The suggestion had been Arokia's, from whom nothing about Ramu and her was ever secret. They left Karuppan and Devi in charge during two days that the school was going to be closed anyway and rode the bus to Tiruchendur.

Once there they did tour the unusual temple, so close by the sea that its wall was lapped by the waves. Ramu had been to the temple before and she could feel him being transported in his mind—she knew him so well, after all!—to a different time, a time about which he never spoke to her. She herself could not bring herself to care about the dim halls redolent with the smell of smoking oil from which people like her had been excluded not so long ago. Later, they let Selvam play in the water, running in and out of the waves under their watchful eyes. They bought murukku and cold, sweet colored water from a man with a bucket filled with melting ice. Selvam had never before had a cold drink. It was a thing of amazement to him. He delightedly rubbed the bottle over his face to feel just how cold it was. Ponni smiles to herself at the thought of it. They sat on the beach sand, munching the murukku, gulping down their drinks, observing the bedraggled peacocks, beloved to Murugan, perched on the roof of the temple and wandering through the surrounding yards.

There was no hurry. They had taken a room in a lodge hard by the temple. They would not return to Athanoor until the next day. The entire day was before them. They went for a walk along the beach despite the blazing afternoon sun, and had gone hardly any distance over the hot sand when a man waved to them.

"What is it?" Arokiasamy yelled back.

The man pointed at a catamaran pulled up onto the sand behind him. "For only a little bit of money, I can take you out on the sea," he replied. His bare body glistened with the ocean.

"Let's do it," Ramu said, excitedly.

Ponni had looked doubtfully at the rough logs lashed together with rope. She did not know how to swim. "I'm not going on that thing," she had said in a voice that brooked no debate, "and neither is Selvam."

Seeing Ramu's face fall, Arokiasamy, who did not know how to swim either, had said, "I'll go with you, Ramu."

Ponni remembers the day only too well. Soon Ramu and Arokiasamy were on the catamaran and the boatman was thrusting them beyond the breaking, frothing waves with his paddle. Holding Selvam by a hand, Ponni watched from the shore as the catamaran bobbed away under the fierce sun. She knew Ramu had not agreed with her, had wanted to take Selvam with him on the catamaran. Selvam was observing the boat intently.

"How long will they be gone?" he asked. When Ponni had decreed that he would not go with his father and Uncle Arokia, he did not protest.

"Not long," Ponni replied. Inexplicably, a wave of sorrow crashed through her.

The catamaran was flat and low in the ocean waves. Ponni could see Ramu and Arokiasamy seated cross-legged in it, facing each other. Arokiasamy was turned toward the ocean, while Ramu faced the shore. Once beyond the waves, the catamaran began to move more swiftly. Ramu raised a hand and waved to Ponni and Selvam over Arokiasamy's head. Arokiasamy turned his head to look back at them—he too raised a hand and waved. Ponni waved back.

Ponni can see the whole scene clearly, even now, with her mind's eye.

The catamaran got smaller and smaller, and as it did Ponni felt as if a stone had settled in her chest in the place where her heart should have been beating. She felt far, far, from Ramu. She did not want to feel so far—she did not want to feel this growing distance between them about the school, about how to deal with Reddiar, or about any of the other things (like raising Selvam) regarding which they seemed to disagree more and more. The catamaran floated on the ocean, a flat, low smudge in the distance. It had gone far away indeed. Ramu was a tiny blob. Had he raised a hand and waved to her again? She could not be sure, but she did not wave back this time, suddenly feeling detached from him, as if it was not just some regular old catamaran that had taken him away temporarily. She did not like the way she felt. She felt heartsick. She gripped Selvam's hand so hard that he looked up in surprise. She gave him a wan smile and said, "Let's find some shade."

The seashell was a gift from that boatman who had taken Ramu and Arokiasamy so far out into the sea. Probably he was pleased at the generosity of their payment to him on their return to the shore. He had fished out the shell from the catamaran and insisted that they have it.

In her ransacked hut, Ponni holds the shell in her hands and thinks back to that day. She says to Karuppan, not without a hint of bitterness, "Nothing is ever simple."

MEANWHILE, BACK IN THE SCHOOL, Ramu wonders why it's taking Ponni and Karuppan so long to return. It will be dark soon. He wonders whether he should send Devi to see what is detaining them. Then his annoyance at Ponni triumphs. No, he will wait. He and the others in the school's office have been talking desultorily of Nehru's death, news of which had not reached Athanoor yet. Now they are done talking. They are silent now, overwhelmed by their own crisis. He does not have much time before it will be too late to go to Reddiar's. He feels it's important not to let the situation fester. Perhaps a compromise is possible. Perhaps Karuppan can disappear for a while, until the situation is under control. The moment the thought occurs to him he feels ashamed. Punishing the victim. How can that be right? He feels confused and helpless. He wishes Ponni were here though he knows they would disagree, and vehemently at that, about how to proceed. Nevertheless, it would be comforting to have her back. Back here with him and Arokia. It would be good to have all his family around him (Arokia is surely family), except for Selvam, who rightly is safe in Paavalampatti with Gomati Paati. It is good that Selvam is getting to meet Gomati Paati. Now, too late, he regrets that he did not take Selvam to meet his grandfather—the man that Selvam knows only through the picture in the hut.

It's been several years since Ramu's father died of some kind of mysterious disease, perhaps heat stroke, though the neighbors in Paavalampatti whispered it was heartbreak caused by his son. Ramu did not take Selvam even on that sad occasion. No one at that time (it angers him even now to remember it), not even Gomati Paati, asked him why he had not come with Ponni and Selvam. As if his family back in Athanoor did not exist! Still, he should have taken Selvam. Instead, he went alone and did what he had to do—his duty as his father's only son. No questions were asked, not even by Aunt Malati or Uncle Siva or any of the other relatives or neighbors, who on this somber occasion held their tongues, at least in front of him. For his part, he gave no answers. But he wore again the sacred thread, just as if he were an unpolluted Brahmin, perfect in all the observances.

Thus pretending to be something he was not, thus masked, he walked with the clay pot of fire behind his father's body to the cremation ground. There he placed the fire on his dead father's chest and lit the pyre. He waited for the fire to catch, the flesh to burn, the skull to shatter in the heat of the flames. The priest handed him the coins that had been placed on his father's eyelids. He dug bones, fragments of his father, out of the cold ashes. He took the ashes and the bones in a clay pot to cast into the river with back turned. He did all this, all this and no more, for he returned to Athanoor then, refusing to stay for the thirteen days of ceremonies that should have followed so that his dead father's spirit might have peace and a proper farewell.

No one in Paavalampatti tried to make him stay. He was not one of them, not any more, not really. Still, he felt guilty all the way back to Athanoor. He remembered his father from years before, from before he went to Loyola. Guilt was not all he felt. He felt fear, too. It was shameful to admit but it was true: he thought of his father's spirit wandering the earth without peace because he, the son, had refused to do all the ordained rituals. He knew that the rituals were superstitious nonsense, but still his heart felt as if a fire had been placed on it and his skull as if it would explode.

Back in Athanoor, he felt guilty all over again. It was, of course, ever like this for him when he went to Paavalampatti to visit his family—he could not return to Ponni without his mind in turmoil. Now he was going back after cremating his father according to the rites prescribed from time immemorial. He could not bear to look Ponni in the face on his return. He felt ashamed, as if he had betrayed her. He did not tell her that in Paavalampatti he had reclaimed his Brahmin-ness for two days—or at least that he had let his Brahmin-ness reclaim him. She did not ask him what he had done, what rituals he had engaged in as the son of his dead father. She did not need to. She knew. Her contrived silence was itself a sign that she had guessed.

Had something changed between Ponni and him in that moment? Sometimes, Ramu feels that the growing coolness between them dates from this trip that he made to cremate his father. Then again, this was the very time that Ponni and he began to disagree about the school. Was it his father? Or was it the school? What is it that has stepped so quietly in between him and Ponni? Whatever it is, he does not like it. He loves Ponni as much as he ever has. He knows he does. He wishes things could be just as they were when they first moved to Athanoor. Then, he and Ponni were of one mind about everything.

When it's almost dark and Ponni and Karuppan have still not appeared, Ramu finally sends Devi to the hut to bring them. Devi returns alone. The hut is empty. They are not there. Ramu says, in exasperation, "We can't wait anymore. We should go to Reddiar's." He has no time to wonder where Ponni and Karuppan have gone.

"What is the use of that? We have already tried," Devi says. "He won't talk to us."

"Arokia and I will go," Ramu says. "He will talk to the two of us."

"I should stay," Arokiasamy says. "In case they try to do something to the school."

"Then Pichayya and I will go."

"What will you say?" Arokiasamy asks.

"Tell me what you think. No use going there to fight. We should offer some kind of solution."

"We can't give up Brother Karuppan," Devi says in a shocked voice.

"Of course not!" Ramu retorts crossly. He feels personally accused. "No one is suggesting that."

"I have been thinking," Arokiasamy intervenes. "Tell Reddiar that this is an issue for the police. Then we'll go to the police station in Keelpaarai in the morning and inform them of the situation. We'll tell them not only of the rape accusation but that we are afraid there will be violence in the village any moment."

"The police are Reddiar's paid servants," Ramu says. "They will surely arrest Karuppan and then he'll be lost."

"Karuppan will have to go away," Arokiasamy says. "There is no choice. He will have to run away. Then the police won't be able to arrest him, but they will be in the village and it will not be so easy for Reddiar to target the school." It appears that Arokiasamy, formerly not so keen that Karuppan vanish, has changed his mind. It is what Ramu has been thinking too.

"Will that work?" Ramu asks, not yet entirely convinced.

"Maybe. We will at least have a chance. Otherwise Reddiar will destroy us. Reddiar's men swaggering about with guns—that is definitely something to worry about."

"I mean to bring that up with Reddiar," Ramu says. "Guns have no place in our differences."

Ramu looks at Pichayya, but Pichayya offers no opinion. He looks at Devi, who too says nothing. Ponni and Karuppan are not here to share their insight. He looks at Arokiasamy and says, "Very well, then. That is what we will do."

Once the decision has been made, Ramu is all determination. He and Pichayya leave as the sun is beginning to set and the bright glare of the summer day is beginning to fade. They walk purposefully down the main dirt trail past the huts of the village, watched curiously by friends and foes—those who are on their side as well as those who have always regarded the school as a troublesome intrusion. There is foreboding in the air. Or maybe it's all the eyes watching. Ramu feels the weight of the eyes as they walk toward Reddiar's white mansion up on its little hillock. *Something is about to happen.* But what? He feels he is walking along this familiar trail toward something unprecedented and momentous. What lies ahead? Something good? Or ill? A solution to the crisis? Or a worsening of it? There is no way to foretell. Turning back, turning aside, will be useless. The moment of reckoning is come. It cannot be deferred. Running away is no solution at all.

Ramu and Pichayya reach Cinema Crazy Susi's shop, where, over a boiling pot of tea, she is regaling customers with the story of *Robin Hood,* the latest Muthu starrer she has seen *first day, first show* in the tent cinema at Keelpaarai. She is a besotted fan of Muthu. Ramu wonders what she would say if she knew Muthu and Ponni—his wife, her Teacher-Amma—were once lovers. There was a time when just the notion of Muthu and Ponni together would have been enough to light a fire of jealousy in him. That time is past. It is good that it is. He knows Muthu does not merit his jealousy. He and Ponni—their fifteen years together have been wonderful; together they have done tremendous things in that time. He knows they have. They have lived enough for several lifetimes. They have had their differences too, but that is of no consequence. Not a bit. He will never stop loving Ponni. Never. He knows that. His love for her surges inside him as he walks toward Parthiban Reddy to save the school Ponni and he have built together.

When she sees Ramu and Pichayya, Susi calls out, offering them free glasses of tea. But they cannot stop. He walks on, grateful for Pichayya's silent company. Belatedly comprehending where they are headed, Susi and her audience fall silent. Ramu and Pichayya keep going until they have passed through the village and are at the tamarind tree at the foot of the steps leading up to the verandah of Reddiar's mansion. The tree rears up, its trailing branches inert in the oppressive heat. Its leaves droop in the perfectly still air. The tree is a squatting lifeless mass, an ominous shape in the gathering gloom. Ramu averts his eyes. He loathes tamarind trees.

On the verandah, Reddiar sits in his great wooden chair, his feet up on a cushioned footrest. His head rests against the high back of the chair and his eyes are closed. His arms are raised up above his head; they too are resting on the back of the chair so that his armpits are exposed. Reddiar is temporarily white. His barber is shaving his cheeks, chest, and armpits—all are white with frothy shaving lather. The barber carefully bends over one armpit, a naked sharp razor poised expertly between his fingers. Despite the gravity of his mission, laughter threatens to explode from Ramu at the sight of Reddiar smothered in white lather. There is something monstrous as well as absurd about him. Ramu controls himself. Laughter would be the worst thing possible. Reddiar is a vain man. He is not handsome—he is too flabby and his facial features are scrunched together under his forehead—but he thinks of himself as a lady-killer. He trims his eyebrows and his mustaches are exceptionally well tended. They spread luxuriantly against his pock-marked cheeks, now covered with lather.

"You have come," Reddiar says, without opening his eyes. "Do you have Karuppan for me?" Two of Reddiar's men stand behind his chair, one on each side. Reddiar's other men are not to be seen.

Ramu ignores the question. "We have come to talk about Karuppan. We feel this accusation against him is a matter for the police," he says. "It is not something we should try to handle by ourselves. If he has anything to answer for, let the police look into it."

Reddiar sighs. "Who is stopping you? Go to the police."

"We will," Ramu says. "First thing in the morning. It is too late now. In the meantime, we would like a promise from you. Please call off your men. Let us not have any more violence. What is the need for guns? What if someone is killed? Let us wait for the police to get here."

Reddiar opens his eyes and waves away his barber, who steps back, razor still poised in his fingers. The barber has scraped away lather and hair from half an armpit. Reddiar glares down at Ramu and Pichayya, who stand at the foot of the steps to his verandah. "Be careful what you say. I know nothing about guns. Why do you talk as if I control these angry people? Do they work for me? Do I pay them? Can you show me one piece of paper that says I do? You do not realize how much anger there is at your school. Until your school came into this village, men like Karuppan were unheard of. There was peace in the village. You have corrupted all the children. That is why there is so much anger at you and the school. I think there is no option for you but to shut your school down." His voice takes on a note of resignation. "I tried to advise you. But you would not listen. We could have worked together. Instead, you insisted on going against me. Now look what has happened. Come back when you are ready to give me Karuppan and lock up your school permanently. Until then, there is nothing I can do for you."

Ramu tries not to show his anger. He says as calmly as he can manage, "We do want to work with you, Reddiar. That is why we are here. That is why I'm asking you to call off your men."

A crafty look enters Reddiar's close-set eyes. "Close up your school and maybe I can convince the villagers to let Karuppan go. That is all I can do. Now go." He dismisses them with an imperious gesture of his head.

Pichayya says, "I have been in this village longer than you, Reddiar. I remember the day you were born. I saw what the village was like before the school and how it is now. I cannot agree with what you say about the school."

Pichayya's words enrage Reddiar. He leaps out of his chair, sending his footstool clattering down the steps. He waves his arms at Pichayya. Lather drips from his cheeks and armpits, sending white streaks across his bare stomach and arms. Again, laughter threatens to erupt from Ramu at the absurd sight. One of Reddiar's men runs down the steps to retrieve the stool. Reddiar shakes a threatening fist at Pichayya. "What insolence! Pichai, be careful! I'll take care of you too. This is my village. Before me, it was my father's. Before him, his father's. Who are you to lecture me about my own village?"

Pichayya remains calm. He says, "We are not here to talk about me, Reddiar. We are here to save the school."

Reddiar laughs and points at the sky behind them. "Look," he says. "It is already too late for that."

Ramu and Pichayya turn in the direction to which Reddiar points. An orange glow is spreading into the darkening evening sky. Faintly, from the direction of the school, they hear yells. Reddiar has been toying with them while something was afoot across the village. Fire! The school is on fire! Ramu begins to run toward the school.

♒

RAMU RUNS IN HIS WORN rubber slippers through Athanoor. When he reaches the school, it is in flames. Men and women, his neighbors for the last so many years, are gathered in front of the school. Some are valiantly ferrying water in buckets from the shrunken muddy pond a short distance away. Whatever little water was stored in the nearby huts has been expended. In vain. It is futile. The thatched roofs of the school are like tinder in the dry summer heat, delectable to the hungry fire. The flames feed on the thatch in devilish glee, dancing on it, leaping from it in yellow joy up into the leaves of the mango tree, flinging themselves at the brick walls in gay abandon.

Ramu stands in front of the conflagration. He is panicking. He should do something. What should he do? He cannot think. He hardly notices Devi when she comes up to him. He only has eyes for the ravenous fire. Devi is gesticulating at the flames, trying to say something to him. She is weeping and mumbling something in a shaky voice. He stares at her, his mind in a commotion. He cannot understand what she is saying. Suddenly he feels fear. Ponni? Is it Ponni that Devi is trying to tell him about? He forces himself to listen: "Arokia-Sar! He is still inside. In the office!"

Arokia-Sar. He. Is. Still. Inside.

Arokia. His steadfast companion from his college days. His confidant. His guide. His refuge in times of trouble. His friend. Trapped in the hungry flames.

Before anyone can stop him, Ramu dashes through the gate into the burning school. Parts of the mango tree have caught fire now. Yellow flames dart here and there from the lower branches. Sparks and burning leaves fly in the air. Ramu calls out to Arokiasamy and leaps past the tree of flames into the fire dancing over the office building. The building is still standing but any minute now it will come crashing down.

⁓

Ponni walks in the darkness along a deep wound in the ground. She has been to the quarry countless times during the day, when heat waves shimmer above it like fiery exhalations of its jagged, gaping mouth. Now the quarry lies deceptively innocent, tranquil except for the occasional stone sent clattering by her or Karuppan down the steep sides into the maw. Once she saw rubble go similarly rumbling down a slope in a sudden avalanche that just missed a group of workers. Tragedy barely averted. In that case, but not always. Hidden in darkness, Reddy's quarry gives no sign of its dreadful daytime reality.

Karuppan walks ahead of her, the homemade gun wrapped in a gunny sack under one arm. Behind her is Athanoor, where a school named for Tiruvalluvar—her school and that of her husband Ramu and their friend Arokia, who was more than a friend—is now a burned-down ruin.

In the gray ashes and still-glowing embers of that ruin are two corpses, burned beyond recognition or recovery.

Arokia, her brother in spirit if not in fact, lies there in the ashes.

Arokia—dead. Murdered.

And the foolhardy man who leaped into flames to save his friend—also dead.

Her husband.

Her lover.

Her beloved.

Dead.

Murdered. Like her father, Murugappa. Like her brother, Arokia.

Yes, he had jumped, but it was still murder.

She had never told him he was her beloved. She had never confessed her love to him. She should have.

Too late now.

By the time she and Karuppan had retrieved the gun as planned and returned to the village, it was too late. Devi, Cinema Crazy Susi, and Pichayya were standing helplessly in front of the leaping flames still feeding, if less ravenously than before, on the thatch roofs of the school. It was much too late to save the school or the men trapped inside. Now the villagers were intent on stopping the fire from spreading. Fortunately, the school was at a little distance from the rest of the village. In addition to the two lines that had formed to urgently pass pots back and forth from the pond, Pichayya's donkey had been pressed into service to ferry water.

As the villagers worked feverishly around her, a false calm possessed Ponni. Her numbed mind heard Devi's account of what had happened. Reddy's men had come while Ramu and Pichayya were meeting with Reddy. Arokiasamy and Devi were alone in the school. Reddy's men had rattled the bars of the gate. They had shouted obscenities, thrown out taunts and drunken challenges. Arokiasamy had gone out to speak to the goondas. There was an altercation.

The goondas had demanded that he open the gate so that they could search for Karuppan. He refused and came back inside. A little while later Devi and Arokiasamy heard whooshing sounds. It was too late by the time they understood that the sounds were made by empty soda bottles filled with kerosene. The bottles, whose mouths had been stuffed with rags on fire, were being flung onto the dry thatch. Who would have thought Reddy's men would go so far? By the time they realized what had happened, flames were leaping from the thatch. Devi had managed to get out. Arokiasamy, intent on gathering up the cash box, the banking and other financial documents, and the school records, had not. And then—Devi's voice faltered; she barely got the words out—Teacher-Sar had arrived . . .

Too late now, Ponni thinks, as she and Karuppan leave the quarry behind and head off into the arid waste beyond. She and Karuppan had slunk away when it was clear that nothing could be done to save the school or the men inside. She had wanted to rush to Reddy's mansion with the gun. Karuppan had persuaded her otherwise. Reddy was sure to be surrounded by his men. It would not be possible to get to him. This was not the right time for such an attempt. Karuppan had convinced her to go with him into the night.

Too late to tell Ramu what she should have when she still had the chance. That she loved him. There had been many opportunities. She had taken none of them.

Ramu. Gone.

How is it possible?

Murdered. Like her father. Both murdered. Is it her? Is it something about her?

She flinches from the terrible abyss that yawns suddenly at the center of her life.

She finds it hard to walk, to put one foot in front of the other on the stony trail.

She finds it hard to breathe.

There is a stone in her chest.

She wants to lie down on the stony ground and weep until the stone inside her is gone, dissolved by her tears.

Too late now.

But it is not too late to make Reddy and his men pay. Not too late for she and Karuppan and the gun to melt into the night. Not too late to find Karuppan's friends, the men and women of the night, who are not afraid of Reddy or his men.

The school was a thing of the light, a beautiful thing born of love for the light. The light had failed. Now it is the time of the darkness—for the fearless soldiers of the night, who have a terrible beauty of their own, a fierce love that is their own.

She must become one of them. She *will* become one of them.

She must breathe. She *will* breathe.

She will carry the stone in her chest. As much as she wants to, she will not lie down on the stony ground. She will become stone herself. No, she will *stay* stone, for stone is what she has always been.

She must put one foot in front of the other on the trail in front of her. She *will* do what must be done.

For her father Murugappa, murdered and cast away under a tamarind tree.

For Arokia.

For Ramu.

For Selvam. Above all for Selvam. Her son. Still alive and safe in Paavalampatti, where he will have to stay for now. She will come back for him. Later. Now duty calls. Another duty. This fight is for Selvam too. And for all the children like him—for the children of the quarries and for the child she herself once was. She will be stone for them.

Ponni walks on into the night. Soon it will be light and they must reach their place of hiding before that happens. She and Karuppan have a while to go before they find his friends, his brave and beautiful friends of the night.

Too late now to say what should have been said.

Her lover.

Her beloved.

Part Four

Prologue Is Past

I BEGIN. I WRITE BY THE dim light of the lamp in the aisle. The train rocks from side to side as it hurtles through the night toward Madras. My fellow passengers moan and mutter in their sleep. The letters are safe in my bag. Leaning on my elbows on the rough Rexene of my bunk, I begin my story here in my notebook. The things I know—I will write them down. Those I don't—I will try to write them too. I know my name. I know that much. I will begin with that—Selvam.

THE KNOCK ON THE DOOR late one night did not wake me. Often, I don't sleep at night. Night, day; they are one to me. Sometimes I shut up the shop in the middle of the afternoon, come upstairs to my bed. I close the wooden shutters of my window against the pitiless yellow of the sun. I fall asleep. At other times, I lie awake at night, reading by the light of my bedside lamp, or else resting quietly in the dark. I do as I please. I answer to no one—there is no one to whom I could answer, even if I wanted to.

So it was on the night of the knock. I was resting with my eyes closed, exiled from sleep. I knew who was at the door but I did not move from my bed. I lay motionless in the dark sanctuary of my room and listened the way a mouse might in its hole: with perfect, undivided attention. A second knock, louder, more urgent. Still, I did not stir. After a while: the sound of feet retreating. I looked at the luminous green hands of the clock by my bed. 3 a.m. The rest of the night, I lay twisting and turning fretfully on my thin cotton mattress. I could not stop thinking of the knock or the knocker. The next day I did not open the shop until late in the morning.

A few nights later, the knocking came again. This time I was neither asleep nor awake. I had just put away my book and was drifting off into my alternative life, my life of dreams. The knock jolted me fully awake. I lay in the gloom, listening intently. More knocking, and then a loud whisper: "Why won't you answer me?" This was followed by a silence, which I made no attempt to disturb.

After a while, she spoke again. "I know you are awake. I saw the light in your window."

I got up and padded soundlessly across the room. I stood close up against the door and listened. I could hear her breathing on the other side of the thick plank of wood that separated us. Perhaps she was leaning against the door, just as I was. Perhaps nothing but an inch of brown painted timber kept our foreheads from touching.

"Why won't you open the door? I only want to talk to you. Please let me in. I am afraid of what will happen if they hear me and find me here, at your door."

At the sound of her voice so close, my hands shook. I felt dizzy. I lifted my trembling right hand and placed it against the door for extra support. The wood felt rough and uncaring to my touch.

"I have seen the way you look at me. Won't you open the door? I only want to ask you why you look at me the way you do."

I trembled inches from her, breathing shallowly, soundlessly, until I heard her make a sound of exasperation. She went away. I remained at the door for a long time after she was gone, listening to the void she had left behind.

Malar. That is her name.

৵

I WENT TO ATHANOOR TO see Pichayya so that I could pose my question to him. He considered my query and replied with great deliberation, "This is what I will say to you, Selvam. I remember your parents well. I was one of their closest companions for many years, until your father died in that terrible way, everything fell apart, and everyone scattered to the eight directions. I met them when they were young and knew them as they grew old, too old. Not in years, you understand—in spirit. Still, they remained devoted to each other. Always. Their love? It was a passionate thing. A fire. A thing to wonder at and pass on for generations. It was a story, a legend, a myth."

I did not believe his little speech.

He looked at me as if he wanted me to understand something.

We stood in the barren field under the headless coconut tree. I had found him in the gray of dusk, under a sky slowly darkening into mystery. So it seemed to me. He was walking across the field with his donkey. Pichayya. Old, gray. Skin loose and wrinkled. And yet the eyes, somehow, ageless, unaging. Perhaps it was nothing more than a trick of the light.

I said, "It is the only time I have been happy, here in this village."

He looked at me with those eyes, steady, unafraid. His donkey too looked at me. He asked, "Only time?"

I replied without hesitation, "Yes. Only time."

"You were ten when you left."

"I wanted to come back many times. At first, I could not. I was too young. When I was old enough, I was afraid."

He did not say anything or make any gesture, but I knew he understood.

"What would I find here? I could not risk it. I was afraid that what I remembered would be spoiled."

"So many years. Such a long time. You have never been happy since?"

I looked away and replied with a question of my own. "Would you lie to me?"

He reached up a hand to touch my face softly, as if I were still that abandoned child of ten, and said, "No, never."

⁓

My shop downstairs—how easily I am able to say that now: *my shop!*—is filled with photographs and negatives. If recent, they are arranged in wooden drawers according to date and name. But there are cardboard boxes going back years, decades, in which black-and-white photos and strips of stiff, smooth negative are tumbled together in utter confusion—the result of the years of neglect I inherited when the shop fell into my possession. In the long intervals between customers I go through the older photographs, many worm-eaten and filled with holes, and organize them carefully. I put them in order, in marked boxes.

How do I arrange them? I do not order them by date or name. These are the categories in which I put them: Happy, Sad, Bitter, Lonely, Loved, Proud, Loving, Meek, Tyrannical, and so on. There are as many as twenty such categories. I study each photograph carefully before assigning it its appropriate place. If the photo is of a single person, I examine the face for clues—the shape of the eyebrows, the thrust of the chin, the look in the eyes, the curl of the lip. If it is a group portrait or of a couple, I pay attention also to the way in which the subjects of the picture are standing or sitting in relation to one another. Happy and Sad are the largest of these categories—each consists of many boxes. Many of the pictures end up in one or the other. Of course, the pictures wander, too. They don't always stay put. They jump from category to category. For often, upon further reflection, I move a photograph from one box to another, sometimes even transferring it from Sad to Happy or vice versa. Some pictures are continually on the move—restlessly hopping from category to category. These are the photographs that make me feel most helpless.

My photographs fascinate me. I mull over them endlessly, examining the clothes and the facial expressions and many other things. I come up with stories for the people in them.

Major Prakasam (if no name is recorded, I make one up) is in the category Deceitful. Look at that weak chin and how the guarded look in his eyes belies his tip-top uniform. He hides deep within his heart the guilty knowledge of his cowardice during the war of '71.

Gopal, on the other hand, is Brave. This is a picture of him on the day he finished school. He holds the government school-leaving certificate against his chest, his fingers gripping it with an intense possessiveness I cannot help admiring. I like, too, the cut of his hair and the tilt of his head. Cruel life will surely test him, but he will prevail—I feel it in the determination writ large on his face.

Vasudha. She is Loving. You can see her love in the jolly shape of her cheeks and in the bright glow emanating from her face that the camera has caught so well. I like looking at Vasudha. She cannot help smiling in her picture and so I too find myself smiling when I look at her. Formerly, I had her in the category Suffering because she lives down the street and I know a little about her life. She sells vegetables from a cart across from my photo studio and I know how little money she has, compared even to the standards of my impoverished neighbors. But then one day I noticed that she never complains. I saw how she dotes on her baby, her daughter, whom she brings with her daily to play on a sheet she spreads out in the dirt under the cart. Suddenly Suffering seemed completely wrong. I moved her to Loving. This is what I learn from Vasudha: you can make the mistake of thinking a person is what is done to that person. Think the other way. Pay attention to what the person does.

Vasudha does not know this picture exists. Hers is not an old photograph left over from a visit to the shop years ago. She has never been inside my studio. I snapped her picture without ever speaking to her, secretly aiming the camera at her from the shadowed refuge of my shop. I do that sometimes. I rove the world outside my shop through my camera. It is not much of a world—a sliver of a busy street in the outskirts of Madras with a mosque, an electrical supply shop, and a bus stop. These are mainly what I see from my shop. Vasudha usually parks her cart next to the bus stop.

As I wait in my shop for my ever-dwindling clientele, I organize and reorganize my pictures. When someone comes to have a picture taken, I make an extra print for my private collection. Sometimes I surreptitiously click someone passing in the street as I did Vasudha.

And then I study them all, my people, old and new, for signs of life.

MALAR TOO IS ONE OF my people.

There are two pictures of her, probably taken by Vivek. The year of the first is marked as 1971, long before I got here. Malar with her father, mother, and two brothers. All standing stiff and formal in their best clothes. All barefoot. The background is the garden scene that still adorns the wall of the studio. A gray stone bench and a peacock, framed by green tree branches. In the distance a brilliantly blue pond with small white waves cresting at most unnatural angles to the surface of the water. Of course, none of these colors is present in the photograph, which is black and white. Malar's father is in a white shirt and veshti with a thundu over his left shoulder. He grips the thundu with a firm hand. Under his shirt, his stomach bulges into a paunch. Malar's mother stands to his right, her well-oiled shiny hair firmly plaited. The brothers, boys still, stand in front in shorts neatly pressed for the special occasion. They glare at the camera just like their parents. Malar, perhaps fifteen or sixteen, thin and awkward in a sari, is to the father's left. She is smiling, so the charming gap in her front teeth is clearly visible. Her hair is stylishly parted at the side and braided loosely. Her gay eyes look at the camera but her exquisitely shaped face with the delicate features is turned ever so slightly away, as if eager to be done and free of the camera's gaze.

The second photograph is of Malar not much later. She looks much older than her seventeen or eighteen years, though. She is with her husband on the day of their wedding. Her rented fake jewelry is resplendent in the picture. Flowers adorn her hair. Arvind, her husband, barely as tall as her, has small arrogant eyes quite unlike Malar's. His mouth is a firm, thin slash under a bulbous nose. Malar looks straight at the camera but she appears lost, frightened. Still, she is beautiful, as beautiful as ever. I know she is not pretty, but she is beautiful. At least to me. This is a picture I try not to look at too much. It must have been taken not long before I got here.

Malar's pictures don't fit with any of the others. Her category should be Loved. It is not. She does not know she is loved, does she? Her category is simply *Malar.* She is simply Malar.

I suppose she is not one of my people.

⁓

Ever since Gomati Paati died I think of her more and more. I will write it out here: Gomati Paati loved me. Her love was confusing. It was strange, fierce, perhaps even shameful. It was love nonetheless.

I know now that it was love that brought Gomati Paati to Forest Glen International School twice a year. Twice a year she made the journey up into the mountains to Ooty to see me. She was the only person to come during all my years there. One week in November during the Diwali mid-term break and two weeks in the summer—these three weeks I spent with Gomati Paati in two rented rooms in Mr. Arnold's cavernous bungalow near Missionary Hill. How powerful her love must have been that it moved her to such journeying at her age. How powerful, and at the same time how furtive and shamefaced.

Mr. Arnold, a gentle old Englishman in his eighties, had once upon a time managed one of the surrounding tea estates. He lived by himself and so was happy to rent out the two rooms to Gomati Paati. He had tried going back to England after '47 but then had come right back. Alas, England was home no longer. But he had pictures of his English relatives in the drawing room with muslin curtains in the windows. He had never married. The pictures showed his brothers and sisters and their families, including grandchildren. He wrote the people in the pictures long letters every week. He wore pants and shoes inside the house, and ate scones from the bakery near the station with his tea, which he poured from a teapot and drank from a cup. He did all this even after sixty years in India.

Gomati Paati found Mr. Arnold through the school. If she felt any unease in Mr. Arnold's two rooms, she never mentioned it. Three weeks a year she lived in his house, but I never once heard her wondering what Mr. Arnold's houseboy might be cooking in his kitchen. Once, she said to me, "The world never stands quietly in one place. It is always rushing along. To live in it you too must move with it." Her words were meant to be an explanation, though I had asked for none. I asked nothing of Gomati Paati in those days.

I only observed her with a barely concealed sullenness. I made no response to her explanation, but noted silently that our two rooms had a separate entrance and that one bathroom was set aside exclusively for our use. At Gomati Paati's request, Mr. Arnold provided a kerosene stove on which Gomati Paati made our simple meals using pots and pans she brought with her. Gomati Paati made no complaint, but nor did she make any adjustments to how she dressed or what she ate when she came to Ooty. I was the only child at Forest Glen picked up at vacation time by a little old Brahmin woman who had shorn off her hair and dressed in a widow's sari.

Such was my childhood after Appa died and Amma disappeared. Three weeks with Gomati Paati in a colonial bungalow with bougainvillea in the garden, and the rest of the time at the exclusive Forest Glen International School, where I very much kept to myself. I felt no bond with the other children at the school. No other child there had spent years in a little drought-stricken village like Athanoor. Some had lost parents, or had parents who did not get along with each other, or were even divorced. But none had been abandoned by a mother, and that too on the very day the father had died in a fire. None had a mother who had disappeared into the night like a ghost. Cruel children taunted me about Amma's disappearance. I kept quiet. What was the point in denying the truth? Eventually they got bored of abusing me and shoving me and trying to pick a fight.

Eight years at Forest Glen! It was not just my school. It never felt like just a school to me. Nor was it ever my home. What was it, then? A warehouse. It was a warehouse. It was where I had been stored, put away on a shelf like a thing with no place in the world. At Forest Glen, I learned to be angry. I nursed my anger deep within me, where none could see it. I was angry at everything and everyone, but especially at Gomati Paati, who was the only person to come and see me in all my years at Forest Glen. My anger at her grew and grew until, one day, it burst like a powerful bomb.

Write it out again: one day my anger exploded like a mighty bomb.

One summer, about a year before I finished at Forest Glen and came to college in Madras, Gomati Paati arrived at the school in Mr. Arnold's black Fiat. Mr. Arnold had sent the car with his driver to pick her up at the Ooty railway station. It was the usual custom: she would let Mr. Arnold know by letter that she was coming, and he would send the car to meet her at the station. She would then proceed to the school to collect me and we would go together to Mr. Arnold's house, a short fifteen-minute drive away. It was the very thing we had done year after year during Diwali and summer, but now I went down to the car park where she was waiting in the car and said to her, "I am not going with you. I am staying here." Around us, the last of the children going away for the holidays were departing with their parents. I paid them no mind. I did not keep my voice down. I deliberately spoke loudly. I knew Gomati Paati was coming to pick me up but I had not packed. I had decided I would stay in the school with the handful of children who had nowhere to go. The truth was that I too had nowhere to go. I was no longer ready to hide from that truth.

"Why?" Paati asked.

"What is the point in going to Mr. Arnold's? I might as well stay here."

"You will get to leave the school for a few days. Won't that be nice?"

"It makes no difference to me."

"Go get your things, child. I have come all this distance to be with you."

I felt cruel. I said, "But I don't want to be with you. I am quite happy here."

Gomati Paati was silent for a while, and then she said, "I know you want to go to Paavalampatti."

It was not true. I did not want to go to Paavalampatti. The very idea revolted me. I said, "Yes. I want to go to Paavalampatti." I watched her keenly. I wanted to hear how she responded.

Gomati Paati corrected herself: "You *think* you want to go to Paavalampatti. You are angry at me because I won't take you there." She spoke as if to herself, as if she were figuring something out.

I felt triumphant. Then I felt rage. Gomati Paati had revealed her treachery. I had always known her betrayal of me. Now she had provided stark evidence of it. She had proven me incontrovertibly right with her words: she was ashamed of me, she would not take me to Paavalampatti. Yet I felt no pleasure in my triumph, only a tremendous anger that I struggled to control. Rage and shameful tears both threatened to burst out. I dug my fingernails into my palms. I would not let her see how she made me feel. I would not let her see my anger or my tears. I said in a voice that I can hear trembling even across all these years, "Go away from me. You are nothing to me. I want to have nothing to do with you." I turned and stalked away under the line of asoka trees leading past the playing field to the boys' dormitories. I lay down on the white and blue counterpane of my bed until Mr. Khan, the dormitory resident teacher, came and said, "Your grandmother has gone away. She has asked that you be allowed to stay in the school. She said she will be back tomorrow."

I did not bother telling Mr. Khan that Gomati Paati was really my great-grandmother. Mr. Khan was dark and had short, thick, curly hair. He lived with his wife in an apartment attached to the dormitory. He taught English, my favorite subject, to the eleventh and twelfth standards. He was a jovial man, liked by all the students. He was kind and I know he liked me, peculiar though I was. He wanted to say something to make me feel better, but I glared at him until he went away.

The next day Gomati Paati returned and waited under the asoka trees by the main gate. From my dorm window, across the pitted brown and green of the playing field, I could see the car. I did not go to her. And so it was every following day, until five days had gone by. When Mr. Khan came to me on the sixth day, he was no longer kindly. He said, "I want you to go to your grandmother. She doesn't want me to force you, so don't blame her for what I am doing. If you don't go you will do one month of detention when the new school year begins. No free play for a month. My advice to you? Go and talk to your grandmother."

I sullenly dropped my book on the floor and got up from my bed—my usual place those days—and strode across the playing field to Gomati Paati. She was sitting in the back of the black Fiat, her covered head hardly clearing the bottom of the window. Every year I saw her she seemed to shrink some more. I hated how tiny she had become and I hated the way she peered at me out of the window from under the hem of her Brahmin widow's sari. I did not open the door. She did not get out of the car. Mr. Arnold's driver was under one of the asoka trees watching us idly. We spoke through the window. I said with barely controlled rage, "What do you want?"

She said, "Do you know why I don't take you to Paavalampatti?"

I made no sign that I had heard the question.

"Because I am not sure I can protect you from Uncle Siva and the others in the village."

It did not matter. Her words made no difference. I did not go to Mr. Arnold's house then or ever again, though Gomati Paati did not give up. She came to Ooty one more time before I graduated from Forest Glen. I stayed in the school. She stayed at Mr. Arnold's house. We met for a few hours every day because of Mr. Khan's compulsion.

Until the day she died, I could not forgive her her shameful love for me.

⁓

GOMATI PAATI WAS RIGHT. SHE could do many things, but she could not protect me from Uncle Siva. When Appa died and Amma disappeared, when for many weeks—weeks stained through and through with a black despair in my memory—I was a terrible vexation, a problem to be solved, Uncle Siva would pace the house in Paavalampatti, stop to look at me, and say, "What is to be done with this thing with no caste? How long can we keep this thing here?" He would pace some more, stop and glare at me again, and add, "Its own mother doesn't want it. Otherwise, wouldn't she come looking for it? What is to be done with this ten-year-old thing? Who will take care of it?"

I see those black days in my mind. I see myself next to Gomati Paati on a swing in a night-filled courtyard lit by a single feeble lamp. I keep my head down but I cannot help watching Uncle Siva lumber back and forth in the murky yellow of the lamp, muttering about me. The words. Mouthed over and over again as if they had a life of their own and would not be contained. I hear them. I see myself watching and hearing with Gomati Paati's frail arm around my shoulders. Only once do I remember Gomati Paati reply to Uncle Siva: "You keep asking who will take care of him. Why not us? This is Ramu's boy. Why should we not raise him? There is no one but you and me left here. Why should we not do it?"

That made Uncle Siva stop in shock. "Here? In this village? This casteless thing? What will the neighbors say? Already I have to put up with all manner of talk." He shuddered his disgust and added, "I can't bear to be in the same house with this thing."

Gomati Paati said in a small voice, without looking at him or at me, "If everyone thought as you do, it would be impossible to live in this world. Not all the neighbors are like you. Now that Ramu is gone, his share of the property is this boy's. He has a right to be here." Gomati Paati still had her arm around my shoulders but I could not understand why she spoke so timidly. Why was she not angry? Why did she not shout at Uncle Siva, fling her displeasure at him, slap her words across his face?

Instead, it was Uncle Siva who rushed over to thrust his face into Gomati Paati's. Anger made the muscles in his withered neck taut as rope; I was once told by Gomati Paati that in his younger days he was an imposing man. He spoke in a voice loud with omen: "Either this thing goes or something very bad will happen in this house! I will not be responsible for my actions if this thing stays."

Gomati Paati kept quiet and I thought, *She agrees with him. Deep down she does.* In that moment, I hated her more than I hated Uncle Siva. Appa had brought me to her. He had said I should trust her. She should have defended me. Instead, she kept quiet. I began to hate my dead father too. Had he not brought me to this old woman who could not speak up in my support? I put away the toy camera Appa had bought me only a day before he died. I would not touch anything that reminded me of him.

A few days later, Uncle Siva announced, speaking defiantly, "I have made enquiries. There is a government-run orphanage in Thirunelveli Town ready to take this thing."

An orphanage. But my fate was not an orphanage. Gomati Paati had been making her own enquiries. Her research into the best boarding schools in South India had led her to identify one in Ooty. Despite Uncle Siva's vehement opposition, I came to Forest Glen International.

"Such an expensive school," Uncle Siva yelled, when he found out what Gomati Paati was planning. "For this thing. Are you mad?"

Gomati Paati replied in a quiet voice, "I still decide some things here. This boy is no orphan. He will not go to an orphanage, not as long as I live. I say he will go to this school. I have the money. He will have the best education I can give him. Don't stand in my way about this, Siva."

Gomati Paati won. In a manner of speaking. I write it out calmly now. Then, I could not forget that she had also lost. I saw that she could not keep me with her at Paavalampatti. I did not stop hating Gomati Paati at Forest Glen.

↝

I REMEMBER LITTLE OF THE weeks—or was it months?—in Paavalampatti before I came to Forest Glen. I have a dim recollection of bits and pieces of days succeeding one another with no sign of Appa. I see in my mind rooms filled to choking with shadows. I stay in the shadows. I move though the shadows as if a shadow myself. Bits and pieces of broken days. I see towering red-and-white-striped walls of a temple at the end of a street of vague shapes. I have no memory of myself ever being out there in the street. The days and places have no order in my head. A few jagged pieces of those shattered days remain; the rest have disappeared, as if swept up by a great broom of forgetfulness. I might have been lied to at first. Then there must have come a time when they told me of Appa's death in the fire that killed him and Uncle Arokia. I don't remember the telling. Just as well. I remember conversations stopping abruptly when I appeared.

I remember one evening when Gomati Paati clutched me to herself and wept inconsolably. I recall the tight grip of her bony fingers on my shoulders and remember thinking with a strange detachment that her old breasts felt nothing like Amma's soft chest when she held me. I knew then that something terrible had happened. I must have been told. But I don't remember. Were there rituals and ceremonies for Appa who had died? Or was all that ignored because he had done the terrible thing of marrying Amma? I don't remember. If there were rituals, did they involve me as they were supposed to, because I am his son? I don't have the answers to these questions because I don't remember.

Amma. I must have been told she did not die in the fire. Did I wonder why she did not come to me? I recall neither the telling nor the wondering, at least not in those days in Paavalampatti. I remember some things. I remember Gomati Paati lying as if stupefied on her mat day after day in the corner of a room full of shadows, rousing herself only when I came near. I remember overhearing her say that the men who started the fire that killed Appa had managed to escape punishment. Just as my grandfather Murugappa's killer had. I remember her making this comparison as if fearfully. That stuck in my head even as I forgot so much else. I remember Uncle Siva's rage, his plans to send me to a government orphanage. I remember putting away the toy camera that I loved, that Appa had bought me. I don't remember much else. Just as well.

~

In Forest Glen, the oldest building was the chapel, built of stone in 1893. Around it, on acres of hilly land and surrounded by tea plantations, a sprawling school had grown up for the boys and girls of the British Raj. There was a pond, overhung by trees, in which the children who stayed back for the summer vacation were allowed to swim—I was one of those children, except for the two weeks with Gomati Paati. The school had two playing fields on which football, hockey, and cricket were played and on which, on Sports Day, track and field meets were held. The principal was Mr. Iyer, a grave man who had never been seen without jacket and tie. He lived in the sprawling Principal's Bungalow. The accommodations for teachers and staff were referred to as "cottages" and were scattered around the grounds.

The boys' dormitories were separated from the girls' by a classroom building and an office block, whose ground floor had a library, an infirmary, and an auditorium. Lore had it that careful planning had ensured the invisibility of the girls' dormitories to prying eyes in the boys' dorms. Each dormitory building had four floors—primary, middle, junior, and senior—and each floor had an attached flat in which lived a resident teacher in charge of the dormitory, usually with family (Mr. Khan, the senior dorm resident teacher, had only his wife). In my years at Forest Glen, I went from middle through junior to senior. The dining hall was on the ground floor, next to the primary dorm. The resident teachers ate with us, sitting up at a separate table on a stage as if at Oxford or Cambridge. The Head Boys of the dormitories also sat up at that table with them. The girls had their own dining hall in their dormitory building. School uniform for boys was gray half or full pants with a white shirt. A similar khaki outfit was for after school. A school tie was to be worn at all times, except at night, though many boys took their ties with them to bed to put to other, furtive use. Each child was to be possessed of pajamas, night shirt, and dressing gown. Lungis and kurtas were strictly prohibited. For girls, the prescribed dress was skirts and blouses. No Indian clothes, as they were called, were permissible.

Forest Glen felt stuck in the past but it wasn't. By the time I was brought to the school by Gomati Paati, its name had gone from Forest Glen Missionary to Forest Glen International. Only the Christian students were now required to attend service in the chapel. Plans were afoot to build a Shiva temple and a non-denominational worship hall. In addition to French and German, Sanskrit and Hindi were now taught. Mr. Iyer had introduced morning meditation before the breakfast of porridge, toast with jam, and fruit. Where once the children had all been British (that was a long time ago; Indians were being admitted even before independence), now they were mostly Indian. The children of the Raj were all gone, though their names were still to be found carved into the wood of desks and doorframes; only a couple of the children were now British, and they were joined by a handful of other foreign students from Malaysia and Kenya and France, children whose expatriate parents were for some reason or other in India. The Indian children came from families that routinely had cooks and drivers and had been raised by ayahs until they arrived at Forest Glen. Though they came from cities like Calcutta or Madras, they often could not speak Bengali or Tamil. When I arrived at Forest Glen, I did not know about ties, let alone dressing gowns. Sanskrit was the same to me as French. I read English well but spoke with little fluency, despite the best efforts of Appa, Amma, and Uncle Arokia.

Unwillingly, I entered life at Forest Glen. Students were organized into houses that competed with each other not only in sports but also in debate, elocution, and other such activities. I was in Indus House, whose color was white. When I was old enough to think about these things, I found it ironic that I was in a house named after a river that was no longer in India but in Pakistan. Every student had to participate in sports and extracurricular programs. I once came third in long jump. In cricket, I was an opening batsman for Indus. I succeeded by putting my head down and patiently knocking ball after ball down the pitch. I did not make runs, but I was not easy to dismiss. In debate, I was a reluctant participant, but calm and collected. In preparing my arguments, I would think, *This is a thing I have to do. This school means nothing to me. These people mean nothing to me.* Somehow that helped. Because of debate, my fluency in English increased rapidly. Soon English was my best subject, while my Tamil became rusty when it came to writing and reading, though I did not lose it entirely. I was secretly proud of my English. Of my deteriorating Tamil, I was equally secretly ashamed.

I revealed little of myself to the teachers and other students. I did not speak in class unless spoken to. Once, in a Civics class at the beginning of the eleventh year, Mrs. Arora asked me to define the subject whose study we were about to commence. I said, “Civics is the study of the right way to govern a country.” My answer was prompted by the turmoil being reported in the newspapers. The war with

Pakistan had made Indira Gandhi very popular. But the newspapers, which I read carefully in the library (my favorite place in the school), were full of disquieting reports about Indira Gandhi's growing authoritarianism and Jayaprakash Narayan's principled opposition.

Mrs. Arora gently shook her head at my answer and said, "No, that's not it. It's the study of the different branches of government; for example, the legislature, the judiciary, and the executive." The class sniggered at my foolish reply, though Mrs. Arora frowned at them. I thought, *They are wrong, she is only partly right, and I am more right than she is.* Later, I went to the library and consulted Plato's *Republic* and Kautilya's *Arthashastra* to confirm my judgment. In the mid-term exam, I added my definition of Civics to Mrs. Arora's, quoting at length long passages from Plato and Kautilya that I had memorized. Mrs. Arora circled in red my personal contribution, by far the more substantial portion of my answer, and wrote a sharp comment in the margin. I barely passed the exam. Throughout my school years I felt clever, much cleverer than my marks suggested. I found little reason to exert myself. I did not belong. In all the years I was at Forest Glen, I had no friends. My friends were books. I knew Mr. Varadarajan, the librarian of the school, well. I was a voracious reader.

Unlike Paavalampatti, alas, I remember only too well my days at Forest Glen. They teem in my head in lurid detail, dominated by the swaggering lords of senior dorm, the boys who excelled at sports, who wore imported jeans with suave flares when out on day passes. These were the boys who had girlfriends whom they met secretly behind the chapel where dead missionaries were buried beneath stone crosses leaning over at drunken angles. These were the rulers of the dorm, who fought with each other and then suddenly became allies to lord it over the other students. At night, after lights-out, the dormitory was their private domain. Cigarettes, prohibited drinks, and contraband foods made their appearance. Pornographic books filled with the most extraordinary sexual adventures were passed around to be read under the blanket with the help of an electric light. In the common room, brazen gambling with playing cards; in the dark corners of the dorm, hidden seductions. Seduction, and worse than seduction. Once there were rumors of the rape of a boy.

I observed, with puzzlement. I was not seduced. I was not invited to the secret feasts of pork and parathas smuggled in from town. When cigarettes arrived, I was not one of the handful of boys to receive a share. I wore a cloak of calculated indifference that made me invisible to the bullies. I survived. I escaped the fevered entanglements. I transcended the wretchedness of it all by keeping to myself.

⁓

OR DID I?

I look back over what I wrote the day before yesterday and read confusion and bitterness. I see evasion and exaggeration. Was this how it really was? Did I really regard Peter's (probable) rape with puzzlement? *Puzzlement.* Is that the appropriate word for what I felt?

Did I really manage to float above it all?

Is what I have written the whole truth?

What is the whole truth?

⁓

IN MY FINAL YEAR AT Forest Glen, I was called to a meeting with the principal, Mr. Iyer. When I entered his office, Mr. Iyer was sitting behind his wooden desk with the tips of his fingers lightly pressed together. It was his usual manner. In my observation of him over the years, I had always felt there was something practiced about it, as if it was a learned mannerism. Now I saw that this was so. On the walls, above wooden shelves stacked with books, were pictures of previous principals, all white. Mr. Iyer was the first Indian principal. Two of these bygone principals held their hands in exactly the way Mr. Iyer did—Forest Glen believed in tradition. In a corner leaned the wooden rod Mr. Iyer occasionally used to chastise boys as the principals before him had done. I recognized the rod, though I had never had occasion to be disciplined in this way.

From the window of Mr. Iyer's upper-floor office, Forest Glen spread out in the Nilgiri Hills like a sylvan paradise. I looked out the window at the stone chapel tower and the green playing fields and the clump of trees that signified the pond and wondered whether I should consider myself lucky for having attended Forest Glen. I could not deny I was approaching the end of my time in a school that took the job of education seriously. The teachers in the school were all highly qualified. The school had justifiable pride in the colleges and careers to which its students advanced. The school counted prominent politicians, artists, sports figures, and industrialists among its alumni. News of their doings was often pinned to the notice board outside the main office. I should have felt lucky to have spent all these years in such a school.

Mr. Iyer removed his reading glasses from his nose and looked at me from across his neat desk. He spoke my name as if sounding out its meaning: "Selvam Raman."

"Yes, sir," I replied, studying him covertly to gauge the reason for the meeting.

"You have been with us for eight years, almost."

"Yes, sir."

"Do you have any opinion of your time here?"

I lied. "I have enjoyed it. I have learned much."

"Good, good. And soon you will be done. Any idea what you might like to do when you are?"

I shrugged in reply. I had spent the past months avoiding thoughts of the future beyond Forest Glen.

Mr. Iyer pulled a sheet of paper lying on his desk toward him and tapped it with a finger. He said, "I have here a letter from your great-grandmother."

I looked at him. He looked back and said, "She is not well. She was planning to come for your school-leaving ceremony. Perhaps she has mentioned this to you? Now she is unable to make the trip. But she has asked me for some help with regard to your future when you leave here."

I thought of Gomati Paati ill. I had never seen her unwell. She had made no mention of her sickness in her letters to me. "What is wrong with her?" I asked.

Mr. Iyer spread his hands to indicate lack of knowledge. "She does not say. An old person like her. It could be anything, couldn't it?" He added reflectively, "I have always enjoyed my meetings with your great-grandmother. An amazing woman. Marvelous, really."

I maintained a noncommittal silence, which Mr. Iyer seemed not to notice.

"She wants you to go to college and she wants me to arrange it. So this is the question, then. Would you like to go to college as your great-grandmother wishes you to? Would you like me to arrange that for you?"

I considered Mr. Iyer's proposition with outward calm. Inside was a crazy mixture of feelings. Mr. Iyer had made no comment on why he had been entrusted with the responsibility of arranging my future. That was because, I was perfectly confident, he knew the reasons. I begrudged him his knowledge, which could only lead to pity. I felt fiercely protective of my uncherished status in the world. It was mine and I did not want it soiled by pity. I felt resentful of Gomati Paati too. Who was she to make plans for me? I resented her concern for me. That, too, was unacceptable. But grudge and resentment were not my only sentiments. Relief, too, was mixed in. I could not deny that college was exactly the answer to the problem confronting me. After Forest Glen, what? After Forest Glen, college. College would buy me time. I took only a moment to contemplate my mixed feelings. I decided to be practical. I suppressed grudge and resentment and said, yes, I would like to go to college.

He tapped the letter again. "She mentions Loyola. It seems your father went there."

True. Gomati Paati had told me that. But I would go to Loyola for my own reasons, which had nothing to do with why Appa had gone there.

"I, too, went there," Mr. Iyer continued, "before proceeding to England. It is a fine college. What would you like to study at Loyola?"

"English."

Mr. Iyer picked up a folder from his desk and examined it. "Your marks are adequate. If you do well in the final exams, I don't see a problem. I will write a letter to the college for you." He looked up at me and smiled. "Shakespeare and Charles Dickens, eh? I can see from your marks that you are not one for the sciences."

"No, sir."

"Have you read R. K. Narayan? He is an Indian who writes in English. Top stuff. You might want to give him a try, too."

"Yes, sir."

"Very well. That is all, Mr. Raman."

And so I left Forest Glen and came to Madras. Mr. Iyer arranged my admission to Loyola as promised. I joined the Loyola College Hostel as my father had thirty years before. Gomati Paati sent Mr. Iyer enough money for my first year in college, part of it to be used for payments to Loyola and part of it to be put in my name in a bank in Madras. That was the last thing Gomati Paati did for me.

I never saw Gomati Paati again. She died only two months after I joined Loyola, as if she had been waiting for me to finish school, as if this was the last duty left for her in life. I received no letter at all from her while I was at Loyola because, I later realized, of her sickness. I learned of her death from a letter Mr. Iyer forwarded to me. The letter was addressed to Mr. Iyer and was from Uncle Siva. It noted Gomati Paati's death and informed Mr. Iyer that neither he nor I should expect any more transfer of funds on my behalf.

I read the letter with a stone heart. I cried neither for Gomati Paati, who in her shameful love had taken me when I was ten years old and brought me to adulthood as best she could, nor for myself, though I was now more alone than ever before. I reread Uncle Siva's letter and thought, *Is there anyone as alone as me?* This was not a self-pitying question. It was meant simply to ascertain a fact. How alone was I? The question required a precise answer. If I was alone in the world, so be it. I would learn how to be alone. That was my promise to myself.

How well I remember that prideful promise! I thought fiercely, *Being alone is better. Much better not to be touched by the restless hands of this hurly-burly world.*

That is what I said to myself.

ూ

I SIT AT THE WINDOW of my room. Outside, clouds are massed in the sky. My wooden stool is placed beyond the rectangle of gray light falling in through the window. I can look out and survey the world but I cannot be seen from the outside. I hold Malar's two pictures over this notebook in which I write. I examine them closely, especially the expression on Malar's face. I note aspects I had missed before. Where I had earlier seen playfulness and anxiety, now I see determination. That thrust of her chin. There is something scrappy about it. Now, as I examine the pictures, I am certain there is.

I sit here with these pictures because I know Malar will soon come into the yard below. It is that time of the morning. She will bring her family's dirty clothes in a large metal tub to the hand pump in the yard. She will sit on her haunches on the slimy green-tinged cement platform. Her back will be to me. I will be able to observe the way her shoulders bunch and relax under her sari's pallu as she scrubs and rinses the clothes. The soapy foam in the tub will be iridescent even in this gray light dripping weakly from the cloud-filled sky. Afterward, she will hang the wet clothes on the orange nylon lines that stretch between wooden poles from one end of the yard to the other. I will watch as she bends to pick up the wrung shirts and veshtis and blouses and lifts them high above her head to fling over the clotheslines. Her bare arms will glisten with wetness. Her hair will come undone from its loose knot as she bends and lifts and bends again. I will watch as she pauses to do her hair up with a quick gesture, hoping to glimpse her face. It will not be easy to make out her facial expression from up here.

Malar's father is in the dirt yard, bare bodied, with just a lungi around his waist. He has just emerged from the direction of the rank-smelling toilets, shared by all the residents, which are beyond the yard. He carries an empty metal pot in one hand. He is small but has an enormous paunch that he massages and strokes and fondles with great affection, as if it is a being separate from himself. The top of his head has a fringe of hair around a bald center. He oils and combs this fringe with great care. From my window, I can faintly hear the film tune he hums as he loafs around in the yard, idly inspecting its corners and monitoring the comings and goings of the residents of our building. He has no job to go to. There is no work he does.

Our building—the building Malar and her father and I share with many others—is shaped like an L. Below me, adjacent to the photo studio, Malar lives in two rooms with her parents. One room is mostly a kitchen, for Malar supports herself and her parents by running a mess. She cooks meals for the men without families who live in the other wing of the building. I too get my dinner from her. I have been doing so for many months now. She leaves my food in tin boxes outside my door. I eat and return them there. Once a week I leave money in one of the boxes. Malar's industry is quite remarkable. Not only does she run the mess, but she does much of the housework. Her enterprise is directly matched by her father's uselessness.

In one room of the other wing of the building lives a carpenter, who is gone for most of the day to whatever construction site his contractor sends him. Each day he returns home exhausted. His four children are always in the yard if they are not in school, which is where they are now. When they are home, they run around the yard wildly chasing one another. Their mother yells at them to do their homework but to little avail. In the remaining two rooms of that wing live an assortment of bachelors who rotate in and out with such frequency that I cannot keep up even though I spend much time secretly observing the yard, as I am doing now. The shyster landlord has filled the rooms with beds. He rents out each bed at exorbitant rates. The men toil in the workshops of Guindy Industrial Estate, to which they can walk from here. Each pays for the bed into which he collapses at the end of the day, exhausted. Sometimes two or even three men, sleeping in shifts, share a bed. A few weeks, or months, and then they are gone. Another job in another workshop in another part of Madras. Or else, perhaps, back to the village from which they boldly came to make a life for themselves in the big city. These are the men for whom Malar cooks.

Malar's husband was one of these rent-a-bed men. That is how they met. I know because Vivek described the courtship to me before he disappeared. He liked talking about Malar, even though I gave him no encouragement. Who wouldn't like doing that?

My room, above my photo studio, is well placed to overlook the yard, which is at the back of the building. The photo studio faces the other way, toward the street. The room is reached by steps that go up the side of the building. It is small, sparsely furnished, with cream walls badly in need of paint. A metal cot with a thin mattress. A kerosene stove on which I cook my morning meal. My few pots and pans. The rolled-up mat on which I used to sleep before Vivek disappeared. A chair and a stool. A table for my books. Under the table, the green trunk that has gone with me from place to place and in which I keep my clothes neatly folded. This list more or less covers all my possessions in the world. And most of these possessions I have inherited from Vivek. Should he return to claim them, they would become his again. I am glad to live so light.

If her father is still in the yard when she comes out with her tub, Malar will not look up at my window. If he is not, she will. She will turn and look straight up, to let me know that she knows I'm sitting here in the shadows. And then perhaps I will be able to make out the expression on her face better.

Why did Malar marry Arvind? Did she love him? This is one of the questions I would ask Malar if I could. What is love anyway? What does it feel like? I don't mean the love Gomati Paati felt for me. I mean the other kind. What does it feel like to receive it? To be the object of it? I would like to know.

I would like to know if Appa and Amma loved each other. Ramu and Ponni. My progenitors. The authors of my very being. Did they love each other? Did they love me? Could they love me if they did not love each other?

∽

Peter and Ranjan. Write it all out.

Write it out. Write out everything that happened. Hold nothing back. Peter was my friend, as much as I had one in Forest Glen. Until he was no longer. He was raped, or at least something as bad happened. Afterward, he tried to reach out to me. I did not respond. Nothing required me to respond.

Then why do I feel as if I should have?

Peter was beautiful, with lips pink as a girl's and skin like gold. Fine, sandy hair that tumbled into his eyes. He knew he was beautiful. But he did not know what to do with his beauty. That was his burden—so clear to me now. His father worked for the railways, sufficiently high up that he could afford to send Peter to Forest Glen but not so well off that the tuition was not onerous. His father had gone to Forest Glen in the waning days of the British in India, when Anglo-Indians went there as if by right. Peter said his father had happy memories of Forest Glen and wanted him to go there too. I saw Peter's father a few times, when he came to pick Peter up. A tall, serious-faced man with a mustache. Peter's mother was darker, had more Indian blood in her. Peter got his beauty from her. Her visits to Forest Glen were an occasion in the senior boys' dorm. Boys found excuses to accompany Peter down to the main office to meet his parents. Peter did not seem to mind. He basked in the reflected glory of his mother's beauty. How he preened when Ranjan teased him about it!

Peter's cot was next to mine in the senior dorm. Often, we talked after lights-out, or rather he talked and I listened. He told me about growing up in a railway colony in Bangalore. I told him very little in return. That did not bother him. Sooner or later, Peter mentioned Ranjan. I listened without interrupting, though I did not understand. I understand so much more in hindsight. So much more. I did not judge, which may be why he trusted me. He saw that I was set apart, that I kept myself aloof. He saw that I cared nothing about the lords of the senior dorm, of whom Ranjan was one. I was immune to them. He was not, but he liked that I was. That is how he and I became friends.

Ranjan. Captain of the school cricket team. Allowed to wear his hair longer than permitted. A boy who did as he pleased. His family owned factories in Bombay. They were generous donors to the school. They had a mansion in Juhu in which the extended family lived. Ranjan's life had been plotted far into the future. Plans had been made. People had been spoken to. After Forest Glen Ranjan was to go to Boston to acquire a college degree in Business

Administration. Then he would return to Bombay to enter the family business. So it had been ordained and so it would be.

Ranjan was not good-looking—eyes too close set, lips too thin. It did not matter. He had no need of good looks. He had a power far greater. I had observed it many times. He entered a room and immediately sucked up the attention. He was big, with powerful arms and shoulders. He was commanding. He was magnetic. Peter could not resist Ranjan. Ranjan enthralled Peter with stories about life in that Juhu mansion. The servants, the imported cars, the weekends at the club—I overhead it all from the adjoining cot, noting the guile in Ranjan's practiced, bored voice as he reclined in his lordly manner on Peter's cot. Besotted Peter saw none of it. I saw Ranjan feed on Peter's adulation and said nothing. It was none of my business. None of my business too how, late in the night, with the whole dorm asleep, Ranjan crawled into Peter's bed. Whispers, giggling, muffled noises. I did not let on I heard. Surely Peter must have known that I did, but he knew too that I would say nothing. He trusted in our friendship. In who I was.

Until that night.

Until the night Ranjan paid one of the gardeners to smuggle toddy and chicken biryani into the school, to be left for him in a little clearing on the far side of the pond, the wilder, less frequented part of the school. Ranjan and his cronies had done this before. It was usual procedure for them. In the middle of the night they planned to creep away to the clearing as they had many times previously. A window in the dorm bathroom had a loose grille. Through this window the intrepid could crawl out onto a ledge, and from there down to another ledge that led to the roof of the dining hall. Shimmy down a drainage pipe and you were free. Few knew of this secret way out of the senior boys' dorm. Fewer still dared to use it.

On the day that something happened to Peter, Ranjan told him about the loose grille and invited him to the illicit gathering in the clearing. Peter was thrilled. And afraid. He had never been asked by Ranjan before. He desperately wanted to go. At the same time, something prescient in him balked. Reluctant to join Ranjan and his cronies by himself, he came to me. He cajoled, he importuned, until I could not say no—I should have but I did not. Perhaps if I had, Peter would not have gone.

Peter and I waited until well after lights-out, and then we followed Ranjan down the ledges and the drainpipe. Peter did not want Ranjan to know he had asked me to accompany him, so he had told Ranjan he was not sure he would come. The idea was that we would follow on our own when we were certain Ranjan and his cronies had left. I had never been out of the dorm this late in the night. The school grounds were transfigured. The half moon had lightly brushed everything with its silver. It was early in the year and a light mist hung around the roofs of buildings and between trees. Familiar shapes had turned into eerie apparitions. We left the dorm buildings behind and ran across the dew-touched playing fields in our pajamas and dressing gowns, the white veil of the mist parting to let us through. It was cold. We had put on our Keds but had neglected to pull on sweaters. Beyond the fields, tunneling through thickly clustered trees, was the path to the pond. Rotting leaves squished under the soles of our Keds as we jogged around the pond along the path. Up ahead, we heard voices. I recognized them—Ranjan, Madhav, Amir, Nageshwar. Cigarette smoke wafted down the path, mixing into the odor of dank vegetation. The mist veiled everything. The world had contracted to this damp clump of trees. The school buildings were just across the small pond, but they felt as if they were on a different planet.

We arrived panting in the little clearing. We were at the very edge of the pond. Before us stretched dark water. The small pond had turned boundless and inscrutable in the mist hovering over it. Nageshwar was opening up the packets of biryani wrapped up in banana leaves and newspaper and tied with white string. Madhav and Amir were taking swigs from a bottle of toddy. More bottles stood on the ground. Ranjan was reclining against a tree, his hands behind his head, a cigarette dangling from his lips. At the sound of our approach, he said without turning his head, "There you are. You came, Petey. Brave boy." His voice was mocking.

"He is not alone," Nageshwar said, rocking back on his heels and looking up at us as we stood at the edge of the clearing.

"He is not?" Ranjan refused to look.

"No."

"Selvam is with him," Amir said, passing the toddy bottle to Ranjan.

Ranjan ignored the bottle. He said, "I see." He pulled on his cigarette and blew a long stream of smoke out from the corner of his mouth. The smoke quickly dissipated into the gloom.

We were shadows in the night. The Ranjan shadow had a throbbing red dot for a mouth. "I thought you didn't want to come. I thought that's why you said you would come by yourself. Now I see what you were planning," the throbbing red dot said.

Amir took a swig from the bottle, laughed harshly, and said, "He's brought a chaperone, Ranjan."

"That's right. A chaperone. Why did you bring a chaperone, Petey?" Ranjan flicked his cigarette in a red arc in the direction of the pond.

"I just thought it would be fun to have more people here," Peter responded. He was peering into the clearing in the darkness, turning his head this way and that, uncertain of himself. He stepped forward, pulling me along by the sleeve of my dressing gown. I freed my arm with a jerk and stayed where I was. I saw immediately that it had been a mistake to let Peter persuade me. I had been weak. I had allowed Peter to tempt me out of my discipline. Ever since I had come to this school my discipline had protected me, kept me safe, and now I had given it up for Peter. Peter paused and said, "What's the problem? It's only Selvam. He's okay." He turned to me and waved me forward, "Come on, Selvam. Come on."

"This is invitation only, Peter. You can't just bring anyone you like," Amir said.

"That's right," Nageshwar added.

Madhav stayed quiet, taking small swigs from his bottle and looking out over the pond. He was a North Indian boy, from Allahabad. A fine scholar and sportsman, much admired by students and teachers alike. A gentle fellow, one of the few lords of the senior dorm who were not bullies.

The packets Nageshwar had been opening were now spread

out on the ground. The spicy aroma of biryani lifted into the night air. No one made a move in its direction.

"Little Peter," Amir said. He turned to Ranjan. "I told you not to invite him."

"Peter's all right," Ranjan said. "He can join us."

I said, "Peter, let's go. Let's go back to the dorm."

Peter hung his head and did not make a move. He rubbed a foot slowly in the damp dirt.

Ranjan said, "Tell Selvam about Chikmagalur, Nageshwar."

Right then I should have turned and left. I did not.

"What do you mean?"

"About your peasants. About what you promised us." Nageshwar was from Hyderabad, but his family owned enormous tracts of land in rural Chikmagalur.

Nageshwar gave an amused snort. He leaned back on his haunches and turned his face toward me. He had understood. He said, "You mean about our trip to my farm at the end of twelfth? About our treat when we are done with this stupid school? Selvam can't come."

Ranjan said, "Of course he can't. Tell him anyway. I'm sure he'll be interested."

Nageshwar said in a boastful voice, "Any woman in the fields. Any woman you want. I just have to say the word and my uncle will make sure she's brought to you."

Amir took a swig from his bottle and laughed harshly again.

Ranjan said, "Selvam doesn't need to come, Nageshwar. He knows all about those kinds of women. Don't you, Selvam? Of course he can't come. What if he has your uncle bring his sister to him? What if he fucks his mother by mistake?"

"That would be incest," Nageshwar said.

"Stop it," Madhav interjected in a quiet voice.

"You don't know where your mother is, do you, Selvam? What if you find her there?"

"That is exactly where he will find her. On my uncle's farm," Nageshwar said.

"Stop it," Madhav said again, more firmly.

Ranjan did not stop. He addressed Peter. "Selvam never goes anywhere, Petey. His grandmother always comes here to visit him. Do you know why?" He answered his own question. "You know why. Selvam's father killed himself to escape his mother." And then he said, "You shouldn't have brought him, Petey."

Peter kept rubbing his foot in the dirt. Rub, rub, rub. He would not look at me. I did not at that moment feel anger at Ranjan's wanton cruelty. I felt an immense sadness wash over me. I said, "Come on, Peter. Let's go. We should not have come." But I knew he would not leave with me. He could not, anymore.

"Go with him if you want, Petey," Ranjan said. "But then don't come crawling to me later."

Peter hung his head and did not move. I turned and ran back over the path through the trees. Behind me I heard someone else running and for a moment I thought I had been wrong about Peter. I stopped. It was not Peter. Madhav ran past, giving no indication as he went by that he saw me standing there by the side of the path. I followed him under the trees and across the playing fields, bitterness in my heart.

The next morning Peter was sick in his bed. Something had happened to him in the night, something bad. I did not care. "Selvam," he said in a small voice without getting up. I ignored him and went to the bathroom for my wash. When I came back, Peter had gone to the infirmary. Throughout the day wild rumors swirled through the school about what Ranjan had done to Peter in the clearing by the pond. *I do not care.* That is what I told myself. I was consumed by myself. I could not forget what had been done to *me* in the clearing. I thought about what Ranjan had said about Appa and Amma. I did not ask myself how in the world Ranjan could know anything at all about them. I could not stop thinking about what he had said. I swore to myself I would not go with Gomati Paati to Mr. Arnold's house anymore. And so I refused the next time she came. That is when she said, "I cannot take you to Paavalampatti because I cannot protect you from Uncle Siva," confirming to me her perfidy, her shameful love for me.

⁓

THERE ARE THOSE WHO CALL themselves the twice-born. They are the Brahmins and others of the high castes. Of themselves, they proclaim they are born first from their mothers' wombs and then as adults into the world of their fathers. I am not one of them.

What am I, then?

What has to be done will be done.

I write now, here in this notebook, many difficult things I could not have known when they happened. I sail the horizonless ocean of my memory with only my need acting as my imperfect compass.

⁓

GOMATI PAATI DIED JUST A few weeks after I joined Loyola. I left Loyola then, so I was not there very long at all. As at Forest Glen, so during my brief time at Loyola I kept to myself. I went to my classes, but I did not make friends with the boys in faded blue jeans, khadi kurtas, and kolhapuris who met under the trees of the car park just within the main gates of the college to drink tea and smoke cigarettes. I lived in the hostel behind the church, where my father too had lived years before. I ate in the canteen, sitting by myself and rebuffing with quiet politeness attempts at conversation. I had with me the green trunk, which Gomati Paati told me had been my father's originally. I knew nothing about my parents' lives before Athanoor, and even of Athanoor I remembered very little. I had no pictures of my parents. I dredged up dim memories of my father, made him younger, and pictured him sitting in the classrooms in which I sat. When I came across a wooden desk with names scratched into it, I looked for his—Ramu or Raman—in vain. I imagined my father walking the halls that I walked. I wondered if my mother had ever come to meet my father at Loyola. I knew Amma had never been a student at Loyola. I knew she had never been to college, and anyhow Loyola did not admit girls.

Still I imagined her striding purposefully next to Appa under the trees that lined the approach to the church, her thick curly hair braided tight. I heard bangles of many colors clinking on her wrists. At other times, I imagined the opposite—Appa and Amma walking away from each other, separating from each other under those very trees. I was not sure what I thought of a father who had jumped into a fire to save his best friend. Was he a hero? Then why did I feel betrayed? And a mother who abandons her child? Is she not a villain? Then why did my anger feel so weak? Haunted by such questions, I struggled toward answers. I thought, *I have no past; I will need to make a powerful past of my own.* Loyola seemed as good a place as any to do this. I filled my ignorance with imagined scenarios.

And then the letter from Uncle Siva arrived and cut me off from my inheritance. I no longer had the luxury of staying at Loyola and searching for solutions to the riddle of my life. I decided it would be much wiser to save the money I had been given for the first year of college. I could make the money go further if I dropped out. Surely there were cheaper ways to live. Thus, I came to room with Vivek, the brother of Chezhiyan, who worked in the Loyola canteen. When Chezhiyan discovered I needed a cheap place to stay, he introduced me to his brother, who offered me a mat on the floor of his room in Butt Road for a small fee. We would share the room here on the outskirts of the city and I would help out in the photo studio. That was the arrangement. I agreed and promptly brought my green trunk here to the Look Nice Photo Studio—but the promptness was mixed in with trepidation. I did not know Chezhiyan well. Vivek I did not know at all. After dormitory life in Forest Glen, I had enjoyed having a room to myself in the Loyola hostel, and now I was to share one with another human being, and a stranger at that.

Vivek was many years older than me. He, I learned over succeeding days, had barely any schooling but he had a grudging respect for mine. He was patient with my ignorance in the photo studio and very quickly understood that all I wanted was to be left alone, which he was happy to do. He was tall and nicely proportioned and despite his bad breath went with an older woman, a proprietor of a shoe shop of some substance, who sometimes furtively spent the night with him. On such occasions, Vivek asked me to take my mat out to the verandah, where mosquitoes tormented me all night long. I did not mind. It was a small enough thing to do for someone who, on the whole, had been obliging.

Vivek was not a bad man. Even so, it was not long before I grew fretful. The room was small and I was being forced to share a life I did not wish to share. I found it hard to be on such intimate terms with another human being when I was still learning—slowly, painfully—to be intimate with myself. I was gratified, therefore, when, a few months after my arrival, Vivek vanished. His disappearance did not come as a surprise. For quite some time, Vivek had not been visited by his woman. He had lain moping in his cot and let me take care of the shop downstairs. I was expecting a crisis of some kind. When he disappeared (one morning I woke up and he was gone), I was left with the room and the studio and his many debts. The room rent had not been paid for months. Bills were outstanding at the lab where Vivek sent film to be developed. I did not complain or refuse responsibility. I settled all the debts out of my own money.

By the time Vivek left, I had learned how the business worked. I knew how to use the two cameras—the 120 mm with two lenses and viewfinder on top, and the smaller handheld one. I knew how to work the three 500-watt lights in the studio. I knew the rates to be charged—Rs. 3 for three passport-size pictures, Rs. 10 for postcard, Rs. 15 for cabinet, and Rs. 30 for full. The lab agent who came to pick up film was known to me. I knew how to file the pictures and rolls of film in their drawers under the counter. And although it was not at all an easy thing for me, I could even talk to the customers, cajole them into arranging themselves in an attractive way in front of the garden scene on the wall or else lower the screen for a more formal picture with a plain background. I managed, if only with difficulty, to keep the photo studio working. It was challenging, but I still much preferred being on my own.

After a couple of months, Vivek returned as suddenly as he had left. I greeted him without enthusiasm and said, "Where did you vanish to?" I was sitting behind the counter in the front of the shop. I had recently discovered the old pictures jumbled together in boxes and begun arranging them into my own categories based on what I saw in them.

I was engaged in this activity when Vivek stepped into the shop out of the blinding sunlight of the street. I put away the boxes while he leaned against the counter and pretended to survey the shop. He made no attempt to come around to his rightful place behind the counter and I did not invite him to do so. He wore fashionable sunglasses that covered half his face and had grown his hair long. His new shirt was bright yellow and unbuttoned to his stomach. He said without preamble, "If you want, you can buy my equipment from me and take over the shop. Otherwise you have to clear out."

I felt no alarm at Vivek's ultimatum. His disinterest in the photo studio was obvious. On a slip of paper, I had kept careful account of all the money I had spent in paying off his debts. I took out the slip and showed him the figures. He glanced at them perfunctorily. I drove a hard bargain with him. We came to a mutual agreement. I could take over the shop and the room for the time being, but I would have to send him money every month for the furniture he had left behind in his room and for the cameras and other equipment in the shop. I scrupulously do so even now, though more than a year has gone by, and even though I sometimes have to dip into the money saved from my first year of college. The shop does not always pay for itself. Some months I have to subsidize it. It is not the shop's fault. There is no other photo studio nearby.

Someone serious about making a successful go of it probably could. I am not that person. I like photographs. I am fascinated by the people in them—their faces, their clothes, their pasts and futures, the loves and hates that I am able to surmise. But the customers who come to the shop are another matter. Sometimes I close up the shop and retire to my bed in a panic when too many customers—as many as three or four—throng the shop in a single morning.

It's true. I like the pictures—arranging and rearranging them in their boxes—more than the customers. That cannot be a good thing.

To live untouched by human beings. To be touched only by their shadows.

That cannot be a good thing.

⸙

MALAR IS MARRIED TO ARVIND, but they no longer live together as they once did in the rooms that Malar shares with her parents.

Arvind is a jealous bully. Once, he even accused Malar of carrying on with me. The accusation was made late one night when I had to use the toilets beyond the yard. I was making my way there when I came upon Arvind and Malar in the dark. I did not see them until I was almost upon them. Arvind held Malar by her hair with one hand and was hitting her with the open palm of the other. I stumbled into him and grabbed him by his arm before I could stop myself. He spun around and glared at me out of malevolent eyes. His protuberant nose quivered indignantly. "It's this clown, isn't it? He is the one you fuck when I'm not around, isn't he?" he cried. He tried to break free from me but he was so drunk that it was easy to hold him. And then suddenly he went limp and started crying. I let go of him then and he lay on the ground, sniveling.

Malar said with contempt in her voice, "He won't do anything now." I rushed away before another word could be spoken.

A few days later Malar saw me in the yard and tried to thank me. I put my head down and hurried past. I brushed past her as if I had not heard her. I was surprised at what I had done in the dark of night by the toilets. I could not understand my action. I was even afraid—not of Arvind, who seemed to have completely blacked out the incident, but of my own instinctive response. Why had I sprung to Malar's defense?

Was it because of what had happened to Peter?

I am still afraid. I am afraid of the impetuous, brave thing I did that night, and of the way that I sometimes feel Malar looks at me when I pass her in the yard.

⸙

Arvind left months ago. I witnessed his departure. Loud voices late in the evening raised me from my bed and brought me to the window of my room. The dark yard below was empty but for two animated figures by the hand pump. At first, it seemed the usual story. Arvind held Malar by her shoulders and shook her as if she were a thing, not a human being. Soon people appeared, drawn by the commotion. The carpenter and his wife stood at the door to their room and watched. A feeble light spilled into the yard from behind them. Rent-a-bed men emerged from their rooms to enjoy the spectacle. Arvind's drunken rages were a common occurrence, but that did not reduce their entertainment value. One man alone threw out an angry complaint without forsaking his bed: "Won't you let us sleep? What insanity is this?" I felt ashamed to be standing at the window, but I did not stop watching.

Down in the yard, Malar's father too stood to one side observing. He stood as if this matter were no concern of his, as if he too were simply a neighbor, while Malar's mother implored him to do something. Soon Malar's mother gave up the futile endeavor and ran to Arvind, stroked his cheek, and cried, "Why are you doing this, Arvind? What has she done to you? Be reasonable."

Arvind shoved her aside and yelled at Malar, "I've seen how you look at other men. That is why you are throwing me out, isn't it? You bitch! You whore!"

Malar had finally asked Arvind to leave, and he was enraged. I was glad Malar was getting rid of Arvind. Though there was more abuse, Malar did not reason like her mother did. She tried to break free from his grip and yelled back, "Let me go! You are hurting me!" It was terrible to watch. I remembered the night I had come upon them by the toilets. I wanted to go down and help, but I did not. I stayed where I was, looking. Arvind pushed Malar down, kicked her. Malar got up and quickly ran into her room and shut the door before Arvind could grab her again. He hammered on her door until a few of the rent-a-bed men finally made him stop. Arvind yelled as they dragged him away, "You want me to go away? I will! You are not the only woman I can get! There are other women like you in the world!"

I felt revulsion at the sad drama. I was glad not to be a part of it. At the same time, I felt ashamed that I had not gone down and done what the rent-a-bed men had.

Arvind still comes around occasionally, usually drunk. He stands in the yard, yells foul things at Malar. Once, he tried to force his way into the room she uses as a kitchen, but Malar took the knife with which she was cutting vegetables to him. After that, he does not dare to get too close to her.

Arvind is wrong. Malar does not carry on with other men. I know because I watch her from my window and know more about her daily routines than probably her mother does. Where is the time for her to be fooling around with men secretly, in a way hidden from me?

Why did Malar marry Arvind? Did she love him?

MALAR HAS A LOAFER FOR a father. Her mother, incompetent and unreliable, alternates between cursing out Arvind and berating Malar for driving him away. Malar's brothers, gone to workshops in other parts of the city, rarely visit. Alone for all practical purposes, Malar runs a business providing lunch and dinner to single men. She does most of the housework at home. She is doing a correspondence course for a B.A. in Tamil. She would like to be a schoolteacher.

Arvind is a fool. Where will he find such an amazing woman again?

I know so much about Malar because I get my dinner from her even though it would not be hard for me to cook. Sometimes, when she needs me to pay in advance, she knocks on my door. Then, she will want to talk. There is no one else like me for her to talk to. I am different from the other men she meets. I know that. She is aware I read a lot. She can see the books in my room, accumulating in piles even on the floor. She will want to talk about what I am reading. I try to keep our conversations as short as possible. I try not to look at her when I give her her money.

Malar does not mention the incident that night by the toilets, but I think she hasn't forgotten it.

I started getting my dinner from Malar after Arvind left. I know why I did. What I don't know is what comes after my decision to do so.

Three weeks ago, Malar suddenly came into the photo studio. She had on a fine green sari with a pattern of mango leaves on it. She had oiled her hair, braided it freshly, and adorned it with a string of jasmine flowers. Her face glowed from her bath and the scent of talcum powder rose faintly from her neck to mingle with the smell of jasmine. She was just as in her wedding picture—no, she was far more beautiful. The gap in her front teeth when she smiled was utterly bewitching.

I said, striving to keep the trembling out of my voice, "Do you need money? I will have to go to my room to get it if you do."

She said, "No. I am not here for that."

"What kind of pictures do you need, then? Passport size? Those are three rupees for three copies."

She expressed her impatience with a low grunt. "No, no, nothing like that."

I waited for her to say more. She looked at me out of those big eyes and asked a question: "Is there something you want to say to me?"

I looked confused. I could not speak.

Her face changed. "Okay," she said abruptly. "Portrait size. How much is that?"

"Five rupees for three copies."

"Fine."

We went into the photo studio. I raised the screen to reveal the garden scene. She stood stiffly before it. I made no attempt to reposition her for a better picture. I switched on the 500-watt lamps, focused the camera, and snapped the picture. She left without another word. She never came back to pick up her three copies. They sit in an envelope waiting for her. In the last many days, there have been many occasions when I could have given them to her. I have not. Nor have I added one of the copies to the two pictures of Malar I already have. Something stops me from adding this new picture to my people collection.

↜

My room and my photo studio. I venture far from them only to buy books. Practically outside my door, I catch the Defence Colony 21 E to Guindy. From Guindy, I go by electric train to Moore Market. Under the grimy arched roof of the ancient brick building, I make my way to the stalls at the back piled high with secondhand books. Sometimes, instead of Moore Market, I go to Mount Road. At Guindy, instead of taking the electric train, I change buses. I wait in the crowd at the bus stop opposite the train station for one of the many buses to Mount Road. In the bus, I sit at the back and watch people getting on and off. I note young men in neatly ironed shirts with frayed collars—silent young men, poor like me, going into the city with their certificates in folders to hunt for jobs. I listen in on conversations. Like those of the women who get on at Saidapet with baskets of bananas bought at the market there. Probably headed to Alwarpet or Nungambakkam to sell the bananas door to door in the hot sun. I listen to them bemoan the rise in prices. I get off at Higginbotham's but I do not go into the bookstore. Instead I make my way to the nearby pavement vendors with their secondhand books spread out in front of them.

If the bus is crowded, I stand in the aisle in the press of people—warm skin rubbing against me, body smells digging deep into me, sandaled feet stamping me. Once I jumped—pure instinct—onto a crowded bus as it was pulling away from the bus stop. Three pairs of hands reached out and grabbed me. If they had not, I would have fallen hard to the pavement below.

I used to hate the crowds in the bus and the train.

Since Indira Gandhi declared the Emergency and placed the country under her iron rule, I am never sure what I will find at the vendors on Mount Road or at Moore Market. Often I see policemen harassing the vendors. Indira Gandhi and Sanjay Gandhi. Mother and son have made despots of themselves. Controversial books have disappeared. But you can still buy novels and poems and classics from distant lands. Such as a slim volume entitled *Letters to a Young Poet* by someone called Rainer Maria Rilke, with a line that sticks in my mind: "Love consists in this, that two solitudes protect and touch and greet each other." And James Joyce's *Portrait of the Artist as a Young Man*. Mulk Raj Anand's *Untouchable*. The story of Bakha the Bhangi boy. That is one I have read and reread. Maxim Gorky's *Mother*. Another time, a worm-eaten collection of Shakespeare's tragedies. "To be or not to be, that is the question." And many other battered books for a rupee or two.

Every time I go to Moore Market or Mount Road I chance my luck, but I always manage to return with a bag full of cheap books that will keep me going for two or three weeks. I freely roam the world in these books.

The bus from Mount Road returns as it goes—over the Gemini flyover, through Teynampet and Nandanam, over the Marmalong Bridge, where the Adyar River glints like dirty silver in the sun. At Guindy, I catch the 21 E toward Defence Colony. Once again I watch the passengers. Or else I look out the window and read the political slogans on building walls. *Indira is India. What the Congress Stands For—A Party That Works for a Nation That Works. Indira Amma Zindabad!*

Indira Amma's face is everywhere. Emergency rule is Mother's rule. That is what Indira Amma would like us to think. But where's the love? The mood in the country feels somber. I read the newspapers, but I don't delude myself that the truth is in them.

I don't know what the truth is, but I know the truth is not on the posters or in the newspapers.

꩜

When I think of Amma, I see her under a mango tree. It must be the tree that stood in the yard of the school in Athanoor. I am up in the tree, straddling a branch with my face thrust into a clump of thick leaves. I am peering down at her upturned face through the leaves. The sharp tree smell reaches deep into my nostrils and tickles my throat. Clambering up the scabrous bark has left gray marks on my arms and legs. I can hear an insect buzzing above my head in the hot air. I have climbed up into the tree to pick ripe mangos before the birds get them. Amma waits down below with an old piece of cloth spread out in her arms. I pick the mangos that are beginning to turn yellow and drop them into the outstretched cloth. Amma's upturned face is laughing at me. *Be careful,* she says. *Don't climb any higher.* I like to see her laugh. I like to hear the love in her voice, and also the way it turns grave when I point to a mango and ask her if it is ready to be picked. *What do you think?* she counters when I do that. Then, feeling important, I touch the mango to feel how hard it is. I feel needed up in the tree. I turn my head to search for more mangos to pick. I find a likely one hidden in a cluster of leaves. *There,* I shout to Amma and point. I excitedly crawl further up the branch to reach it and cry again, *There.* But there is no answer. I look down through the leaves. Amma is gone. I push the leaves away and look again. She is not there. I hear voices. Amma has stepped away to speak to some of the schoolchildren. A trivial, childish crisis of some kind. Her gentle voice consoles them. Suddenly, the ground feels far away, terrifyingly distant.

That is one of the few memories I have of Amma.

And of Appa? My most vivid memory of him is of a conversation in a small room with a desk and a shelf of books. I am sitting on the hard cement floor in a corner of the room, drawing pictures on my slate with a piece of chalk. The chalk makes a scratching noise on the slate. Uncle Arokia says, "Is this necessary, Ramu?"

"You know how bad the situation has become here in Athanoor," Appa replies. "I don't have to tell you that."

"But do you think Selvam will be welcomed?"

I become alert at the mention of my name, but pretend to continue with my drawing.

"What else can I do? Where else can I send him? Ponni has no family anymore. We don't know where anyone is. We have long since lost contact with her family."

"But think about where you are taking him."

"I trust Gomati Paati," Appa says. The sharp note of defiance in his voice makes me look up. Appa's eyes meet mine, and then he looks away, unable to return my gaze. Uncle Arokia shakes his head but says nothing.

I have no memory of Appa and Amma together. Not a single one. I wish I did. It might have helped with some of the answers I seek.

ঌ

When I went to Paavalampatti, the first thing Uncle Siva said was, "I knew you would come." He spoke the words with smug satisfaction even as he lay dying on a cot in the front room of the house from which Gomati Paati came twice a year to visit me at Forest Glen. This was the house in which my father had grown up, the house to which he had brought me before he died. I remembered little about the house. I entered it with quiet dread—filled equally with resolve and with fear. Uncle Siva had sent a message through Mr. Iyer in Forest Glen: "I am dying. Come immediately. I have something important to give you." The letter had been redirected from Loyola. I thought about it for several days, shuffling my photographs in my photo studio, and then decided to go. I did not trust Uncle Siva, but what could I do? I wanted to know what he had for me.

I found Uncle Siva old, emaciated. Gomati Paati had stayed strong well into old age. Not Uncle Siva. He could not have been more than seventy but looked much older. The ten years since I had last seen him had wasted the man I vaguely remembered. An ox of a man in his prime—so I had heard—had been brought to this. Skin and bones, finding it difficult even to raise his hand. A storm of emotions raged in his eyes, though. One moment the eyes glowed haughtily; the next they were frantic, or else abject. It was death. Impending death had raised up a tornado in Uncle Siva's heart. I realized with a shock, *The monster is afraid of dying.*

A young man with a sacred thread across his chest, hardly older than me, had let me into the house. Uncle Siva pointed at him with a trembling finger and observed, "Son of a neighbor. Looks after me. He comes in the morning and leaves in the afternoon." He added with a challenge in his voice, "He is a Brahmin." The young man emitted an involuntary sound of annoyance and disappeared into the house, leaving Uncle Siva and me to stare at each other for a long moment of silence in that front room into which the morning air drifted through a barred window. The village street was peaceful. But in Uncle Siva's eyes a fire smoldered. He inspected me with sharp, glinting eyes that cut into me. Then the light in his eyes dimmed. The eyes turned old, gray, watery, and he said in a subdued voice, "I have something for you."

"I came, as you wanted me to," I replied. I waited, standing over Uncle Siva's bed with my bag on my shoulder. I did not bother to put the bag down. There was a chair by the cot. I made no move to sit in it. The room also contained a sofa and an old, battered radio, and there were pictures askew on the walls. Everything was raggedy and the dust was thick everywhere.

"I have cancer," Uncle Siva said, as if he had in an instant forgotten that he had something to give me. A distant expression came into his eyes. He looked at the ceiling above. "Do you know where my children are?" I knew Uncle Siva had a son and a daughter. My father's cousins, my uncle and aunt. I knew their names—Kumar and Sharada—but I had never met them. Last I had heard, they were in Bombay. "In Chicago. In America. Both of them." He turned mournful eyes on me and said, "They never write to me. Maybe once a year I'll get a letter. *I'm fine. Children are fine. Hope you are fine. Sorry we won't be able to visit this year either.*" Fear mixed with anger quickened his voice. "How do I know they are still alive? Last letter came six months ago. Will they come even when I die?"

Chicago. Pictures of American cities I had seen in newspapers and magazines sprang to mind. Rows of brick houses with stoops in front. Forests of TV antennae on the roofs under wintry gray skies. In streets filled with snow, long American cars with extravagant fins. Huddled figures in overcoats and hats around overturned garbage cans. Streets of ice like glass. Slush. I imagined a younger version of Uncle Siva trudging through the brown slush, cold hands thrust deep into an overcoat. I thought of Uncle Siva's son in a distant land while Uncle Siva lay dying alone in the house in which he had been born. Superstition had it that the son's inescapable duty was to carry fire to the father's funeral pyre, so that the father's soul might attain peace. Would the son return to honor the father's superstition?

A hunted look slid into Uncle Siva's eyes. He whispered to me, as if afraid of being overheard, "There are ghosts in this house, you know." His colorless lips trembled as he nodded his head, affirming his own observation. "Yes, yes. The tamarind tree out back. There were always ghosts in that tree. Your grandfather's murdered body was found under that tree. Did you know that? Now the ghosts are here. In the house. Murugappa. Chellappa. Even Ramu, your father. And other ghosts whose names I don't know. I see them. They have come right into the house." He looked stricken. "Before she died, Gomati Paati had a dream about the tree. Next day she had it cut down. I did not want it cut, but she would not listen. Now the ghosts are all in the house." He repeated vehemently, "Gomati Paati would not listen! I said, *Don't cut down the tree!* But when did she ever listen to me?"

Uncle Siva lay back on his bed, exhausted by his emotions. I examined him quietly while I waited for him to gather his strength. I thought about him on his cot after the neighbor's son departed. Daily the darkness slowly gathered in the house as the old man sweltered in the heat and listened to furtive sounds welling out of the gloom. Ghosts. Creeping ever closer to the monster who lay there, dying and fearful, in the dark, while his son was so far away.

I understood. I hated that I did, but I understood.

I thrust pity out of my heart and said, "What is it you wanted to give me?"

Uncle Siva was quiet such a long while that I thought he had not heard me. Then with a quick movement, he felt under his pillow and drew out faded blue "inland" letters folded over. He thrust them at me in a shaking hand. "Take them! Take them! I don't want them. They are for you. From your mother."

I looked at the letters stupidly. "From my mother?"

Again, fear flooded his eyes. "I kept them. No one knew. Not even Gomati Paati." He thrust them at me again. "Take them! They are not mine!"

My stunned silence was met by panic. "Don't you want them?" Uncle Siva cried, waving the letters frantically at me. "They are from your mother. No one knows of their existence. I hid them. They are yours. Don't you want them?"

The letters were folded together in a tight wad. The moment I had hold of them, Uncle Siva withdrew his hand as if from fire. His shallow chest heaved and he took great gulps of air as if he had just completed a tremendous ordeal. I held the wad of letters just as he had given it to me and said, "From my mother."

Uncle Siva gazed at me from newly calm eyes. "Yes. From your mother. Now go. I have given you what is yours. Go!"

I looked at him foolishly. "Amma's letters. Why did you not give them to me when they arrived? Why did you hide them away from Gomati Paati?"

Pure hate exploded in Uncle Siva's eyes. "Go!" he cried. "Get out of my house!"

I left. I had gone no farther than the front room of that ancient house. It had been enough. I walked out and left the monster to his ghosts.

ঌ

I READ THE LETTERS MANY times. The letters from the mother who had abandoned me. There were three of them. The first was from five years ago, the last from only four months. I read them again and again on the train from Paavalampatti to Thirunelveli. All the letters say the same thing in three or four brief lines: *Come and see me. Please come and see me. There is much I want to tell you.* The letters had been sent from Madras Central Jail.

In Thirunelveli, I took the bus to Athanoor. My reservation for the train to Madras was not until the next day. I had given myself an extra day in Thirunelveli just in case. Because of the letters, I used the extra day to visit the scenes of my childhood, to walk where once I had walked with Appa and Amma. I remembered Pichayya vaguely. Pichayya and his donkey. I had an urgent question to ask him if he was still alive. Or if not him, then someone else. Some of the answers to the riddle of the letters, and of my life, were there, in Athanoor.

The bus let me off at a Mariamman temple in the middle of a rocky barrenness. A small cluster of shops surrounded the temple—a tea stall, a cycle repair shop, a woman selling buttermilk in a clay pot alongside wilting sliced cucumbers sprinkled with salt and black pepper. Where were the people who brought their business to these poor little shops? Far into the distance, no human habitation could be seen. Where was the village? The woman from whom I bought a cup of buttermilk indicated a barely visible trail in the stony ground and told me to follow it over a ridge to Athanoor. I poured the cool buttermilk down my throat and trudged along the trail. From the top of the ridge, the village came into view. I descended the ridge and walked toward Athanoor through scrub and stone. I soon came to a blackened shell of a building choked by weeds and rubbish. It was the school. I knew it immediately. I could not bear to look. I averted my eyes and walked along the dirt track on both sides of which the huts of Athanoor lay scattered. One of these huts might very well have been where I had lived with Appa and Amma. I had little recollection of it. Nor of the most substantial building within view, a white mansion sitting on a rise in the distance, at the far end of the track.

A woman covered with fine white dust and carrying a battered metal pan passed me along the trail, and then a man on a bicycle who threw a curious glance at me. I kept going, looking for some likely person to query. I found an old man with white stubble on his chin sitting on his haunches against the slender gray trunk of a palm tree. I did not introduce myself to him. I said only, "Do you know where I can find someone who was connected to the school that once existed here?" I pointed in the direction of the ruined pile of bricks behind me.

The old man stood up and adjusted his cloth around his waist. His bare feet were covered with dust. He was tiny. He noted my clean shirt and trousers and asked, "Why do you want to know?"

"I was a student there at one time," I said. After all, it was the truth.

He squinted up at me and said, "There used to be a Teacher-Amma. She vanished. No one knows what happened to her. Teacher-Sar and Arokia-Sar died in the fire. You could talk to Devi. Perhaps you remember Devi? She too used to be a student in the school. And then she became a teacher herself. Now she has a school just like the one that existed. But that's in a different village. In Keelpaarai. That's a good two miles away."

"Another school?"

"Yes. Many of the children go there now. For a few years, there was no functioning school in the area. Then we heard that Devi-Amma, who had gone far away and studied a lot, had taken up where Teacher-Amma and Teacher-Sar had left off." He nodded his head in the direction of the mansion on the little hill. "People said they would burn the new school down too. But that hasn't happened yet."

I too nodded in the direction of the mansion. A vague memory of Parthiban Reddy came back to me. Though I knew the answer already, I asked, "Those people. Did they pay for what they did to the old school?" I had not forgotten Gomati Paati saying despairingly that my father's killers had gone unpunished. Just as Amma's father Murugappa's killer had.

The old man gave a derisive grunt. "The police came and pretended to investigate. They sat for a few weeks at Cinema Crazy Susi's drinking tea and bothering the women coming back from the quarries. Then they said they couldn't find any of the men who had attacked the school and left. Devi-Amma was present when the old school burned down. She can tell you everything that happened on the day of the fire, everything you want to know about the school. But you will have to go to Keelpaarai to talk to her."

"What about Pichayya?"

The old man nodded. "It's true. Pichayya too can tell you everything you need to know." He cackled. "Pichayya is an old man, the oldest I know. Much older than even me. He didn't teach at the school. How could he? He doesn't even know how to read and write. But he loved that school still. His hut is by the dried-up pond."

I was heading in the direction the old man had indicated when I found Pichayya in a field with his donkey. The light was fading out of the world when I came upon him. It was turning toward night.

I said to him, "Do you know who I am?"

He said, "You are Selvam, Ponni and Ramu's child. I knew you would come one day."

I was not surprised that he had so easily identified me. "Why were you so sure?"

"Because you had no choice. You had to. You have to do what has to be done."

I told him about my conversation with the old man under the palm tree. Pichayya said, "Devi-Amma is continuing what was started. People think only the bad things continue forever and ever. But if you do good things, they too leave their marks upon the world. The past goes before the present, but the present need not always follow from the past. Sometimes you can break the past and leave it where it belongs—in the past."

Pichayya's donkey shook its head impatiently in the gathering gloom. It pawed the dirt and looked in the direction of the dried-up pond, where Pichayya's hut was.

I screwed up my courage. I asked Pichayya my urgent question about Appa and Amma. He did not hesitate in his answer. He said their love was a great thing, a tale for the ages. I doubted him. He insisted he would not lie.

I said, "I have letters from Amma."

"From Ponni?"

I explained to him how I had come by the letters and added, "The first one was sent five years ago. Only four months have gone by since the last one. Do you know what happened to her after the fire ten years ago?"

He shook his head. "She disappeared when your father died. With Karuppan. Some said she went into the jungle. When Reddiar was killed, some said she and Karuppan had done it. But that was only rumor."

"Reddiar was killed?"

"He was going home on his motorcycle one night about a year after the fire. Someone shot him dead. Now his son has taken over the quarries and lives in the mansion."

"Amma is in jail," I said. "Amma sent her letters from jail."

Pichayya saw how my mind was working. He said, "As far as I know, Reddiar's killers were never caught."

"Amma is in Madras Central Jail. She wants me to come and see her. I don't know if I should."

"Why would you not go?"

"After the fire, she left me in Paavalampatti. She did not come to get me."

Pichayya nodded as if he understood. Then he said, "Maybe she couldn't, child."

"What could have stopped her? What was she doing for the many years before she sent me that first letter?"

"Ask her that. Go and ask her. Maybe she won't be able to give you a good answer. Then that is something you will know. But unless you go, how will you find that out?"

"I'm afraid."

"I know. But go anyway. What truth there is for you is in that jail with your mother. You have to do what has to be done."

That is what the old man Pichayya said. He also said Appa and Amma's love was a legend for the ages.

⁓

THE DAY AFTER I MET Pichayya, I bought this notebook at Thirunelveli Junction before I got on the train to Madras. I began writing in it on the train. My mind was in turmoil. One moment I thought one way, and the next another. One moment I wanted to go to Madras Central Jail in Park Town—how many times I had passed the jail's walls on my way to the secondhand bookstores in Moore Market!—to visit the mother who had abandoned me; the next I was afraid. I thought writing in the notebook would help. My life, haunted by ghosts past and present, was an enigma. I wanted to solve the riddle.

That was more than a month ago. I have written both more and less than I meant to.

∽

I SENT MALAR A NOTE in one of the tins in which she brings me my dinner: "Please forgive me. You are right. I watch you from the window. I would like to know you better. If you are not angry, please tell me where and when we can meet."

There was a knock in the middle of the night. I opened the door. Malar stood there with my note in her hand. I let her in. I switched on the bedside lamp. I sat on the bed, she in the chair. She had come in the old cotton sari in which she had been sleeping. Her hair had come loose and fell over her shoulder. When I looked at her I was afraid, but I made myself speak. I said, "You are beautiful." It is true. She is. Despite the gaps in her teeth and the marks on her cheeks.

I started talking. I talked for a long time. I said many things. I told her about the pictures of her that I look at over and over again. I told her how I admired her. And then I began speaking of Appa, Amma, Uncle Arokia, Gomati Paati, Forest Glen, Peter. I told her about my visit to Paavalampatti and Uncle Siva, and Athanoor and Pichayya. I told her how both my grandfather and father had been killed and the killers had never been caught (though perhaps justice of a kind had been done for my father). I showed her the letters my mother had sent me. She left her chair and came over to sit beside me on the bed. She touched my hand softly and took it in hers. I started crying. She took me in her arms, then, and held me and said nothing. She touched my head and my cheeks and my eyes and my lips. She gently wiped away my tears. When finally she spoke, she said with a smile, "Aren't you glad I'm not a picture you can only look at?"

We sat like that, holding each other, until the new day began to fill the window with its light. We made plans. She went away.

It is time to be done with the writing.

It is time to go to Madras Central Jail.

It is time to visit Amma. And to ask her about Appa.

Acknowledgments

It would be tedious to list the books that have contributed to the research that has gone into this novel—let me just say they are very many and range from histories to biographies to cultural studies, and also that a guide to some of the research is to be found in other (scholarly and journalistic) work I have written, especially in the last ten years or so. The following people, however, deserve the warmest gratitude for providing references, talking through ideas, introducing me to the right people, reading, or otherwise helping: S. Anandhi, Cristina Bacchilega, V. Geetha, Jennifer Lyons, M. S. S. Pandian, Nirmal Selvamony, and John Zuern. Pamela Kelley of University of Hawai'i Press has given the novel an excellent home; I am grateful for her invigorating confidence in my work. I appreciate too Jennifer McIntyre's careful work with the manuscript. I want especially to thank Cynthia Franklin for her rigorous and generous reading of multiple drafts; the book has certainly benefited enormously from her enthusiastic support at every stage of the long journey. It is no exaggeration to say she has significantly shaped the novel in tangible and intangible ways. Ujjayan Siddharth went from middle school to college during the years that it took me to write this novel—thank you, Ujay, for your spirit as well as equanimity.

My father, K. S. Subramanian, discussed many aspects of the novel with me during the early years of drafting and redrafting, and especially during a research trip to Thirunelveli, supported by the University of Hawai'i, that I took in 2006 with him and my mother. I regret that he, who read everything I wrote, is not here to read this novel. The novel is dedicated to my mother, K. S. Champakam, a marvelous teller and connoisseur of stories—some of your stories have found their way in here, Amma.

About the Author

S. SHANKAR is a novelist, critic, and translator. He is the author or editor of seven previous books, including two novels: *No End to the Journey* (2005) and *A Map of Where I Live* (1997). He teaches at the University of Hawai'i at Mānoa, where he is professor of English.